12/13.

THE QUEEN'S WAR

Also by Jeanne Mackin

The Frenchwoman: A Novel of the French Revolution

THE QUEEN'S WAR

A Novel of Eleanor of Aquitaine

Jeanne Mackin

St. Martin's Press   New York

Grateful acknowledgment is made by the publisher for permission to reprint *Lancelot: The Knight of the Cart* by Chrétien de Troyes, translated by Deborah Webster Rogers, copyright © 1984 by Columbia University Press. Used by permission.

Design by Karin Batten

Library of Congress Cataloging-in-Publication Data

Mackin, Jeanne.
     The queen's war : a novel of Eleanor of Aquitaine / Jeanne Mackin.
         p.   cm.
     "A Thomas Dunne book."
     ISBN 0-312-04960-9
     1. Eleanor, of Aquitaine, Queen, consort of Henry II, King of England, 1122?-1204—Fiction. 2. Great Britain—History—Henry II, 1154–1189—Fiction. 3. France—History—Louis VII, 1137–1180—Fiction. I. Title.
PS3563.A3169Q45   1991
813'.54—dc20   90-15542
                                                          CIP

First Edition: April 1991

10 9 8 7 6 5 4 3 2 1

For my husband, Steve

There be three things which are too wonderful for me, yea four which I know not: The way of an eagle in the air; the way of serpent upon a rock; the way of a ship in the midst of the sea; and the way of a man with a maid.

—Proverbs 30:18

In 1173 the sons of Henry, King of England, rose in angry rebellion against their father. The King, at that time, was out of favor with his wife and Queen, Eleanor of Aquitaine.

It was suspected that Eleanor, wroth, had much to do with the rebellion.

Acknowledgments

My thanks to Ellen Bonn for her enthusiasm, careful reading, and thoughtful questions; to Tom and M.K. for their support and encouragement.

Author's Note

Most people interested in Eleanor of Aquitaine have already formed their opinion of her. This novel constitutes my opinion. It is based on research and wide reading but is, nonetheless, speculation, just as this book is fiction and not history. We can "know" Eleanor only through the various contemporary historians who wrote about her, bearing in mind that those historians were less than objective, especially when writing about women in general and Eleanor in particular. This, then, is how I have envisioned the legendary Eleanor, and that time and place that was twelfth-century Aquitaine.

BOOK ONE

Lucie: Ordeal by Water

Easter 1173

But know that you will meet many hardships and ugly passages: it's not an easy place to get into, except by leave of the king. His name is Bademagu. Actually, one can get in, by two very dangerous routes, really bad entrances. One is called the Water-bridge, because the bridge is under water. There is as much water between the bridge and the bottom as there is flowing over it, no less, no more; the bridge is exactly in the middle. And it's only a foot and a half wide, and the same thick. It's a good dish to refuse—and that's the less dangerous route.

—Lancelot: the Knight of the Cart

1

The pear tree waited like a sentinel on the horizon, its blossom-laden branches dark against the grey dawn sky. It was alive with motion and seemed to dance in the mild wind. From its boughs streamed ribbons of every color, tied there by maidens with secret wishes.

Lucie, weary and soft-eyed from lack of sleep, paused under the tree. She plucked at a bough of white blossoms that danced invitingly overhead.

It was hard to reach up because she dragged the shared weight of the cart behind her, but she could not resist the beckoning hope of those ribbons, the beauty of the blossoms. The wild pear tree was heavy with flowers and throbbed with busy, humming bees. It would yield a good harvest that summer. Lucie sighed, knowing she would never taste its fruit. Godfrey had a dread of ever passing the same way twice.

The cart ropes cut angry welts into her shoulders. She shifted their weight, seeking momentary release from the discomfort, and then tucked the fragrant, just-plucked flowers into her bliaut. If only they could stop and rest for a while. It was just past dawn, but the day already grew warm. Sweat streamed down her face from the exertion of pulling the cart.

She sighed loudly, intending that Godfrey should hear, and then hummed a tune that was a secret message between them. *Godfrey m'aime, Godfrey ma'a.* Godfrey loves me, Godfrey has won me. But she was certain of only half of that rhyme: that Godfrey had won her. Two weeks ago they had lain together in a fragrant apple orchard, but not since then, and she craved his touch.

Sadness, despite her fatigue and chafed shoulders, was as distant as last winter's snow. Fair, verdant spring wrought a green and white tapestry over the land. The forests and meadows frothed with wild, fragrant bloom, and musical streams coursed sweetly over the hillside.

All nature rejoiced. Spring was upon them, ripe as a wanton lady, making the blood run faster and the skin tingle with delight where the sweet breezes brushed over it. Christ was resurrected, the world and men's hearts were made new. And the Queen was come back.

It was three summers since hot-tempered, vengeful King Henry had brought fire and sword to the rebellious villages of Aquitaine, three summers since he had relinquished his struggles with the recalcitrant southern barons and left his wife, Eleanor, to restore order. Since Becket's murder, Henry was too busy trying to iron out his wrinkles with the Church and his own soul to bother with Aquitaine. Let Eleanor take care of the South. And Eleanor was glad to do so . . . It removed her from his presence, a presence that had grown increasingly distasteful to her. Aquitaine was glad to have the Queen with them again; she was one of them, golden-skinned and warm of heart, not cold and fishy-eyed like the English King Henry.

Lucie had been but a child when the last war started, and had a child's memories of the troubles—the smell of burning straw huts and singed cattle, the horse-trampled gardens and fields, the soldiers with red-stained clothes who rode through the castle village taking what they wanted—chickens, sacks of winter wheat, maidens.

4

But now she was a grown woman of fifteen and the world was at peace. The burnt huts were rebuilt, the wounds of the men healed; the large-bellied village women carried babes fathered by men of choice, not rampaging warriors. When knights appeared on the road or in the woods, the people waved gladly, no longer expecting merciless massacre. Traveling knights, this spring and for the two past, journeyed only to mock tourneys, not real battle.

The land smelled of prosperity, of newly plowed earth and germinating crop seed, of warm hearths and the acrid reminders of new building. It was Eleanor, the Eagle, who had brought peace to this, her golden, southern homeland. And all of Aquitaine who were not bound to field or cloister traveled in the direction of Poitiers, to Eleanor's court, to rejoice in the new spring and her homecoming. As surely as the spring-quickened sap rose in the trees, so did the free people take to the roads in penance, pilgrimage and sheer, joyful wanderlust. The mud roads were thick and difficult with ruts from the many cart wheels, horse hooves and feet that had traveled them.

Lucie and her companions were different from the many others who had passed the same wild pear tree that spring. They wore neither the drab garments of serfs nor the richly embroidered silk robes of the nobility, but outlandishly dyed garments and strangely cut tunics. Their gaily decorated carts, a row of five traveling one after the other as docile as cows, displayed the good luck charms, magic eyes, fringes and banners of minstrels and jugglers. The carts explained why they were not busy plowing a lord's field or manning a merchant's booth at one of the many spring fairs: they were traveling players.

The leader, Godfrey, heard Lucie humming and turned to look at her. He was a tall man with wheat-colored hair, and young, handsome face clean-shaven in the southern style. He had the far-seeing eyes of one accustomed to scanning distant horizons.

Three women followed him. Lucie, she who wore pear blossoms tucked in her bliaut, was the youngest and the tallest. Her height suggested maturity, but her face was still round and soft as a child's. A dark-eyed Moor, with unbound black hair and tinkling bells tied at her ankles, followed; the eldest was a stoop-shouldered, wide-hipped matron of twenty-three with eyes small and black as raisins in a bread pudding.

Behind them trailed a giant of a man whose long grey locks contrasted with the open vulnerability of his childish countenance; a bearded, overly thin man whose clothes hid the puckered scars of chains once worn at the neck and ankles; and a stately, turbaned Moor, mate of the raven-haired woman. These were the members of Godfrey's traveling company. Two were former slaves, two were runaway serfs, and three were freeborn but of low station. They slept where the wind took them, ate what they could steal or beg, and called no man master and no place home.

"We will rest here," Godfrey pronounced, unyoking himself from the lead cart and still looking at Lucie. Her face was burnt by the sun, but where her bliaut occasionally gaped open, the skin was whiter than the pear flower.

In the year in which she had been with his troupe, he had begun to measure his own appetites by the hourglass of her needs, without even knowing he did so. He denied her little, never realizing that she asked even less.

The others, following his lead, undid the ropes that bound them to the carts. They sighed with relief and exhaustion, eager to leave the thick mud of the road for the green welcoming pasture and the silver, serpentine spring. The Vienne flowed gently here, but just steps away, where the meadow ended and the steep incline to the town began, it gathered force and wore a mantle of frothing white urgency.

In the grey, misty distance of the young morning, the spires of the Cathedral of Saint Pierre stood sentry over the red-roofed ducal city of Poitiers. Its new, polished stones and graceful statues—renderings of saints so lofty and elongated, they were said to be based on Eleanor's own exceedingly tall, slender build—caught the first rays of dawn. Graceful, ornately carved pillars supported the walls of the many-windowed church. From a distance, the huge cathedral reminded Lucie of a great ship that has been sadly landlocked and awaits a new deluge to free it.

The morning was still innocent with sleep, new as the Garden of Eden before man was placed in it. None yet stirred but the players, who had pulled their carts all night through the wolf-prowled emerald forests of Poitiers. The players turned as one toward the cathedral.

"It's as fair a cathedral as I've ever seen," Godfrey said approvingly. "We'll stop here and wash the mud from the carts. Make them shine like Venus at dawn, which even now is smiling down on us, and then prepare your costumes. We perform Noah and the Ark today. A cathedral fair and large as that will provide a good crowd for us."

As he stooped to clamber into his own cart, which was acting platform, sleeping loft, closet, pantry and warehouse to him, his multicolored cloak caught on a vagrant breeze and billowed like a sail. His tall figure was like a mast, and his beauty so great that the audiences which beheld his face in its many disguises loved him equally as Lucifer or the Virgin Mary. Free of beard and long sidelocks, he could play young warrior and shy maiden alike, as his trade required. But now his cheeks were covered with several days' stubble, for he had barely stopped to rest, and not at all to bathe. A layer of dust covered the costume trunks, which had not been opened in a fortnight.

He had been in a hurry to reach Poitiers. They had marched quickly along the course of the silver Vienne to reach the court of Queen Eleanor, to put behind them the long winter months spent unsuccessfully at the court of the Duke of Avranches, where cold, salty winds blew constantly and their plays and songs had gone unappreciated. In Poitiers Godfrey would seek his fortune, there where Queen Eleanor bided her time and plucked at the roses given her by troubadours and love-struck pages. The Duke of Avranches had no ear for music, and no heart with which to appreciate a love poem. But Eleanor of Aquitaine had both . . . and great generosity for those who pleased her.

Lucie and stoop-shouldered Udele, hitched to a common cart, watched Godfrey with hungry eyes, glad for a moment's rest, glad to have his voice rise again above the stillness of the spring world about them. They shared another yoke besides the one that bound them to the same cart. Both loved Godfrey. For a brief moment

7

this shared passion united them in sisterly friendliness. Udele, hands on hips, leaned backwards in a feline stretch and yawned with pleasure.

"I could sleep for days. Godfrey's been pacing as though his soles were on fire; even in his sleep he grumbles orders and twitches as though the road were still underfoot," she complained, proudly reminding Lucie that wherever he might wander during the day, Godfrey shared her pallet at night. "Can't see that this cathedral is any different than the others, for all his rush."

"Nor I," agreed Lucie, peering through the haze into the distance where the great church hovered like a heat mirage, tall and ornate and shimmering. She, too, glad to undo the ropes that tied her to the cart, yawned and stretched. But as she dipped sideways to loosen the stiffened muscles in her weary back, her hair tumbled to the ground and shimmered against the mud of the road.

Udele observed for the hundredth time how the girl's brown hair caught fire in the sun and gleamed like red gold. Her short-lived sisterly feeling began to churn and twist in her stomach like a worm, quickly metamorphizing into the emotion she normally showed this girl:

"Don't just stand there, then. We'll need water to wash down the ark," she grumbled, pulling her hood closer about her own mouse-colored head.

Because Udele was Godfrey's common-law wife, it was she who gave the domestic orders to the traveling troupe. And because Lucie was just his leman, with no authority or status other than that bestowed by his secret kisses, the girl fetched the buckets and trotted to the stream. She was free by design, not birth. Taking orders was as natural to Lucie, the runaway serf, as breathing.

"Wait! Wait! I want to come with you!" Broderick, the grey-haired giant who pulled their largest cart as easily as if it were a toy dog on wheels, fumbled at the ropes that yoked him. Unable to undo the intricate knot Udele had tied, he pulled the rope in two, rending the thick hemp into a mess of frazzled, itchy threads.

"Lout! Fool! You've ruined the rope!" Udele shrieked, but Broderick was already gone, plunging through the grassy meadow after Lucie on legs thick as tree trunks.

"She'll beat you later for that," Lucie said when he caught up with her. "Why do you let her beat you? You could thrash her with just one hand."

"It's wrong to hurt people," Broderick said, kneeling beside her on the grassy riverbank. He plunged his hands into the cold water and giggled.

"But she hurts you when she beats you. So Udele is bad."

"No, Udele takes care of me," Broderick protested. "Brother Thomas said I was to be grateful for all people of intelligence who feed and shelter me, a poor idiot." The words, long-since memorized, tumbled out slowly. He had no idea what they meant, other than dumb, animal submission.

"Brother Thomas, I suspect, used you badly, and taught you punishments that a monk would never endure. Gratitude. He made you so grateful you ran away."

"Bad Broderick." Tears clouded the giant's eyes. He ducked his head and wiped at them.

"No, Broderick, you're not bad. Don't cry. It's good you ran away, because then we found you and we needed you. Brother Thomas did not. Who else would play the giant or the cyclops, or Samson?"

Broderick brightened instantly. "Samson! Samson!" he yelled, splashing his hands in the water again. "Pull the castle down!" chanted grey-haired Broderick, the six-year-old boy locked in the body of an aging giant.

"Not Queen Eleanor's castle, please." Lucie grimaced. "I think Godfrey hopes to win her favor, not destroy her palace." She looked over her shoulder into the distance, past the tall towers of the cathedral to the crenulated turrets of Aquitaine's ducal palace. Dawn was advancing fast as a brigand; Lucie could discern parti-colored banners hanging from several fenestrations, and the distance-spanning gleaming helmets of guards.

It looked winsome enough. But she felt foreboding. Too many nights now, she had dreamed of water, flowing over her, suffocating her and forcing the air from her chest. "It is nothing to dream of water here," Godfrey told her. "Aquitaine means 'the land of waters.' Haven't you noticed that we are always in hearing of a stream or river?"

It was more than that, though, but what, Lucie couldn't say.

And what mischievous demon had whispered in Godfrey's ear that they should perform Noah's Ark today, when any sensible man would have chosen a play from the Easter cycle? Godfrey went even against the seasons in his angry rebellion. Even now black clouds leaned on the tallest spires of Saint Pierre's Cathedral, promising rain to come.

"Come, Broderick. We must hurry."

Sophia, the queen's astrologer, leaned on a moss-covered allure of the Maubergeonne Tower. Dampness seeped through her fashionably tight, pale blue sleeves, making her shiver. The dawn smelled of rain, and rain made her bones ache. What a misery the flesh was, no more than an instrument to remind her of the tainted brevity of life. We eat and then defecate, we sleep and then rise and are weary. And what was the point of it? The flesh was no more than the *caput mortuum*, the residue left after what is pure and usable is emptied from the flask. The flesh was the enemy.

She longed for her small, spartan sleeping room opposite the scriptorium. But Eleanor, filled with disquiet, had insisted she sleep in calling distance, in the Queen's Tower. Sophia hated the secretive corners, the colorful tapestries with their amatory scenes, the overabundance of silk pillows and brass vases, in these rooms. They reminded her always that this tower had been built to house La Dangereuse, the whore kept by Eleanor's grandfather. The place reeked of sin and sensuality, of earthly things with their scent of decay.

She thought again of her little cell in the convent of the Paraclete, missing and not missing it at the same time. It was the only home she had known for the past twenty years, since her aunts had sent her there as a child of five. She, Sophia, had been one of the first girl children to be educated at that famous nunnery established by Abelard's discarded lover, Heloise. It was Heloise herself who had taught the young Sophia that the pleasures of this world were short-lived as a rainbow. By then the beautiful Heloise was tough and dried as old leather . . . That was what great love had done for her.

Once she was established in the convent, her childhood had passed happily enough. Sophia studied and learned the four sciences of physical matter and the three sciences of the intellect. She read Pytheas and Strabo, Alcibiades and Theophrastus. And some days she even forgot that she was lame, and plain of face, and a runt not destined to live long, according to her aunts. It was peace and happiness of a sort.

But when grown, Sophia had been a restless novice, unwilling to leave her manuscripts of Boethius' *Consolation* and Aristotle's *Metaphysics* for the chapel, unwilling to give up the pursuits of the mind to insure the peace of the soul. She had been unable to make her vows, and equally unwilling to give up the peace of the convent. There was part of her that wanted to be as other women, those who lived on the outside, but did not know how.

Till Eleanor, hearing of how learned and wise she, Sophia, had become, had sent for her to come to court. Sophia had accepted gladly, loath to take those vows which would bind her for all time to the routine, unquestioning life of the convent. There was much that could not be learned within the cloister, and she was by nature filled with a lively curiosity.

But it seemed that her three years away from Paraclete had proven just one thing—Sophia was made for neither convent nor court. One was too tedious, the other too taxing. The one left insufficient time for her studies because the prayer bells never stopped ringing; the other left even less time because Eleanor could be even more demanding than God.

A yawn pulled at her thin, pale lips. Fresh from her bed with the whole of the long day stretching before, she was already tired. Curse her weakness. What good to have the heart of a philosopher when her woman's body was as weak and fragile as a moth caught in a spider's web?

11

The court had been at Eleanor's ducal castle for less than a month, yet already the Queen was talking of removing herself to one of her other castles. Sophia was sleepless with worry. Eleanor was usually as good as her word. Hadn't she, the Queen's astrologer, followed her on one *chevauchée* after another for the past three years, crossing the channel from France to England and back again with as little regard as if they were merely crossing from one chamber to another? Each voyage had meant weeks away from her translation of St. Boethius' *Consolation of Philosophy*, and weeks of jolting, tooth-grinding back pain caused by horse and ship.

Curse Eleanor, she thought, but quickly swallowed the emotion, calling up the gratitude that was the Queen's due. Restless Eleanor would cavort over the entire of Gascony and Aquitaine, moving her court on the whim of a morning, breaking fast at one castle and dining at the next.

But no matter how quickly or how much she moved, the Queen could not outpace the demon at her heels.

Eleanor was fifty-one years old that spring and had already outlived many who shared her year of birth; the Queen's thoughts were autumnal and her moods often wintry. Age, and the loss of power that comes to all wives whose husbands warm their nights with young mistresses, was the demon she fled.

And if the wife be Queen, and the errant husband King, the loss of that husband's love is that much greater a tragedy, Sophia thought, hugging her arms tightly across her thin chest. If only Henry shared the Queen's age, they might have reached an understanding. But Eleanor's second husband was a man eleven years younger; she was growing old, and Henry was in his prime. It was not a happy situation.

"Human nature was originally one and we were a whole, and the desire and pursuit of the whole is called love." Sophia recited aloud Plato's words. The desire and pursuit of the whole. Eleanor, cast off, was no longer whole. She paced her court and her land in search of that which was missing, that part which Henry had loved and revered, that part she would never have again.

12

Sophia rejoiced that she had never known that destroyer of peace and happiness, love.

She had hoped that passing spring in the beloved, memory-filled palace of Poitiers would calm her Queen, help resign her to the inevitable. Poitiers was the jewel in the verdant setting of Aquitaine; it was here that Eleanor was most content. But Eleanor could not be resigned, would not be calm. Even with her court filled with vassals, adoring troubadours and the loveliest maids and bravest youths of Aquitaine, Poitou, Brittany, and Anjou, even with her sons Henry, Richard, and Geoffrey and their brides or betrotheds, Marguerite and Alais of France, Constance of Brittany and Alix of Maurienne wandering in and out of the Poitevin court at will and for various holidays . . . even then, Eleanor was bored and restless.

Sophia sat on a low stone bench and put her head into her hands, sighing. The pain in her back made her fidgety. And her head ached so. All last night she had studied her charts and diagrams, trying to find when Aquarius, the water-bearer of the zodiac, would find harmony and balance with Capricorn. The charts only showed continued unrest and yet more travel, a bad sign.

"My Lady." Sophia looked up to find Amaria, Eleanor's maid, peering round a corner of the balustrade at her.

"What is it?" Sophia asked in irritation, knowing already what the girl would say.

"The Queen is calling for you. She had a dream you must interpret." The maid's voice was soft and bore hints of fear.

"Now? Before mass and breakfast?"

"Please. I beg pardon." The girl ducked her head. She, like most other maids in the castle, feared this astrologer. It was rare enough to find a man who could read; yet Sophia, a woman, was said to be as learned as any of Paris' left-bank masters of philosophy. She was also small and sickly and misshapen, with one leg that was several inches shorter than the other. Sophia was different, she was set apart, she was not as other women. "Now, my lady," the maid insisted shyly.

Sophia rose from her bench with a sigh so loud that her heavy-lidded watchman jerked to attention, called away from his dreams of the fair Celia, who poured beer at the Golden Merlin Inn.

"I'm coming. As quickly as I can." But Sophia's movements were slow with annoyance and fatigue.

The bells announcing first mass were already ringing by the time Godfrey and his troupe had reached the great cathedral's west portal and set up their carts. Washed and lovingly dried, the gilded sides of the large-wheeled carts shone brightly, catching the eyes of the town people who hurried by.

Godfrey's wagon stood in the middle of the row of five carts. Its flame-painted helldoor had been covered over with flimsy wood panels through which the animals of the story would disappear. After the miming of Noah's Ark was over, the players would change from their animal costumes into the rags and tails of de-mons and leap out through the helldoor, scattering curious chil-dren and making the women scream with delight.

It was the demons and goblins the people loved most, not the good saints and beneficent angels. Godfrey never ended a mime without throwing in a good rousing game of tag with cloth-tailed devils.

In the first cart, where the costumes were kept, Lucie painstakingly braided her hair. It had to be bound tightly so that it wouldn't show under her cap. Her breasts, too, small and hard as they were, also had to be bound, to hide her sex. It was forbid-den for women to act in mimes.

When she had first joined the troupe, she had been small and skinny enough that passing her off as a boy had been no problem at all. Now, a year later, even with Udele's miserly meals, she had grown, developing telltale curves and that startling abun-dance of wavy, tawny hair. But Godfrey's troupe was small; he needed her to mime, whether she be female or not, and so she continued to mime, risking hellfire, interdiction and many chapel dungeons to do so.

As Godfrey wanted, so would she give. Willingly and gladly

14

had she left her home and mother to go with him; willingly and gladly she did as he bid.

But today, she was afraid.

"You are slow this morning, Lucie. Your hair is not even bound, and soon the mime must begin." Her master, quiet as a cat, had crept into her wagon and, standing behind, put his arms about her. She felt his warm breath at her neck, his hands clasped her breasts. Her heart quickened at his touch. This was the center of her world, this slowing of time when Godfrey came to her.

She kissed his long-fingered hands, first one, then the other, silently, remembering that Udele was probably prowling around outside, listening, waiting. Lucie had already lost several handfuls of hair to the older, stronger woman's terrible jealousy.

"We should leave this place," she whispered to him as he lifted her tunic and kissed the hard, strawberry-colored tips of her breasts.

"We have only just gotten here. The crowds will be large, the coins in the cap many, I think."

"There is something here I fear," Lucie insisted. Godfrey caught her up in his arms and pitched her lightly onto the straw mattress in the corner. The cart was so small he could not stand up straight, nor could they sprawl full length together on the bed, but only curl about each other in a tangled mass of arms and legs.

"A tupping for luck." He grinned at her.

Obediently she pulled up her skirts and opened her legs. She hoped this time would be different, that he would be gentle and reach that unreached center of her that loved him but as yet had not been touched by him.

He did not. Hurried and impatient, he entered quickly, giving her pain. They coupled with little noise and only enough touching to achieve his immediate goal. Lucie was used to this; her mother had told her that men found joy in coupling, but for women it was a service to be rendered to a master, a way to get babes and regular meals. Still, she wished he would hold her a little longer, after. He did not.

"There is naught to fear, little Lucie," he said, rising, remembering that she had spoken of fear a moment ago. "Now put on your costume. We must perform well this morning, if we are to be invited to the Queen's castle."

His wanton mood disappeared as quickly as it had arrived. He was serious, preoccupied; his eyes looked to the distance even in the small confines of the cart. He slapped her behind to get her moving, but there was no love or gentleness in the touch.

"Sometimes I wish my mother had lost her speech before she ever convinced you to steal me away," she said slowly, searching for words that would hurt him the way his quick, sudden coolness hurt her. She had lost some of her serf's meekness in the past twelvemonth of wandering with Godfrey and his troupe. She often spoke up where once she would have bitten her tongue to keep it silent.

"Do you mean that, Lucie?" Godfrey smiled at her. It was his strongest weapon, one that even sharp-tongued Udele could not resist. His pale blue eyes grew warm and soft. His full, red lips stretched in a pleasant curve over white teeth. His arms opened again to her.

"No, I don't mean it." Lucie stepped within his arms and let him give her the kiss of peace. It was no good trying to be angry or sullen. She could not hold out against that smile. When he released her, she pulled off her ragged gown and donned the boy's breeches he held out to her.

Minutes later the bells for the communion began to ring from the cathedral, and the small troupe gathered outside the central wagon, flanking both sides of the helldoor. Lucie flushed red as Udele stared accusingly. She had seen Lucie and Godfrey leave the cart together.

Huge Broderick was dressed as an elephant, all in grey and with a rag-filled hose hanging from his face. After going through the helldoor into Noah's Ark, he would have to reappear as a mule, an ape-man and even a wolf, despite his bulk. Each costume was more ridiculous than the last, each change more difficult, and purposely so. Haram, the Moor, would circulate through the crowd making surreptitious bets that the idiot-giant could not get through the whole mime without a mistake. Haram always won, and the troupe would grow richer for Broderick's clumsiness.

Haram would then change into a colorful Arab robe, complete with veiled headdress and unsheathed sword stuck into his girdle, and mime the role of Noah's troublesome son. Haram always had to play the troublesome roles, the evil villains, the devils. His black complexion roused warlike memories from those in the audiences who had gone with King Louis and Queen Eleanor on Crusade those many years before.

Cedric, the runaway serf whose neck was ringed with puckered scars, would play the other son, while Godfrey would recite the part of Noah.

Farther away waited Udele, and Haram's woman, Lillah. Udele was thick and stubborn and would do naught but help set up the platforms and cook their meals. Lillah, who was beautiful and exotic, danced while clanging little hand bells, undulating her hips and slender arms in movements that made men sigh with longing.

Lucie, dressed in the orange-and-black-striped sackcloth of the tiger costume, huddled between Cedric and Broderick. The slits in her face mask hampered her vision. She squinted to see better all those who passed, or stopped to stare. Most were villeins, some were merchants, but one or two were squires set free for an hour to run errands in the town or bishops' palace. Lucie checked to see if any wore the black and red device of Sir Foulkes de St. Servan, the owner she had fled that night she joined Godfrey.

They were many leagues away from St. Servan and the looming keep of Black Oaks, a year away from St. Servan, yet the fear was still there. There wasn't enough land or time in the whole universe to put between herself and the wrathful lord of Black Oaks.

Godfrey, sensing Lucie's nervousness, gave her a pat on the shoulder as he passed. It was the touch a man would give to a youth, not to a beloved woman, and it did not reassure.

The final set of bells for the morning mass rang out. The great wooden doors of Saint Pierre's were flung open and a broiling stream of humanity flowed between them, powerful as the strongest spring currents.

17

"Fair and virtuous ladies! Generous and brave sirs! A mime! A mime for your entertainment this fine morning! A mime for your edification! A mime to stir the senses and redeem the soul!" Godfrey's voice, almost as loud and clear as the bells themselves, rang out. He fought his way through to the middle of the human stream and, like a rock breaking the path of a river, directed as many of the townspeople towards the semicircle of carts as he could.

Broderick began to giggle. A little tributary of excited children had already flowed to the helldoor, where he and Lucie waited for the play to begin. They pointed to where huge Broderick stood with a stuffed grey hose hanging from his face. Under the hose, his mouth trembled with fear. The tiger next to him reached for his hand and squeezed it. Crowds frightened Broderick.

Lillah, dressed in her silken veils sewn with little metallic moons, tapped on her tambourine and moved through the throng, a beautiful swan gliding seductively through muddied water. Lillah spoke no French nor English nor the langue d'oc, but she did not need words to convince the youths and grown men of Poitiers to follow her swaying lead.

Their good wives, distracted from their after-mass errands, had already gathered in a tittering circle around the good-looking, well-formed Godfrey. As they whispered and nodded at him, their linen headdresses frothed like white water. He smiled in a way that convinced each wife and maid he had spent lonely years searching just for her; his eyes and mouth were as eloquent as Lillah's dance.

Soon a large, noisy group of men, women and children, captured by the alluring Lillah, comely Godfrey and comic Broderick, had pooled in front of the carts.

"The story of Noah!" Godfrey called out then, exultant.

Udele, standing to the side with her hands wrapped in her apron, watched him through narrow eyes. Jealousy, the worm within, churned in her stomach. How the women stared at him, their mouths open, their eyes wide. That little vixen Lucie watched him as eagerly as the others. She looked ridiculous in that costume, even more so than she had a year ago, when she had donned it for the first time.

Ah, why had Godfrey thought to do such a thing, fetch away some serf's brat! The child had been pretty, the mother tearful, the night soft and sweet with spring. Godfrey was softer than other men, and daft; Udele could remember a time when her tears had moved him as easily as Lucie's did now.

But Lucie was a child no longer; she was a woman, with hard, high breasts. Udele squinted at Lucie's chest. The small mounds of the girl's breasts were visible even through the thick, painted sackcloth.

Now here is trouble, she thought. If it is discovered that Godfrey is letting a woman step on the players' platform, we'll spend the night in the bishop's jail. Many nights. The thought of Lucie being led away in chains brought more pleasure than the fear of time in a rat-filled keep, though, and Udele smiled. If only she could turn in the girl without endangering him!

Across from Udele, nearsighted Anselm, canon of Saint Pierre's, stared at Lucie, too, but for other reasons. What the priest saw was a tawny-haired, fair youth, young and unsure of himself, about to begin a mime. He sighed with longing and nostalgia.

Anselm had been such himself, all these thirty years past. He had been a gifted mimic; all who had beheld him said so. His poetry and songs had been second to none. The ladies and knights had ceased their clatter and sat in awed silence when Anselm recited his love poems. That was long ago, when Queen Eleanor went on Crusade and took half of Aquitaine with her, including her favorite troubadours. She had not taken him, despite his pleading. How he had hated her cold, beautiful voice as she spoke the word "no." How he still hated her.

Anselm sighed and reached deep into his robes for a coin to buy strawberries a merchant held out. Regret for the beautiful archer, Nicholas, who had gone on Crusade and never come back, made him bitter and wrathful. But deeper longing for the youth he had been, not the paunchy, bald canon he had become, made him move in the direction of the platform. He became part of the humanity that washed up in front of the helldoor.

"The story of Noah's Ark," Godfrey called out again, and this time the crowd applauded gleefully, ready for the play to begin. He stood in front of the cart, where the crowd was thickest.

"Pardon, Lady," he whispered to a dwarfish woman whose small feet he accidentally stepped on.

Sophia nodded pleasantly, well accustomed to being trod on and pushed about because of her diminutive size and unimposing stature. The crowd smelled as crowds did, and judging by the mimes and their poor props, the play would not be a good one. Yet it would be a diversion, and diversion was what she wanted. Let Eleanor call for her, and pout and rage. This morning Sophia would amuse herself. She tried not to think of the morning scene in the Queen's bower.

Eleanor, trembling with Henry's letter still in hand, had been restive and puffed up with dangerous anger, like a furious eagle batting its wings.

"He writes that we are to spend the Christmas season in England with him. Again." Eleanor's voice had been cool and unruffled water, but there was a deadly glint in her eyes.

"What is the harm in that?" Sophia asked, not as innocent as she feigned.

"His intent was not kindness to let me know so far in advance. I'm certain he was hoping to ruin the whole of the spring and summer with dread anticipation. Well, I will not journey again to his miserable, wet domains across the channel, as long as Rosamonde is by his side and in his bed. Nor for as long as the matter with the Young King remains unresolved. Henry wants to play at family to impress his subjects. I will not be used."

"If the King calls, we must surely go, Lady," Sophia had said, standing first on one foot and then the other. Her legs were cramped from the dampness of the morning. If she had to wait for the matter of the Young King to be resolved before peace would reign in Eleanor's court again, then she would have to wait for a very long time. True, Henry had crowned his son, Henry, as his heir and successor to the kingdom of England. But everyone knew that Henry had no intention of actually letting the Young King rule. Not while there was breath in Henry.

"Must we, my friend? I think not. I weary of this game. If he wishes his Queen and wife back, he will have to be rid of his harlot, Rosamonde. I will not be cast aside like an aging bitch, left to dream and twitch in front of the master's hearth, while he cavorts with sluts. Nor will I sit back and let him make a fool of my son." Eleanor emphasized this vow with a pounding of fists against her cherrywood writing table.

"Henry is his son, too," Sophia said. Eleanor glared at her, but did not respond. Sophia tried another strategy. "Then Rosamonde is still at Woodstock?"

Not a sympathetic person by nature, Sophia felt a tug of pity for this aging Queen's problems. Henry's mistress was younger by many years, and so beautiful she was known as Rosamonde the Fair, although no one made flattery of her intellect. The Fair Rosamonde was passive and sluggish of mind—just the kind of woman a man would want after a quarter of a century with Eleanor, Sophia thought. The calm after the storm. The rest after the battle.

In a loutish manner, instead of easing for his wife this matter of taking a mistress, he had installed the wench in one of Eleanor's favorite properties. In a specially built bower secluded in a magical maze, to protect her from Eleanor, the gossips whispered.

The insult, the implications, were all too clear, and unforgivable. As if Eleanor of Aquitaine would stoop to private murder, even given the opportunity. Did he think that all in Christendom were as corruptible as he, who had the blood of Thomas Becket on his hands?

"He does not mention her, of course, but the message reeks of her perfume. He lies in her arms, ignoring his sons, his wife. We are to sit in our bower and grow aged with good grace while he makes himself into an old fool and deprives the kingdom of its heir. We are to look the other way, powerless, while he uses the wealth of our lands, our sons' wealth, to support his lechery." Eleanor's mouth curled with disgust.

Sophia said nothing. Her mentor, Sister Alicia of Paraclete, had taught her many years ago that a wise woman answers direct questions and leaves the rest to the village idiots and lecturing almoners. She waited for the next barrage of anger. It didn't come. Instead, something like regret crossed Eleanor's face.

"Rosamonde is very beautiful," Eleanor said. "You have not seen her, I believe. But I have. She is beautiful as the rose she is named for. And young. She has what I have lost . . . youth and beauty, and a womb still ripe for seeding . . ." Her voice caught on a note of sadness and disappeared.

She still loves Henry. I should have known as much, Sophia thought. The hate could not be half as strong, were not the love even stronger yet. Or perhaps it is just possessiveness. She wants Henry to belong to her despite the ill will between them.

"You have already given Henry more than his fair share of sons," Sophia reminded her. "And daughters."

Eleanor had been a fecund queen, certainly, providing four heirs: Henry, Richard, Geoffrey and John. And her daughters would ally the English throne with most of the kingdoms of Christendom. Matilda was wed to the duke of Bavaria, Eleanor to the king of Castile, and little Joanna in a few years would be wed to the king of Sicily.

"I have," Eleanor agreed bitterly. "And he cares for none of them. Except for John Lackland." She almost spit the name. John Lackland. The last child born, the son she despised because he reminded her of all that had gone wrong between her and her once-beloved king. Eleanor, unique in many ways, was also unique in this: She had married Henry as much for love as political purpose.

"He wants more sons to choose from. Sons from fair Rosamonde." She banged her white fist on the table and then, wanting to hide her face even from Sophia, cradled her head in her open hands.

"You are the fairest," Sophia murmured, going to Eleanor and putting a small hand on the Queen's shoulder. A little lie is no sin, if no sin is intended. Hadn't Abelard preached that? And Eleanor was tall and slender, with thighs and hips kept shapely from riding. Grey streaked her hair, which had once been the

22

color of ripe wheat, and lines framed her large brown eyes, but for a woman who has passed fifty summers, she was a marvel of beauty and health.

"You lie with such earnestness, such sincerity. I could almost believe you, were not my looking glass more honest than you," Eleanor said. "I am betrayed by my own flesh. This is where time has led me. Time and Henry."

Aged or no, wroth or not, Eleanor had lost none of her famous vigor and energy and could not be sorrowful for long. A rueful smile crossed her face, lighting the dark eyes from within.

"I'll have my revenge," she said. "*Deus le volte*. God wills it." She voiced the old Crusaders' slogan, those words which had guided her early years of married womanhood with the monkish Louis, her first husband. Even just saying them reminded her of other spring mornings long ago, when the air lay sweetly on her unlined brow and all the world was fresh and waiting for her in the shape of a prancing grey mare which would carry her to foreign shores and adventure. Where had the golden mornings fled?

"To begin with, I'll have Raoul write a new song and see to it that it is played all over France and Aquitaine. He is not as clever as Bernart de Ventadour was . . . who could ever be? . . . but he is quick enough at satire. Rosamonde shall be named a toad, a creeping, slimy thing who crawls into bed under cover of darkness, afraid to be seen in the light. And Henry shall be named an old fool, a traitorous Nureddin who will not relinquish the power that should be in the hands of his sons. Old man. I'll show you," Eleanor said again, forgetting that Sophia was still there, awaiting instructions.

Quill in hand, forehead creased in concentration, the Queen clearly would write the song herself, rather than trust her vengeance to a troubadour.

Minutes passed as Eleanor, lost in concentration, poured venom onto the paper beneath her quickly moving hand. Sophia, still standing and now all but forgotten, shuffled from foot to foot, trying to ease the pain in her back.

"My Lady sent for me? A matter of a dream needing interpretation?" she finally said, reminding the Queen of her presence.

"Yes. A very strange dream." Eleanor turned in her chair and motioned for Sophia to come closer to her. She took the astrologer's hands in her own and looked pensively into Sophia's tired eyes. It was a gesture that, years ago, had won the heart of two kings.

And Louis she had cuckolded, while she tore Henry apart with anger and jealousy over her courts of love. Strange for a woman who thought so little of loyalty to make such a fuss over a husband's wanderings, Sophia thought. And the pursuit of the whole is called love.

"I dreamed of water. Of a deluge, closing over me. But I did not drown. I was breathing, and walking, although I was deep in water, and all about me was afloat. What does it mean, Sophia?"

"Water is always a symbol of good fortune." Sophia thought for a moment before answering. "In our mother's womb we float in warm water; out of the womb, water brings all those things we need for sustenance. But a deluge. That is no simple matter. I must think more on this." Indeed, a dream of deluge meant ill luck, catastrophe. But no need to point that out at this moment. Not when your back is killing you and all you want to do is go back to bed.

"Do so. And also ponder this, Lady Sophia. We need advice and information as to the disposition of the stars." Eleanor looked up to the ceiling, her eyes glinting with unspoken plans. Sophia knew that look. It meant trouble.

"We must know the most auspicious time for a great change in our lives. It is to take place this summer. The planets must favor me and my sons. They must frown on Henry. Find such a time, Sophia. Look into your charts and tables and find the day when I may triumph over Henry and regain what is mine, and my sons'."

So, Sophia thought, biting into a strawberry and waiting for the mime to begin. So, the Queen thinks to best the King. It will be an interesting summer, but probably one filled with discomfort. What form would Eleanor's revenge take?

"And God looked down from the heavens, and was sorely distressed by what he saw," Godfrey recited. His eyes shone; his hands trembled as he pointed at the crowd before him. "The world was filled with evil. In all the four corners, only three good and godly men could be found, Noah and his two sons."

Cedric, dressed in a robe and carrying a shepherd's staff, appeared on the first cart. The crowd moved as one toward the first station of the mime. The carts had been set up in a row, and the audience would move from cart to cart as the scenes changed.

Cedric knelt carefully so he wouldn't trip on his long robe, and lifted his arms up to heaven in supplication. Next to him rested a bundle of sheep's wool tied and twisted to resemble a lamb.

"The lamb! Sacrifice the lamb!" the crowd roared.

Cedric lifted the bundle onto a large plank which passed as an altar. Staying his arm as long as he dared, rousing the crowd to a fever pitch, he paused, and then plunged his knife into the bundle of wool. The knife found its target. Blood spluttered out from the pig's bladder, dousing with a scarlet rain those who stood nearest the cart. The crowd screamed with delight.

Broderick, watching from inside the helldoor, shuddered and giggled.

"Now," said Lucie. They scurried hand in hand to the second cart, while the audience was still distracted and whooping in front of Cedric's sacrifice. Here, a little trestle and two chairs had been set up to indicate a domestic scene.

"But the Lord saw that Noah and his sons, and their wives, were virtuous in his eyes, and walked in the way of the Lord." Godfrey's voice quieted the crowd again; they turned to the second cart, where Lucie and Broderick stood by the table. Broderick carried a scythe to show that he was a hardworking husband; Lucie had a long white robe over the sackcloth tiger costume and a yellow girdle about her waist. She wore a wig of straw over the tight cap and her own braids; she was a woman playing a man who was playing a woman.

"Husband, I do revere and obey you," Lucie recited loudly and with some effort of concentration. The trick was to make her voice deep enough so that she would sound like a man who was trying to sound like a woman. She moved stiffly, trying to quell the

25

feminine grace of her limbs. "As the Lord instructs you, so shall you instruct me in all that I do. You are my master. You are the good wheat and I the useless chaff."

In the audience, the wives booed and jeered; their husbands guffawed and pinched them, saying, "Listen, woman, to how a good wife speaks to her man!"

Broderick was supposed to speak a piece, too, but he had forgotten the words and stood knock-kneed and quaking on the platform, scratching at his wiry grey hair.

"Well I know you love me, with your heart and body. It is pleasing to the Lord," supplied Lucie, filling in the silence of Broderick's forgotten lines. "Yea, it is pleasing to me, too. Tup me again so we please the Lord that much more." She threw her arms around the giant and pretended to kiss him. The audience stamped in delight. Godfrey had added those lines to the traditional script of Noah and the Ark. He knew men's hearts; he knew that their reverence for God filled one side of it, but the other side was human and venial, and even the purest of saints would laugh at a good bawdy joke.

The play continued at a good speed, with Lucie and Broderick and Cedric moving from cart to cart as the scene changed, and Godfrey and Lucie between them filling in the silences of Broderick's oft-forgotten lines. Lucie's nervousness began to disappear. She enjoyed the playacting. Miming the actions of Godfrey's spoken words made her feel at one with him, as though he were the soul and she the body.

She forgot the woolly, dark clouds gathering overhead, forgot the tight band that constricted her chest and made it difficult to breathe. Forgot Udele, who glowered at the side of the platform like an ember that wouldn't be doused.

The time for the procession of the animals came. This was the tricky part. It was easy enough to please an eager Sunday morning crowd with bawdy jests and a quick pace. But everyone knew the animals went two by two, and in Godfrey's small troupe they went one by one. There weren't enough actors to present the animals in couples. Mayhap the rich town guilds that performed the Easter plays could find mates for all the animals that march into the ark. But this company, not tied to a guild and lacking resources because of its independence, could not. Had the people no imagination that they could not picture two elephants when already presented with one? Godfrey insisted over and over.

Hence, when he began to call the roll of the animals, a lone tiger jumped out at the audience. Lucie growled as loud as she could and leaped at a group of children, bringing forth a cacophony of playful shrieks. But after she disappeared back into the helldoor, there were mutterings from the audience and a few boos.

Anselm, finished with his packet of strawberries, wiped his hands on his brown robe and grimaced. What was this? A Noah's Ark with only one of each animal? Part of him was filled with sympathy for the fair youth with the sweet voice. Surely his talent should earn him a place with a more prosperous troupe. But the other part of Anselm was cold and speculative. Last week the bishop had complained that Anselm was lax in his duties; he did not strenuously enough pursue the task of bringing the parish sinners to a greater knowledge of God's commands.

There had even been rumors of heresy within Anselm's own household, of secret meetings with Cathar goodmen. Anselm was sympathetic to the new doctrine which preached that the fleshly joining of man and woman, even to make new souls, was sinful.

But here on this platform might heresy be better blamed, in the guise of this troupe which disdained the word of God, and sent animals one by one. If he brought this to the bishop's attention, perhaps his own household would no longer be scrutinized. Anselm drew closer to the platform, squinting to see better.

Behind the hellhole, Lucie struggled with Broderick's costume. He had fidgeted with the strings of the elephant trunk, and now they were knotted tightly behind his ears, refusing to come loose. Broderick's eyes shone with fright and tears.

"And the mules and horses came into Noah's Ark," Godfrey was calling. He repeated the line three times, and each repetition grew darker with impatience.

"You'll have to go out in the elephant costume again," Lucie

27

sighed. "Then Godfrey will see you're stuck in your costume, and he'll move on past the rest of the animals' roll call."

"He'll be angry." Broderick cringed.

"I can soothe him. It's Udele you'll have to watch out for tonight. Here, wipe your eyes, and go back out to the animals' platform."

As he left, Lucie peeped out the curtain. It had grown dark, and the sky overhead was heavy with rain clouds. A before-storm uneasiness filled her; the birds had stopped singing in the oak trees, and the audience no longer laughed as easily at Godfrey's bawdy jests. It would pour soon. They must hurry or God would have a finer jest on them. The players would be rained out before they finished the story of Noah and the Ark, and it was bad luck to begin a performance and not finish it.

When Broderick returned in his elephant costume, the crowd no longer laughed at his clumsiness and forgotten lines. Instead, small stones and handfuls of mud were thrown, insults called. This was no proper mime; the costumes weren't right and the animals didn't go two by two. They yelled for Haram to come back and return the coins they had thrown into his basket.

Godfrey, trying to yell above their noise, felt his neck prickle with fear. There was real danger here. He had seen smaller crowds rampage and destroy the players' carts for fewer errors than his troupe had committed this day. Maybe Lucie had been right, maybe the day was ill-starred.

Udele, still standing off to the side and red with fury over Broderick's mistakes, began cursing aloud. It was all the girl's fault. Things hadn't gone right since she'd joined them. If only she could be free of her! There were things she could do. Turn her in to a sheriff for stealing, sell her to a brothel keeper when Godfrey wasn't looking, or even tell a clerk that the woman appeared in mimes although the Church strictly forbade it. But Godfrey would discover what she had done, and be angry, perhaps even cast her off. No, it must appear that she, Udele, had nothing to do with it. But how arrange such a miracle?

Godfrey, pausing from the play, contemplated the sky. The clouds overhead were sooty with unshed rain; there was a tension in the air that suggested the storm would break at any moment. Perhaps, he thought, I can use the coming tempest to my purposes. I must try, at least. He grinned, realizing it was a trick that could make a man an instant reputation, if it worked. Or make him appear a total ass if it did not.

He waited as long as he dared as the crowd around him grew more restive. He took a deep breath, and when his instincts dictated, he lifted his hands high, palms facing the blackened sky, and cried aloud for the clouds to render themselves. At that precise moment the first flash of lightning appeared in the sky.

The crowd hushed and drew closer together. "Did ya see that?" a toothless old woman spoke aloud, and others around her laughed nervously. Anselm scratched at his bald head, awed by this seeming miracle. It was a trick, of course. The man had a goodly knowledge of the sky and gambled that lightning would come in that strange hush in the atmosphere he had perceived. Still, it was a good trick for all that. And look how the fair youth stared adoringly at his master! Anselm snorted.

Sophia, huddled between two merchants' carts to avoid the jostling crowd, nodded in admiration. This player knew how to turn a bad day to his advantage. She put her hood over her hair to protect it from the rain that would come any minute now.

"And the Lord said: Thou shalt not disrupt the player of the Lord, those who seek to spread His word and mime the story of the Gospels," Godfrey improvised in a ringing, proud voice.

"Then get on with it before we all get a soaking," the miller called out. "Though it's a strange player who brings his own deluge with him to float a paper ark!"

Godfrey hesitated just a moment. He was a young man, half arrogant and half self-doubting, and sometimes not even he knew which half would rule. But the audience looked to him expectantly and ceased their grumbling. He judged the sky to be as black as sky can be before it gives full vent to the storm it carries. Satisfied, he raised his arms and voice and continued. "And the Lord said, 'It shall rain for forty days and forty nights!'" His voice was triumphant.

The rain came, sharp and slashing as Damascus daggers.

The crowd broke up and scurried in all directions like a pile of leaves whipped by the wind. Blinded by the rain, they ran in frenzied circles, bumping into each other. Many, confused, stopped where they had started, in front of the players' cart, and this, too, they took to be part of Godfrey's magic.

Anselm was pale with the new cold, and with fear, his feet were frozen in place. Now this is a strange and terrible thing, he thought. What powers of darkness is this man in league with? I must rescue the youth from this devil. The canon's heart brimmed with newly found love, warming him so that he didn't feel the pricky cold of the raindrops. He already envisioned himself and this fair youth together, late at night, heads bent together over a manuscript of Bernart de Ventadour's pure love cantos. Anselm, ducking his head against the driving wind, moved towards Lucie.

She, frightened by the loud storm and the confusion of the crowd, leapt from the cart to find Godfrey. She made her way through the panicked audience and fought her way to his side, unaware that the drenching rain made her tunic and breeches cling like a second skin.

Udele, her hair and face streaming with rain, saw the way the rain revealed the woman's curves under the man's clothing and opened her mouth to call out a warning. Then closed her mouth, said nothing, and smiled. She moved closer to the moony-eyed canon who was clumsily making his way towards Lucie.

"They think it magic, the fools," Godfrey whispered to Lucie when she reached his side. "All of Poitiers will talk of this; Eleanor will hear of it and send for me." He put his arm around Lucie's shivering shoulders. "She will hear, and send for me." Bending, he placed a tender and triumphant kiss on her lips. Anselm, still struggling through the eddies of the frenzied crowd, felt his heart contract in jealousy.

"A pretty youth, is he not?" Udele whispered into Anselm's ear, positioning herself on his left side, the devil's side. "Look closely," she hissed, and then disappeared into the confusing throng.

Lucie, comforted by the kiss, was leaning back in Godfrey's

arms. Her head tilted. The straw wig, heavy with rain, slipped off and her long braids tumbled free.

Anselm, seeing what he had not seen before, the swelling breasts pressing against her wet clothes, the woman's long vanity of plaits, started in alarm and disgust.

"By God . . . the player is a woman! Sheriff's men! Quick! Seize her!" He roared, first in surprise, then fury.

He had lost his golden youth. But he had gained a heretic. His nights would be no less lonely, but he could prove to the bishop he did his share to bring sinners to justice.

Lucie was still as a hare that has been cornered and sees no escape. The sheriff's men surrounded her on all sides, grabbing at her hair and arms although she offered no resistance. Only her eyes moved wildly, from Godfrey, who was still at her side, to a far corner of the churchyard where a small, sad-eyed woman wearing tight blue sleeves watched with sympathy as Lucie's arms were bound behind her back.

Godfrey struck out and hit a guard on the jaw; he toppled over. Another guard lunged at Godfrey, raining blows on his chest and head. Soon, Lucie stood alone. Godfrey was bloodied and crumbled at her feet.

"Take her to the bishop's keep," Anselm ordered, standing closely over her so that even his nearsighted eyes could see the swell of her breasts and the red of her lips. Anselm wondered how he could ever have mistaken this wanton peasant girl for a noble youth.

"Godfrey!" Lucie screamed as they led her away. The blue-sleeved woman, who was quiet and different from the others, who cheered and roared, flinched. Over her shoulder Lucie saw Udele stoop to where Godfrey lay sprawled and bloody in the mud.

"I'll take care of Godfrey. You see to yourself," Udele said. "See they don't burn you at the stake." Her eyes were bolder than her words; they said Udele would be just as content if Lucie did burn.

The crowd, gleeful and whooping at this unexpected and exciting turn of events, parted to let the shrieking maiden and her captors through. The rain had stopped and the world was a muddy, drenched place. Yet the villagers were in no hurry to return to their fields or hearths. This was more excitement than they had seen since the abbey pigs had burst their pens and charged through the streets of the town on the feast day of St. Secundus.

"A woman acting in a mime," they whispered as Lucie passed. "The harlot. Oh, the sin and the shame of it!"

Sophia, shivering in her drenched blue gown and already astride her horse, watched from a distance, musing indifferently on the injustice that fills this world. Dressed in fine robes and sheltered within the walls of a strong castle, the girl's playacting would have been an innocent, playful thing. But out here, dressed in peasant clothes and facing the rules of the peasant's world, it was a crime.

She was tempted to step in and question Canon Anselm's authority in this matter. Perhaps with half a distraction, the girl could contrive to escape. But Anselm was no stranger to Sophia; she knew him for the narrow-minded, small-hearted man he was. Interfere, and he might well try to bring Sophia herself to the bishop's court, even protected as she was by Eleanor.

No, the best she could do for the girl was send a basket of bread and ale to her cell to make her stay more comfortable, for it was obvious the girl would have to answer to the bishop for this and do her penance.

I will tell Eleanor about this event. It will help distract her from her own problems for a few moments, Sophia thought. Eleanor always enjoyed a good tale. Especially if the damsel was beautiful, as this maid was. But as soon as her horse began to canter up the hill, familiar prickling pains raced along her back, and the old, nagging pain made her forget about the pretty maiden who had dared play a man's role.

Broderick stood in a corner and wailed in misery as Cedric and Haram dragged Godfrey out of the square and into the shelter of his own cart. Lillah was still moving through the crowd, tapping her tambourine and draping a veil so that coins and other offerings could be tossed into it. Godfrey would have wanted it so, she knew. Why waste a good crowd because a man's wounded face needs bathing? For Lucie, she felt nothing. For her man, she would kill—she always carried a small, deadly dagger in her girdle—but all others were as leaves in the wind, to be tossed this way and that as kismet wished, with no interference from her.

Udele, her face a study of bliss, arranged pillows under Godfrey's back as they laid him on his cot. Lucie's tunic, discarded earlier in the day, still rested there. Udele picked it up and threw it in the rag pile. Godfrey was hers again. Through no fault of her own—what had she done but whisper in Anselm's ear?—the girl had been discovered and captured. When they also found out she was a runaway serf, she would be whipped through the streets and returned in bruised shame to her owner in the dismal swamp where they had found her. Godfrey need never see her again.

Udele hummed happily as she cleaned the dried blood from her beloved's face and shoulders.

"Pack up the carts. Quickly. We are leaving," she yelled to Cedric and Haram, who were pacing outside.

Broderick would not leave without Lucie. He sulked and stood as unmoving as an oak till Udele came out of the cart and lashed him with a torrent of words that would have frightened Lucifer himself. But by the time the costumes and props were put away and the ropes uncoiled and ready to be harnessed, Godfrey was conscious, and asking for Lucie.

"Where have they taken her?" he demanded, trying to sit up.

34

A hammer pounded at his temples; his long hair was wet with rain, mud and blood.

"Who knows?" Udele said, smiling. "I'm sure she will be well taken care of."

"No. We must get her back." Godfrey struggled to rise. Udele, with a great sigh, tried to push him back down onto his cot, but even after his beating, he was strong and stubborn.

"Well, then, if you insist, fool that you are, let me help you," she said. Pretending to reach behind him for a cloak, she reached instead for a kettle hanging from the ceiling and gripped it securely in her fist.

"God forgive me. And Godfrey, too," she muttered, bringing the kettle down on his head as hard as she dared. He slumped down. Udele tucked him in lovingly, and then scrambled out the small door of the cart, feeling strong enough in her joy to pull the cart alone.

The bishop was a wealthy man. But his keep was poor. Comfort and courtesy were not necessary for such as she, for prisoners. Rats scurried at her feet in the dank, smelly straw littering the mud floor. Although it was not yet noon, a midnight darkness filled the windowless, high-walled cell.

Lucie bunched together as much dry straw as she could find and curled up on it in a corner. She shivered, hoping her wet garments would dry soon. Her hair, as long as it was, would be damp till the next morning, with no sun to dry it. It would be a very long night.

She was calm now, realizing that no storm on her part could win her release. Minutes ago she had been a wildcat, kicking and biting. She had drawn blood from both her guards and cursed Anselm so roundly, his ears were still red. But once the door had thudded shut behind her, all that was useless. Better to rest, to pray. To wait for Godfrey. He would come for her.

Something rattled at the thick wooden door. Her eyes were still not used to the dark. She had to creep all the way to the lock itself before she saw through the wide crevices the wizened gaoler standing there.

"Ah, a new friend!" he exclaimed, showing her a toothless smile. "A pretty one! Let me pet your hair, girl, then I'll fetch a bucket of water for ya." He cackled.

Lucie spit on the floor at his side, then repented of her rudeness. She might well need a friend in this place. Swallowing her disgust, she bowed her head and kept her face expressionless as the ancient gaoler put his trembling, gnarled hands through the meal hole and stroked her hair, the hair that Godfrey had playfully twisted around his fingers in the heat of late afternoons. He left and minutes later returned with a dripping, moldy bucket and a stale trencher that was soggy in the middle with the remains of a thin meat stew.

"Eat," her gaoler said. "The bishop only sends food down once a day, and if you leave it till later, the rats will eat it for you."

She hadn't eaten yet that day, and as foul as the trencher smelled, her stomach grumbled in hunger. I will suffer one meal here in this keep, and then before the next meal comes, Godfrey will have come for me, Lucie promised herself. She did not let herself wonder what he would say or do to win her release, nor consider how a mere jongleur would gain an audience with a bishop to plead for the freedom of his paramour. He would find a way. In Godfrey was her trust.

The choked-down trencher sat in her belly like a lump of lead; her hair was like strangling seaweed as she crouched in the straw. She was drowning in misery. She had never before been bound and imprisoned, never been as completely alone as she was in this dark keep. Tired and frightened, Lucie closed her eyes and forced her mind to go many leagues away from this dank cell, to travel where she wished it to be.

She felt a floating sensation and, with eyes still closed, imagined she could look down below and see the four stern towers of the fortress of Sir Foulkes of St. Servan, her birthplace. She was an angel flying over them, free and holy and beyond harm and fear. Beyond the towers, salt marshes and weedy pastures stretched as far as the eye could see, all the way to the sea. Her nostrils twitched, remembering the feel and smell of salty air, and then she remembered other things.

Smoke from the cookhouse ovens rose from the wooden sheds that leaned against a postern gate.

A woman, back bent in work, arms covered with cinders, fed the oven bits of wood. She was singing quietly to herself. Warmth creeped up from Lucie's toes and fingertips to the middle of her chest, meeting in a soft rush of comfort. "Mama," she whispered into the dark cell. And then she forced her mind to travel, not just over land, but into time itself.

A small child with sun-golden skin and tawny hair scurried from under the huge oak worktable, chasing a wooden ball.

"Lucie!" the woman yelled. Even when angry, her voice was soft. It was still the time when there was much love between them, the early time. "Don't get in the way. Go play outside."

"Yes, Mama." Lucie went to her for a hug, which she quickly received, and then, with the ball tucked under her arm, made for the door. It swung open from the other side, almost knocking her over. The lord of the castle, Sir Foulkes, strode in, his sword clanging against his boot top. Half-hidden by the door, which had stuck open, Lucie hesitated, sensing a change in her mother. Her back was no longer bent, but stiff, like a hunting hound's that has sniffed wild boar. Her face went white despite the heat that emanated from the brick bread oven.

The baker had always been a coward. As soon as his lord entered the kitchen, he left it, taking with him his helpers and cleaners. Lucie, her mother, and Sir Foulkes were left alone amongst the pots and pans and flour barrels.

"You honor us, Lord," her mother said, curtseying. The young child heard the fear in her voice.

"Douce, don't be cold," Sir Foulkes said, grinning. He was a powerful-looking knight, thick as a bear and quick on his feet. He covered the length of the room in three strides and took Lucie's mother in his arms. She struck out at him; he struck back, hitting her cheek with the stinging flat of his hand.

Lucie whimpered. Startled, both her mother and Sir Foulkes turned to discover her hiding behind the door, which, in her memory, was caught for all time in a swing open.

"The cat has a kitten," Sir Foulkes said, staring down at her. "A kitten that promises to someday give as much pleasure as the mother." He took Lucie's chin in his grimy, callused hand. Her mother stepped between them.

"Leave the child alone," she said. "I won't hit you again, Lord, I give my word."

"You will come tonight, then? No more of this coyness?"

"Yes," her mother agreed. "But leave the child alone."

That night, when she was supposed to be asleep, Lucie listened to her mother dress in the dark and then creep out. Her steps were heavy. Some women liked coupling, but her mother did not. Even so, it was necessary. No man lived in their bare, thatched hut with them, no one claimed them. Their small cornfield barely fed them. Such women did not say no, especially not to the seigneur.

After that night, their lives changed for the better. They slept in the oven-house, where it was warm and food was always available, even meat once or twice a week. Her mother sang as she worked, and she had new coins to buy a ribbon for Lucie's hair.

But one day Sir Foulkes' lady, Maria, came down to the kitchen and stared at them for a long and icy moment. The next day the seneschal came and scooped up their bundle of clothes and tossed it outside, into the mud. "Go back to your marsh cottage," he told them. "You're not wanted in the kitchens anymore. There's a new girl to tend the ovens."

In her dark cell Lucie shivered, remembering how cold that next winter had been after the warmth of the kitchens. There hadn't been enough bread or gruel to keep their stomachs full from one dawn to the next. Her baby brother, born just a few months later, died quickly, and her mother no longer sang, nor hugged her.

On the coldest days Lucie walked long hours into the distant woods to collect scraps of bark and twigs, for a fire. Her mother sat pale and empty-eyed and silent.

As Sir Foulkes had predicted, Lucie grew as fair as her mother had once been, with the same curling, tawny hair and sparkling brown eyes. Other men of the area—Robert, the miller; Berengar, the woodcutter; James, the coin-clipper—would sometimes come and knock at Douce's door and sit with her of an evening. But when Lucie grew tall with long legs and a shy grin, they winked at her and told rude jests. Douce began to frown and encouraged Lucie to sit deep in the shadows, away from prying eyes.

During the spring of her fourteenth birthday Sir Foulkes, fresh from a tourney, had ridden his black gelding through the salt marshes to their cottage. A black tunic lay over his chain mail; red and black ribbons streamed from his lance. He was famous for his skills in the tourneys. He had unseated the renowned Aliksander of Toulouse that day, and the victory had made his blood hot. His eyes flashed.

"Bring out the kitten," he told Lucie's mother, giving her no other greeting. Hawks circled and cried overhead in the large, white sky.

"She is too young," her mother protested, standing in alarm and dropping the peas she had been shelling. Douce, who took three days each to birth the children she brought into this world, feared that her young daughter would get with child.

"Come, woman, she's old enough to have a man and well you know it. As lord of the manor, I claim my right to instruct her in the ways of a woman." Sir Foulkes threw his lance at her feet as if claiming a foreign territory for his own dominion. Lucie watched from the shadowed interior of the cottage.

"Come back tomorrow," Lucie's mother said, narrowing her eyes at him. "I will prepare her for you."

"Tomorrow, then." He had ridden off again, relieved that the woman had pleaded for time. The tourney had wearied him; he would be more vigorous on the morn.

Lucie knew Sir Foulkes' reputation, the stream of servant girls that entered the castle and left weeks after, bruised and pregnant and cast off, while Lady Maria brooded in her tapestry-hung feather bed. She knew Douce was one of the castoffs, and that their own lives had been made worse, not better, by his attentions.

"Mama." Lucie went to her mother. For the first time in many months, Douce hugged the girl and patted her on the back with a friendly fluttering of her hand.

"How tall are you, my child." Douce looked at her in wonder. "The lord is right; you are child no longer. It is time to make your way in the world." The two women looked at each other. Lucie was bound by the rule of serfdom to St. Servan's and Sir Foulkes, as was her mother, and her grandmother and great-grandmother had been, back to the time before the first Crusade. This niche of servitude was her place in the world. She belonged to it, and likewise, it belonged to her. She could not leave, by the laws of God and man. But they both knew she would. Lady Maria was more to be feared than the great unknown outside the mesne of St. Servan's.

"The Lord will show us a way," her mother said, trying and failing to sound confident.

That evening, Godfrey and his troupe came.

Sir Foulkes, in a merry mood because of the day's victories in the tourney, permitted them to enter the great hall and play for his guests and household during the evening feast.

Godfrey, seeing that the great hall was no more than a crude pile of stones with a roof on top, was dubious of collecting a good fee from this marsh warlord. "Then we'll get our supper and be grateful for it!" Udele hissed in his ear when he hesitated. "We'll stop here for the night, or are you too good for it, Sir Paris Student?" She always called him that when she meant to berate. He gave in, and unpacked his lute.

The hall was lit only by hearthlight; this lord was too cheap to provide candles. Just as well, perhaps. Judging from what he could see of the hall, it did not bear closer inspection. Month-old mutton bones littered the straw underfoot, and no hall servants had bothered to remove a great accumulation of brown piles left by the packs of dogs that freely roamed about. The company was drunk and boisterous.

Godfrey, sensing that the evening's mood required tales of

bloodshed and seduction, recited the *Song of Roland* and some new love poems of his own composing. But the company was unappreciative and tightfisted. No coins or tidbits from the table were forthcoming until Lillah, sensing the mood of the crowd, took out her tambourine and performed her sensual, lyrical dances. Only then were they fed and showered with coins.

Later, when Sir Foulkes and most of his guests lay under the food-littered trestles in snoring, drunken heaps, Godfrey led his tired company out of the hall, richer by several silver goblets. Thievery was dangerous, but Sir Foulkes had promised a fee and paid none. He owed him something for the night's entertainment.

They left hurriedly by way of the postern gate, passing by the salt marsh cottage where Lucie and Douce lived. Lucie, having heard that there were jongleurs and minstrels in the hall that night, had waited for them, guessing they would leave by the lowly back gate, where the guard was liable to be asleep, or at least uncaring about any bulges in the pockets and tunics of the hurriedly departing company.

"Good sir," she pleaded, when the troupe finally appeared through the thick curtain of fog and darkness. She pulled at Godfrey's russet tunic and brought him to a halt. He put down the pulling ropes of his cart and stared at the girl, startled. Her pale face and shining hair gleamed eerily in the moonlight. He made a quick sign of the cross over his forehead and breast to ward off evil spirits, so unnerved was he by the startling appearance of this beautiful and wild-eyed maid.

"Friend, how may I assist you?" he finally stammered.

"I would like to come with you," she answered shyly.

He ran his eyes over her, taking in the poor clothing, the slightly bowed head that spoke of servitude. "That cannot be," he told her. Already he regretted it could not be.

Douce, who had been waiting in the shadows, stepped beside her daughter. "Take her with you," she also pleaded.

Now, Godfrey liked to think of himself as a practical man. But faced with two sad-eyed women seeking a favor . . . and to boot both fair of face and gentle of voice . . . he felt his resolve weakening.

"Should I take the girl with me, we will be pursued. It is a risk I don't need," he protested feebly. But the girl's face was like a candle, shining with hope.

Lucie watched the quick emotions flicker in the eyes of this tall youth—first surprise, then fear, then something else, the same thing she had seen in Lord Foulkes' eyes when he took her by the chin and called her a kitten. But she liked it when this youth looked at her. She did not feel like cringing behind a door to avoid his gaze.

Against his will, he smiled at her. Lucie smiled back. Their eyes locked and it seemed it was dark night no longer, but bright day. The two of them stood together in a field of light that touched no one else, binding them. It was the first time either of them had felt this strange binding. They shyly looked away from each other. Lucie's heart was beating fast in her chest, as though she had just run the whole distance from the miller's house.

"Godfrey?" Udele crept out of the shadows to see what kept him. She saw the mother and the girl standing there, quiet and still as statuary, and impatience moved her lips before she had considered her words.

"Leave them, Godfrey. We have no need of more in our company." Her voice was shrill.

She could not have chosen a better way to force his decision. Udele was bossy and quarrelsome; Godfrey had taken to doing things just the opposite of what she commanded, to spite her.

"She can learn lines and add to our company," he said. "Often enough you remind me how paltry we are." The girl was tall and slender, he had already noted. With her hair bound up, she could pass as a youth. Udele flung up her hands in exasperation, realizing her mistake.

"If I take her with me, she may be found and taken back on the morn. And I and those with me branded as thieves for stealing the lord's property," he said to Douce, forming one last argument, although the case was already won.

"There is a deep pond behind the kitchens. It is cold and brackish," Lucie said. "A kitchen girl threw herself in five Eas-

42

ters ago and her body never came up to the top of the waters. If they think I am in the pond, they will not search for me."

"Why would they think you were in the pond?" Godfrey asked.

"Because the lord comes for me on the morrow, and I would rather be in the pond than in his bed." She said it simply and without self-pity, and Godfrey knew it was the truth.

A few minutes later Lucie, half-dressed and cold in her bliaut, watched as her mother took her worn, filthy tunic and wrapped it around a large rock. "Mama. Who will plow the wheat field in the spring?" Lucie whispered, worried now for her mother rather than herself. Douce was not strong enough for hard labor.

"Robert will have me," Douce whispered back. "He was waiting for you to leave. No sense feeding a grown daughter." Lucie thought maybe her mother was just saying that, to ease her leaving. But there was an edge in Douce's voice that prohibited more questions.

With Godfrey following at a distance, Lucie and Douce crept to the pond, carrying the rock between them. They threw the bundle into the murky water. As it left their fingertips and arched through the air, Lucie felt the bond between herself and her mother arch in the air with it, free, and then it was no more. She had a past now. And a future. The drowning of the rock was the dividing point between the two.

The splash sounded loud and final. Douce waited till the rock carried her daughter's bliaut well beneath the murky surface of the pond, then screamed and wailed till all those who slept in the nearby huts were roused by her feigned agony.

Godfrey and Lucie had already disappeared into the night, followed by a muttering Udele.

"Let us be quickly on our way," Godfrey whispered, flinging clothing and curtains and rugs over Lucie, where she crouched in the corner of his wagon. "The further away we are by the time Sir Foulkes hears of this, the happier I'll be."

And so, Lucie had left with the players. Her last glimpse of her mother had been of her kneeling by the pond, weeping. But she knew there was joy in her heart.

*   *   *

Something small and furry was sniffing at the mud on her wooden shoes. A rat. She kicked at the vermin, cursing aloud. They were losing their fear of her. This one scurried away to the corner; she could see its small, evil eyes glowing in the dark, watching her. Lucie sat up stiffly. The damp straw had stolen what little warmth she had; she shivered.

What hour was it? Where was Godfrey? She wished she had a candle notched with the hours so she could see the time burn away while she waited. Never before had she slept alone. Always there had been her mother or the bread-baker's sister, or Lillah or Godfrey or even foul-tempered Udele, to share the darkness with her. Such solitude as this was not to be suffered. She fought back tears.

The gaoler was back, rattling the heavy-timbered door.

"Time to break fast," he wheezed. "Come get it, girl, or do you expect it to arrive on a silver plate?" He cackled and wheezed. Another meal, and he had said the prisoners were fed once a day. Had she been here a full day, truly? She felt her hair. It was matted, but dry. For the first time, her heart contracted with real fear. She tried to eat the trencher, but it tasted of dirt and rancid fat. She put it aside and let the rats take it.

Sophia toyed with the chunk of meat speared on her jeweled dagger. The noise in the great hall was deafening, even though all there conversed in the gentle, well-modulated tones that Eleanor bid them use. No yelling, drunken brawls or pinching of ladies' maids was allowed at her feasts.

Eleanor demanded courtesy of her company: they were to converse over their meals, making intellectual stimulation as important to daily fare as the meat they ate. They were to come to the table with clean hands and combed hair. The knights and squires were to show gentle courtesies to the ladies seated beside them, always offering them first choice of the communal dishes and cutting their meat for them in small, delicate bites before offering it

44

on the tips of their daggers. The ladies were to accept prettily and not too eagerly, chewing with closed mouths and lowered lids. They dabbed often at their lips with fine napkins so the grease would not trickle onto their chins. And they spoke of love, that fine metaphysical state of the soul in which all emotions and desires were purified in a fire of appreciation for the beloved.

These were the manners that the barbaric English and monkish French courts scoffed at; these were the manners that befitted a court of love, a palace of poetry, music and philosophy.

Sophia, unpartnered, a foreigner in the court of love, cleaned her dagger with a napkin and sighed.

Never had a knight willingly sat next to her, mincing her meat fine enough for a babe and offering it with grand patience though his own stomach rattled with hunger. She was the court astrologer and a reader of books. That set her apart. That, and her afflictions, her childishly small, unwomanly body, with its flat breasts and one leg longer than the other, which made her slow and ungainly. All looked away when she approached, and no knights clamored to sit by her side. Sophia pretended indifference.

Sweet melodies from viols and lutes wafted through the air, along with the odors of roasted venison, pheasant stuffed with apples, gingered carp in huge ponds of golden aspic, and silver-coated honey cakes shaped like beehives. The divers dishes were carried in by young pages who began their apprenticeships in chivalry by learning to graciously serve. An hour before, they had formed a timorous, fidgeting line in the buttery, where Eleanor personally inspected them to see that boots were free of manure, tunics free of grease spots, and no dirt lurked under their nails. There were those who grumbled that Eleanor thought too highly of cleanliness.

Now, all straight backs and youthful eagerness, the pages were everywhere—cutting meats, pouring wine and seeing to the comfort of the large host of diners seated at the long rows of trestles. The great hall was a sea of faces; more than a hundred knights and ladies had gathered to pay homage to Eleanor, their Queen, for the Easter court. Enough candles to light the cathedral for a week blazed in the hall, and musicians played from each corner of the room, striving to be heard above the unavoidable din of such a large feast.

It was a marvel of a feast, Sophia admitted to herself. The ladies wore gold crucifixes and tapered sleeves that trailed all the way to the floor. The knights had donned formal, full-length robes and jeweled surcoats. The cooks had outdone themselves, and what she could hear of the music was lovely beyond compare. Yet she would have preferred a small meal in her room to this over-done splendor. Her back was killing her. And that half-witted page Raoul smirked every time he served her.

But Eleanor, regal and self-assured in a sky blue gown trimmed with ermine, had requested that her astrologer dine with her in the hall. Only those in the infirmary were excused from the feast.

Increasingly, the unhappy Queen surrounded herself with crowds the whole day long. "Solitude oppresses me," she confided. "At night I dream of small towers, and of being shut in them, where it is cold and dark and no sounds of music can be heard. Do I dream of death, Sophia?"

Sophia understood pain but was still too far from her own demise to appreciate her aging Queen's preoccupation with death. Such talk chilled her. "No, My Lady," she said with a frown. "Death is not a tower, but a dungeon. You dream of your own restlessness and melancholy."

The greasy odor of the venison turned Sophia's stomach into a knotted pit that rejected food. She put her dagger back into its little jeweled sheath in her girdle and tore a hunk of white bread into little pieces. She fed them to the hounds that crept about under the table. And she waited.

The hall was alive with anticipation. Eleanor had promised them a surprise that evening, one of great magnitude. It would be timely, Sophia thought, if Eleanor could produce a miracle, even a small one, to please this gathering. Courtesy reigned in the hall, but too many of the southern barons were thin-lipped and frowning.

Peace sat heavily on their shoulders, like a vulture, pecking at their wealth and ambition. Peace was good for the countryside and the peasants, but the barons and knights of Aquitaine were showing the strains of idleness.

Sacking castles was how they increased their reputations; ransoming nobles caught in battle was how they filled their coffers and paid off their retinues. To be at peace was to be on the road to poverty. After three years of truce with Henry's English armies, the warriors spoke through clenched teeth and complained that their horses were fat with lack of exercise.

Eleanor, not deaf to their mutterings, had sponsored tourney after tourney, inviting all knights who would come to her court to compete for sacks of gold and glory. Still, the older knights spoke of the better years of before, and the young knights clamored for battlefield experience. No, peace was not to their taste.

Even now Sophia could hear a knight telling a long-winded tale (a bit too loudly, she thought) about the time he had captured the chaplain of Clairvaux Castle and ransomed him for two war steeds, although all of Christendom knew this worthless priest couldn't even recite his confiteor without stumbling over the Latin.

Across the table from him, Benoit, the young Count of Clairvaux, affably gritted his teeth and tried to share in the general laughter, although it was his own father who had been cheated of the valuable horses.

Sophia watched the two men, intrigued. Their natural inclination was to reach for battle-axe and sword; the courtesy of Eleanor's hall required that they treat each other as brothers-in-arms.

Count Benoit of Clairvaux, in the flower of his youth, was still young and slender; he had been knighted only two years before, the same year as his father's death. The other knight had the first streak of grey at his temples, and was burly as a bear. His arms and neck bulged with muscle. If they should fight, the winner would be the elder.

She would mention this matter later to Eleanor. It would not do to have young Benoit murdered right under their noses. Although the killing of this unknown knight might be a pleasant thing. He had loud, uncouth manners and eyed the ladies in an unseemly way. He had even kept his black beard, which curled defiantly over the lower half of his face, although other knights shaved their chins and wore neatly trimmed mustaches in obedience to Eleanor's preference.

The older knight's face suddenly lighted with lust. Sophia followed his eyes to where Marie of Champagne glided in on the arm of her court poet, Chrétien de Troyes. Those two made a habit of coming late to the feasts, appearing only when all others had gathered. And each appearance was greeted with a mass intake of breath, for the beautiful Marie knew how to draw and hold all eyes, even those of her Queen Mother.

"Forgive us, Lady Mother. We were hard at work in the solarium and lost track of the hour."

"Beloved child, you need never apologize. Here, I saved a place next to me," spoke Eleanor, who could not abide tardiness in any others but this daughter. Marie was the first child to issue from Eleanor's womb, the child whom God had finally seen fit to send her and Louis of France.

Other mothers would have mourned the birth of a daughter, those many years ago when the throne of France begged for an heir. Eleanor had not. Daughters were as useful as sons, she protested to Louis. And, she thought to herself, they were in many ways far superior to men. More intelligent. Greater able to appreciate the worthy things of the spirit. More cunning. What a fool St. Paul had been, and those of his ilk, who preached that women were no more than the manure on a pious man's boot.

Although God had eventually rewarded her with many sons— God and the virile loins of her lusty Henry—she had never regretted the birth of that first or later daughters. And now see how God sent solace in the form of this grown child, so beauteous and wise! So like her own mother!

She and Marie had been separated most of their lives. Soon after the birth, she and Louis had gone on Crusade, leaving behind their comely little Marie. Upon return from the Crusade had come the divorce. On that last day of her unhappy marriage to Louis Capet, she had ridden south from Beaugency, and Louis rode east, taking their two daughters—a second girl-child had followed the first, not the desired son—with him. Oh, the years of separation, of wondering if the French court was turning her beloved child into a piously meek maiden fit only to bring forth children and order about servants.

And then the surprise, the miracle, when tall, comely Marie, now a married woman and countess, rode into Poitiers three springs ago! Never had daughter more favored mother, both in body and spirit. God could be fair. He took Henry's love, but gave her back her daughter.

"How goes the work?" Eleanor asked, waving aside a page so that she herself could serve Marie from the heaped platters littering the white-clothed trestle. Marie and her court poet, Chrétien, had begun a long romance about the legendary King Arthur and the exploits of his court. Marie was a great patroness of the arts, rivaling even Eleanor in the amount of poetry that was conceived and brought forth in her court.

"We have begun a new verse. One devoted to the love between Lancelot and Guinevere," Marie answered, sipping delicately at her spiced wine. Chrétien, farther down the trestle, bit into a huge chunk of venison, splattering juices on his own surcoat and those of his neighbors. As much as he loved poetry and song, he loved his food equally well.

Lancelot and Guinevere? Sophia closed her eyes in concentration. Geoffrey of Monmouth's spare account of Arthur had said nothing she could remember about such an affair. It was as she had feared when she first heard of this literary project. Marie and her poet would take little effort to preserve the truth. Already they had invented some nonsense about Arthur finding a sword in a stone.

"An adulterous love, is it not?" Eleanor asked, smiling. "The best form of love. Only between unwed men and women can true, pure passion exist."

Sophia's eyes narrowed when she heard this. She knew Eleanor had not forgotten the great passion that had existed between her and Henry. This, then, was a part of her revenge, this insistence that husbands are not to be loved but merely tolerated. It is the plucked chicken asking for the warmth of the soup kettle, Sophia thought. It is the fox's sour grapes.

"Adulterous love is wicked," spoke up slow-moving, fat Andreas Capellanus, who had followed Marie and the poet into the hall. His fingers were ink-stained, his watery blue eyes bloodshot from close work and smoky candlelight.

"Sir Priest, God give you good appetite. Does work on the *Treatise on Love and the Remedies of Love* progress nicely?" Eleanor asked. Her voice was grave, but there were curls of disdain at the corners of her mouth. She disliked this ill-kempt, unpleasant cleric.

Marie, with her wide-searching mind, wasn't content with her work on the life of King Arthur; she was also dictating a lengthy work that coded all the rules of love. And there were many. It was Andreas' task to finalize the codes into formal language. He, a fervent woman-hater and defender of the commandments, hated this task. But yet more did he hate poverty, and Marie was a generous patroness. Grudgingly he kept at his work, but already he planned his revenge: an epilogue that would show women for what they were, unclean beasts who led men to eternal damnation.

"It progresses," he muttered, taking a seat below the great silver salt cellar which marked the boundary of who was in Eleanor's favor and who was not.

"Then you should have learned by now that such love is not wicked at all, but a way for the pure in heart to transmute passion from earthly goals to heavenly rewards. The adoration of a lady, who leads the worthy from the path of despair to the pinnacle of hope, is the true purpose of any goodly knight," Eleanor argued.

"Hummph," snorted Andreas.

She is light of heart tonight, whereas this morning she was downcast, Sophia thought, watching the queen. What has happened to cause this change?

And not once has she mentioned her son, Henry, the Young King. It was unlike Eleanor to let that absence go unmarked. "See. See how Henry holds his own son prisoner" was her usual comment, referring to the rather short leash on which the elder Henry was keeping the younger these days. The Young King was,

50

by his father's orders, cooling his heels in Chinon, never far from his father's side.

It was several years since the Young King had been crowned. They had been years of humiliation and frustration. First, Henry had refused to crown Margaret of France. That had insulted the Young King, her husband; infuriated King Louis, her father; and given the girl herself a fit of bad humors that lasted for months. Then, Henry had refused to give the Young King power and money. He still treated him as a lad, miserly counting out coins and all but patting him on the head. All in the land knew that the Young King's coronation had been an empty political maneuver meant to keep his sons under stricter control, not empower them. The Young King was crowned, but Henry Fitz-Empress made it very clear it was an empty title. Henry Fitz-Empress intended to keep the throne, and all the power associated with it, for himself.

And then came the catastrophe of Montferrand, in January past. Henry decided his favorite son, John, known as Johnny Lackland, should be wed to Alice of Maurienne, and to insure this, he promised the powerful castles of Chinon, Mirebeau and Loudon as a marriage portion. The Young King, sulking and forced to sit in on these impossible negotiations, listened as Henry generously planned to give away three of his most important holdings. The Young King was beside himself with impotent fury.

"Over my dead body. Or yours," he yelled to his father, stalking out. Since then the youth wasn't even allowed to piss in private, for fear of the sedition he might plan.

It was wise of Henry, Sophia thought, playing with her food, to keep close watch on Hal. The seventeen-year-old had a temper and was unpredictable. And his fury was understandable.

But it wasn't just his son whom Henry kept a watchful eye over. After the Young King's outburst, Raymond of Toulouse had pointedly, and without subtlety, reminded Henry that his wife, Eleanor, was also wroth. The Young King's cause was her cause. In fact, all of the southern kingdoms, including his own family, thought that ambitious Henry was overreaching himself, and that his plans for eastern expansion of the empire were a threat to what they already held. What good to possess Maurienne if Chinon, Loudon and Mirebeau were lost? What good to take from one son to give to another?

King Henry paced and scratched his head whenever Eleanor was mentioned. At best, she made him nervous. At worst, she roused him to fury. Her pride was the undoing of them; she should meekly obey and support him like other more sensible wives did. But no, not Eleanor. She had to have equal say, equal power, even challenge the King himself. Southern women were overweening in their demands, they did not know their place, and if that place was pointed out to them, they would not keep to it. And now she encouraged her sons to challenge him, too.

The King's desire should be law, but Eleanor had become even more intractable with age, not less. For years they had slept side by side, her skin warming him, her blond hair tangled in with his red hair. And now they were strangers, because Rosamonde slept next to him, and he had three grown sons who filled him with consternation and confusion. Only the seven-year-old John seemed to love him.

"The Queen is fierce," Henry agreed, nodding. "Set a man to watch her. But don't run to me with tales not worth hearing. The least said of the Queen, the better." When he thought of her, something in his chest twisted, and his head started to pound. A younger man would confuse the sensation with love. Henry remembered the time when it had been love, but knew now it had turned to fear. And guilt.

And so a man was secretly sent to Poitiers to discreetly press his ear to doors and keep his eyes open. This man, Maingot, a middle-aged knight of smooth disposition and bland features who asked ten questions for every two he answered, sat now at the feast, chatting with Richard, Duke of Aquitaine, Henry and Eleanor's second son.

Sophia watched them, wondering what they discussed with such avidity. Maingot she did not like, although she couldn't say why. His black eyes were handsome, his manner polished. But there was something furtive about him.

52

Richard, seated next to him, was openness itself. This fair youth of sixteen, with his red hair, ruddy cheeks and flashing eyes, glowed like flame, attracting the moths of all attention as his just due. He was comely, brave and filled with the ideals of chivalry. His love cansos, despite his tender age, were already famous throughout Aquitaine.

Eleanor was besotted with love for this second son. Not even intense conversation with her daughter, Marie, could keep her eyes from straying regularly to the shining face of the young and beloved Duke of Aquitaine.

Sophia, growing yet less hungry for every new platter carried into the feast, turned her attention to Marie and Eleanor. They talked and occasionally laughed, their two fair heads pressed together, their profiles showing uncanny resemblance one to the other. Their conversation was a lighthearted debate about whether or not a wife could kiss her husband after she had recently kissed her lover knight, without sullying the love between herself and the knight.

It was, Sophia thought, an exceedingly silly debate. But Eleanor's court revolved around such discussions. Sophia was eager to leave the hall and return to the scriptorium, but she needed Eleanor's permission, and it was not forthcoming. She sighed, and pushed food around on her trencher, and waited.

At twilight—the feast had begun at midday, when Eleanor returned from the hunt—she was still waiting. Fingers of night crept into the room as the pages scurried about, replacing burnt-down tapers which had created pools of wax on the trestles. Sophia stifled a yawn. The black-bearded knight who had been taunting young Sir Benoit was sound asleep, his face resting on a damp stain of red wine. His snores resounded through the hall, and the pages giggled as they cleared the debris around him.

Eleanor and Marie still debated whether or not a wife should freely kiss her own husband. Just as Sophia was preparing to feign illness and ask permission to depart, a fanfare sounded at the entrance of the great hall. All turned in the direction of the guards, who now stood quickly aside to permit entrance to a messenger, newly arrived.

53

The hall grew silent. Ladies stopped gossiping in midsentence, knights turned away from the maidens they had been flattering, the fatigued pages put down the emptied platters and sullied cloths they carried. Only the steps of the messenger, a knight clad in gleaming chain mail, could be heard as he crossed the long hall. His face was obscured by the visor of his helmet; the tabard over his chain mail tunic was pure white.

Even Sophia sat up to see better. Who was he? Why did he approach the Queen in full armor, dressed as for battle? Eleanor and Marie smiled knowingly, and Sophia realized this mysterious appearance was as staged as a miracle play; the messenger had arrived earlier and already delivered his message. This second arrival was for the benefit of those others gathered in the hall.

The messenger knelt when he reached Eleanor's dais. She stood and extended her hand.

"I bid thee rise, fair knight. Rise and let the company know you."

He stood and lifted his visor. All in the hall craned their necks to see better.

The youth, standing proud and smiling before them, was Hasculf of St. Hilaire, the Young King's boon companion. The buzz in the hall grew louder. Henry had thrown the youth out of Chinon, saying he was an evil influence on the Young King. And now he was at Eleanor's court and obviously carrying a message of great importance.

"I bring news of your son, Henry, King of England," Hasculf announced in a ringing voice. He is enjoying this too much, Sophia thought, alert and suspicious. The message pleases him. "Henry, your son, sends his love and devotion to his fair Lady Mother, Eleanor of Aquitaine. He bids her know he is safe and well. He is in Paris, with his friend and ally, Louis of France." Hasculf's voice, still not arrived at dependable manhood, broke at the end so that "Louis" came out as a very loud squeak, but none in the hall remarked this. The message itself had caught their full attention.

The buzzing ceased. Now the hall was silent as they tried to make sense of this.

In France? The Young King with Louis? But how is this? Sophia, too, thought, fidgeting. Henry is with his father, a prisoner there.

Nay. He *was* with his father. Now he is with his father's enemy, Louis of France. When the King hears of this, he will be greatly angered.

Then Sophia almost laughed aloud. God's knees, but Queen Eleanor was brazen. She was going to set son against husband, by allying the Young King with Louis of France, who had been her first husband and was Henry's sworn enemy!

At that moment, others came to the same realization. There would be a battle. There would be war between the King and his sons, and his wife.

A round of applause sounded through the hall. Even the blackbearded knight, who just a moment before had been snoring, jumped to his feet and banged his great fists against the wooden trestle.

"God save Young King Henry!" he shouted, inflamed with excitement.

"God save the King," all the company yelled. And it was not old Henry in England they were cheering on. It was Young King Henry. Eleanor's son. Eleanor would have her revenge.

Hasculf, seated now and with goblet and platter set before him, regaled them for hours with tales of Henry's escape. It had been a daring one. Eleanor, encouraging, fed him tidbits with her own hands. Richard and Geoffrey, eager for adventures of their own, listened avidly and with more than a little jealousy to the escapades of their elder brother.

To escape Henry's watchful eye, the Young King had risen in the middle of the night, donned his armor, and made for France, with Henry hot on his heels all the way. He had been promptly welcomed by Louis, who awaited him. This was planned in advance, Sophia realized. This was not the decision of a moment. Her eyes narrowed as she watched Eleanor more closely. The Queen had been busy indeed that spring.

But Eleanor's eyes were soft and almost meekly downcast, as she prompted the young knight to continue the boastful story. Her

55

face revealed little emotion. She reveled inwardly, carefully keeping her face masklike.

What was it like for Henry, she wondered joyfully, knowing that the son of his loins had fled for protection to the King of France? Did it hurt as much as she hoped? Did it stir up the old jealousy?

No matter how much he had denied it, Henry had been jealous of the years when Louis and Eleanor had lived together as man and wife, Eleanor was certain of that.

And what of Louis, who now entertained her son, the son they had not been able to produce between them? Did he dream of her at night, remembering her as she had been thirty years before, young and slender as a willow, as untamable as the wind? Eleanor sighed.

"Go ahead. Finish," she said, noticing that young Hasculf had grown silent and was watching her with a slightly peeved expression. "I am all attention."

"Louis greeted the Young King at the gate and held the stirrup cup himself," he continued. "He told all there that he welcomed him as fondly as if he were his own son . . ."

That was generous. That cost Louis something, Eleanor realized . . . unless his hatred for Henry was stronger than his regrets of his failed marriage to Eleanor.

". . . and that he recognized him as the rightful King of England. Which he is."

"Of course," Eleanor said. "There is no doubt of that. He was crowned three years ago. It is only a matter of gaining what is his, what Henry refuses to relinquish."

"Henry will relinquish, Lady. He will have to. When he sought the Young King at Louis' court, he announced himself as the King of England. And you know what Louis said?"

"What, my darling boy?"

"That that could not be. The rightful King of England—was already sitting in his hall."

"Louis is on our side," Eleanor mused.

There will be battle, the barons and knights thought, rejoicing and banging their fists against the table.

56

There will be war, Sophia thought, frowning.

There will be war. The thought saddened Eleanor, for she knew what war would bring to her beloved peaceful countryside. But only through war could she see her son on the throne. Then let it be. And her heart, that heart which had been scorned and cast aside by her liege lord, the King, beat faster. So far, all went as planned.

Later, when the trestles had been cleared and put aside to make room for the many knights who would sleep in the hall, Sophia crept to her rooms, so tired she feared she would not be able to sleep. Her back pained her beyond words; her limp was more pronounced than ever.

On the way to the garderobe she passed the black-bearded knight, who had just relieved himself outside in the Queen's rose garden. He smiled at her but did not bow. After they passed each other, she heard the rhythm of his steps change. She turned in time to see him mocking the way her right foot dragged as she walked.

Caught in the act, he stuttered an apology and hurried away. The squires with him laughed behind their hands.

"Who is that uncouth bear?" Sophia asked, for Eleanor had appeared behind her.

"Sir Foulkes of St. Servan. Has he troubled you?"

"I dislike him," Sophia said.

"So do I," answered the Queen. "But he brings war-horses and knights with him. We need his support."

There was something else Sophia had meant to bring up with the Queen, but she couldn't remember what it was. Lucie, tossing and turning with fear in the bishop's dungeon, had completely slipped her mind.

The world throbbed with pain. Every time he moved, a tempest exploded in his brain. Slowly, very slowly, he sat up and looked around. He was in a long, bare dormitory with narrow pallets lining both walls. A large crucifix hung over the wooden double door, and a strong smell of crushed herbs insinuated itself through the room.

As if from a great distance, he heard the monotonous plainsong of monks at prime, but the music blended with the roaring in his head.

Godfrey groaned.

Udele was there instantly, trying to cradle his aching head in her lap.

"Let me be!" He pushed her away.

"Are you feeling any better?" she whispered, penitent.

"What happened?"

"They beat you. Knocked you silly. You've lain still as the dead for a full day, now. Oh, Godfrey, I was so worried!"

"Now, woman, don't carry on so." He put a friendly arm about her quaking shoulders, for Udele was weeping by then. A memory lingered in the back of his mind and would not come forward. In the cart . . . something had happened to him after the beating by the bishop's men. But there was a more important matter.

"Lucie. Where is Lucie? Stop your bawling and speak up."

"They took her away." Udele's eyes, wet with tears, now grew wide with insult. Asleep for a day, and the first thing he thinks of is that slut? she thought, wounded.

"Then I shall go fetch her." Godfrey tried to stand, but the room whirled around him. He tried again and gained his feet.

Real fear replaced Udele's feigned tears. "You can't." She clutched at his hand and pulled him back down beside her on the cot.

"Why not?"

Udele thought quickly. "I heard the bishop's men say that if you ever came back to Poitiers, they'd throw you in the deepest dungeon and leave you there," she lied. "Godfrey, we have to leave Lucie, for the good of the others. They'd put Broderick in jail, probably torture him." Godfrey would never endanger the idiot, she knew. Put it on Broderick's head.

Godfrey lay back down and covered his eyes with trembling hands. Everything on him ached, even his eyeballs. And now, his conscience. Poor Lucie, in the bishop's keep. And he had promised to care for her, had vowed to her mother she would eat regularly and not get in trouble.

"I can't just leave her, Udele," he said in a dull voice. Nor, it seemed, could he go fetch her. He wasn't an outlaw . . . nor had he lived completely above the law in recent years. He passed as law-abiding . . . as long as the matter was not too closely examined. Which it would be if he went knocking at the bishop's door. He hadn't yet sold off the silver goblets taken from St. Servans. They would be found in the carts if he pressed matters.

"Mayhaps it's what she wants," Udele suggested hopefully. "I heard the bishop's men say that the palace majordomo has a soft eye for maidens. One night in the dungeon and then she'd be in his apartments eating roasted chicken and drinking unwatered wine."

Godfrey felt a sudden spasm of jealousy. He would rather have Lucie be hungry than eat roast chicken off another man's dagger.

"You heard the bishop's men say quite a mouthful," he commented dryly, not knowing if Udele could be trusted. She had always disliked Lucie. But what if she told the truth? What if Lucie was safe in Poitiers, and he would not be?

Just then Abbot Robert came into the infirmary. He was tall and thin with a strangely round, merry face that belied the gauntness of his body. The gauntness came from rigorously following the fast days, as few monks did. The round, jovial face came from his father, who had been a soldier of high spirits who never stayed in one place overly long. His length he had inherited from his mother, along with her complacent trust in God. He never questioned life too deeply, not because he lacked intelligence, but because he had an abundance of faith. Man asked questions; God withheld the answers. It was better that way.

"And how is our patient feeling today?" he asked with a large grin. He had a fair knowledge of medicine and knew from the swellings and bruisings on Godfrey's head that he must feel as beat-up as a well-used tilting dummy. "Drink this. Quickly, while it's still hot."

Godfrey accepted the goblet of calf's blood and spiced wine and swallowed it in three gulps. His tongue was so swollen, he could not taste.

"We have no money to pay you," he told the white-robed monk. "Udele was wrong to bring me here."

"Payment? Who spoke of payment?" Abbot Robert raised his eyebrows and feigned shock. "This is a house of God, not an inn. But of course, even if you have no coins, you might consider an hour or two of work in the vegetable patch, once you're feeling up to it. We are always short of labor, my son." Robert meekly bowed his head, but his eyes stayed on Godfrey.

"I am no field hand," Godfrey protested, trying again to sit up.

"I can see that." Robert smiled, eyeing the pile of ragged but now clean clothes resting on the floor by Godfrey's pallet. "You're a baron of France. The King's nephew. Or perhaps a wandering trouvère seeking a friendly court at which to sing his songs. No

60

matter. Our Saviour was no carpenter, yet he worked with his hands. Pride, as the Bible reminds us, goeth before a fall. Rest now. We will talk more of this later."

God's blood. A world filled with corrupt clerics and Udele had to bring him to a truly pious monk.

Godfrey mouthed an answer, but his tongue was tiring; all he could do was splutter like a babe too new for language. His eyes closed of their own accord as his head again found the soft, warm center of the pillow. Soothly, I am weak, he thought. How badly things have gone. Instead of writing love songs for Eleanor, I now owe labor to a monastery. And I have lost Lucie.

He rolled her name on his tongue. It tasted of emptiness, and only yestermorn it had tasted of pride and hope. He would fain have Lucie with him; he would fain not be put in the bishop's oubliette as a criminal. Between the two lay a painful choice. He had been imprisoned once before for feasting on one of the King's deer, and he hadn't liked the experience. For it is a sad truth that while the world is filled with pretty damsels, freedom is a harder thing to come by.

"Pride goeth before a fall," Robert repeated, tucking the covers in around his patient. Udele, standing behind him, smiled cheerfully. Hers was the last face Godfrey saw before sleep washed over him again, gently as a spring zephyr. His dreams were filled with the restful plainsong of the white-robed Cistercians who marked the hours in the chapel near the infirmary, regular as sunrise, sunset and the slow, relentless movement of time in between.

When next he woke, morning sun had scattered night and flooded the infirmary in a brilliant deluge. Godfrey, stronger, sat up to take better inventory of his surroundings.

Thankfully, they had placed him at the end of the row, separate from the others. Godfrey knew there was a difference between illness brought on by sword and fist and those illnesses caused by invisible vapors that sometimes spread from one patient to the other.

The narrow pallet under the central window was occupied by a man so old, he seemed already dead and embalmed. His chin was collapsed into his neck, his eyes sunk into their surrounding sockets. His stentorian breathing, Godfrey perceived, had been the cause of the sounds of the waves that had pounded in his dreams.

In another cot rested a man of fewer years, but he, too, seemed nearer death than life. He lay still as stone, staring relentlessly at the ceiling, his body tense with impatience as if death could not come soon enough. Feeling Godfrey's eyes upon him, he turned once and looked at the young man; his eyes were emptied of life. Then he resumed his meticulous study of the ceiling, and made no more movement.

Godfrey reached under the covers to scratch his balls. His member had its familiar early-morning stiffness, and joy of being vigorous in this room of illness made him restless. The throbbing in his head was gone and he could clearly distinguish the hymn the monks were singing for matins.

Haec dies, quam fecit Dominus: Exsultemus, et laetemur in ea. This is the day that the Lord hath made: let us exult and take joy in Him. Blessed be the Lord, for He is good.

Godfrey sang the familiar words aloud, breaking the stillness of the infirmary. It was a joyous song, one favored by younger monks who remembered the sweetness of May mornings and the softness of a woman's skin. Godfrey's heart quickened with a sense of homecoming that was both love and hate. He had grown up within the echoing sound of plainsong; it had circled his nonage and youth like the curtain wall of a castle.

Abbot Robert appeared, bearing a tray of bread and small ale. His tonsure gleamed as pale as eggshell, his smile was saucy.

"You have a goodly voice. I am impressed, but I don't know that your fellow sufferers have enjoyed the disturbance," he said, balancing the tray on the leverage of his sharply angled hip and a window ledge as he patted smooth a place on the pallet.

"From their morbid looks, nothing further will disturb them but the archangel's clarion." Godfrey hopped from the bed, naked and goosefleshed in the brisk morning air.

"Hold. What are you doing? It is not wise to move so quickly after a long rest," Robert reprimanded as Godfrey trotted quickly down the aisle toward a door that opened into the yard.

"To piss. With your permission, good brother," Godfrey called cheerfully. When he returned, Robert was munching on a crust of bread he had brought to break his fast with his new patient. Robert did not question God, but he did like to question mortals, and this fair, young, healthy if bruised man intrigued him.

"No meat or cheese?" Godfrey protested, peering at his meager meal after returning to the warmth of the bed.

"It's a fast day. Any lad who knows the hymns as well as you should also recall that today is the feast of the Invention of the Holy Cross. Where did you learn Latin?" Robert asked casually. He fussed with the covers, trying to pick off a spot of dried soup with his fingernail.

"You can stop counting the reward money in your sly brain. I'm not a runaway monk," Godfrey said, swallowing the mug of ale in one gulp.

"Pity. Just when I thought our Savior had arranged a way to finance the repairs to our oratory roof." Robert sighed in feigned disappointment that was actually relief. He liked this raw, strong youth and—God forgive him, he thought, touching right forefinger to head, chest and shoulders—was just as content that such a splendid lad was not given to the Church. There were too many of those already—second sons, unloved stepchildren, those infirm in body or mind, unwanted by parent or future spouse or liege lord—who sulked along monastery corridors, always wanting to be elsewhere. Many a good and holy monastery had festered under the injury of their rue and melancholy.

The abbot was in good spirits that morning. The Moor who came with this youth had given him a recipe for the stomachache, a new Spanish one, and the monk was eager to try it. "Eat slowly. Methinks your stomach, after its emptiness, will be aching and in need of medicine," he suggested, already fingering the vial he had brought with him.

"Nothing is bothering my stomach but the lack of morning

cheese," Godfrey protested around a mouthful of coarse, black bread.

"Then if you won't sample my new stomach powder, amuse me with the tale of how you come to know Latin," Robert repeated.

Godfrey stopped chewing and put down the slab of bread he held. The good humor in his eyes fled; his once open face closed like the lid of a smoothly carved chest.

"I grew up in the guesthouse of the abbey of St. Lucullus," he said in a low voice.

Robert showed the surprise he felt. "A guesthouse? I know a goodly share who were born in a guesthouse because their mothers insisted on making a pilgrimage too close to birthing time. But raised in one? Only monks, widows and bankrupt knights spend more than a month at a time within the walls of monasteries."

"My parents were neither, but close enough." Godfrey was loath to discuss this painful matter. There were still great wounds in his pride and heart. But Robert had been charitable, and he owed him some explanation in return. "My father owned a manor in Clermont. He put it up as security to pay his way on Louis' crusade . . ."

"A saintly gesture. He will be rewarded in heaven," Robert said.

"Perhaps. He was certainly not rewarded on earth." Godfrey grinned mirthlessly. "He came back from Jerusalem a pauper. All the yield of the farms and laborers went to paying the interest, and he himself worked the fields like a villein."

Robert had heard this story before. Many nearly impoverished knights had risked what little they possessed to venture to Jerusalem, hoping to return with lands and treasure that would enrich them. Louis and Bernard of Clairvaux had deemed it a holy war. Robert had his doubts; for most it had been a commercial venture, and an unsuccessful one at that.

"How came he to lose the manor?"

"Upon his return, he found his wife and only child, a son, had died of fever two years before. Seeking solace and companionship, he wed again, to my mother, a childless widow. And after twenty years with her, when he was bent and weak with age and she just past her time of childbearing, he despaired because God had given them no children. And an injury to his back made it impossible for him to work as hard as was required of him to keep the manor. So he bestowed the manor on the monks of St. Lucullus, in exchange for a lifetime tenure in their guesthouse." Godfrey picked up the bread and tore another bite out of it, but without relish.

"That is common enough, for an elderly couple to retire to the shelter of a monastery and live their last years in peace and prayer." Robert prompted the youth to continue his tale. The heart of it had not yet been revealed.

"Yes. Common. But my mother, it seems, wasn't elderly enough by nine months. I was born the year after the papers were signed. Much to my dam's surprise. For seven months, so she told me, she thought I was a case of indigestion. I was her first and last child."

Robert sighed with pity and then thought better of it. The youth needed encouraging, not sympathy. "You must have been a most beloved child," Robert said hopefully. But in such circumstances . . . a father given up to despair, an aging mother who knew naught of mothering, no patrimony, no lands with which to secure service or wife . . .

"My father was bemused. He was already half-monk and only awaiting my mother's permission to take vows. My arrival upset those plans. When the truth finally sank in, that he had an heir after all, he asked the monks to annul the agreement. They refused, saying the heir came after the agreement was legalized, and the law upheld their claim. So we stayed in the guesthouse, having nowhere else to go. Guests, on our own lands."

"Unfortunately for you. Methinks you have no great liking for monasteries or monks because of this."

"I was glad to leave when I came of age," Godfrey admitted mildly, not wanting to hurt Abbot Robert's feelings. Not all monks were avaricious, and this one had cared for him although he was under no obligation to do so.

In the near chapel, the monks were beginning the last hymn of the morning service. Their voices chased each other in joyously repeated rising and falling ebbs of plainsong. *Regina caeli laetare, alleluia*, they sang in exultation to Mary, Mother of God and Queen of Heaven. The canticle was thrilling as a lark's song at dawn, and unfamiliar to Godfrey. The monks of St. Lucullus were remarked for their dour gravity.

Robert remarked the way Godfrey's blue eyes narrowed in concentration, trying to place the song.

"It is a new one, sent to us by Queen Eleanor's chaplain," he explained.

"A song in praise of Mary?" Godfrey asked. "That is uncommon. She was but a woman, a sister of Eve the temptress."

"Times change, and so do ideas. Sister of Eve, yes, she was that, but also mother of our Saviour, and therefore worthy of worship," Robert corrected. "Eleanor's chaplain is commissioning many such hymns, many even less modest than this one you hear now. He would have it that Mary's Godhead is as highly placed as her Son's."

"Mary divine? Nay, any creature with a maidenhead can never be a Godhead," Godfrey scoffed.

"The monks of St. Lucullus who taught you were backwards," Robert protested. He himself was no great follower of this new Mary worship; it was excessive. Neither did he hold that all women were vessels of sin, as did many older clerics who frowned on new ideas. "But you are young, and with years ahead of you for repenting of error. For now, you may begin your payment in the scriptorium. I assume you can also write Latin in a fair hand?"

"I can, but I never agreed to be a scribe," Godfrey protested, sliding deeper under the covers. A moment ago he had been bursting with energy. Now he was already fatigued and his head ached. One of the bishop's men had really thumped him on the skull.

"Too late to play the invalid," Robert laughed. "I saw how quickly you moved when nature called. Can you not move as easily for the spirit as for the body?"

Godfrey scratched at his head, rousing shocks of gleaming gold hair to stand on end till smoothed down again, and refused to answer.

Abbot Robert, experienced in coercing labor where no labor was due him, pulled his saddest face. "We are poor. And your mending was costly. I slaughtered a calf for you. We are also near the completion date of a prettily illuminated Book of Hours which will greatly ease our debts, once finished. Alas, Brother Dorus is suffering a stiffness of the joints and the manuscript is nowhere near completion. So you see, dear friend, how desperately could we use your skills in the scriptorium. Unless, of course, you prefer to help break up clods in the cornfield."

"The scriptorium," Godfrey agreed.

The monk raised his eyes heavenward in thanks. The youth had the hands of an artist, not a laborer. God had not yet seen fit to send the means by which the roof would be repaired. But the future of the Book of Hours for Lady Lusignac was assured.

Two hundred knights, all loyal to the Young King and ready to journey to battle when the time came, soon arrived in Poitiers, doubling the population of Eleanor's already crowded castle.

Knights played at chess in the hall, camped and jousted in the bailey, hunted hare and boar in the near forest, wrestled playfully in the baths and loitered at the wells. They were everywhere, loud and frenzied and quick to quarrel, as men who await battle are wont to be.

The knights had brought one thousand armed and unarmed foot soldiers, who stayed not in the castle with the lords and ladies, but in the town with the merchants and the merchants' daughters. They flooded Poitiers, raising clouds of dust and annoyance and fear as they roamed narrow lanes in search of food and adventure. This great cacophony of soldiery which stormed dirt streets and green meadows made villeins and merchants quickly miss the former peacefulness of the new spring. Prices tripled overnight. Wise mothers began to hoard supplies of grain and dried beans, a little at a time, not to arouse their neighbors' suspicion. If everyone began buying extra at once, the prices would double again.

"Mayhaps the Queen is planning another tourney," the merchants speculated in the late afternoon, when a lavender sunset and the end of the day's work encourages a glance at the brighter side of life.

"Mayhaps battle," they grumbled in the morning, bleary-eyed and wary.

Even in the Maubergeonne Tower, the corridors and outer wall-walks were so crowded with newly arrived knights that Sophia could make her way only by pressing closely to the damp stone walls and squeezing through. Some knights had brought their ladies. Eager to see the famed wonders of Eleanor's court, they were constantly underfoot, peering into closets and shadowed chambers with the ill-mannered curiosity of children.

Sophia longed for the quiet solitude of the convent of the Paraclete, where no knights clomped up and down the circular stairwells and where lady guests kept their places.

She made her way through the keep to the Queen's walled rose garden, moving faster than usual because of her errand. Sleepless the night before, she had of a sudden remembered the jailed maiden whose cause she meant to plead with Eleanor.

The bailey was awash with the smell of vinegar, used to dissolve peacetime rust from armor and weapons. Its pungent fragrance was the smell of war to come. Great, rearing war-horses neighed in the castle stables, and a constant stream of carters brought in supplies of spring produce and slaughtered livestock to feed the appetites of the knights and their men.

Sophia had seen a great castle prepare for battle just once before, and that her father's when she was four. It had been all tense excitement then, cheering from the walls as the knights wrestled in the greensward to gain flexibility, while their men-at-arms polished sword edges till they sliced through the waxy grass.

The preparations now, though, did not excite her. They reminded her of death, of her mother's face as they pulled the white shroud over it. Sophia, the grown child, still remembered the long mourning for the only person who had found her winsome.

A stray arrow meant for a near warrior had found the mother instead, during that month of siege. The punishing metal head further tore the white flesh as it was pulled out. The wound festered and turned green and black in a sickly ebb tide around the wound's cruel red center. Sophia remembered the odiously sweet smell of gangrene, and then the smell of the orange field lilies filling the chapel where they kept vigil over the body.

The castle had been preserved, but its lady was lost. Broken, her father embarked on the lengthy and dangerous pilgrimage to Jerusalem, leaving his daughter in the care of the nuns of the Paraclete. The last she had seen of him was his slumped back, wide as the penitent's mule he rode off on, with the straw hat of the pilgrim tilted sadly over his face. He never returned from that pilgrimage.

Eleanor, craving a precious moment of solitude, sat on a stone bench, partially obscured by arching boughs of dewy spring roses. Their frothing pink heads filled the private garden with the scent of cloves. She had pulled one apart, and the curling, dawn-tinted petals lay in her lap. Lost in reverie, she rested her long-fingered hands on her thighs, palm up. It was this posture—the gentle tilt of the head, the open generosity of the hands—that her court illuminator used to depict Mary as she gazed at her infant son.

Sophia hesitated. It was miraculous, this quiet peace that Eleanor found in the midst of confusion. Loath to disturb the Queen's daydream, she leaned on a rose arbor to rest. Her back was prickly with pain.

Unaware of this new presence, Eleanor inhaled deeply the spice perfume of the roses. It was this very species of rose that her mother had once held under her chin to see if she would find lasting love.

"If it reflects pink on your chin, then you'll be loved by the knight of your dreams," she had said somewhat listlessly.

"Is my chin pink? Is it?" the worried five-year-old Eleanor had asked as the rose tickled at her throat.

"Pink as can be, my daughter," the mother said with a hug. It had been a strong hug, Eleanor remembered all these years later;

her mother had clasped her tight enough to keep away the winds themselves. Was it the grown woman's sorrow, rather than the daughter's future joy, that had put such strength into the woman's arms?

The gardens of her childhood had smelled of rose and myrrh, quince and horehound. They had sounded of her grandfather's boasts and her father's pounding laughter. They had both been men larger than life, great in their need for food, wine and love. They compared themselves to Arthur of the Britains and Julius Caesar of the Romans, and were not wanting in courage or skill. Nor did they bring much happiness to their women.

"Choose the man's castles and stables when you wed, not the man himself," her mother whispered with a voice soft as rose petals. "Steeds and castles you can count, but not the wayward deeds of a husband's heart." As if Eleanor would have choice in the matter. She, heir of Aquitaine, must marry a man at least as full of promise as her own future. Louis of France had been the only reasonable choice.

Now, there was a husband with a true and loving heart. And how boring it had been, after the first thrill had worn off. How unhappy for both of them. The first rule of love: The knight must never exceed the wishes of his lady. Louis, till he learned better, trailed after her like a lap dog hungry for tidbits. In Paris with him, she had sought rooms with locks on the doors, just for a moment's peace. Certainly he had been faithful to her. Between his prayers and his pursuit of his wife, he had no time for infidelities.

But he had been lacking. It required unnamed potions and hours of prayers to rouse Louis to lovemaking. She wanted many children, but would not get them of him, it seemed.

There had been others willing to do the work. She had been young and fair and high-spirited. Of course there were others. And by the time she first met Henry, her honor had been shredded by the angry French, who distrusted and disliked the southern Queen. That had helped her case with Henry. He disdained the cold-blooded Parisians as well as she . . . especially cold-blooded Louis.

Sixteen and just knighted when they first met, Henry had fallen instantly. He still had freckles on his nose, but the homage in his eyes was not childish. Nor was the desire. At sixteen, he was more knowing, more worldly in the ways of love, than was Louis at twenty-six.

They were Antony and Cleopatra, Helen and Paris. She was a tall poplar, he the loving zephyr that stirred her at morn and eventide. He was the mother-of-pearl coffer, she the pearl nestled at its heart. Ah, the sweetness of his love words that spiced their stolen hours in Paris!

Nay. We were dust in each other's mouths, Eleanor thought, trying to harden her heart against him. Our love was no more than the secret worm that consumes the apple. The golden spring sun that warmed her throat reminded her of love's fire, now dead, of her faded beauty, of her passed youth, consumed in the flame of time. She plucked unhappily at a rose.

"My Lady. Don't be saddened," Sophia croaked gently from the trellised arbor, sensing the Queen's mood change from reverie to bitterness. The rose pollen was making her nose itch and throat sore.

"Ah. Lady Sophia." Eleanor shook her head as if cobwebs clung to her silken wimple and she would remove them. "Sit by me for a moment. It is good to be away from the clanking and banging in the hall, isn't it?"

"It is." Sophia sat next to Eleanor on the stone bench. Side by side like that, dark-eyed Eleanor looked even larger and more regal; Sophia looked even smaller and more wan. Her feet dangled helplessly, not touching the gravel path beneath the bench.

"I am daily amazed at how many knights are called forth through love for you. Your heart commands a wide kingdom," Sophia said. A little flattery—and it was truth, surely—would ease the Queen's mind. Be useful. And win the friends you need, Alicia of Paraclete had instructed her. This is no child's game you go to, in Poitiers.

"There are those who would have me rule no more than my own bower," Eleanor said, frowning, thinking of Henry. "But you look worried, friend. Are you fearful?"

"I am," the astrologer sighed. "I have no great longing to be in a castle under siege."

"It will not come to that," Eleanor said briskly. "Henry will never try to bring troops as far south as Poitiers. The whole quarrel will be over in a matter of weeks."

Quarrel? Sophia thought. She sends her son to Paris to join with Louis, to certain war, and calls this a quarrel? Henry will call it war. Henry will rage, and when the King rages, the land trembles beneath his feet. Distracted, Sophia plucked at a rose but caught her thumb on a thorn. It drew forth a spot of bright blood.

"He has too many enemies between England and Poitiers for us to fear him," Eleanor continued. "Since the murder of Becket, he seems to have lost the knack of friendship. And he takes too much power for himself, leaving too little to the barons. They are tired of his many laws and his taxes. No, there are few enough that will fight with him. This will be quickly won and over. It is but a matter of weeks before my son will sit on the throne. Here, clean your thumb with my handkerchief."

"But if Henry should march south, then his soldiers may try to take the bishop's palace . . . and all the prisoners in it could be killed as a matter of course?"

Eleanor nodded. "But it won't come to that, Lady Sophia. I tell you, the Young King will quickly defeat Henry. With Richard's help, and the aid of the barons."

"Of course," Sophia agreed, still unconvinced. "But, My Lady, something occurred the other day which I forgot to speak of at the time. There is one in the bishop's prison—a maiden—whose release we should obtain. Her sin was an action with which we would not think to find fault; rather, she may help amuse you and pass the time."

"Well, bring her here, then, if you so advise. The matter is in your hands, Lady Sophia." Eleanor obviously did not wish to be bothered with trivial matters. She rose and quickly departed, leaving Sophia alone on the bench. The astrologer, who normally stayed clear of such dramas, wondered what errant planets had caused her to take interest in the unfortunate maid-player, and why she should bother. But she knew she would.

"Come, Godfrey. Here, sweety, sweety." Lucie used a honeyed, coaxing voice.

The sleek brown rat, sulking in a corner, sat up on hind legs and contemplated her with beady red eyes. Lucie crumbled the bit of bread to release its yeasty fragrance and held it closer to the animal's nose. Its whiskers shook with indecision. Finally, with a delicacy that pleased the maiden, the rat reached forward with its two paws and accepted the sop.

They had been companions of sorts for several days, sharing bread and damp darkness.

"There, sweety, eat your dinner." Lucie leaned back against the moss-slimy wall and ate the last of the black loaf, licking her fingers clean of crumbs. "And when you're finished, tell me how you come to be here, instead of in some sweet cornfield where you can eat your fill and warm yourself in the sun."

Lucie had unburdened herself freely to her lover's namesake, recalling all she could of her mother, early life in the salt meadows, the year of traveling with the troupe . . . and of Godfrey. "Godfrey, the true vermin, the one who abandoned me," she berated the dark, fetid air. For now she knew she had been abandoned.

She was half-afraid that if she was alone in the small cell for many more days, she would hear the vermin answer.

It was the solitude that preyed at her. After the first day, there had been plenty of food, albeit coarse and good only for filling the stomach, not whetting the appetite. And once her long hair dried, her own youthful strength had kept her warm enough. Now that tawny hair that had caused Udele to ache with jealousy was strewn with molding straw and debris; the hint of gold in it had been obscured by mud.

She had tried talking to her wizened gaoler. But he was hard of hearing, and what little wits he may have once possessed had been sacrificed to his great age. As much as she had feared being called to the bishop's court, she now hoped for it . . . for anything that would release her from her prison for a few moments and let her try her voice with other humans who could answer in kind.

The rat moved closer, hoping for another sop.

"No more," she said, showing her empty hands. Godfrey glared at her with his red pellet eyes and then disappeared into the darkness of the corner where his hole was.

"Lout!" she called after him.

The page shuffled his feet and stared intently at the intricate mosaic floor. His brown hair had been slicked down with spittle; his rosy cheeks burned even more fiercely under the bishop's penetrating gaze.

"What is Eleanor's interest in this girl?" Bishop Jehan's voice was smooth and easy as the deep blue satin of his rich robe. As smooth as the road to hell, his canons described that voice.

"It says in the message," the boy replied, pointing at the vellum he had just delivered. He wished with all his heart that Lady Sophia had sent some other page on this errand. Angry words and a boxing on the ears would not have bothered him; but the icy glare of this powerful cleric made his ears tingle.

"It says next to nothing," Jehan purred, "except that I am to release a prisoner from my keep." He leaned back in the ornate diocese chair, covering with his broad back the wealth of garnets and pearls inset into the mahogony wood.

"As always, Eleanor is interfering with the bishop's mission to save his flock," protested Canon Anselm. The message had arrived in late afternoon, calling Jehan from his well-laden board and Anselm from his bed, where he had been seeking solace with the cook's son.

Jehan stared at Anselm, a cold, withering glance that made the tousled canon take two steps backward toward the door, as if he would flee.

"Leave us for a moment, child," Jehan said to the page. "There is a bowl of figs in the outer room. Help yourself, and stay there till I call for you." The youth, only too glad to leave, darted for the door, leaving the bishop and Anselm alone in the huge, marbled chamber where voices rang cold and metallic.

"You are indiscreet, Anselm. To cricitize Eleanor in front of one of her own pages. Tsk, tsk." Jehan waved a beringed forefinger at Anselm. The gesture could have been a playful one. Coming from this bishop, it was not. Anselm quaked.

"The woman is a busybody," he protested in a small voice.

"The woman is powerful. Don't you recall, Anselm, only three springs before, when Eleanor rid herself of all clerks she disliked? That is to say, all clerks who had sworn homage to Henry, her husband?"

"Who could forget?"

"And do you forget that it was Henry who made you a canon of Saint Pierre?"

"Both Henry and Eleanor together," Anselm corrected the bishop.

"You remember that small detail. Eleanor may not. I suggest, Anselm, you go along with her wishes, unless you want to be sent on long pilgrimage to Canterbury . . . and ordered to stay there."

"If you ordered me to remain in Aquitaine, Eleanor would not countermand your order."

Bishop Jehan, known as Jehan aux Belles-Main, held up one of his long-fingered hands and admired the large ruby ring he wore. It was a gift from Eleanor. And even at this distance he could hear the laborers hammering at the new choir for his cathedral, a work commissioned by Eleanor.

"I would not go against Eleanor's wishes," Jehan said smoothly, no longer smiling.

"Now, Anselm, fetch the girl. You, yourself, shall accompany her to Eleanor's court, in safekeeping. Her sin cannot be so great. If the Queen is willing to forgive her, so should we. Forgiveness is a divine trait."

"A purchased trait," Anselm muttered, turning to leave.

"You spoke?" Jehan's voice was at the zenith of its cool, dangerous smoothness.

"Nothing, My Lord. Nothing." Anselm hurried from the chamber.

Although it was dim twilight, the remnant light in the sky made Lucie's eyes ache. She rubbed at them till they were red, all the while trotting along obediently behind Anselm. A small hope was spreading golden warmth through her—the hope of freedom. They were taking her to Eleanor, they had told her. And now the same evil clerk who had first denounced her to the crowd led her through narrow paths and guarded gates, away from the bishop's keep. He was in a great hurry to be done with his chore, it seemed.

First, she had been led to Bishop Jehan, where he sat on his throne, fat and clothed as richly as a statue of the risen Christ.

"So this is the wench who has caused the trouble," he said in a bemused voice. Lucie was caked with dirt; her hair hung matted over her face, like a wild woman's. She still wore the men's breeches and tunic, which no longer revealed taunting curves but hung in limp, muddied folds.

"Interesting," Jehan concluded with a yawn, turning away. "Go, child, and sin no more." He gave her a penance of a hundred Ave Maria's, and then turned his attention to a plate of sugared almonds resting at his elbow.

76

Through narrow streets lined with town houses and guild halls, up a steep hill fragrant with honeysuckle, Anselm led her to the very gate of Eleanor's palace. His heart grew heavier with each step; hers lighter.

The bailey was awash with knights and squires who were brushing down chargers, cleaning weapons, and wrestling each other, stripped down to hose and smallclothes. The still air was heavy with the smell of sweat, and Lucie thought longingly of Godfrey for a brief moment. Godfrey the betrayer. Godfrey the abandoner.

Anselm forced his way through the throng, to the Maubergeonne Tower, where Sophia awaited them in a brilliantly lit doorway.

"We sent the message hours agone. What delayed you?" she asked, perturbed. She had lost valuable hours of daylight, of writing time, waiting for the maid. And then, "God's knees! Is this the same maiden? What have you done to her?" she cried, seeing Lucie's muddied and rumpled condition.

"Nothing that her sin didn't warrant. Less than her sin required," Anselm muttered testily. "Throw a bucket of water over her and her punishment will wash away; 'tis but the dirt of the cell has transformed her. This be what women truly are, vessels of corruption and filth," he finished in some satisfaction.

"This be what men make of them," Sophia sniffed angrily. "Go, Anselm. And beware. Neptune enters Mercury tonight, which bides ill for men of the cloth, such as yourself. Cleanse your heart of ill will and mayhaps you will escape harm till Neptune passes."

"Don't preach to me, woman."

"A word of warning, then. Your eyes have a vengeful look to them. Leave this maiden alone in the future, Eleanor has claimed her." Sophia, standing on a step so she could do so, put her arms about the tall Lucie in an authoritative and protective gesture.

Anselm snorted and turned to leave. Relieved of his charge, his heart bristling with anger, he noticed then that the bailey was even busier than usual. There is a wealth of knights and war-horses here, he told himself. If Eleanor is planning another tourney, she has outdone herself. There must be warriors from all over Aquitaine and Poitiers gathered here.

Now what has the Queen up her sleeve? Anselm rubbed his chin in speculation. He knew matters were strained between Eleanor and Henry; he wished the King would find it in his heart to beat his interfering wife, as all wives deserve beating. It made them softer and more compliant. And that witch, Sophia, should be locked in a tower. Surely she had the evil eye, and the deformity of her body must give evidence to the evil of her soul . . . Further speculation was rendered impossible as a group of knights, young and rowdy as a spring storm, washed over him and carried him away in their wake.

As soon as Anselm was lost in the thick of the crowd, Sophia pushed Lucie away and put a cloth scented with attar of roses to her long nose.

"No offense meant, but you stink like a cesspool. You can't enter the Queen's apartment smelling like this. Amaria! Amaria!" She called to a handmaid, who quickly appeared. "Take her to the baths and scrub her. Bring her to me when you're done. I'll find some suitable robes." Sophia enjoyed giving the orders. She rarely had the opportunity to do so.

Lucie, in a passive mood of confusion, let the maid lead her through the bailey to the castle wall, where a row of wooden lodges, brown and rough as swallows' nests, leaned into the curving grey stones. Smoke curled through their chimney holes. The middle one sent forth the acrid smell of lye and wood ash.

Four youths came out from one of the lodges, their naked skin red and glistening, their shoulder-long hair still dripping sudsy water. They hooted at the pretty Amaria, who ignored them, knowing that the baths—and the young maidens who were the bath attendants—made men high-spirited.

But when Lucie discerned her intent, she set up a shrieking that intimidated even the warriors.

"No! No!" she screamed, bending her knees and leaning backwards against Amaria's determined pull. Like most of her caste, she had never been dunked in a bath, finding an occasional damp rag scrubbed over various body parts to be sufficient a wash. It was unwholesome to cover the whole of the body with water; physicians said it led to death. Priests claimed baths were mortal sin; the holy desert anchorites had gone decades without touching water to skin.

"I'll die! I'll die!" Lucie yelled, digging her heels into the mud. Had they set her free from the cell just to torture and drown her?

Amaria pulled harder, and the tunic covering Lucie tore off with a hissing of torn seams. Lucie didn't care that she was bare to the waist and the youths were ogling her; she would not be dunked.

"It won't kill you," Amaria yelled back. "It will refresh you. And even if it doesn't, it will make it possible for others to stand near you. God's knees, but the stench is overpowering."

"No!" Lucie insisted, biting into Amaria's arm to try to gain release.

"Demon!" Amaria roared. "Help me, help!" One of the youths, enjoying this uncommon spectacle of maid against maid, both of them pretty and one half-naked, broke from the circle of his companions. With one arm he lifted the slender Lucie over his shoulder. Grinning, he carried the kicking girl into the bathhouse and unceremoniously dropped her into a large wooden tub, breeches and all.

Lucie felt soapy, warm water close overhead. Her hair floated about her like pondweed; the bottom of the tub was slippery and she couldn't get her footing. She swallowed a great mouthful of the soapy fluid and then rose to the top of the tub, buoyant with fear and animal despair.

The anvil-ringing blacksmith's stall was nearby. Sitting on a stool there, waiting while his much-cosseted black charger was newly shoed, Sir Foulkes heard a maiden's lyrical voice proclaim the loudest, most profane curses he had yet heard from a woman's mouth, between strikes of the anvil. The voice had something of the salt marsh in it, a wild quality like the sound of hawks winging and crying overhead, that made him miss his own manor in the North.

He grinned and shook his head, remembering the tall, strong women of his demesne. In the South, women were shorter and

79

stouter and dark-haired, many with a hint of mustache over the upper lip. They were lusty creatures, for all their piously lowered eyes and unhealthy liking of poetry. Unlike his own Lady Maria. Bed had been torment for her, not play. He was only too content to leave her to her prie-dieu and headaches. She was cold, and blond, and Sir Foulkes liked dark-eyed maids with hot blood.

There had been that very promising maiden who had disappeared. What was her name? Lucie. The mother said she drowned; he didn't believe it—how could a maid who promised such brilliant beauty and bed sport end her life before she'd had a taste of pleasure? Yet to hunt her would have been costly and, ultimately, perhaps not worth the trouble. Runaway serfs tended to repeat their crime over and over till they were fit for nothing but leg-irons. There were always more urgent errands to attend to than running to ground a worthless chit of a maiden.

Lucie. Sir Foulkes patted his fretful charger and chuckled as the screams and salt-marsh curses from the bathhouse grew even louder. I envy whatever man is bedding that spirited damsel, he thought. And then he wondered where his serf, Lucie, had got to in her twelvemonth of freedom.

"Easy, man!" He jerked to his feet as the blacksmith aimed a clumsy blow at the horse's foot. "Harm this beast and you'll eat your own balls for supper!"

An hour later, when night was full on them and yellow candlelight showed through the loopholes of Eleanor's castle, Lucie and Amaria emerged from the bathhouse.

Lucie was dressed in a pale blue tunic with cream sleeves and chemise underneath. She looked composed, even indifferent. She was exhausted. Her hair, still wet, curled down the length of her back, leaving dark trails where it rubbed the blue cloth.

Amaria was soaked to the waist and bruised, but triumphant. "Didn't I tell you it wasn't that bad?"

Lucie gave her a look that ended the maid's impulse to conversation.

The two young women walked quickly to the Maubergeonne

Tower, where Sophia awaited them. The evening was growing cold. The knights taking their ease in the bailey gathered around fires and exchanged tales of battles and adventures.

Amaria recognized the voice of one of them, a northern voice with harder consonants and the edge of boasting in it that produced skepticism in the hearer, not admiration. Sir Foulkes. She drew her hood closer about her head and gave that bonfire wide berth. Castle gossip already said that this warlord drew no fine difference between ladies and whores. Best to avoid him altogether, especially with this young maiden in her care. Now that the crust of many weeks had been washed away, even Amaria admitted that the maiden was exceptionally pretty. Just the kind that Sir Foulkes and his like would waylay in some dark castle corridor.

Lucie had been away from St. Servan's for a year, which is more like many years to those as young as she, and she was preoccupied with the gripping emotion of self-pity. Fatigue was reminding her of the many injustices she had suffered in the past few days, beginning with Godfrey's abandonment and ending with the bath. She heard the northern voice boasting in the darkness, but it did not disturb the train of her thoughts. The runaway serf passed by her seigneur with never a recognition or thought of what that boasting voice could mean to her future freedom.

Only outside the Queen's rooms, where Amaria finally released her grip on her hand, did Lucie begin to see some redemption in the situation. She was freed from prison; she was well dressed, and it appeared she would be well fed and well housed, else why would they make such a fuss? She smiled, thinking of how Godfrey's eyes would light when next he saw her. She frowned, remembering how he had abandoned her.

"Lady Eleanor is with her sons," Amaria informed her. "We must wait."

Sophia sat on the stone bench with the two younger women, the one tall and dark-eyed with tawny hair, the other with merry green eyes and hair dark shining as a raven's wing. Her back was paining her, and the proximity of so much youthful beauty made her feel like a toad.

"What is your name?" she finally thought to ask the rescued maiden.

"Lucie." Her voice was sullen and wary.

"A pleasant enough name. When were you born?"

Lucie's eyebrows shot up in surprise. She had been asked few questions in her brief lifetime, and never this one.

"Sometime in winter, I think my mother once said. Why?"

"I will need to know what planets rule your houses," the astrologer said.

"Does that have to do with more water?" Lucie asked, suspicious.

Eleanor sat at her tapestry frame, her silver needle gliding in and out with a circular sweep of her hand. Her head was serenely bent over the tapestry, an allegory of the hunt in a just-begun condition, albeit she had started it ten years before. She hated working at needlepoint: a woman's life could pass away in the constant in and out of the needle, and all she would have accomplished would be yet another wall adornment.

But needlework was soothing and reassuring. Not to her . . . but for those who watched. A few steps away from Eleanor's frame, crouched by the hearth because the spring night was cold, were her son, Richard, and her kinsman, Raoul de Faye, who was seneschal of the ducal palace. They watched the dancelike, repetitive motion of her hands, and their brows grew less stormy.

"All went well with Louis, then?" Raoul asked again. He had asked the same question four times this evening. He was a nervous man, always in a state of mild agitation. Tonight his agitation was exceedingly unmild.

"All went well. The Young King went to him. Louis greeted him and called him friend. Louis rebuffed Henry's ministers. Surely he has already declared which side he will take," Eleanor repeated, forcing her voice to remain mild. "Louis and the Young King stand together. Henry must fall."

"I should be in Paris with them," spoke up Richard loudly enough that the hunting dogs, roused from their sleep before the hearth, barked in alarm. Eleanor turned and coolly eyed her flame-haired son.

"In time, my son. In time. If all my knights ride now to Paris, Henry would be on the alert. And we need the element of surprise in this if we are to succeed," she said.

"You speak truly. But how I hate the waiting." Richard, sixteen, was eager for battle. It would be his first. He was gifted with great grace, and even when he sulked, as now, it seemed the air and all things in the room parted to ease his passage. Gracefully he approached his Lady Mother and went on his knees before her. She reached out and touched the flaming hair on his brow and her heart rejoiced.

"My own son," she whispered, kissing the palms of his hands, where calluses from wielding lance and battle-axe rose pale against rosy skin. "I am tormented by the thought of where this may lead, should we fail. If harm should come to you . . ."

"Ah, but we won't fail," cried Richard. "Justice is on our side. God defends us. God, and the largest army that Henry Fitz-Empress will ever have faced."

Eleanor sighed, pushed away the tapestry frame, and considered this son of hers. He was the thirdborn, after William, who had died as an infant, leaving only the memory of swaddling and tears, and Henry, who grew tall and dark-eyed like herself. After Richard had come Geoffrey, who resembled her one moment and his father the next, and his allegiances seemed just as wavering. And John. The baby John, whom she could not stand to have near her because he was so distinctly Henry's favorite. Poor John. Did she so hate him because Henry favored him, or did Henry favor him because she so disliked him? It didn't matter. John was with Henry, and there he stayed.

But Richard, her Richard was here, with his startling, fiery hair and square jaw so like his father's. Even when just born he had that shock of hair, that stubborn jaw. Nursing him had been like holding her own husband, new and small and helpless in infancy as the man had never been in maturity.

Richard was youth-slender, but in maturity he would have Henry's stouter build. Like his father, he had unusually long arms ideal for wielding the sword, and the long legs to match. His complexion was ruddy, quickly turning to brilliant crimson under the inspiration of strong emotion.

With every passing day he became more like the Henry she had first loved twenty years before, both in appearance and manner of speaking and moving.

And in his tendency to exaggerate, she thought with another sigh.

"Surely the army is not yet that large?"

"No," he admitted with a shrug. "But it will be. More knights arrive daily. When we depart we will have a force that will make the Old King turn tail and run."

"That lacks respect," she reprimanded him.

"Respect?" Raoul de Faye almost screeched but controlled himself at the last moment. He hated Henry Fitz-Empress with a rare passion. Many of the southern barons did, considering him a cold-blooded English foreigner who knew naught of the South and had even less right to rule it.

"Sir Raoul. This will be accomplished according to the rules of God and chivalry," she whispered. Talk in low voice when you most need to be heard. Louis had taught her that.

"The rules of God and chivalry have had little respect from Henry Fitz-Empress," de Faye protested. "He is a priest-murderer and wife-abandoner . . ." He stopped, biting his tongue, wishing he could take back those last two words.

Eleanor pulled her tapestry frame closer and proceeded to ply her needle again. She bowed her head over the chase scene and her wimple fell forward, hiding her face like a veil.

"What do you mean, sir? It is I who left Henry, not Henry who left me."

"You left Chinon when Henry was there, that is true. But there are rumors . . ."

"Any rumors concerning me should be told me . . ."

"Rumors that Henry seeks to put you aside so he may wed Rosamonde . . ."

The room grew silent except for the hissing of a log in the hearth. Eleanor's needle quickly moved in and out, in and out.

No one noticed that she was wrongly using a rose-colored thread to tint what should have been the brown throat of a hart. She bit her tongue to keep from crying out and said nothing. Rumor dies fastest if it is ignored. But if the rumor be true . . .

"By Lucifer! I'll kill him," Richard yelled, banging his fist against the table with such force that their three goblets jumped into the air.

No, Eleanor thought, I will kill him myself, and save you the deed, my son. Rather than be put aside.

Seeing the mistake in the tapestry, she plied the little silver scissors she wore chained at her waist, and picked out the rose threads. She poked fiercely, harder and faster, faster and harder. A moment later, the tapestry lay ruined at her feet, and she was standing and trembling as if caught in a fierce wind.

Richard and Raoul de Faye averted their eyes from the destroyed needlework. Eleanor kicked the tapestry into the hearth, and the room filled with the bitter smell of burning wool.

"Sir Raoul, you must not believe all that comes to your ears. Most of it never comes to pass. Surely you know that Henry cannot put me aside. All he has indebts him to me. Without me, he would have nothing and be nothing."

Henry sees it differently, de Faye thought. He hadn't known that Eleanor still cared for the English pig. That was dangerous.

"Richard." She turned from her seneschal to her son. "You must not vow, nor think of murder. You are hotheaded, and need to learn coolness."

"Yes, Lady Mother." He grinned at her in agreement.

I wish they would leave me, Eleanor was thinking. I must be alone. To think. Henry wed Rosamonde. It will never be. It will never be. She forced herself to believe that, to will it to become true. She moved to her worktable and pushed the rumor to a far corner of her mind.

"Have you yet given thought to which castle we should first put under siege?" She laid her white, slender hand on the map before her in a careful manner and invited them to approach.

Strategy must be discussed. It was her fate as well as theirs they would be fighting for; she fully intended to participate in the making of the war plans. The important things of life—the battles as well as the lovemaking, the plans, the schemes—should not be left entirely to the men. They could so easily botch things. Hadn't her husbands Louis and Henry proved that over and over? If only Henry had listened when she first encouraged him to be rid of that righteous little clerk, Thomas of Becket . . . But this was not the time to go over that again. Henry and Rosamonde. They must be parted.

"If we can convince Count Philip of Flanders to march on Normandy, at the same time as you and the other two"—she often referred to Henry and Geoffrey in that tone, as merely addenda to her beloved Richard—"then it would be well for us to strike Driencourt Castle at Neufchâtel, while Louis strikes at Verneuil. Henry Fitz-Empress will be divided into three camps and weakened at the very outset."

She looked up from her map to find Richard watching her with a wary little smile.

"You shouldn't trouble yourself, Lady Mother," he said, tenderly stroking her cheek. "But I will put your ideas to Geoffrey and Henry, if that is your wish."

Eleanor felt a burning flash of anger. His condescending tone was all too like her husband's. What nitwits men could be, even this darling son. And how easily did they take offense, she reminded herself, especially when a woman could ill afford to give offense. She swallowed the anger. Suddenly she was very tired.

"Then go now, my beloved child. Amuse yourself while you may. When summer comes you will have little time for pleasure, I'm afraid." Eleanor eyed her box of writing materials. She would send the messages to Louis and Philip herself.

"When summer comes I will have the opportunity to avenge a most evil wrong done to my Lady Mother. There could be no greater pleasure."

"Richard, you speak well." Eleanor smiled as he took her hand.

He grinned brightly, basking in the praise, and looked so like the father had all those years before that Eleanor's heart thudded with unhappiness.

As he left, though, Richard's thoughts were most un-Henry-like. Instead of drinking and being rowdy and bawdy with the knights in the great hall, he would go to his sister, he decided. Perhaps she will sing for me. We can compose a canso together. And he found it not at all strange that a youth would rather hear love songs from his half-sister's lips than from any other maid.

In the dark corridor, he remembered how her pearl circlet had made Marie's fair forehead even paler in last evening's candlelight, and smiled. His step was light. Why should it be heavy, when exhilarating spring beckoned the sun to linger longer in the sky, bringing forth buds and birdsong—and when a great battle was in the offing? Now would his fortune be made, his reputation written in large letters for men to admire in the ages to come. How had that tune gone? Chrétien was cunning with lyrics. Richard sang under his breath.

"*Ecce gratum et optatum ver* . . . See, pleasant and longed-for spring restores delight; a blaze of color, the meadow is in bloom, the sun lights up everything. Now let sadness be gone! He is a miserable soul who does not enjoy life . . ." Richard, blessed with a fine voice and strong ego in equal measure, sang lustily as he left his Lady Mother's bower and made for Marie's rooms, unmindful of the maidens waiting in the hall for audience with Eleanor.

Raven-haired Amaria knew the courtly skill of shutting out all sounds when she so chose. It was the only way much-needed privacy could sometimes be obtained. This song, though, she harkened to intently, word for word, hoping that Richard would see her love for him in her face.

Ah, he is beautiful, she brooded, sighing, as he passed by. She watched his back, admiring the way his tunic flared from broad shoulders to a slender waist. His dear shadow in the rushlight grew longer and longer and then disappeared entirely as he turned a corner and could no longer be seen. For three years she had watched that departing back; always did he seem to stride further away from her desire, not closer. She sighed again.

I wonder he didn't feel the holes she burned into him, Sophia thought, observing. Human nature was originally one and we were

87

a whole, and the desire and pursuit of the whole is called love, she recited to herself, trying to understand the nature of that turmoil that is called love.

Well, it will be a very long time before Amaria finds wholeness with that youth, Sophia thought. Anyone with eyes to see—or the will to look—would know that Richard shared the proclivity of the great philosophers. Otherwise known as the priest's sin. Perhaps Richard himself did not yet know it. But Sophia doubted he would ever find much pleasure with womankind.

No wonder he courted his half-sister, Marie, so avidly. By giving his heart where love would be a sin—the grave sin of incest—he need never bother to give his heart where it would eventually have to prove a true lover's devotion.

Should she say something to the handmaiden?

Amaria's eyes were still soft and shining as she rose from the bench and adjusted her veil for the meeting with Eleanor. No. Such knowledge must come from one's own heart, not another's observation. Besides, why become involved in this knotty vexation? It was Amaria's problem; let Amaria solve it.

A small voice whispered that if Amaria had been less beautiful and Sophia more so, she might be willing to solace the lovelorn maiden. Sophia determinedly ignored the voice. Ayyyye, how her back was paining her!

Lucie, no longer sullen and indifferent to what was befalling her—the roughly forced bath was already becoming memory—entered the solar after Sophia and Amaria.

The chamber smelled of perfumes and purifying incense, like a chapel at Easter. And, strangely, of burnt wool. It glowed with riches. Bright tapestries hung on all the walls, there were silken coverlets and cushions on every bench and stool. Polished looking glasses framed in hammered brass cast her reflection as she moved. The sumptuous pleasures of the East darkled in each corner and nook, brought back to this more moderate clime by a younger Eleanor fresh from the Crusade. The maiden's eyes widened.

Sir Foulkes' hall had been bare, even miserly, compared to this wealth. His wide-planked floors were overspread with straw, the walls covered with smelly, ill-cured sheepskins to keep out the north wind; those who wished to sit had to comfort themselves as best they could on crude wooden stools. His tower was in constant night to avoid the expense of candles; his pages dirty and surly for lack of training.

Lucie saw that even great lords sometimes suffer the chastening of poverty. It cheered and bravened her to realize that Sir Foulkes, whom she feared so greatly, was poor as Job's rooster, compared to this southern queen.

"Come here, maiden," beckoned a warm voice. Lucie turned toward that voice, obedient as a seedling that turns toward the sun. She walked in the direction from which the voice emanated, toward a dais obscured by layers of sheer silk suspended by a golden ring in the ceiling. Amaria followed gracefully at her side; Sophia dragged behind.

He will not put me aside. He will not have Rosamonde to wife, Eleanor repeated to herself over and over, like the prayers on a rosary. Why, then, did her eyes smart? Tears made it even harder to see. She had little interest in this maid Sophia had fetched, but once here, the damsel should at least be viewed, she decided.

Eleanor had to wait till the maiden was but an arm's length away before she saw her clearly. She would admit it to no one, not even Sophia, but the eagle's eyes were no longer as sharp as they had once been. Like everything else, age was dulling them, taking the brilliant edge and leaving obscurity. Age, and sorrow.

The girl stared at her dumbly.

"Kneel!" Amaria hissed. The girl fell clumsily to her knees. When Eleanor extended her hand, she merely held it, not knowing the Queen expected a kiss of submission.

"Child," said Eleanor, "it's clear you are unhampered by an education." Some of her good humor returned. She liked young, unschooled things, with their eyes wide as the first dawn of genesis, and smiles of promise, not regret. "Rise, and tell me about yourself. You were caught playacting in a youth's guise, were you not?"

"Yes. We were playing Noah's Ark, outside the cathedral."

Lucie spoke shyly, but there was no fear in her voice. That pleased Eleanor, who disliked cravens of either sex.

"Noah's Ark? During the Easter cycle?" Eleanor was surprised, and wished to keep the child talking. She had a sweet, musical voice.

"Yes. It was . . . the jongleur's idea. But then it really rained, and the canon found me out . . ."

That would be Anselm. Eleanor had never cared for him. He was a troublemaker with very low ideas of woman.

"And are you well, since your stay in the prison?" Eleanor prompted.

"Now, I am very well." Lucie smiled ingenuously. Eleanor smiled back.

Sophia, who had caught up by then, was speculating that Eleanor might well indeed be pleased with this damsel. The child was tall and fair, and slender as a willow. Unschooled, she yet had a natural grace that invited eyes to follow her movements. And her coloring was not unlike the Queen's. The maiden showed what the older woman had once been, the older woman showed what the maiden would yet become.

"By Mary's milk!" Sophia exclaimed, irritated. Why hadn't she noticed this before, and how would Eleanor take it? A woman in the midst of grief over lost youth may be less than overjoyed to see her spent beauty in another's face.

Eleanor noted Sophia's distress and raised her hands, as if in blessing, to show there was no anger, only curiosity. The damsel was of apparent low birth, but her beauty recommended her. And she is so very, very young, Eleanor thought, allowing herself a small sigh. She is so young, she is not aware of the years that stretch before her . . . or how quickly they will disappear.

"Come, look." Eleanor, intrigued, rose from her dais and invited Lucie to step in front of the large mirror. They stood side by side, shoulders touching, Lucie's blue tunic girdled at the same height where the gold mesh rope girdled Eleanor's red tunic.

"Sic transit gloria mundi," Eleanor sighed, looking at Lucie and then herself. "Thus fades worldly splendor."

Lucie stared intently at the steel mirror. She had never before seen her face so clearly. I am much prettier than Udele, she thought. Why, then, did Godfrey forget me so easily? Her bravado fled. Tears started, encouraged by the warmth of the solar, the kindness being shown her and the sleepless nights of the past week.

"There, child, it is nothing to weep at," crooned Eleanor, putting her arms about the girl. How thin she was! Despite her great height, she was still so young, so unformed. The Queen, who had left her own children behind for years at a time while she attended to Crusade, war, pilgrimage and matters of the heart, felt a sudden thrusting of maternal energy in the pit of her stomach. God had sent her his child. His purpose was unknowable.

Forgetting that the beloved son, Richard, had recently acquired a habit of treating his mother as though she were a doddering fool; forgetting that the favorite daughter, Marie, was a grown woman who, even as a child, had not needed her—forgetting for the nonce that Henry was recapturing youth in the arms of Fair Rosamonde—Eleanor found solace in comforting the adventurous young damsel.

"Amaria, fetch some meat and cheese. And red wine. Are you hungry, little one? Good. Now, sit. We must fetch the roses back to your cheeks. You are wan." Eleanor, distracted as Sophia had intended, oversaw the laying of the table herself.

5

Grey-bearded Broderick strained with all his strength, bringing beads of sweat that collected and ran in rivulets down his sunburnt forehead. The tendons in his neck flared like the sinuous, above-ground roots of a great oak. The cart behind him, weighted with bushels of soil and rock, creaked and groaned in protest. And then, as the leather straps yoking Broderick tautened, stretched, the cart moved forward a slow, painstaking foot's length.

A cheering, stamping row of white-robed Cistercians squinted into the bright sun behind Broderick and yelled encouragement. "Pull, man, pull!"

Godfrey yelled as heartily as the next but, out of habit, looked guiltily over his shoulder to be sure Lucie wasn't watching. She babied Broderick, cosseted him as if she were his mother, not a damsel half his size and less than half his age. With a pang, Godfrey remembered Lucie was gone. Abandoned, left behind. He could not reconcile himself to the fact that he might never again see her. Half the day he spent looking back over his shoulder to see if she was coming, and the other half he spent missing her. How had a maid come to make such a difference to him? He hadn't meant to care by half as much.

Next to Broderick, the monastery's two mules, led by Brother Dorus, brayed in frustration, unable to budge the cart to which they were yoked. Brother Dorus, his bald pate gleaming in the sun like a brass bowl, mumbled words of encouragement mixed with threats and curses, but Anne and Jacques could not budge their sorely laden cart.

Broderick, red of face and soaked with sweat, made one last great effort. His cart groaned and moved the last foot to the finish line. Godfrey ran to embrace the victor.

"I told you, Dorus," he yelled from under Broderick's armpit. Even tall as Godfrey was, he could not peer over the giant's shoulder. Dorus mumbled an unhearable answer and gave a carrot each to Anne and Jacques for their efforts.

"I know no man here would fall to sin," Abbot Robert called to them as he made his way through the rutted field of the contest. "Of course, there were no wagers made on this mad contest. I know the brothers of this holy monastery would not try to profit from the labor of others . . . nor would our honored guests."

The monks, half of whom had gained a week of another's midday ale or an extra hour of sleep while one of the losers attended to chores for them, nodded in pious agreement as they hastily made to leave. Only Godfrey, clasping his hands behind his back and intently peering at a stone by his feet, blushed.

"Your wagering distresses me," Robert addressed him. "But your honesty pleases me." That, in a voice loud enough for the monks to hear. With lowered eyes—how Robert spouted at them!—they went their separate ways, to apple orchard, stables, barley field, kitchen and scriptorium, to resume neglected chores.

"And you, my child, you should not let others goad you."

"I won," Broderick said, grinning.

"You could have injured yourself. The Lord frowns on self-inflicted injuries."

"He's pulled heavier loads," Godfrey protested.

"Then you have taken advantage of him even before this. He looks like a giant, but he is a man. And I have noticed that the larger among us often have the weakest hearts. Keep that in mind when next you seek to profit from this man's trust in you. Go, Broderick. Rest for the remainder of the day. If you feel any faintness or pain, come to me immediately. Understand?" Robert talked to him lovingly, as if he were a child, reminding Godfrey again of Lucie's affable voice. How had Udele never learned to soften hers? She spat sharp words as if gentleness would choke her.

"I would not knowingly hurt him," Godfrey said after Broderick had left.

"I know. Your sin was one of ignorance, but no less dangerous for that. Tell me, what was the bet, and what did you profit from your friend's success?"

"Ten sheets of parchment from the scriptorium stock," Godfrey admitted sheepishly.

"I see. Then I shall take the cost out of Brother Dorus' Christmas travel allotment. And what was your great need for this parchment?"

"Something in my head I would like to put on paper. A song."

"I will assume it was not a hymn or prayer you were composing but some lines meant to please a woman." Robert chortled with returning good humor. "For your penance, you will sing this song so that I may judge it." The elderly monk remembered the many songs he had once written for a certain Clarisse and wondered if he would find Godfrey's songs as touching as he had once found his own. Clarisse had been totally unmoved by them, preferring the wooing of her merchant father's partner, a wealthy widower.

They had been walking leisurely through the muddy field and arrived now at the charterhouse door.

"First, though, have some ale and a roll," Robert said. It concerned him that the youth, for all his raw strength, was losing weight under his care. Other than undetected illness, only one thing in God's world could make a strapping young man like Godfrey lose his appetite. The song would likely provide a key to the problem.

Godfrey accepted the ale but not the bread. His throat well moistened, he asked for another mug and then, with a wry grin,

began to sing. The lyrics, as Robert had anticipated, were red-
olent of worldly emotion liberally doused with a young man's
overrefined sense of injustice, which so quickly turns to self-pity.

"The heaviness of my heart seems a weighty matter . . ." Godfrey's voice hesitated and then accepted the challenge of Robert's
disapproving look and sang all the louder. Having no instrument
with him, he beat out the quick pace of the song with two large
wooden spatulas left lying on the table.

Youth makes men feel things too strongly, the monk thought,
listening. They see injustice and personal misfortune under every
rock. But the tune was merry and Robert's foot began to tap of its
own accord.

> ". . . sporting is pleasant, and sweeter than honeycombs;
> whatever Venus may command, the task is delightful.
> On a broad road I walk like any young man,
> and I am bound up in vices, unmindful of virtue,
> greedy for pleasure more than for health,
> dead in spirit, I take care of my skin."

Robert's foot ceased tapping. His sunburnt face blanched, and
the large, echoing room was silent for a long moment. Here was
bitterness strong enough to warp a soul for a lifetime. For eternity. This youth was in great danger.

"It would have sounded better if I had my lute for accompani-
ment," Godfrey apologized, sensing Robert's disapproval.

"It was not the quality of the music that distresses me," Robert
admitted, "but the words themselves. They praise sin and disdain
virtue. Is such a philosophy your purpose in life? If it is, I tremble for you."

"Purpose? What do I know of purpose? I go where the road
takes me." Godfrey grinned, but there was no mirth in his eyes.

"Life is unfair, I grant. But that is not justification for bitterness. Indeed, show me the man . . . any man . . . who thinks life
has given him his just rewards. That creature who is content with
his lot has not yet been fashioned. But Christ forbids us to keep

95

anger and despair in our hearts. They become canker sores on the soul, eating away at it."

"Then what is your complaint, Abbot Robert?" Godfrey taunted, putting down the spatulas. He liked Robert well enough, but the hint of lecture in any man's voice made the fine hairs on his neck rise in rebellion.

"You are thinking I should be happy enough, with my full belly and soft bed, and enough years on me that I no longer feel the pull of the flesh or the heart," Robert said. He looked away from Godfrey, through an open window where vegetable garden gave onto pasture, and pasture gave onto forest fringe, and beyond that forest was a road that led to Narbonne, and the illusion of freedom.

"It is the common mistake of youth to think that need and desire pass when youth have passed," Robert told Godfrey. "But it is not so. Love grows stronger, not weaker. I do not know if this is God's blessed design, or a lure of the devil. I only know it is so, and that the young must be careful of what they pursue in youth, because it will pursue them in later years. You will be pursued by your own vices."

"Then I'll have women aplenty at my heels, and not complain," Godfrey retorted.

"Are you, indeed, no more than a Goliard, who can't think beyond pleasure, who disdains God to pursue a life of sin? You are satisfied with a life of constant wandering, of attachment to things that decay and are lost?"

"I would have been attached to my land, but that was robbed from me. I would have sought virtue in hard work, but I had not the money to buy a position. I could have stayed in Paris and instructed some rich canon's young niece . . . but look where that got Abelard . . . severed from his manhood. No, thanks, Robert, the open road is safer."

"Safer for your skin, but not your soul. And for a strapping young man, you stress safety too highly."

That insult to Godfrey's courage disrupted the smooth surface of his bitterness and showed the rough anger beneath.

"Tell me, Abbot Robert," he spoke loudly and angrily,

". . . in heaven, where time is past and only eternity exists, does virtue exist?"

"In heaven the souls are all pure and free of corruption. There is no need to practice virtue in heaven, as there is no vice. As no evil can be done, there is no possibility of practicing virtue. It is too late," Robert replied warily, sensing a trap.

"Then virtue is of this world? You nod yes, even if it be unwillingly. And did not St. Paul tell us, 'Set your affection on things above, not on things on the earth'?"

"You, in the way of Goliards who have some education but little intelligence, twist his meaning. St. Paul also told us, 'Harden not your hearts.' Yours, it seems, is exceedingly hard."

"Maybe yes. Maybe no. Sometimes I wish it were harder." Godfrey rose to leave, but Robert pulled at his sleeve.

"Tell me what is truly worrying you. You argue like a true Goliard, but your words hide meaning. Forget this specious reasoning, this lure of the devil which you call by the name 'logic,' and try honesty. The change will do you good. Are there troubles between you and Udele? Troubles in love, I believe, are most common to men of your age."

"Udele?" Godfrey laughed. "Aye, there are love troubles. But not with Udele. Why would you think of her?"

Robert's eyes narrowed. "Perhaps because she is your wife."

"Priest never joined us. Udele only says she is my wife."

"Ah. That explains somewhat." Robert was beginning to see the lay of the land. "Who is this other, then?"

Godfrey, tired of argument and relieved to have a listener, told Robert the story of Lucie, how he had stolen her away, lain with her, convinced her to wear boy's clothing and act parts on the platform.

"That was grievous sin. You stole another man's property, and then stole her chastity," Robert reprimanded. It was a rote answer; he himself did not believe the words. Women should not be counted as property, and if they freely gave, then what was the harm of love? If he had been able to steal Clarisse from her father, never would he have counted it sin, but more of a blessing. Ah, well, better to forget that and concentrate on this more immediate problem. The youth was in pain, the kind of pain that can't be healed with splints and medicines, that will twist and ferment inside until the soul is fouled as a brackish pond.

"And to have her play roles. That was wrong, but surely a minor wrong," he continued, gentling his words for Godfrey's sake.

"The bishop's men thought it not minor. Udele said I would be imprisoned should I return to Poitiers and claim Lucie."

"Udele said that, did she?" Robert turned his face to hide the smile. God bless women, how cunning they were. And God save men, who trust in them so readily, not realizing the formidable foe that can be contained in their small, seemingly fragile frames.

"Out of fear for my own safety, I abandoned her." Godfrey turned his head away in shame. "Imprisoned, starved, probably tortured, she who trusted me . . . I left her there . . ."

One day's journey away, cushioned by a soft silk pillow, sat the damsel responsible for Godfrey's troubled confession. Eleanor herself poured wine into the maid's silver goblet. Amaria brushed the stream of hair that flowed over the maid's new blue gown, and whispered praise into her ear. Grown docile by their fuss over her comeliness, Lucie bit into a sugared almond. Sated, she let her hand hover over the tray of sweetmeats, searching for one she had not yet tasted.

"Easy, child." Robert patted Godfrey's blond head. This was the problem, then. The youth was punishing himself for a moment of cowardice. His mind, filled with malaise and dread, had enlarged the evil possibilities of the situation, and his own culpability, to unreasonable proportions.

"I know Bishop Jehan. He is righteous, but not cruel. Lucie will not have been harmed. Nor will you be, when you return for her." Robert cleared his throat and peered off into the distance. "Udele may have exaggerated the danger in order to keep you at her side. Did that never occur to you? Do you love this other maiden?"

"She was pleasant company, meek and compliant and merry. She had ways about her that could make you forget your troubles."

"Well, that might be a beginning to love, I suppose. Though it seems to me that any man who prizes meekness in a woman must yet learn much about their sex. And it was unmanly of you to leave behind the girl. No friend should act in that manner. When your work with Brother Dorus is finished, you must do this. Rise at night, when all is quiet, and leave. Return to Poitiers and seek her. Mayhaps she is there waiting for you. Leave Broderick with us. I will see that he is cared for and well treated."

And he, generous and childish soul that he is, will see to it that our roof is well mended, Robert thought but did not say. He crossed himself quickly and asked forgiveness for his greed. He was greedy for Broderick; not just for the man's soul, which was clean as an innocent child's, but for his body, which had the strength to do the work of six other men.

"What of Udele?" asked Godfrey, frowning. Only Udele was left of Godfrey's little traveling company. Cedric had run from the monastery the day of their arrival, fearful of being forcibly returned to his master. Lillah and Haram had disappeared two days later, slipping away with no farewell but with Lillah's purse heavy with the coins that should have been shared by all.

"If you have truly made her no vows, you must leave her behind. Udele is safe here, and seems contented tending the bread ovens in the hostel. When she discovers you have gone, she may count her losses and console herself elsewhere."

Then again, maybe she wouldn't. One of the monastery's paying guests who had complained about her cooking still bore the marks of her nails on his cheeks. She had a tongue that would frighten Satan himself. I will cross that bridge when I come to it, Robert thought, wondering if he might absent himself from the monastery on the day of Godfrey's departure, when Udele would discover his absence.

"And the carts?" the youth asked.

"You will travel faster with just a pack. Leave one cart for Udele to sell—you owe her that much—and one for the monastery, out of charity. The others I will tend. You can claim them at a later time."

"I will do it," said Godfrey, jumping to his feet with a quick movement. His heart was lighter than it had been for many a day.

"Where are you going?" Robert called.

"To the scriptorium. Time is wasting and I've work to do." There was a spring to Godfrey's walk.

"One other thing," Robert said.

"Yes?"

"Your song lacks inner rhyme. Don't commit it to parchment while it can be yet improved." Robert smiled indulgently, willing to overlook the song's secular faults. He had struck a profitable bargain. God forgive me, he thought, for taking advantage of the child's lovesickness. But it will be pleasant to keep next spring's rain off our heads while we are at prayer.

Robert rose to go about his chores, his knees creaking like castanets from the effort. Amazing, how quickly the problems of youth can be solved. Even in their sinning they were innocent as babes, lacking complication and needing only a finger to point direction. I don't believe, though, that Udele will be quite as simple, he thought.

And what was it Brother Dorus, the keeper of the monastery's records, had said about their wheat tax being increased a triplefold? To pay it, they would have to send their entire crop of first spring beans to the castle. Queen Eleanor was scouring the countryside and her own properties for foodstuffs . . . What had she in mind, to house and feast the great gathering of knights assembled at her court?

Abbot Robert mumbled a quick prayer. It was always bad luck for the peasants when the nobility met in war council. Maybe, like the coming storm with Udele, it would blow over without casualties. And then again . . .

And then again, mayhaps Eleanor did have something up her sleeve. The King, on hands and knees, tapped heavily at the wood beams supporting the gallery. It sounded hollow. Worms had feasted here. Gingerly Henry moved back till he felt the rougher surface of the wall-walk safely beneath his knees.

The wooden galleries would have to be replaced with stone parapets, the drawbridge reinforced with large bands of iron, and new wells dug. These were improvements he had meant to make for a long time. The castle at Gisors was strategically important and must not fall into disrepair.

I will repair it now, he told himself. What he could not admit was that the castle was being readied for warfare . . .

My son has fled to Paris, to Louis. It is a young man's anger and bitterness that has caused him to do so. He will not go to war against his father. He will not.

Henry stood slowly and looked down at the red-roofed village laid out at his feet. It lacked the beauty of Chinon, and the hunting here was not so good. But it was a good place for battle, and the castle was well located to withstand and drive back a siege.

Eleanor would not drive her own sons to battle against their father, the King told himself again. She was angry. Bitter. Frustrated. He smiled, remembering how easily he had cured her frustration in the past. But he could not now. Rosamonde had made that impossible. His body was Rosamonde's, it would obey Eleanor's call no more, and he was glad of it.

But she must not war against him. She would not.

Below, in the village, a shepherdess was driving her flock through the narrow street. The sun was low in the sky, yet Henry could make out the nans with their kids bleating and trying to thrust their heads under the mother's belly, seeking the teats even as they walked. In front, leading the others, was a large, weary-eyed buck who walked with head high, knowing that where he went, the others would follow. The Judas goat. The one who, later in the year, would lead them not to safety but to the butcher.

Henry watched the Judas goat, and bile rose in his throat.

Some days and many pages of manuscript copying later, Robert and the weary-eyed monks were already chanting the second service of the still dark day when Godfrey awoke. The air smelled of release and pleasure to come. Quickly he dressed for travel.

The blood sang in his veins. He had been still too long. It

would be good to feel time pass the way it passed for journeyers, as a movement of road underfoot, hours measured by changing scenes and the changing fall of light. To be errant, in quest of adventure and riches, that was the only thing worth the doing. It was misery to linger for long in one place . . . Life is no more than a journey from here to there, from birth to death. The journey is everything, the destination nothing.

Although it would be good to see Lucie again. She had a way of lurking in the shadows of his thoughts, never far from what he was doing or thinking, yet never in reach, either. The memory of her satin skin and the long veil of her hair as it fell over her modest nakedness stirred him to faster movement.

He crept out of the men's guest dorter and peeked down the cloistered walk, to be sure none stirred in the women's house. Only sleep sounds, snores and mutters, the rustling of bed covers, disturbed the air. Udele was not yet up.

On tiptoe, mouth pursed for whistling but no audible tune issuing from it, he disappeared through the monastery gates and into the large, welcoming last hour of night. A cock crowed in the distance; Godfrey understood its exultation. It was good to be alive, to be young and in quest . . . in quest of what? he wondered. Love? A maiden? Adventure? All of them, he decided.

"I'll kill him! I'll kill him!" Udele shrieked several hours later. "He's left me!"

Robert, inspecting a new planting of comfrey in the herb garden, decided it was an appropriate time to make himself scarce.

"Here," he said, passing his trowel to an assistant. "I just remembered a chore I must attend to in the village." With a quick glance over his shoulder, he was gone. He could not lie to Udele if he was not there to answer her questions. A debate with her could easily turn into a physical contest, and he feared her sharp claws and sharper tongue. Hasty retreat was the least sinful option.

In the monastery kitchens Jacobus, the baker, made a hasty

decision. He could duck, and sacrifice the expensive timeglass for which a just-fired pot was headed, or stand his ground and take the punishment instead. "Not the timeglass!" he pleaded, deciding to duck. Too late. The hourglass was already in a thousand pieces at his feet. He was awed.

My God! He hadn't seen such spirit since his dear departed Agatha, bless her soul and may it rest in peace, had found him with a scullery maid. "Udele, my dear, calm yourself, this will lead to injury," he pleaded.

"I'll kill him!" Udele repeated.

But the storm was passing, Jacobus could see. Her shrieks, thickened and reduced like a good sauce by the heat of passion, were already mere wails. Braver than many another man, he approached. Albeit with due caution. Udele's fury, already mollified by the admiration in Jacobus' eyes, turned into a deluge of tears.

She wailed piteously, cursing her father and mother, who had let her go off with such a lout in the first place, what did it matter that they had twelve other daughters at home, they should never have let her. See what it had come to.

"Have no fear. I'll take care of you," widower Jacobus said, his eyes on Udele's full and heaving bosom. Warily he tried one arm about her shoulders. She peeped out from under the apron she had thrown over her head. Not bad, she decided. A bit long in the tooth and soft in the middle, but better than no man at all.

Emboldened by her speculative glance, he put the other arm about her and tried a tentative hug. She did not hug back. Neither did she try to scratch his face. Jacobus smiled.

"Pious Queen, most illustrious Queen." Eleanor held the letter by her fingertips, as if it were a soiled object. She held it at arm's length, putting a good distance between the sheet and her celebrated dark eyes, which at that moment were squinted and narrowed as a clerk's.

The company in the Queen's bower waited as Eleanor pulled a lamp closer and tried to hold the sheet at even greater distance than her arms could stretch. Her eyes refused to focus on the

fine, spidery writing. Around her sat Sophia, Richard, Raoul de
Faye, and Lucie. Because Lucie had been given in to Sophia's
care, she followed her everywhere . . . and was admitted everywhere, much as a pet dog would have been.

Sophia, impatient with fatigue, shifted on the cushioned bench.
It had been a long day and she was longing for her bed. The
prelude to battle was as tiring for the inhabitants of the castle as
the war itself would be for the warriors.

There were inventories to make, supplies to be readied, con-
tacts to be made, letters to be answered. Horoscopes to be drawn
for the most important of the arrivals because Eleanor needed the
guidance of the stars even to keep peace in the ladies' dormito-
ries. Just yesterday a lady born under the sign of growling Leo
had been assigned to a bed with a stinging Scorpio. The resulting
fiasco had produced torn pillows and divided camps in the
women's bower, until Sophia, correctly judging the problem, reas-
signed the Scorpio to share a bed with a more tractable Cancer.

The castle was so crowded that ladies of lesser birth shared
three and four to the bed, while their knights camped in the
courtyard under the stars. Sophia herself, who had never before
shared a bed, now slept with Lucie at her side. The girl did not
snore, thank the Lord for that much, but she tossed and turned
and mumbled in her sleep. The nights were long and filled with
wakeful hours spent trying to decipher the girl's words—as much
as she longed for sleep, Sophia was curious by nature. Who was
this Godfrey who was called for over and over, and who did not
appear?

The days were even longer than the sleepless nights, made
busy with feasts meant to keep spirits high, tourneys, and hours
of reception to greet the newly arrived.

Diplomacy had never been one of Sophia's virtues; she preferred the directness of the philosophers. Her stature, deformity,
and bookish penchant had kept her removed from the patterns of
worldly courtesy. But now she must flatter silly brides who
thought only of baubles, for if they were offended, or even neglected, they might leave, and their lord's support flee with them.
She must laud peacock knights, singing exaggerated praise of

previous battles so that they would fight even harder in the battles to come.

What a silly business it all was. And deadly, after all the gallant songs were sung and armed knight faced armed knight on the killing ground.

Lucie, sitting bolt upright next to Sophia, heard her sigh. She watched her warily from the corner of her eye, waiting for a movement, a gesture, that she could repeat. Always in unfamiliar situation within the walls of Eleanor's castle, Lucie had decided to follow Sophia in all she did. The results were sometimes droll, sometimes troublesome. What was preoccupation in a scholarly astrologer appeared as arrogance in a young maid.

Unbeknown to her, Lucie had already snubbed many damsels who expected better. She had earned few friends and many enemies, who called her La Caulde, because she seemed cold as a mountain stream and passed by just as quickly.

"Before matters come to a worse end, return with your sons to your husband . . ." Eleanor read from the parchment. "When Satan wears a halo," she interjected mildly before finishing the letter. ". . . whom you are bound to obey and with whom you are forced to live; return lest he mistrust you or your sons. Most surely we know that he will in every way possible show you his love and grant you the assurance of perfect safety. Bid your sons, we beg you, to be obedient and devoted to their father, who for their sakes has undergone so many difficulties, run so many dangers, and undertaken so many labors."

Raoul de Faye, listening to this stern warning from the archbishop, turned white and then red. Richard, furious, jumped to his feet and began to pace the length of the room. He had just come from a hunt, and his silver spurs rang on the stone floor. Amaria, seated behind her tapestry frame, watched him with burning eyes.

"What difficulty has this paragon of fatherhood undergone for me?" argued Richard, raising a gloved fist to the ceiling. "Mayhaps he will permit me to retain my dame's dower of Aquitaine. Mayhaps not. He made me duke, yes. But he made Henry King, and see what good that has done him. Behind his back they call him the schoolboy king. Did you know that, Lady Mother? Henry treats us like hooded hawks, taunting us with power he will never relinquish from his own grasp. He hasn't the decency to retire or die."

"You and the Young King are both wronged by your father," admitted Eleanor, a little coolly. Henry was, after all, more than a decade younger than herself. What was this talk of death, of retiring? "But the letter continues and so shall I, by your leave. 'Either go back to your husband, or by canon law we shall be compelled and forced to lay the Censure of the Church on you. Although we say it unwillingly, unless you return to your senses, we shall do this with grief and tears.'"

"He threatens you with the interdict," Richard roared, furious. Amaria, trying to imagine what the voice would sound like in peaceful lovemaking, mistakenly jabbed a needle of blue thread into the crimson tapestry field.

"Your hand is trembling," Sophia pointed out to her cruelly. Amaria burst into tears and fled the chamber.

"The damsel seems unduly frightened, don't you think?" Richard asked after the heavy wooden door slammed shut behind her.

"No matter. I have quarreled with the Church before. What most worries me is not what the archbishop says, but what he leaves unsaid." Eleanor patted the cushion next to her, signaling for Richard to sit and calm himself.

"How so?" her son asked.

"This letter follows quickly on your heels. Too quickly. Whoever informed the archbishop of the forming of our army knew of our plans in advance."

"You are saying we have been betrayed." Raoul de Faye, more nervous than ever, began pulling at his beard.

"I expected as much. When you have called together as many knights as we have, human nature itself dictates that at least one will be a Judas. There is one here who has sworn homage to us, but is in Henry's pay."

"When I discover him, I'll personally see to it that his hands, both of them, are cleanly separated from his arms," Richard vowed.

"Till then, we must all be on our guard. But now that is said,

106

let's pass the time more pleasantly. Richard, doesn't our rescued damsel look charming in blue?"

Lucie sat up straighter, knowing that the Queen referred to her. She smiled winningly at the Queen's son, who was almost as comely as Godfrey. Unlike Godfrey, he ignored her glance. "Mmmmm," he mumbled, peering out the window.

Vagrant late-afternoon light washed the bailey with a golden cast. Alberic, his squire, had set broken pieces of pottery on the stable roof and was about to release the first arrow. Richard had forbidden target practice within the castle walls; yet he chuckled, watching the other youth's face grimace in concentration. Alberic, holding his breath and counting to three, let fly the shaft after a mighty draw of the bow. It found its target, a shard of old pitcher, and knocked it off the edge of the roof.

"Well done!" Richard called from the embrasure of Eleanor's bower. "But if you hit a passing knight or lady in this turmoil, I'll not answer to the seneschal for you."

"Come down, then," Alberic called. "There's time enough to ride to the east pasture and aim our arrows at something more profitable than pottery!"

"I will," rejoined Richard. With a quick kiss of his mother's hand, Richard was gone from the room.

Eleanor, tired but straight-backed and regal, saw how quickly the son who had never yet declared a love fled the maiden.

"Sophia, bring me a compress. I shall have a headache tonight," she said in a voice that had an edge of disappointment to it.

Sir Benoit leaned against the passageway, letting the rough, en brosse surface of the stone taunt his back under its thin green tunic. His senses were enkindled; all day his vision had been tempered with golden flame. Surely she would have to pass this way before retiring for the evening.

Never had dusk seemed so enchanted by sorcery. The lively bailey was quick with light and shadow, emphasized by the bonfires already lit for the evening. A great murmur of voices surrounded him—knights and their esquires, grooms and pot-stirrers, washerwomen and ladies—but he had no ear for them. He strained to hear the sound of her approaching footsteps, small and gentle as raindrops on a roof. Surely she would pass this way.

Young Sir Benoit had found love.

He was Tristram to her Isolde, Aucassin to Nicolete, Sir Orfeo to her Heurodis. For her would he face unjust kings and menacing demons, leap rivers wide as a country, pick apples guarded by dragons, go to hell and back to keep her by his side. Ever since that moment two days ago when he had first espied her, he knew the meaning of life. It was to worship, to adore, to serve. She was all beauty, all grace.

Sir Benoit sighed, joy and pain mingling in his chest, for love brings both and the greatest honor is in pain. Through pain is the soul purified, perfected, made worthy of love.

He was already well instructed in the rules of courtly love and chivalry, having spent the past three years in service to the Lady Marie of Champagne, daughter of Eleanor. But never yet had there been a domina, an *amica* . . . the lady who would command his heart and soul. Now, ah now, the saints had seen fit to send him this grace, this blessing!

Benoit, transported with ecstasy, rolled his eyes to heaven, unaware that a small gathering of women had collected in the wall indent opposite him. He heard the music of the planets as they danced in the night sky, not the giggles of the pointing women.

He whispered her name as he had heard it pronounced by Amaria, the Queen's maid. It spoke of murmuring streams and spring morns. There was a mystery to her. No one could say where she was from, except that her voice hinted of the North, and the Queen had chosen to protect her.

She would be his Holy Grail, his meaning, his redemption, the mission he had sought since being dubbed knight. Lucie, he prayed, pass this way soon. Let me but reach out and touch the hem of your gown and I'll not ask for more.

A second of Alberic's prankish arrows flew across the bailey, letting loose a small volley of loosened stones and pottery shards over Benoit's head. The women laughed; Benoit indifferently

108

brushed dust and pebbles off his shoulder and continued his vigil.

The one they called Soiette, for her well-used bosom was white and smooth as silk, made much to do about pressing thumb and forefinger together to form a small, tight, circle. This she waved at Benoit. He, just feet away, neither saw the obscene gesture nor heard their laughter.

The whores, for such they were, became peevish. Wherever knights and foot soldiers gather, there too gather the women who ease their less spiritual needs. The ones of this group, hearing of the grand migration of knighthood to Eleanor's court, had traveled from as far as Avignon. They, the queans, counted themselves the best in the trade and looked down on the trulls—the ones with torn gowns, hunger-swollen bellies and wild eyes—as avidly as the veiled ladies of the castle looked down on them. They were not used to having their charms ignored by knights; they expected better of hot-blooded lords.

More, the last repast of the day would be served soon, and Soiette as yet had not been claimed for the evening. No one approached her. It was assumed that Foulkes, as usual, would claim her when all the torches in the great hall were extinguished, one by one, and men and women went to their private deeds. But he had gone to the hunt and not yet returned.

Soiette's stomach rattled with hunger. The camp followers could light no fire nor set table of their own; it was their calling to be always the guest.

"Dead," she exclaimed in a voice thick with the feigned treacle of a woman wanting attention. She pointed at Sir Benoit with a forefinger as slender and long as Queen Eleanor's, but it was crusted with dirt. "Dead to the world. But I could rouse him."

"Bet," said a little dark one, Brangoene.

"Your leather girdle against my silk purse," Soiette agreed with queenly confidence. She knew she was irresistible; hadn't a score of men told her so in the past few days? The leather girdle in question was worked with silver thread embroidery and even boasted three pearls. Soiette had hungered for the girdle since a Spanish soldier had bestowed it on Brangoene two years ago.

"Go to it, then," cheered the other queans.

Soiette spit into her palms and rubbed them over her curling black hair. Then, with more delicacy, she licked both forefingers and traced them over brows and lashes to darken them. With a grand gesture she brushed dust from her skirts and tugged at the neckline of her tunic so that the tops of round, white breasts showed clearly above the homespun crimson cloth.

Humming a tune she had heard years ago—it was an introit for a requiem mass, but of that she was unware, knowing only that it had a catchy air—she sidled across the passageway to where Benoit stood.

"The air is sweet tonight, isn't it?" she asked, looking up with a hint of shyness. Youths of this age are often frightened by a too bold approach; better to play the maiden a bit.

On close inspection, Benoit proved to be most pleasing. His eyes were the soft grey color of a dove's wing; his brown hair curled nicely to his shoulders. His face still had a childish ruddiness and little hint of harsh stubble. Soiette guessed that this youth applied razor to face no more than once a week. How smooth that cheek would feel against her bosom! He had the youth's fault of being overdeveloped in the shoulders and too thin in the hips and legs, but time and gravity would remedy that. It made no difference in the straw anyway; a skinny rooster was as good as a fat one.

God's passion, this gentle youth would make a soft and pleasant switch from Sir Foulkes, who was all prickly beard and impudent hands! Soiette was pleased with her choice.

"Did you speak?" The reverie was broken. Benoit looked down at the woman beside him, uncertain of what she had said or what she wanted. The queans across the way giggled into their hands.

"I said, it is a sweet evening," Soiette repeated. "Company would make it sweeter, my honey." She threw caution to the wind; his gentle eyes roused fire in her loins. There were those who did not enjoy the work; Soiette was not among them. She followed her calling with true and ready ardor.

"Come lay with me." She stood on tiptoe to whisper it softly in

110

his ear. As she balanced, she wound one long leg over his thighs and pressed herself against him.

The next moment she lay stunned, in a pile of mud and manure at the feet of the laughing queans. Benoit's arm, which had struck out soon as she finished the words, was still poised in midair. His face was twisted with disgust.

Soiette wiped her mouth, where a bruise was already rising. She watched him through narrowed eyes and saw what she had not seen before.

"He's a virgin." She said it once in wonder, twice in scorn. "He's a virgin," she yelled to her comrades, hoping thereby to redeem her damaged reputation. "God's balls, this knight is a virgin!"

Benoit reddened with embarrassment and dishonor. He had struck a woman. It was against every code of honor he had ever learned in Eleanor's courts of love.

At being a virgin he was not distressed at all; hadn't Countess Marie instructed him that love was to be pure, spotless? That carnal cravings damaged love? The first passage he had been set to memorize was St. Jerome's "Praise of Virginity." But to strike a woman, even a woman such as this . . .

"I ask your forgiveness," he said, extending a hand to pull Soiette out of the mud and manure where she sat.

She spit at his hand and swatted it away. To be struck was nothing new; but this raw youth would not condescend to her. She had her pride.

"Forgive," she spat out. "I curse you. There." She put both hands together and pointed two forefingers at him.

"Witch!" cried Benoit, backing away.

A torch was coming their way, splitting aside the dark curtains of newly arrived night as the bearer approached. Benoit and the queans backed against the walls of the passage in surprise.

Ayeeee, my back, thought Sophia. And isn't it just like Richard to insist on quartering with his knights rather than making himself comfortable in the Tower? If he were more considerate, she wouldn't have to make her way through the crowded courtyard six, seven, even eight times a day, when Eleanor summoned them to Richard's side to watch the two of them play chess, compose lyrics or just to keep them company.

She could see, though, how the mother could be so taken with the son. He was as fair a man as ever walked the earth, the true personification of knightly being. Ayeee, foolish Amaria to think or hope he would look her way. How he had dashed down to answer Alberic's call!

And therein lay the problem of statehood. The Young King had already fathered many bastards and promised to sire a large stable of boy-children, once he and that French wife of his got around to it. If she didn't stray first. The wife's eye wandered as quickly as her husband's, especially if the Young King's man, William Marshall, was near. Now that Marshall was gone with Henry to France, Margaret, left behind in Poitiers, was dejected and wilted. She spent most of her days alone, which also suited Eleanor. She had no great love for her daughter-in-law.

Yes, Henry would likely proffer progeny. As for the rest of kingship . . . he didn't have it in him. He had lived too long in his father's overweening shadow, been made content with display and luxury. He spent his days in tourneys, mock battles, his nights in drunken play with knights and unsavory women, and was satisfied. His ambition, the true ambition that came from his own soul and not his mother's persistence, wouldn't fill a thimble.

The fuss he was making now, this escape to Paris to side with Louis and war against Henry, had more to do with being deprived of his allowance and his boon companions than a real thirst for power, Sophia suspected.

Whereas Richard, the younger son never destined to be King . . . now, there was a choice the saints would favor. And Eleanor, his mother, too. He was intelligent, courtly, diplomatic and brave. And ambitious. Without ambition the other qualities were as nothing. Richard's penchant for youths presented no problem; many such knights did their duties to God, wife and overlord, producing a stable of children in between flings with boy lovers. But Richard had another virtue that could be his undoing. He had no tolerance for hypocrisy. Eleanor might maneuver him into a diplomatic marriage, but he would not bed with a person not loved. There would be no heirs. That would break Eleanor's heart.

The desire and pursuit of the whole is called love. Love, ultimately, was no more than a *res nihili*, it had no more consequence beyond the troubles it wrought.

"Have you pain?" asked Lucie, solicitously, hearing Sophia's sigh.

"Child, I always have pain. But that is not why I sigh. I sometimes think God was besotted when He ordered this world of His. Nothing is as it seems, nothing is as it should be."

"I know what you mean," nodded Lucie with new wisdom, thinking not of Richard but of Godfrey. "Careful, Lady Sophia. There is a step here." Lucie took her gently by the arm to guide her through the dark passage. The torchbearer was walking faster than the tiny lame woman could manage, and the darkness was encroaching upon them. "Hold up!" Lucie called to him.

Sophia was startled and pleased by the new note of authority in the girl's voice. She learned quickly and easily by mere imitation. Her mannerisms were acquiring dignity. Was she fleeing a cruel father or bestial husband when she decamped with that traveling company? She was frequently sad; she avoided company as much as Sophia herself did. What frightened her, so that she called out in her sleep? In time it would be revealed; to force the damsel to answer questions now would probably only result in lies.

It is her voice, thought Benoit as the company approached. His heart jumped in expectation.

It is La Caulde, thought Soiette, rising hastily to her feet.

The torchbearer walked between them. Sophia and Lucie followed at his heels, intent in private thought and not noticing the two camps that eyed them as they passed.

Benoit, not expecting a greeting or glance—he had not yet done anything to deserve his beloved's notice—leaned towards Lucie as she passed like a tree bending in the wind. His face filled with love; he sighed as the hem of her cloak brushed his leg.

All this Soiette noticed, and it brought burning fire to her cheeks. So. He pines for La Caulde, does he? she thought. Of course a limp virgin would pine for a seemingly cold fish like her. But I see through her. She pretends to be a lady, but is not. She pretends innocence, but this one is no unused child. She hungers for bed sport, although no one sees it but me.

Jealousy and bitterness coursed through Soiette's veins like molten lead. Because of this pale fraud she had been rejected and thrown to the mud.

When Foulkes returned from hunting, he soothed the ruffled Soiette with fresh rabbit stew and eager lovemaking. She made bawdy jokes at Sir Benoit's expense, omitting mention of her mud bath and making much of Benoit's sheepish virginity, and the foolish way he mooned when La Caulde passed.

"From what I've heard of her, most men would swoon over the damsel." Foulkes grunted with pleasure. Soiette's hands were knowing and experienced; she was doing tantalizing things between his aching, bruised legs. When had a day in the saddle begun to take such a toll? Just yesterday he had been young and invincible; now even mild exertion left him tired and panting.

Despite the skill of her hands, he was still limp; he feared the time to come when even a woman like Soiette could no longer rouse him. God. Take me on the battlefield before that happens, he prayed. Let me die first.

"Take my word for it. She's a cold fish. Not to your taste at all," Soiette murmured, still burning with Benoit's scorn and the haughty way La Caulde passed without so much as a nod.

"You think you know my taste, woman?" Foulkes teased. "You

may be right. And you may not. It would please me to see this La Caulde, although it's said she keeps muchly to the women's bower. Ouch. Easy. If you don't control that temper, you'll ruin both our pleasures this night. Gently, gently."

Moments later, as the familiar and pleasant sensations roused him: "Christ's passion, woman! Where did you learn that? Ahhh. You say Benoit's a virgin? I always thought him a fool—no don't stop—now I know he's one."

In Eleanor's chapel, all was quiet. The candles were doused, all but the one that burnt constantly in front of the Virgin Mother. Benoit kissed the statue's feet and then prostrated himself on the floor before her. Dear God. Make me worthy of her. Make me a worthy vessel to hold the precious will of pure love, he prayed. He looked up again. The statue of the Madonna resembled her, with its deep shadowed eyes and thick coils of hair which slipped from a loosened veil. Had the statue nodded at him?

Lucie and Sophia lay side by side in bed. Both pretended to be asleep; both stared at the obscured ceiling with wide-awake eyes.

If I sleep, I will dream of Godfrey. I can't stand it, Lucie thought. Her limbs were on fire with the need for his touch. She stayed as still as possible, trying to distance herself from her body, which was all desire, and her heart, which was all pain.

De integro. It begins again, thought Sophia. The way he looked at her, and she not even noticing. How did beauty so change women, that they could be adored and yet be indifferent to it? If just once a gently born youth had looked at her in that way . . . better not think of it. It will never happen. I have a score and five years, and that much more to live through, God willing, yet will no man look at me in that way. She closed her eyes and willed elusive sleep to come. Tomorrow, whether Eleanor permitted it or no, she would spend the morning in the scriptorium, attending to her translation of Boethius. There was healing in labors of the mind. There was no healing in the matters of the heart.

*   *   *

In the hour before dawn the air was sweet and fresh as a maiden's breath. Rosy-fingered Dawn danced before the Sun chariot, scattering pink hues against the grey sky.

In the court of love, the sleepers tossed, turned, sighed, groaned, smiled and cursed in the darkly secret landscapes of their private dreams. Lucie, asleep against her will, lay in Godfrey's arms atop the wardrobe chest, as she had that first morning in Poitiers. He was no longer hurried and impatient; in the oft-repeated dream he took his time, was loving and gentle and did things that produced sensations unknown to her in the waking world. She sighed happily, willing the dream to continue, willing him to continue.

Next to her, Sophia again kissed her father's cheek in farewell. After her mother, he was the only one who had ever loved her. Her mother was dead. He was leaving on pilgrimage. She knew in her heart she would never see him again. "Papa!" cried eight-year-old Sophia. "Hush, daughter. Don't fret. You'll always be taken care of. But tend to your letters. You'll not get much pleasure elsewhere, I'm afraid." He held her one last moment and then turned to leave. Sophia frowned in sleep.

In the damp postern turret, Alberic called out. Richard wakened immediately. The youth was having a nightmare. Tenderly his liege lord and friend pulled the cover tighter over his squire, tenderly he placed a kiss on the smooth cheek. Amaria, sharing a sleep-quieted bed with a young bride from Troyes, sighed with joy as a phantom Richard admitted he loved only her, he could no longer keep it secret but must declare his adoration to the world.

His mother, Eleanor, smiled with pride and joy in the fulgent splendor of her bedchamber. The young Duke of Anjou, Henry, knelt before her bed in her favorite English manor of Woodstock. He kissed her bare instep in a manner that was both adoring and provocative. "If you came to me with naught but a shift on your back, I would worship you," the young man vowed the woman who was already a crowned Queen. "Forever, Eleanor. Till the

117

mighty seas evaporate and the mountains are leveled, will I love you, only you." Eleanor sighed and turned over in sleep, encouraging her young lord to place his kisses on the back of the knee, there, that very sensitive, very secret place . . .

The floor was cold and hard, but passion kept Benoit, asleep against his will to keep vigil in the chapel, warm. Lucie floated overhead on a cloud, her tawny hair made even more shining by a halo hovering over her dear head. "I am waiting for you," she called to him. He climbed a silver ladder; for every rung he gained, a new one appeared at the top. "Wait for me, Lady Love," he called, but her chariot-cloud was already passing by. He climbed faster and faster, never gaining the end of the ladder.

Sir Foulkes and Soiette, sound asleep, still rolled in each other's arms, moving as one, snoring in abandoned unison. These two, sated, did not dream but only continued the reassuring contact of chest to chest, thigh to thigh, as they renewed their vigor for the day to come.

As the dreams ran their course, the sleeping sun stepped closer to the horizon. Godfrey's step was only slightly less vigorous than it had been the morning before, when he first set out. The day of walking had cleared the monastery cobwebs from his head; he breathed deeply, and each breath was a paean to the glory of this world.

The maiden spring was bursting into ripe bloom under the push of God's thumb, just as the tight wild Iris burst into bloom when snapped by a maiden's finger. The air smelled of sweet hay, for it was already the time of the prime mowing. Even in this early hour, laborers were in the field, making the air hum with the sound of scything. The creatures of the pasture had been delivered of their calves and lambs and stood, contented and docile in maternity.

The journey had been an easy one, filled with warm days blessed with the kiss of sun, and an easy night passed pleasantly enough in a woodcutter's hut. The woodcutter and his wife had

118

accepted a song in exchange for supper. Godfrey's purse was as heavy as it had been when he set out.

He was dressed in a fine russet suit and new hose that showed the good shape of his legs. He felt rich as a King. And like a King, abundance made him generous. He would buy a present for Lucie in Poitiers, some ribbons or a bauble to please her vanity. Otherwise his fine appearance, compared to her poor misery, would make her feel too keenly the difference between their stations in life.

Of Udele, he had but a single thought: good riddance. There was guilt mixed with the pleasure of that thought, but not enough to spoil the fineness of the morning. Nor did it interfere with his appetite, which was strong again, now that he had left behind Udele, monastery and dim scriptorium. He was free, and with a purpose, and with pleasure expected at the end of the journey. Could even a knight errant ask more of life?

Whistling, he sat in an emerald glade and laid out the remnants of his bread and slab of cheese. No need to arrive in Poitiers hungry. The thought of laying with Lucie that night doubled his hunger for bread; he bit into the loaf and chewed with no less content than the creatures of the field.

"Aye, he'll be carrying silver in that purse." Ebles chortled, and his face, already twisted, grew even more twisted as the long, ragged knife scar on his cheek turned up in glee.

"Silver, perhaps even a gold piece or two," amiably agreed the man who was known to his comrades as Rouge-Raoul, for the sight of blood pleasured him greatly. "And look at that tunic. Like new. And just my size, I'm thinking."

"Get down, man! He's ripe for the plucking, but if you stand up like that, he'll spot us, and then a lot of good both the purse and tunic will do us, till we get a few steps closer." Ebles pulled his partner back down behind the dew-slippery hillock. The force of his jerk made them lose their footing; they tumbled together,

119

arms and legs askew, to the base of the incline, with much breaking of twigs and graveling of pebbles.

Godfrey, mouth full, stopped in midchew. Something was
prowling at the skirt of the forest behind him. Mayhaps just a wild
dog. Mayhaps more. He stood and gathered together his bundle.
No need to delay longer. The noise reminded him that he was
eager to reach his destination.

"Now. I'll go right. You'll go left," Ebles whispered to Rouge-
Raoul, who was fierce but not cunning. Dressed all in greens and
browns, the two brigands melded into the verdant background of
wood and pasture as they circled their prey.

Rouge-Raoul, the first to reach the victim, stepped out from
behind a tree directly into Godfrey's path. He was smiling, but
Godfrey didn't like the hard glint of his eyes.

"It's a fine morning!" Rouge-Raoul exclaimed heartily, squinting at Godfrey the way fishwives squinted at the morning catch,
trying to assess its tastiness.

"That it is," Godfrey agreed, warily, taking a step backward, a
step that brought him, unbeknownst to him, closer to Ebles.

"And it'll be no trouble to you if I lighten you of your purse,"
said Rouge-Raoul.

"It would be much trouble." Godfrey hoisted his heavy walking
stick, prepared to do battle.

"Now, now, man. Don't take it so hard. Have you never been
robbed before?" said Ebles from behind.

Godfrey struck without further thought or invitation. Rouge-
Raoul was in sight and within reach, so it was his head that took
the first blow of the walking staff. It was a wise choice, although
Godfrey didn't know it. Rouge-Raoul was the kind of thief who
would joyously break your head if you didn't break his first. The
thud of wood against skull was loud and sickening. In slow motion, it seemed, Rouge-Raoul collapsed in an untidy heap and
was out of the fray.

"Ayeiiiiii!" yelled Ebles, jumping on Godfrey's back and beating him about the ears with his fists. Godfrey hopped about in
fury, trying to get this monkey of a brigand off him. He would
have succeeded had he not tripped over the supine mound that

120

was Rouge-Raoul. Down went Godfrey and Ebles both, and before Godfrey could so much as curse, the second bandit had his purse, and tunic too, for the garment had split at a seam.

Ebles' scar, earned in a tavern brawl, had taught him the valuable lesson of quickness. There are some trades that allow a man to stand back and admire his pretty and cunning handiwork; brigandage is not one of them. And so it was with great speed that Ebles disembarked from this scene and back into the woods, where dawn had not yet vanquished the concealing darkness of night.

Godfrey, bloodied and shivering in his torn shirt, gave chase through a cow-littered pasture and into the crackling-floored forest. Fruitless. The bandit had disappeared.

Soiette had slept well and wakened even more pleasantly, thanks to Sir Foulkes. But then, roosters his age are more vigorous in the morning, she thought, rubbing sleep from wine-reddened eyes. The knight was already gone, but had thought to leave her a thick slice of bread and cheese and small skin of wine. And, of course, a few coins to spend at Troyes Fair when next she was there.

She stopped rubbing, stretched, and looked up to the heavens with a glance that was half curiosity, half challenge. The sky over the bailey was a pale blue circle rimmed by grey stone walls. The day promised to be fair. That was important to Soiette, who, because of her calling, had to remain out of doors or seek shelter in chapel. She preferred mild days spent in ease, or even rainy ones, for that matter, to a day at chapel. Mary's womb, how those monks and priests would lecture when once they spied a quean on the premises. They carried on as if the Magdalene hadn't been one of the chosen few, as favored by Jesus as his own mother.

Bread and cheese. A warrior's breakfast. Her stomach churned for something more toothsome. A plum pastry or baked apple wrapped in a flaky crust oily with butter. I'll to the kitchen, she decided. Mayhaps Gislebertus is there. He's an easy one. A few grabs at my teats, a peck at his ear, and he'd feed me till the second coming. Too bad he was never at his ovens for the last part of the day, but only the first. Rabbit stew, especially as it was prepared by Sir Foulkes' squire, with bits of fur and claw still floating in it, quickly lost its appeal.

In the Maubergeonne Tower, Sophia choked back a mouthful of bile and painfully sat up. She had not rested well, and if the day continued as it had begun, she would spend it in bed. Her courses had started, her head ached, her stomach churned and her shorter leg was contorted with the cramp.

Morever, after a mere hour of sleep, she had spent most of the long night poring over her ephemerides, seeking that moment in time that Eleanor requested. A time of secrecy and caution when Richard, to best advantage, could make his way to Paris.

Eleanor had already decided that Richard and his brother Geoffrey must join the Young King there. The rebellion was already more than quarrel between father and son: now, with Richard and Geoffrey committed, Aquitaine and Brittany must also do battle.

But the ephemerides and the stars had pointed to this day as the day of departure. How could that be? If Richard and Geoffrey marched today, all in the castle would remark it, and hence all Poitiers would remark it. The key was in the sign of Pisces, the water sign, but Sophia had not yet made sense of it. Even so, she must send a message to Eleanor: Look for the chance. Today is the day. Astrolabe already in hand, Sophia turned to Lucie, who was just rising.

Judging from the hollow-cheeked, red-eyed look of her, her sleeping companion had not fared much better in the arms of Morpheus last night.

"You are ill," Lucie said, sitting up to look at Sophia.

"Not truly. Only ridding myself of foul humors. It is that time for this weak vessel which passes as a body to purge itself of excess moisture and blood."

"Your monthlies," guessed Lucie, who had no training in medicine.

"To use a simpler phrase. But you, too, look less than bloom-

122

ing. What ails you, child?" A quick, painful cramp made the astrologer's voice waspish.

"Dreams." Lucie looked away.

"What kind of dreams? Speak. Give me the reason for your tossing and turning and my loss of sleep. Mayhaps I can purge you and we'll both rest better."

"Of . . . a man. He comes to me and rides me all night. Like an incubus." Lucie turned again to look at Sophia. Her eyes were wide with fright and sincerity. "Every night since . . . since we did Noah's Ark and the rain came, and the bishop's men took me. It's a demon, I know it, it's stealing my soul." She was close to tears but did not shed them. She already knew how Lady Sophia detested weepy women; low birth and a gentle disposition made Lucie eager to please and obey.

"Drivel. There is no such thing as an incubus. Only a disturbed mind. But tell me, does this . . . creature . . . have a familiar visage?"

"Oh, yes. It is Godfrey," said Lucie, as if all the world should know the name and the man who went by it. Sophia quickly rid her of that notion.

"Who, child, is this Godfrey?" she asked in a peevish voice. The direct question left Lucie in a perplexing position. To fully explain Godfrey's identity would require revealing hers; that would result in being returned to Sir Foulkes as a runaway. That, she could not do.

"He . . . he is the knight I love."

"Ahhhh! Now, that does explain everything!" The heavy sarcasm of Sophia's voice made Lucie flinch. "'Why am I kept awake all night by insomnia, thrashing around till every weary bone in my body aches? If Love were my assailant, surely I'd know it. . . .'"

"Lady?"

"Words from Ovid. The poet of antiquity . . . never matter. Tell me, does this knight love you?"

"He never said."

"He never said? You declare love, and he hasn't said?"

123

Lucie slipped deeper under the covers. "He abandoned me. I will never forgive him," she answered.

"You already have, foolish child. Why else would you dream of him every night? At the cost of my sleep, I might add. No, forgiveness seems not to be the question. Revenge is. If ever you see this so-called knight again, you must revenge yourself. And do not be so innocent. No lady declares love before the man. 'Play stubborn, you get a far more thorough going-over than those who admit they're hooked . . .' Ovid, my child. Yes, if this knight should reappear in your life, you must play the game with him. Sir Benoit will be happy to assist you. No, don't tell me you've not even noticed him? The grey-eyed one. A bit thin, but comely and brave. Only look his way, and he's yours. That will make you that much more attractive to your knight errant."

"You know much about love, Lady Sophia."

Sophia looked quickly to see if Lucie taunted her. No. Her face was all open sincerity.

"I have read Ovid," Sophia grumbled. "Now that I have solved your problem, you must solve mine."

"Gladly."

"Run to the kitchens and fetch hot broth. Tell them it must be boiling hot. Watch and see that it is properly heated. Then bring it back anon—no delays, you understand. Broth with ginger is the only thing that will quiet this foul, heaving stomach of mine when it is purging."

"It is done," declared Lucie, scrambling to her feet and quickly throwing a bliaut over her chemise.

In the maze of corridors and paths that led to the kitchens, though, her purpose and confidence ebbed. She did not like going about without Sophia hobbling at her side. There was nowhere within the castle gates where she properly fit; she was like a newly captured marsh hawk, cut off from her own kind and wary of the kindness of her keepers.

Alone, unprotected, she sensed that the castle was even more frightening than the wolf-prowled forests. In the forest, she knew her place. God had given her dominion over animals. And He had given her Godfrey. But here, she had no place, no Godfrey, no dominion. At her mother's side, and then at Godfrey's side, she had possessed a selfhood since lost. Not a lady, yet dressed as one. Lower than a servant, yet waited upon. Maiden with no protector, yet not a virgin.

I'm all at odds, she thought, recalling a verse that had oft been quoted by Sir Foulkes' chaplain to discontent villeins. What good to gain the world if you lose your soul? The question had new meaning here, at Eleanor's court.

They are kind to me, yet I must leave. Tomorrow. I will go into the village. I will ask for work as a laundress by the riverside.

The thought made her laugh. "Where is my damsel?" the Queen will ask. "My Lady. She is washing smallcloths down at the river." No. Not that, she reconsidered. I might fall in. There is still that nightmare of drowning.

She was frowning when she entered the cooking-house, and the frown, coupled with her height and natural grace, made her look extravagantly haughty. She, dressed in borrowed silk, with scented plaits hanging one over each shoulder and gliding to her knees, did not notice the other woman, whose clothes were dirty from sleeping in the mud of the bailey, and whose unbound hair smelled of camp smoke and ale.

Soiette drew back to make room for the lady. Then stared in wonder and hatred. It was La Caulde. And if she knew her women, this one was no gentlewoman, no matter where she slept and how much rosewater she used.

Bald, rotund Gislebertus stuttered in unabashed delight when Lucie entered his humble domain. He had heard of La Caulde. Who hadn't? Never yet had she deigned to visit and ask a favor, although Eleanor allowed her ladies complete run of the place. She who could not stand confinement never imposed it on those who pleased her.

"Ginger broth? Certainly, My Lady, certainly. You sit here, and I'll fill a pot for you before you can blink twice." With a great show of clumsy courtesy, of dusting of stool tops which were coated with flour, of hand clapping and calling of assistants to fetch small ale and dainties, he insisted that Lucie sit and refresh herself, while he turned to his bubbling caldrons and shifted them on the hearth to make room for a new pot of ginger broth.

Soiette, concealed within a shadowed corner and licking apple pastry from her fingers, contemplated Lucie. Lucie, aware she was being watched, stared down into her folded hands and blushed. Gislebertus leered at her over his shoulder as he grated ginger into a vessel of soft rainwater.

Pretty as a gold piece, Soiette was forced to admit. And she hated her more for her prettiness than her faults of deceit and haughtiness. Suddenly she knew how to get her revenge on this damsel who had enchanted the young knights so that they disdained the tasty favors of the famed Soiette. Witch, he had called her. Well, we'll see about that.

"Witch!" she said, walking to where Lucie sat.

"Easy, my girl. What's this? Have you gone daft?" said Gislebertus. He rose from his crouching position by the flames and grabbed Soiette by the arm.

"Let me be. She's a witch. Yesterday I saw her give the evil eye to your milch cow. And how much has she given this morning?" Not a cupful, Soiette already knew, for she had asked for milk and been denied it for that reason. "Witch!" cried Soiette in a louder voice, sensing that the milkmaids, manure carriers and pot cleaners of the lower bailey would rally to her cry, for excitement, if no other reason.

"I am not!" exclaimed Lucie, rising in alarm. She tried to quiet the wild-eyed woman by putting a hand on her arm. Soiette flinched back as if she'd been burnt by a poker where Lucie's fingers had touched.

"See! See!" she exclaimed in triumph, waving her arm like a war banner. "She tried to burn me with her touch!" There were no marks, but all who were there, and there were many already, claimed they saw fiery red burns.

Gislebertus, as superstitious as any cook who feeds fires that will sometimes not catch and stirs pots that will sometimes not boil, stared at Soiette's arm in dismay.

"I am no witch!" cried Lucie again, too loudly. The cook's assistants dropped their wooden spoons and lancing needles and rushed to the front room, eyes wide and spirits ready for a good, rowdy dunking.

"She's a gentlewoman," said Gislebertus, pulling at the stubble on his chin, his watery blue eyes reddened with sudden confusion.

"She's not," a new voice added to the growing cacophony. Lucie recognized the voice and turned in an agitated circle, seeking escape; she was surrounded by a forest of faces grown animated with hostility and malice.

"She's already spent the calends of May in the bishop's prison for her crimes," said Canon Anselm. "She was dressed in men's clothing."

A hush followed by a murmur of shock went up around her. Anselm stood taller, yet his tonsure barely reached Soiette's chin. All eyes turned to him. The youth next to Anselm, one of Gislebertus' many nephews, gawked at the clerk in shy admiration.

The Lord provides, thought Anselm with satisfaction, eyeing Lucie.

Not often did he visit the lower bailey. He had come this morning on two errands: to see for himself if Gislebertus' new nephew from Normandy was as pretty as the wags said, and to warn Soiette that the bishop would tolerate no more knifings. She had slashed Brangoene's face, just over an embroidered girdle, it was said. Things like that made for hard feelings, and hard feelings could cause complexities for the bishop. He was willing to overlook many faults and sins—too many—but not these unruly complexities that result when certain elements of a society come to the forefront. Women like Soiette and Brangoene must of necessity keep in shadow, not come to the bishopric seeking charges against each other.

And now here was a third reason, much sweeter by far than the other two combined. He could revenge himself on interfering Eleanor and her deceitful maid, Lucie.

"The Lord sayeth, 'Ye shall not suffer a witch to live amongst you,'" Anselm preached, quoting one of the few Bible passages he had got by heart.

"The test! Put her to the test!" One voice began the call, many soon echoed it. Anselm, with a commanding wave of his black crucifix, sent Gislebertus' nephew off to the stable to fetch the dunking pole. Lucie turned and turned within the human wall confining her; there was no escape and no mercy.

Godfrey, clad now only in torn breeches and soiled shirt, his face marred with mud and dried blood, made his way through the seething, crowded streets of Poitiers. He muttered as he walked, cursing the bandits who had robbed him, and was not gentle as he elbowed people out of his way.

He was penniless and solitary. This was not the way he had imagined his rescue of Lucie would be. Nor was Poitiers as he imagined it. The townspeople were in bad humor. Not that he could blame them. The streets had been taken over by mounted knights who rushed to and fro, upsetting carts and splashing mud on the pedestrians. Was there a tourney planned for Poitiers? If so, why didn't these rude, loudmouthed fellows gather on the jousting field, where they belonged?

He cursed loudly as yet another group of knights rode by, forcing him and many others to flatten themselves hastily against town house walls to avoid being trampled. The riders were Richard's men. He was in their midst, dressed in unmarked chain mail, and they were in a great hurry to leave the city behind.

At the ducal palace, there was a great, distracting commotion in the courtyard, and Richard, awaiting just such an event, had seized the moment to make his departure.

Godfrey, once the knights passed, continued on his way, eventually arriving at the huge gate that separated the ducal palace from the surrounding town. The gatekeeper at the bishop's door had already sent him on his way, saying there was no maiden to be fetched from the bishop's keep.

Godfrey walked through, surrounded by carters and laborers. A guard spied him, quickly pulled him out of the crowd and tossed him to the side, yelling at him to go away.

128

"We've no more need of vagrants. We've quite enough already. Go away, my man. We've no tolerance for beggars."

Godfrey, weak from lack of food, the day of walking and the beating, choked on his anger and the insult. He had planned to enter in honor, with a gift for Lucie and a song praising Eleanor's mercy and beauty. To think, his Lucie was in the castle itself, had been for many a day, protected by Eleanor, eating at her table. If what they said in the town was true. But why would they lie?

A twinge of jealousy made him frown. Here was he, dirty, poor as a beggar, hungry, abused. All because he had decided to rescue a damsel in need. And there was she, well fed to the point of growing fat probably, doing nothing all day but listening to lute players and brushing her hair.

It was unjust. He would not tolerate it. He would enter the castle and somehow find the opportunity to sing the song he had composed to win Eleanor's favor. He would need a new tunic, an embroidered cloak, a well-made lute, but those problems he would overcome later. First, he must gain admittance.

He retreated from the gate and slipped behind a pile of rubbish, watching carts come and go. There was much business this morning, a constant stream of carts entering, heavy with squawking chickens and piles of vegetables, and leaving emptied and light. And other carts, heavy and creaking with a burden of quarried rock, for Eleanor was building onto her chapel.

These carts Godfrey watched with great interest. They were pulled by carters, freemen who did the service for no reward except the penance they gained from the task. To pull a cart in the service of the Church was to gain grace and favor from the saints. Only the most desperate of men fell to such a task, those who had beaten their own mothers, robbed their own children, raped a nun, or committed some other deed so foul that only hard labor could redeem their souls.

No freeman of good conscience became a carter; the task brought instant dishonor amongst men, and that dishonor was part of the penance.

An idea came to Godfrey. He waited till one of the carters, one of about his height and build, undid his yoke and made off to answer nature's call. Godfrey quickly walked to the cart and strapped the yoke about his own chest. Towing the heavy burden of rocks and disgrace, he entered the castle unquestioned and unchallenged.

Sir Foulkes felt the familiar rattling in his stomach. The warrior's illness would set in any day now, that burning watering in the bowels that grew ever worse as the day of battle came closer and closer, so that the soldiers would feel the mess running down their legs even as they fought. They would be already weak even before the battle started, and that was God's joke on men who made a livelihood in warfare. God was no soldier, that was certain, and Sir Foulkes couldn't help but think that was a great fault in God.

Well, let it be then. If God wants him to fight again with shit running down his legs, then Amen. But maybe a dose of rice water sweetened with honey would lighten the pain. There was no cowardice in trying to ease the illness.

Slightly bent in concession to the twisting, gurgling travail of his stomach and intestines, Sir Foulkes made his way to the wooden sheds of the kitchens.

Lucie walked in a daze. They had rope-bound her, strapping her arms tightly to her side so that only her hands could twist and turn in the fear that made the sunny morning go black and stormy in her head. There was a great roaring in her ears, as if the water already filled them, and it seemed not familiar ground beneath her feet as she walked, but soft, enveloping, suffocating water, ready to rise up and claim her.

The mad crowd—the cook's assistants and stable cleaners, camp followers and laundresses, led by Anselm and Soiette— roiled about her, a human, frothing current forcing her in the

130

direction of the deep, still kitchen pond. Chickens and ducks fled at their approach, dogs barked and mules brayed.

Let me die quickly, Lucie prayed as they fetched a new set of ropes and began to tie her to the dunking pole. Quickly. Quickly. Quickly. The one-word prayer echoed in her head, a stone skipping over the waters of fear.

Sir Foulkes heard the frenzied tumult. Temporarily distracted from the gurgling of his stomach, he headed towards it. As he did, he bumped into a tall, towheaded carter who had momentarily unstrapped his burden. The two men, urged forward by the ever-increasing din coming from the kitchen pond, paid no attention to each other in the riotous confusion.

Godfrey, longer of leg than Sir Foulkes, was the first to reach the pond. He saw the mass of yelling, cheering menials, the maiden with the long, swinging plaits who was strapped to the cruel pole, the canon who sanctimoniously blessed the pole even as it was lifted in a laborious arc to the pond's deep, unforgiving center.

This is my nightmare, Lucie thought. This is the water I have feared, this is my ordeal and my death.

"Lucie!" Godfrey shouted, fighting his way through to the pond's edge. "Lucie!"

Lucie? Sir Foulkes, panting and newly arrived at the tumultuous scene, looked about in confusion. Why did the witch-maiden look familiar? And then he knew her, the runaway, who had peppered many a long night with the spice of his lusty invention.

"Lucie!" he, too, yelled, just as the pole was lowered and the girl disappeared into the murky pond. This was his maid they were dunking, his property!

Godfrey and Sir Foulkes met at the end of the dunking pole, where, with shouts and threats and much pushing and shoving, they forced the villeins to raise the pole and haul in the damsel.

She was half-dead from fear. Her clothes were sodden and added great weight to her already heavy limbs. She looked wildly about and twisted her hands in their bindings. Rivulets of water

131

blinded her. But through the blur of water she saw Godfrey standing before her, and she rejoiced.

Standing next to him, though, she saw her master, Sir Foulkes.

As soon as the ropes were undone, she collapsed to the ground in a swoon.

Anselm and Soiette, sensing trouble to come, stalked away, and no one gave more thought to them. The villeins were already dispersing back to stable, kitchen and laundry, watching wide-eyed over their shoulders as the knight and carter pushed and argued over the maiden. At least they had the satisfaction of proving her innocence. Lucie had started to sink like a stone as soon as she had touched the water.

BOOK TWO

Sophia: The Serpent of Knowledge

Summer 1173

When the Knight of the Cart heard his prayer for mercy, he neither
touched nor struck him, but asked, "You want mercy?"

"Now that's an intelligent thing to say. A fool should ask. I
never wanted anything so badly as I need mercy now."

"Then you'd have to get into a cart. You have no hope in
anything you might say to me, if you don't get into a cart, because
you have a fool's mouth as to basely reproach me with it."

The beaten knight answered, "God forbid that I should get into
one."

"No? Then you'll die."

—Lancelot: The Knight of the Cart

1

Well, I was right about one thing, at least. The maiden has proved a great distraction. For Eleanor, and Richard.

Sophia angrily stirred the spiced wine and tested it to be sure it was not overly hot. Raoul de Faye would have let her drown. And unnecessarily. A half-dead damsel was as interesting to a crazed mob as a dead one. Had he let the ordeal by water reach its culmination but then interceded, Richard and his men would have stolen away just as easily.

With an exaggeration of her limp—anger always made her exaggerate everything—she hobbled to the bed where Lucie lay.

"Drink this," she said, and while her intent was kind, her voice was not. Sophia's anger was like a rainstorm that must fall on the entire countryside and not just the seeded fields.

Lucie smiled wanly and sat up.

"Thank you, Lady Sophia. You are kind."

"Hmmmph." Aside from a fever and flux of the lungs, the girl had never looked better. Indeed, she was blooming with joy and contentment. Certainly a far cry better than she had looked yesterday, blue in the face and wet as a drowned kitten, her eyes rolled back in her head and not knowing anyone about her.

The nonsense of it, trying to drown the girl to test if she was a witch or not. Ah, but what could you expect of scullery maids and cook's assistants? They need distraction as much as a Queen, and is a war any less gentle or more noble than murdering a maiden in the kitchen pond, just to liven the day?

What a coil that had been, when the truth was out. She wouldn't be surprised if Anselm swam all the way to England, after his part in it came out. The one they called Soiette had slunk off like a beaten dog. The porters knew her face. She'd not be back.

But Sir Foulkes. There was the real trouble. Sir Foulkes carrying on as if Eleanor had known the girl was his runaway, yelling and thrusting gloved fingers at her and threatening to leave, with all his knights and archers, if she wasn't returned to him.

That had been his mistake. And the saving of Lucie, who would surely have been beaten, had Sir Foulkes his way. You don't storm at Eleanor. You don't threaten her. To do so is to insure she will do just the opposite; hadn't Louis and Henry both found that out? Sophia had watched her lady's face change from ivory to red to pale blush as Foulkes had raged and ranted about the deceit of women, and Sophia had known that never would Eleanor grant his request. At that point if Foulkes had insisted that Eleanor breathe, she would have held her breath to spite him.

"Your property, Sir Foulkes? I understood that you had sworn homage to me, Good Knight!" Eleanor retorted coolly, and the man had stuttered and turned red in fury.

"Aye, homage! But I never swore to give up all my vassals to you," he had roared back.

"It is not all your vassals we are contending. It is but a maid who has sought shelter in my court. Would you deny me the use of the maid, sir?"

Of course, he could not. Eleanor was his Queen, his liege; by his honor, he must give her whatever she asked. But how the point made him sore!

136

Lucie had been returned, sodden and swooning, to Sophia's chamber, to be nursed—and for safekeeping, for there was a vengeful gleam to Sir Foulkes' eyes that neither Sophia nor Eleanor trusted.

Sir Benoit, fresh from the hunt and just hearing of this sport, had dashed through the bailey and great hall, boots and quiver clanging, paler and weaker with trembling than Lucie herself. If there had been any doubt about which court damsel was the cause of his wan trilling, those doubts were put aside once Sir Benoit gazed openly on his beloved's face.

Marie and her poet, Chrétien, also heard of the happenings and came to see, bringing several of Marie's ladies with them and one or two gangling sycophants who pointed Chrétien's quills, hoping for more gainful employment from his beauteous and generous sponsor. For a few moments this carrying in of the supine Lucie had been as busy as an Easter procession led by the bishop himself.

"Ah! How lovely she is!" Marie had exclaimed, while Chrétien rubbed at his chin and examined the girl as if she were a blurred page of manuscript.

Sophia had to admit that even in this condition, mayhaps because of the situation, which was not bereft of a certain glamour, the maiden was unusually pretty. This was how Eve, the temptress, must have looked in the garden, after the world's first thunderstorm. Her wet hair clung to her like dark seaweed, flowing all the way to her knees in small waves; the blue gown was transparent with wetness, showing the gleam of ivory and rose-colored skin beneath.

Sir Benoit beheld her and blushed; Sir Foulkes devoured her with his eyes.

"A verse. We should compose a verse about this event," Marie decided. "About a maiden who dies of love and then floats in a barge downriver to her beloved."

"Wasn't love she almost died for but the accusation of witchcraft," Sophia pointed out, to no avail. Marie and Chrétien were already off, discussing the details of the new story to add to their life of King Arthur.

And there was the other, the carter, who in the madness had followed Lucie's procession into the chamber itself, where no carter should be allowed nor go. He was probably no more than a common criminal. He, of all those keeping watch, had shed a tear of genuine grief. Sir Benoit had finally forced him out, back into the bailey, at sword point. The carter had roused Sophia's curiosity. There was a connection between those two. He had something to do with the new contentment in the damsel's eyes.

Lucie sat up and sipped at the proffered wine. She smiled sweetly at Sophia, never minding that the astrologer's face was dark and stormy as St. John's Eve, when rain always falls. He had come back for her after all. Godfrey had come for her.

Sophia went to the casement and stared moodily into the dark night. Blue Regulus, the brightest star of Leo, shone in the south, a diamond shimmering against blue velvet. Soon it would follow the westerly path, making way for the great heat of summer, when the sun would pass Regulus and enter the sign of Virgo.

And then we will be fully at war, thought Sophia. When the sun enters Virgo, the fields that should be ripe for a first harvest will more likely be burnt and trampled, and too many of them watered with the blood of young men. Because a husband wanted a younger woman in his bed, and his grown sons were tired of mock battle and craved the real . . . along with the father's throne.

Love. For women. For power. For gold. If love is the pursuit of the whole, then the lecturing friars are correct, Sophia thought. We have been cursed since Eve bit into the apple and Adam followed her lead.

She continued her examination of the spring sky. Under Leo sprawled the Water Serpent, a long stream of bright stars that splashed over a major portion of the southern sky, if one followed it from shining head to shimmering tail.

For this constellation, Sophia had a particular regard. Its chief star, Alphard, was known as "The Lonely One": It was the only star in a large and dull area of the night sky, and thus did Sophia often regard herself. She walked apart from the others.

The ancients thought the Serpent was the Hydra itself, the hundred-headed monster slain by Hercules. Theologians claimed that the Serpent represented the creature that led Eve astray, and thus befouled all of humanity. Sophia thought they were both right. The Water Serpent, large and ancient as it was, symbolized the getting of wisdom—for Hercules, who learned that the sword will not slay all dragons, and for Eve, who learned that the price of knowledge was the fall from grace and innocence.

Corruption might be a fair price for knowledge, Sophia thought with bitterness. She had spent some months now translating St. Boethius into Provençal, and the work was not progressing well. Each time the great philosopher ranted against the sins of the flesh, she would stop and try to imagine those sensations he preached against. How can one avoid what one does not know?

Nor was she likely to know those particular sins, her with her ugly face and ungainly gait. Sighing, she returned to her worktable and patient.

Lucie's adventure in the pond had put her in a unique position. Sophia was, for the first time of her life, the nurse and not the patient. She who had always been the weak, ill and pampered one now must care for a strapping lass whom others—only the devil knew if they were right or not—saw fit to suffer the ordeal by water.

Nursing made her feel important and useful. It agreed with her, as much as she tried to convince Lucie otherwise.

"Finish the wine," she commanded in a loud and authoritative voice.

Lucie sneezed; she blew her nose on a lace handkerchief donated by Eleanor. The situation was a unique one for her, too. Never before in her short but now exceedingly varied life had anyone so much as fetched her a skin of water, much less attended to her through long days and nights of illness.

Being Sophia's patient was a grave responsibility. Aware of this, Lucie kept her voice low and her face wan, not wanting to rob Sophia of the evident pleasure she found when the fever went back up a bit, or the sneezes came more frequently. The chamber smelled of bitter herbs and purifying incense and was busy with the astrologer's constant toing and froing from the stillroom to her worktable.

"The carter was here again this morning, pleading admittance," Sophia grumbled. "Do you wish to see him?"

Lucie smiled.

"With all my heart. But I won't. I'll make him wait for me, as I waited for him. And may his days pass even more slowly, before I give him the kiss of peace."

Sophia, feeling a cramp in her leg, leaned against the open casement and regarded Lucie with surprise that was not entirely happy. How quickly the girl learned. Mayhaps the thirty-two rules of love were contagious?

Sir Foulkes, when pressed, had recalled that this maid had been born during the fortnight after the Epiphany. Under the sign of Aquarius, the Waterbearer. According to Albumazar, whose astrological theories Sophia favored over Ptolemy's, Lucie was, then, ruled by the heart, sensual, and fiercely loyal. But there was a perverse streak in the Aquarian's nature, lingering under their comely form and sweet brows.

Eve, she who would taste of forbidden wisdom and knowledge, had been an Aquarius. Hence the troubles of the world. Aquarians had a particular fondness for fruit trees—hadn't Lucie first asked for last summer's preserved pears when her appetite returned?

"I assume then that this carter is the knight you spoke of before. Only love brings such cruelty." Sophia sighed. It would not be an easy summer, it seemed, not restful and uneventful as she had hoped.

"He is. I don't know why he is so strangely dressed, but yes, the carter is my own love, Godfrey. He doesn't look as fair in those strange clothes," Lucie mused. She had never before seen him in anything less elegant than his flowing cape and peacock green quilted tunic. Strange, how the beggar's clothes made him seem not as tall, not as impressive.

"Carters are known for their devotion, not their pretty vest-

140

ments. Three, four times a day he comes to the door and begs entrance. And you refuse to see him." Sophia returned to the bedside and checked the damsel's forehead. Even as her fingers lingered, the ivory brow seemed to grow cooler. The maiden was a paragon of health, healing so quickly that Sophia could not keep her medicines apace of the waning symptoms.

"Mayhaps you should reconsider this hasty course," Sophia said, thinking ahead to the time soon to come when Lucie would be well and they two sharing a bed again. Before she grew old and died, she, Sophia, would like one more night of sleep unbroken by a maiden's distressed call for her own Godfrey.

"My lady!" Lucie protested hotly. "You yourself instructed me in this. You said I should never declare love till the man declares his own first, that I would get more by giving less. That making him wait only increases his ardor."

"So I did, so I did. And it seems I must live with the consequences. God help me to keep more sparing of my words in the future; they come home to roost in a most irritating manner. It was Sir Benoit I spoke of, not this Godfrey."

"Is there a difference in the way I should behave between the two?" Lucie was genuinely confused. Like Sir Foulkes, she was inexperienced in the ways of courtly love.

"There is a difference between a knight who seeks you through dangerous adventure and a knight who is . . . is merely nearby when adventure befalls. More than that I can't explain. You must be instructed by your own heart. But remember, there comes a time when illusion and pretense must be set aside in favor of the truth."

Sophia made to leave, but before she could, Lucie took her hands in her own and kissed them.

"My Lady. My friend. I am so happy," she whispered. Her eyes shone with more than fever. "I know now that what I feared has come to pass, and I am none the worse for it. Even better, mayhaps. I survived the ordeal and now Godfrey will love me."

Sophia felt the heat in her words, in her hands, in her breath, and was amazed that a maiden could burn so hotly.

"Sleep now. You are safe, and soon you will be well." With the resilience of youth, Lucie was soon lost again in the fair land of her dreams.

Sophia, who had been surprisingly moved by the childlike touch of the girl's hands, returned to the casement and her examination of the night sky. She, excluded from the company of men, had also never been fond of the company of women. She had grown as alone and wary as the owl that sits solitary in the circle of the moon. How, then, this quick affection for this unlikely damsel who moved Sophia to smiles and anger so easily? She is passable, Sophia protested quickly to herself, in Lucie's favor. What was more, the girl needed her. And to be needed was a rare luxury.

Albumazar had speculated that Alphard, "The Lonely One," was not truly alone in the heavens. It was just that her companions, lesser stars sheltered by the larger sun, could not be seen by frail human eyes.

Louis of France welcomed Richard and Geoffrey as warmly as he had welcomed their elder brother, the Young King. They feasted daily, and each feast was greater than the one before. Knights and messages arrived continuously, pledging themselves to young Henry's cause.

"William of Angoulême, Geoffrey and Guy of Lusignan, Geoffrey de Rancon, William of Parthenay . . ." Louis reeled off a long list of names got by heart. "All the great families of Aquitaine are with us in this," he said, smiling at Henry, Richard and Geoffrey, and toasting them with his goblet. The sons of Eleanor raised their goblets and drank.

Louis' eyes, watching them over his gold goblet, became dark with regret. These were Eleanor's sons, gotten on her by Henry. They might have been his sons. Might have been. Fourteen years of marriage, and not one son had he and Eleanor got. His physicians had told him it was the Queen's fault.

But she'd had no problems getting sons . . . too many sons . . . off Henry.

Water under the bridge. Why couldn't he forget it? It was not possible that he still loved Eleanor. She was an old woman by now, and he'd had two other wives since then. His third, bless her for eternity, had finally presented him with a son, his own Philip Augustus, the God-Given. He'd been forty-five when that first son was born; Henry had been getting sons since the age of nineteen.

The old hurt, jealousy and anger flooded over Louis as he watched Eleanor's sons drink and make the proud, boastful jests of young men. My God, how proud they were. How sure of themselves. His own son, Philip Augustus, not yet nine years of age, watched them with dark, brooding eyes.

The God-Given was both intrigued and repelled by these visitors from Aquitaine. They were large and loud; they could smash him like a fly. But someday I will be grown and larger than they, Philip Augustus thought. And I will smash them. He went to his father's side and stood there, stiff and unsmiling.

Louis was not demonstrative. He did not put his arm around the God-Given, or smile at him. But there was a knowledge between them, a unity. They feasted these sons of Eleanor. And for a time they would fight side by side. But never could Louis forget that these were the sons of his enemy.

He would enjoy this battle against Henry, enjoy using his own sons as the hammer against him.

Godfrey pulled at his blond hair till it stood on end, beside himself with anger and perplexity. What was this, that the villein maid he had rescued should be cosseted in Eleanor's chambers, while he, son of a knight and finely educated besides, should be left to the louse-infested straw of a stable?

He cursed the night he had stolen Lucie away. To elope with a maid, and love her, come to her rescue, and then be refused her door! He should have gone back to Paris. There were women there who knew better ways of greeting him. There were women there who knew gratitude. But in his heart he knew he was doomed. It was Lucie he wanted, not them.

He kicked at an orange mongrel dog who was sniffing at his

143

wooden shoes. The dog yipped and backed away, but soon was back, more curious than before. Godfrey, unbearably alone, let the dog come closer and lick his face.

Eleanor sat alone in her bower. The fire was cold, the candles unlit, the lutes rested silently against the tapestried walls. Her maids and ladies, dismissed from her immediate presence, tiptoed aimlessly up and down the long corridor outside her door, and whispered. Only Amaria sat quietly, content to dream of a red-haired lover who brought her wild violets from the emerald forest.

The Queen pressed a cold compress of rosewater to her forehead. There wasn't a day now when her head didn't ache. It was because she was born under the sign of the Ram, Lady Sophia said. It was the Ram that gave her energy, intelligence, wit. And her headaches.

Well, Amen then, it was a fair enough trade. She could be witless like Henry, who, not even in his dotage yet, was acting like a senile fool. How he flaunted his Rosamonde. How even now he hid in his wattle hunting lodge outside of Rouen, trying to forget his shame.

It was the baneful day that Becket had been martyred, that things started to go against Henry. She could almost pity him. Almost. But not quite.

She had warned him that Becket would be his undoing. How many years ago was it that she had first seen the way Becket looked at Henry, his eyes soft with love and jealousy? For a time she had worried that Henry and his chaplain would become lovers. Instead, they had become the worst of enemies. Love, it seemed, curdled as easily to sour hatred as milk left in the too-strong noonday heat. Love, which brought forth life, could also summon death. Death, in the form of four overeager knights hoping to please an exasperated Henry, had found the archbishop in his Canterbury cathedral.

It was more than two years since Thomas had been murdered. And instead of forgetting, the land and the people remembered

144

better each day. It was said that strange winds arising in Canterbury blew over England, carrying away the soil's fertility and making women miscarry. And in Poitiers and Aquitaine, barons who never before would have spoken against their King openly mocked him. How easily, how thoroughly, had it all gone wrong. An archbishop murdered, a Queen put aside, a throne toppled . . .

Eleanor gritted her teeth and the pain worsened. She forced herself to relax, to take a deep breath, to swallow the pain so that it would not furrow her brow. To distract herself, she remembered the last interview with Richard.

He had come late. The darkness of the room had been deep as the shadows in her own heart. They were to be parted, and it might well be a parting for all time, if things went badly.

Richard arrived dressed in his armor. It flashed and gleamed like polished silver each time his red overcoat parted and revealed the warrior's garb. His pale eyes were clear and shining from last night's fast. She knew without asking that he had kept the knight's holy vigil. Oh God, if this beloved son should die!

"Your thoughts should be of victory, Lady Mother." He smiled at her. Of all her children, only Richard had this gift, to look closely into her eyes and see the thoughts that sheltered behind them. It was one more sign of the closeness between them. She remembered how her grandfather, on the eve of war, would stir the battle-fever by yelling "Do you want to live forever?" No, *she* did not want to. But this beloved son, Richard, must live a long, long time, she thought, as Richard knelt for her blessing.

This was how Henry, the young husband, had looked twenty years before, all raw courage, noble bravery . . . and adoring, as he knelt before her chair. She reached out and touched the weather-roughened forehead of her son, remembering how the father's skin had had that same dry feel.

Suddenly she had a premonition of that same beloved forehead growing hot and damp with blood from a battle wound. Her heart faltered.

He is a warrior, she thought, and overlord of Aquitaine. Should God give me that greatest of joy, he might one day even be King.

But he is, above all else, my son, and if he should die, there will be no joy left for me in this world.

Richard lit an oil lamp. She could see the elaborate embroidery on his red overcoat, the fine nap of his boots. Although it was not visible, she knew that the quilted vest under his armor would be equally beautiful. And strong. Richard was no peacock who cared for appearance above all. His garments, although handsome, were also purposeful in their details. The heavy gold- and silver-threaded embroidery, the thickly padded quilting of the vest, could protect him from arrowheads that might slip through the chain mail armor.

But what of the crossbow? It was an invention of the devil, this new weapon that penetrated armor and quilting as easily as a pin slipped through silk.

There will be no crossbows. Only mercenaries use them, not noble knights, Eleanor reassured herself. This will be a battle between princes, not highwaymen. No proud and God-fearing knight would lower himself to use the crossbow. It was forbidden by honor, and by the Church.

"Have no fear," Richard whispered, again reading her mind. "We will be victorious. When I return, it will be in triumph."

It was not natural for a son to hate a father, she thought. Yet wasn't this what she had plotted for, the past years, to claim Richard as her own child, not Henry's?

Henry has John, I have Richard. She realized that she hated John, her last child, as fully as Richard hated the father. She had been big-bellied with John when she first realized that Henry's obsession with the harlot Rosamonde had made her, Eleanor, the joke of the English court.

It was a moment frozen in time: the throbbing headache that had made her keep to her bedchamber for two days . . . the sudden inspiration to put aside the illness, don her finest dress and jewels, and join Henry in the great hall, thinking he had missed her.

The jewels missing from their coffer. The silence in the hall as she entered, all eyes peering at her in sudden fright over raised goblets. Even Frederick, the dwarf jester, was pale and grave.

146

Rosamonde, lolling in Henry's lap before them all, glittering and vain with Eleanor's own diamonds and pearls wrapped at her throat and wrists and strewn in her dark hair.

If she hadn't been pregnant and already weakened, she would have fought back, would have pulled the jewels from the strumpet's throat, torn loose her plaits, and slapped her before all. But because she was great with child, all she could do was flee and hide her disgrace in the darkened bedchamber.

She had prayed for the child to die in her womb. But John, already perverse, had thriven and, in his impatience for life, came several weeks early. She denied him her breast, hoping to wound the father through the son. Henry, tiptoeing through the rooms of his raging Queen, took John and placed him with a wet nurse of Rosamonde's recommendation. Since then, John hadn't left his father's side. John Lackland, as his father had nicknamed him in a moment of black humor, was seven years old, and never had Eleanor, his mother, embraced him.

"You will be victorious all your days," Eleanor told Richard, loudly and with a conviction that challenged God Himself to contradict her. She untied a ribbon from her girdle—she had worn it especially for this moment—and tied it around his muscular arm, where the sloping, dropped shoulder of the vest would conceal it. The length of blue satin was studded with ruby cabochons. They glowed like fire in the light of the lamp. Their worth would be enough to ransom his life, should he be taken captive. A surgeon's care, a roast chicken and fresh white bread, a few healing hours in the sunshine of the bailey—those things came expensive, should a knight find himself in an enemy's keep.

"I shall wear it with pride and return it safe and complete to your own hands."

"God will protect you." He'd better, or she'd rail against the heavens and all the saints themselves. She had already made her bargain with God. A vanquished Henry in exchange for a new and expensive chapel. A mass a day for St. Hilarius, St. Radegonde and St. Joseph, and a holy procession on each of Mary's feast days, in exchange for obeisance from her husband. It was a good bargain, she thought, a generous one on her part. But she knew

God could be as capricious as any husband, and as unpredictable as the weather which showed the varied moods of God.

Eleanor gave her son the kiss of peace as he knelt to her, and thought of the other two. Henry, the firstborn, was flawed by a too quick and unreasonable temper, by self-indulgence and a streak of cruelty. It was apparent that he held no great love for anyone, including his Lady Mother. His favor was not to be counted on, for virtue, with him, was as fleeting and momentary as the froth on a mug of ale, all air and no substance. He fell short of greatness, which is no problem for a vassal but a great flaw in a King.

For half a moment panic welled in her. And then: No matter if he is not ready. Richard and I will guide him.

Geoffrey, too, was a disappointment. He was a born follower, a flatterer, a youth who without hesitation could say one thing and mean just the opposite. He lacked integrity. He had already made his farewell, and a short one it had been, void of sentiment. He, too, had promised victory, but he would not meet her eyes nor did he ask her blessing. Geoffrey was for himself and no one else. Still, she prayed for his safety.

They were hers; they would fight for her, champion her, further her goals. These sons were hers as her husbands had never been. Ah, what a King that middle son would make, given the chance! Why hadn't Richard been first from her womb?

Richard had been restless to be gone.

For many days small groups of knights and soldiers had been leaving Eleanor's ducal palace and riding north into the wind and east into the dawn, for those were the directions of Henry's holdings, where the battles would take place. They left when night made all movement into fluttering shadow, all clatter into the echo of bad dreams, so that this migration of axe and sword-laden warriors would draw as little attention as possible.

But where a minion of young knights who normally trod the spring-muddy roads from tourney to tourney could march forth unremarked, Geoffrey and Richard's own sergeants could not. Their departure would have been noticed and buzzed through the countryside faster than sunset in winter.

So they waited in sweating, armored discomfort, watching for a moment that was all too slow in the coming . . . until a camp-follower took it into her head to be jealous of one of the Queen's maids. Then had such a hue and cry happened that their departure was easily made under cover of the din and confusion of dunking a supposed witch.

There was no magnificent riding forth of knights in polished armor, no marching forest of proud banners and trumpets to announce the coming battle. Stealth and secrecy marked their progress. Eleanor regretted this. It smelled of deceit, and deceit was dishonorable.

But deceit is another word for cunning, she reminded herself. And cunning is a warrior's virtue and a woman's salvation. Nay, this is different, a smaller, evil voice had whispered back. I am sending off my own sons to war against my husband, their father.

But what kind of husband? What kind of father? A vainglorious one. A foolish, selfish one. A husband who flaunted his mistress before the courts of Europe rather than hiding her in secret shame, as mistresses should be hidden. A father who kept his sons weak, dependent and powerless, who withheld their futures in order to prolong his own past. A husband and father who grabbed at crowns and wenches like a drowning man reaches for a rope.

As if crowns and mistresses could save him from what was to come. Eleanor's nostrils flared. He fled the same demon that pursued Eleanor and clipped her, the Eagle's, wings. Age. Increasing powerlessness. The feeling that one should take up less space in order to make room for those to come. The betrayal of the body, the obscuring vision, creaking bones, toothache and bad digestion, the body and mind growing feebler together like an old husband and wife who must carry the bucket between them.

He shall not escape, she thought. He flees from what cannot be fled. His future soon will taste as bitter as the dish he has given me to eat from. He will beg for mercy, plead for me to take him back.

That's better. Show some spirit. Curse and rage, don't sit and fidget and frown like an old woman. The die is already cast; now

149

it only remains to see the game through. If I fail in this, it won't be for lack of trying.

For a long time after his footsteps had died away, Eleanor had sat alone in the darkness. Richard, knowing his mother's preference, had extinguished the lamp before leaving.

Now, Henry, you will see the form of my revenge, she whispered to the night.

Becket, who was dust now but lived fully in Henry's nightmares, was speaking in that special voice he used, low and rich and heavy as velvet. It was the voice Gabriel would have if the archangel who defended Paradise could still be heard by mortal ears.

"Take care of young Henry. He is too much in his mother's influence," the voice warned.

"He's a mere child, not long weaned from the breast," Henry protested. "And there is nothing for me to fear in his mother's ambitions. She is all for me, always has been. Eleanor is my Queen and a true wife."

Henry blushed fiery red, reading the lurid thoughts in the mind of his beloved friend, Thomas à Becket. Ah, yes, all the court knew how Eleanor was all for Henry. She made no secret of her passion for this young husband of hers, especially not since this son had been born to the woman who had gotten only daughters from her first husband, the monkish Louis of France.

"Your Queen's passion is not the question," said Thomas with an evil smirk on his face.

Henry raised his hand to strike him, to wipe away that offensive grin, but thought better of it. It was impossible to win a quarrel with Thomas. Besides, it would be Christmas soon. His thoughts were of Eleanor, of the coming festivities at Chinon. He would bed his Queen and make another son; Christmas, with its good cheer and long nights, was a fine time for making heirs.

Thomas spoke sternly: "It is a sin to love a wife too passionately. You must moderate your feelings."

"It is no sin to want more sons to safeguard the throne," Henry protested in a rising voice. Why did Thomas always make him angry, always make him want to strike out? Could there be no peace between them?

"Too many sons are as dangerous as no sons. They will turn against each other. And perhaps against you."

Thomas turned to the open casement. When he turned back to Henry, he was aged by many years, no longer the gallant knight dressed in fine garments and jewels, but the pious archbishop, gaunt and dirty in his proud asceticism. He repeated his warning. "Too many sons. Against you." Then, with thin, dirt-encrusted hands, he opened his robes and revealed the dagger wounds in his chest. Blood flowed out in a strong, crimson arc and splattered at Henry's feet. Thomas laughed.

"You have murdered me, Henry," the voice said.

Henry woke up with his mouth opened for a scream, but no sound came out. He leapt from his bed and began to pace the earthen floor. The chamber smelled of peat fires, needed year-round to ward off the chill that haunted the King since Thomas' murder; it stung his nostrils like the smell of dishonor.

"Thomas!" he called aloud in his grief and anger. "Leave me in peace, Thomas. I meant you no harm! Why did you insist on fighting me? You should have submitted to your King, to him who made you all you were!" No, that wasn't true. There had been that part of Becket that had been all his own, that Henry had never seen or suspected, else the man would never have been appointed archbishop.

He had a thirst for death, Thomas Becket. A hunger for martyrdom. He used me! Henry yelled to the dark and chill night.

The King grabbed for the sword which was never far from his side and slashed at empty air.

The hissing of the blade aroused Charles, who slept fitfully in the antechamber. Henry's man-at-arms peered through the curtain and watched as his King, stark naked, struck at moonbeams and nothingness as if an invisible army attacked him in his bedchamber. He had watched this macabre dance many times before; it no longer astounded him. Charles had been in too many battles, parted too many men from their own lives, to be overly affected by death anymore. Yet even he, whose imagination was as hardened as the palm of his sword-yielding hand, felt the presence of the dead archbishop, the demon who robbed the King's sleep.

Strike hard, my King, Charles thought. Lay the ghost, and mayhaps in the nights to come we will learn again what sleep is.

Soon Henry would tire and grow calm. He would send for Rosamonde, who would soothe with her cool ointments the taut muscles of his cramped arms and legs. Her words would soothe his roiling thoughts. And then Henry would rest as the fair, fragile Rosamonde guarded him from vengeful shades.

Charles lay back down. Thank God for Rosamonde. Without her, Henry and sleep would be total strangers to each other. And to him, Charles, who followed Henry in all things.

Whispers. The heavy thuds of a page's footsteps. A moment later the consoling, whispering noise of a woman passing. Charles turned on his side and watched as Rosamonde, following the flickering light of the servant's lamp, glided into the chamber.

Now, here was a mistress as unlike the wife as husband was ever able to find. Short and plump as a kitten, whereas Eleanor was all height and willowy slenderness. Grey-eyed and pale, compared to Eleanor's dark-eyed beauty. Slow and gentle of speech, in contrast to the Queen's quick and sharp intelligence, which bit as often as it soothed. Meek enough to be a nun, and in fact, when she wasn't with Henry, she preferred to live in a convent.

When all was said, though, Charles preferred Eleanor's vigor and challenge to Rosamonde's sweet passivity. Stupidity is easier to be turned and twisted than intelligence, and Charles measured

all people by their potential loyalty to Henry. Rosamonde, because her passivity would make her so vulnerable to the will of
others, including those who would dethrone Henry, could not
measure up to that other, Eleanor, whose wit made her always her
own person and the King's.

Still, there were those rumors. Would the Queen really openly
defy Henry? Impossible. Yet . . . Charles remembered how easily
anger flashed from the Queen's eyes, and her habit of never forgiving a slight, no matter how long it took to get revenge.

Mayhap the King was right, softer women who could soothe and
comfort rather than provoke were the better answer for sleepless
nights.

A murmur of two voices, one high, the other low, then a creaking and stirring as Henry clambered back into bed. A second
creaking and stirring, lighter, as Rosamonde slid next to him.
Charles dutifully closed his ears to the noises that would follow
and went immediately back to sleep. His thumbs were prickling,
though. He thought there would be a battle sometime soon.

A messenger arrived that morning, while Henry and Rosamonde still hid within the bed covers, finding peace there and
nowhere else.

Charles received the man, a cleric, judging from his shaven
pate and soft hands and belly. He was still damp and shivering
from his long ride; he smelled of horse and sweat and something
else that made Charles' nose twitch. He smelled of deceit, of
cravenness.

"I have to see the King himself," Anselm panted as Charles
blocked the door with his huge bulk. "I have important information for him."

"You could have sent a message; why come all this way yourself?" Charles asked, suspicious. The man had the look of a
fugutive. Had the guards searched him for weapons before letting
him ascend the stone spiral stairs that led to Henry's sleeping
chamber?

"I left Aquitaine hurriedly." Anselm, whose journey had been an arduous one, eyed the chill, smoky chamber, hoping to find a warm meal, drink, even just a stool so he could rest his feet. He expected that much, and more, much more, for his loyalty to Henry . . . and his betrayal of Aquitaine.

"For what purpose? And why such a hurry?" Charles asked.

"There was a matter that required my immediate departure." Anselm was loath to explain the turmoil between Lucie and Soiette and the fishpond that had led to his decision to seek friendlier surroundings.

"And another matter. Richard and Geoffrey have left Aquitaine, and most of their men with them. They are riding north and east, to met with the Young King and Louis in Paris. They ride against Henry."

"Man, you've worn out your boot leather for naught. Your news is old."

"Old?" Anselm was weak with hunger, fatigue and disappointment. He had expected a reward for this. Instead, he was being laughed at.

"Old as week-old fish. We've known of this for days." But Charles would not say how they knew. It was no one's business that Maingot, living in the ducal palace and posing as Eleanor's friend, was Henry's man.

Anselm had one small twinge of conscience. He had betrayed not just Eleanor, but the whole land of Aquitaine with her. For naught.

Charles wagged his head sorrowfully and clucked his tongue.

"These are evil times we live in," he said. "Revenge is a terrible thing."

Anselm started; then he realized Charles was referring to Eleanor, not him.

It should not be said that young Sir Benoit was sulking. He was a goodly knight well taught in courtesy. There was, however, the hint of a pout on his thin, noble lips, and his eyes were stormy as he plucked the white rose and tore it apart, petal by petal, there in the Queen's pleasance. The bees in the rose arbor buzzed as if in reprimand for his trespass into this private garden, but he paid them no attention. The day was fair with promise and a green loveliness, but his thoughts were dark.

Sophia, bristling with concern for her ward, had again chased him out of Lucie's bedchamber. He had been sitting there quietly, holding his beloved's hand, when in hobbled the old witch (it did not matter to Benoit that Sophia was but seven years older than he), declaring that her ward needed rest more than wooing and he was to leave.

"Out," she had screeched, waving a bunch of newly picked, pungent herbs in his face. "What are you thinking of, sir, to sit alone like this with a damsel? This is no honeycomb for you to sample at will!"

He had resented the implication. As if he, Sir Benoit, would ever do anything to harm his beloved, or bring ill repute to her good name. He knew the rules of love. Already past the stage of *fegnedor*, an aspirant, he was Lucie's *precador*, or supplicant, allowed to declare his love and wait patiently for hers.

Instead of defending her suitor from Sophia, Lucie had slid deeper under the covers and laughed, pleased to be the center of so much attention. Indeed, she seemed to have a habit of laughing at inappropriate moments, he reflected, little realizing that for a suitor in his grave frame of mind, any laughter is inappropriate. Benoit did not have, need or want a sense of humor. Life in general, and love particularly, was a serious business. What was there in it to laugh at?

No, Lucie had been wrong to laugh at his discomfort, no matter how fetching the dimples that laughter brought to her rosy cheeks. He was willing to forgive her that . . . except so many of her reactions seemed wrong. She did not grow pale and tremble when he entered. Instead, her cheeks blushed with an almost unseemly vigor, her eyes grew large with expectation. It was confusing.

Lucie did not love him, but she was more than willing to let Benoit comfort her. She hadn't forgiven Godfrey for his desertion of her; he would have to wait and suffer, as she had. But she had no intention of suffering further. It was spring, and she was young and alive, and here was a knight all set to worship, and who was she to say no to any joy the saints might send her way? Especially if her pleasure would at the same time wound Godfrey?

But of all that, Benoit had no inkling. His mind was such that it saw problems, no matter how small, and not opportunities, no matter how large.

And there was that other slight, even worse than his beloved's laughter, worse than his suspicion that his beloved's chastity was not all he hoped for.

"Why me?" was the unvoiced question that shook him with injustice and compelled him to distractedly tear apart the fragrant white roses that leaned towards him as he sat on the stone bench. All the knights had ridden off to glorious battle. Yet here was he, doomed to stay behind, coddled and safe in the very thick and secure walls of Eleanor's palace.

"We need a true and gallant knight to stay with us and protect us," Eleanor had explained, half concealing her face behind a handkerchief, as if she would not have him see the timorous fear in her dark eyes. If he had looked closely, he might have seen that Eleanor's eyes were crinkled at the corner, and that she was smiling behind her handkerchief.

"I wish to join the fray," he had protested hotly. The weight of his disappointment was too great; his voice broke on a quivering note and ascended from a manly low to a childish high in the midst of the word "fray." He blushed, thereby adding to his overall impression of being unripe and callow.

"You are needed here," Eleanor insisted gently.

"As My Lady wishes," he said, although his heart revolted against the order to stay behind. Glorious battle was his destiny; why was he refused the opportunity to claim his due fame on the battlefield?

Eleanor, only half hiding her impatience with this interview, signaled that he might leave. Inside her sleeve, the newly arrived letter rubbed against her wrist. Sir Benoit's mother had written, pledging payment of a scutage fee that would support fifty knights and one hundred horses . . . if Benoit would be kept at Poitiers. He was an only son, and too precious to risk on the battlefield.

Eleanor, although scornful of such cowardice and avoidance of duty, granted the mother's plea. Benoit truly did not look to be an overly promising warrior, and his family's goodwill would, in the long run, probably be worth more than his contributions in battle. She did not consider his easily wounded pride.

Of this, as of many other things that directly concerned him, especially Lucie's willingness to make him an object of Godfrey's jealousy, Benoit suspected naught. He tried to be flattered by the Queen's decision to elect him her personal protector, and he would obey her wishes.

How, though, to win the fair Lucie if he could not win glory in battle? According to the court of love, a knight must prove his valor three times before a lady of virtue can honorably accept his love. And here sat he, plucking at roses when all the world was off to battle. Sulkily he abandoned the ravaged arbor and made his aimless way through the creaking wooden gate to he knew not where.

Now, crossing the half-deserted bailey, kicking the abandoned litter of dozens of campfires out of his path, the full burden of the Queen's command washed over him and drowned his hopes in despair. How would he dare kneel before his beloved, once she learned he had no brave deeds, no glorious feats, to his credit? His only avenue of proving himself worthy of love had been closed to him by Eleanor. Sir Benoit violently kicked at a stone.

The disappointment of being denied battle was nothing compared to the earlier peevish grief of seeing his beloved, sodden and unconscious, in the arms of his enemy, Foulkes. Of the carter who helped pull the maid from the pond, he gave not a thought. Carters were beneath a knight's consideration. If he had known that Lucie was of even lower birth than the carter, events would soon change course. But he did not know, and being by nature not overly given to speculation, he did not question the origins of his beloved. Did one question the origin of the moon when it glows jewel-like in the velvet sky? Sir Benoit took delight in comparing Lucie to the moon. It was, he thought, a highly original and poetic device.

Left with much time on his hands till he might dare breach the dragon's breath of Sophia's vigilance and visit his beloved again, he kicked at another stone. The strength of his ruminations propelled it half across the bailey, which flight was ended only by the sudden barricade of a laborer's backside.

The equally peevish Godfrey, who had stooped to lift a heavy sack of stone, stood, insulted and angered. He was dressed in coarse peasant garb, streaked with the dirt of his labors, and his transformation from jongleur to carter had not left him in good spirits.

Godfrey heedlessly flung the stone back at Benoit, who merely kicked it again, this time in the direction of the stables. A thought had occurred to him, and he dashed off to have his horse saddled and hunting gear put in order.

He would hunt a boar for his beloved. Single-handedly he would bring back the rare and esteemed delicacy to tempt her dainty appetite. This was how little Benoit knew of his beloved. Godfrey had sometimes gone without dinner so that Lucie could eat hers and his, too. It had not helped endear her to Udele, who counted crusts of bread as parsimoniously as a miser counts grains of gold.

A roast boar for his beloved. This would be the first of his three labors to win her love. He almost shouted with delight, and the scarlet-tasseled toes of his shoes danced as he raced to the stables.

Sir Foulkes couldn't remember a morning when the pain had been this bad before. It twisted and churned in his stomach like a living serpent, biting and rending.

Doubled up on his cot, he cursed and groaned and was glad that Soiette was not here to see his unmanly misery. The sun was high, and he was still abed like a mewing infant. She, thick-skinned slut that the wanton thing was, would have laughed at his weakness, called him old man and other names. His lady wife, Maria, would only go to the chapel and pray at such length that the calluses on her too pious knees would grow even thicker.

No, a sick man was better off alone, or with one of his own

men. Was it that bad that he would have to call for someone to fetch him a pail and hold his head? No, by God, he could still make it to the privy. Was he a warrior or a doddering grandfather? He was, in fact, a grandfather thrice over. His three living children were all daughters, and his three grandchildren to howl into life so far were red-faced girls. He did not hold the post of grandfather in high esteem.

He pushed himself into a sitting position, casting aside the old and mangy fur coverlets that had covered him against the morning chill, and then rose, swaying, to his feet. The beaten-earth floor under his feet seemed as unsubstantial as water. Water. He must drink some water. The weakness came when the body lost too much of its own wet humors. Water. Shit on water. He reached for his wineskin and downed the heady red wine made from the southern vines. He belched hopefully and waited for the warm vigor of strong drink to reach his stomach, head and heart, that holy trinity of the warrior.

Better. Much better. He felt like a man again, filled with life to the fingertips. His stomach gurgled once and then was silent. The cramps eased enough that he was able to take a few steps without fear of soiling his breeches. The ground felt solid again, and the lackluster day brightened.

The now empty wineskin had restored him to that higher state where colors are more vivid, the scents of horse and womenflesh more delightful, and life in general is a more worthwhile prospect. If asked, "Do you want to live forever?" at that moment, he might well have answered, "Yes."

Because his ailing guts would not allow him to enjoy food, and Soiette was fled and the pleasures of the bed gone with her, he decided he might as well pass the day hunting in the woods. At least he was not likely to run into that milksop, Benoit, there. He disliked Benoit for three excellent reasons: He had loved Benoit's mother, but she had chosen to marry elsewhere; Benoit might well have been the son he had never had; and Benoit, as even a surrogate son, was a sore disappointment. What can be said of a youth who wears crimson velvet shoes that curl up at the toes?

160

The first flush of joy bestowed by the wine was already growing pale, as Sir Foulkes contemplated his many problems.

It was, for him, a difficult time. It was three years and more since the first tentative message had arrived from the Queen, asking in an incredibly roundabout way what he thought of a plan to take Henry, the old King, off the throne and put Henry, the son, on. Three years was a long time to wait and consider.

Though Foulkes placed a great store on loyalty, and he had sworn loyalty to the old King, he had no love in his heart for King Henry. How could he, when Henry had reduced the Foulkes holdings by a third, giving back to the fat monks of St. Servans the acres his father had spent years wresting from them?

The quarrel with Becket had wrought havoc in many castles and families. It was good and well to mourn a martyr, as Becket had become, but more than a few in the land said "good riddance" and "Amen" to the whole affair with some relief when news of the murder arrived. The relief had been short-lived. Henry, in an attempt to do penance and make peace with the Church and its powerful princes, had had no choice but to give in to some of their demands, and hand back over lands and villeins that had been captured by more secular warriors.

That had been a black and bleak winter, when the abbot came with his damned ledgers and pipe rolls, demanding title to some of Foulkes' best pastures. He had been left with the marshes, where nothing but hawks and weeds thrive. When Prince Henry—nay, he was crowned King, but you'd not know it—had sent surreptitious messages offering to restore the lands, Foulkes had not wasted time considering the offer. A simple change of loyalties to add acreage to Black Oaks? There was nothing to even reflect upon.

His message had been brief and not at all roundabout: Yes, his scribe had written, and underneath it splashed the large X of Sir Foulkes' own eager hand. Piss on Henry, who was near to taxing his vassals out of existence, and who so freely gave away his vassals' lands.

Then had come the waiting, seasons and seasons of it. Waiting

161

in the dark hall lit only with rushes like a peasant's hut, because the abbott claimed all the fat and tallow of his autumn slaughter . . . waiting and fuming as the abbot's men took the best cornfields and left only husks for the starving villeins. How he hated the waiting, the time that washed by and could never be regained. All must be right: the weather, the time of year, Henry's frame of mind, the Young King's health, the disposition of the warlords and barons. Years of waiting, of toing and froing, of sending and receiving coded messages, of plotting and scheming. That had not been to his taste. That reeked of woman's devious ways. Battle, to Sir Foulkes, meant meeting the enemy on the combat field and honestly, forthrightly, bashing at each other till one or both dropped.

But Eleanor, like others of her sex, waged a different campaign, a cat-and-mouse game. Send a message, wait for an answer. Count vassals and oaths of loyalty like eggs in a basket. Wait till this baron's treasury is larger, or that baron has wed his eldest daughter. Three years, and Sir Foulkes had yet to go head to head with the enemy in open battle. His nerves—and his treasury—were wearing thin, and his men were as testy as tomcats, traveling back and forth, back and forth, in case, just in case, Lady Eleanor should finally decide to get this war of hers under way.

Now, crossing the courtyard, newly emptied of queans, tents, boisterous groups of knights and even his own men, Sir Foulkes hugged his stomach and cursed and railed against the waiting.

When knights were finally marching, he was still waiting . . . for his own body to come to an agreement with him. The illness had robbed his strength; he was too weak to ride to battle. Exercise would cure that: he would hunt. Muttering fiercely as he made toward the stables, he pushed a villein out of his way.

Again, Godfrey was forced to drop the heavy load of stone and soil he had stooped to pick up. He cursed. The proud Godfrey was not used to being treated in this fashion; being a carter was not a role that came easily to him. "Your mother suckled pigs!" he yelled after Foulkes, who paid him no attention whatsoever.

The sun was high in the sky and shone hotly. It was a summer sun, fierce in its golden promise, not the pale, indecisive sun of tentative spring. The giddy miracle of spring was already giving way to the more seductive pleasures of summer. A pleasant buzz of insects hummed in the air. The paths leading to the forest were bone-dry and sent up fine puffs of dust as his horse cantered down them in the familiar three-beat gait.

Foulkes carried a quiver of arrows with him, and his sword. The sword never left his side; the arrows were to bring down some quail or pheasant for dinner. Roast boar would have made a fine meal, one that would have eased both his sore heart and queasy stomach, but his men-at-arms—those fortunate bastards—were already making their way towards the first of many battles. And no fool hunts the wild boar alone. It was the most dangerous, the most cunning, of adversaries. After women. No, he'd not risk his life nor his strong-hearted horse's, either, not for a year's supply of boar. Quail would do. His mood grew lighter with every three-beat canter of his mount. Castles and towns were not to his taste; the open forest was.

After an hour's pleasant ride, he was deep into the green and golden wood, where red squirrels darted over last year's rustling dried leaves and sparrow hawks filled the firmament with their high, piercing cries. Feeling more at ease than he had for many a day, Foulkes was overcome again by thirst. He put the sun at his back and turned Ceres downhill, in the direction of the Clain. The wineskin was empty. Water would have to do.

The swift-flowing Clain water was sweet and cool. He drank greedily, sprawled on his stomach and leaning into the river so that his reflection, haggard and dirt-streaked above the full black beard, rose up to meet him. After leaving Ceres to graze at will, he leaned against an ancient oak. The day was as sweet as youth, and it was of youth that Foulkes thought—Lucie's youth. Strange, her turning up like that, just when he assumed he would never see her again. The past year had improved her. She had lost her childish thinness. Too bad she was guarded so fiercely by that hobbling demon, Sophia.

Foulkes grimaced. Now, there was a woman he would never warm up to. Even aside from her lame leg, she was too scowling, too spindly to be pleasing. The fact that she could read and write made her all but inhuman to this warrior who proudly signed his clumsy X and left letters to the squinting scribes.

Warriors, who can't be certain when the next meal will come or the next opportunity to rest, learn to sleep at will, and instantly. Sir Foulkes, comfortably cuddled by the gnarled roots of the tree and with humor restored by imagining a naked Lucie curled up on his bed, fell asleep.

His horse caught the scent long before he did—the pungent, strident smell of wild swine. Sir Benoit smiled confidently. His father had always complained of the difficulty of tracking boar, but how easily he, Benoit, had done it!

It could, however, be said with greater accuracy that the boar was now tracking him. She had a litter of piglets down by the river, where the land grew soft and marshy and the wild yellow orchids poked their graceful heads through the spongy moss. She shuffled querulously through the undergrowth, alarmed by the trespasser and anxious to see that he did not get too close to her darlings. She was an old sow, filled with worldly wisdom and strong feelings for her most recent brood.

Now that Benoit had found the boar, he wasn't too certain how to proceed. He must draw it out into the open, he supposed, and do battle with it. But how draw into the open a boar who prefers cover?

Unintentionally he did the one thing that could have made the sow give up her cover and face him, unabashed and furious. His horse trod dangerously close to the litter, where little squeals and movement of fright made the bristling row of stiff hair on the sow's back stand up straight in angry warning. To draw this clumsy horse and its strange, sweet-smelling rider away from her piglets, she moved onto the path and stood in Benoit's path, challenging him. Her red eyes glowed like coals in the sooty brown face.

Benoit, gingerly sitting his mount and not knowing what to do next, now that he had forced his quarry into the open, eyed the sow with a reasonable amount of trepidation. For Lucie, he re-

164

minded himself. She will be pleased by roast boar. But the boar didn't seem in a mind to cooperate.

Covered with brutish, grey-black hair, the animal was over three feet high at the shoulder, and four feet in length. Her beady red eyes were wary, and the mane of black bristles that grew along her spine stood straight as a war banner. Long, sharp teeth curled up from the lower jaw on either side of her blunted snout. She could rip a man open from throat to belly with one well-placed lunge of her head. She swayed her large head from side to side, and the teeth, recently rubbed clean and sharp against a fallen log, glinted dangerously.

For the first time, Benoit thought perhaps he should have set his sights on a more easily obtained goal, such as venison, or even quail. Too late. He had found her; she had found him. They had a destiny to fulfill, these two.

As quietly as possible, he reached back to his quiver, drew from it a straight arrow with a broad feather, and fitted it to the bowstring. Holding his breath, he pulled back, squinted the length of the arrow, and then sped the shaft.

It whistled through the air with soaring promise. The sow watched with more curiosity than fright. When it grazed her ear and then continued its flight into the base of an old oak, where the arrow found home with a strong *thump*, she felt no pain, only anger. Her instincts told her this man was a greenling, and this greeling was challenging her, when he should turn and flee.

Benoit watched, transfixed, as the first drops of the sow's blood splattered onto the dry leaves under her hooves. The scent of blood drove her to frenzy. She knew she had been more insulted than wounded, yet for that insult he would pay. She lowered her head, pawed the ground twice, and then charged.

Foulkes was woken by a whistling twang ominously close to his left ear. "Christ's balls!" he roared, reaching up instinctively to find the arrow that had narrowly missed his sleeping head. But before his curiosity could turn to anger, he smelled the pungent scent of boar and knew there was more afoot than a misshot arrow.

165

He stood quickly, reaching for his sword. His keen eyes saw the sow just as her violent, foaming head arrived at the belly of Benoit's horse. The long, sharp teeth tore into the horse, bringing her down in a nightmare of shrill screams and blood. Benoit went down with her, half-crushed, half-protected by the flesh of the mortally wounded horse.

In four unhesitating strides, Foulkes covered the distance between himself and the killing ground.

Sir Foulkes was fifty-seven years old that summer. The only reason he lived to celebrate a fifty-eighth summer was because he ungallantly attacked the boar from the rear, while she was still busy burrowing her tusks into the screaming, disemboweled horse. Foulkes slashed with all his might, his arms awhirl with a purposeful movement that turned the patch of woodland into a turmoil of bloody activity. He did not stop until his instinct, not his senses, told him the animal was dead.

But before the death rattle came, the sow managed to turn her head, as if to see the identity of this other strange-smelling creature who had so surely numbered her days. In doing so, she was able to pierce his arm with one of the bloodied, sharp tusks. A red current flowed freely from the man's wound. The boar died without bitterness, knowing that the ground under her was also wet with the blood of the enemy.

"Benoit," screamed Sir Foulkes, when the sow no longer twitched with bloody convulsion and the birds, frightened into silence during the battle, resumed their songs. "I should have known it would be you in the midst of this mess!"

Benoit, prostrate under his screaming horse, looked up with eyes gone black with shock and fear.

Ruefully Foulkes stroked the dying horse's head and then gave the mercy stroke. Benoit was injured, too, but it was the horse, the ruined, wasted, loyal beast, that Foulkes grieved for, not the youth.

"What imp of Satan possessed you? Did you take a fancy for some new pigskin gloves?" he accused the youth when he pieced together the puzzle of a lone hunter, a dead horse and the sow.

"I wanted a roast boar for the lady Lucie," Benoit protested sheepishly.

3

Benoit would never forgive Foulkes for saving his life. That much was immediately evident to Sophia as the two men were brought in to her by the plow-hands who had found them, bloodied and white in the face, in the field nearest the west wood.

Sir Foulkes was walking, if barely, and kept protesting that the wound from which the blood still flowed freely in great spurts was only a scratch. Sir Benoit, his shin broken, had to be carried in a litter.

Sophia, bustling about happily giving orders, was pleased by these unexpected events. Nursing Lucie had awakened new feelings of power and authority in her. And now, just as Lucie was too bored with the invalid's couch to tolerate it much longer, here came two more needing her potions and safekeeping! Within minutes she had converted an antechamber into a sickroom and had her most potent brews fetched up from the stillroom.

Eleanor was not as content. She left her rooms to watch, cold-eyed and frowning, as the two knights were brought forth into the bailey. A large procession of townspeople, pages and other bystanders newly bored by the restored serenity of the almost empty palace, followed.

"Carrying in litters of the wounded is becoming a routine event," she remarked dryly and with displeasure. Her eyes narrowed. Benoit, evidently, had managed to break a leg even without the benefit of battle. And Sir Foulkes, whose age and maturity she had thought reliable, if not his manners, was in a worse condition.

"Do what you can, Lady Sophia." Eleanor flicked at a fly that was buzzing near her, dismissing the wounded knights and the irritating insect with the same gesture. She quickly left the motley assemblage to return to her maps and the little pieces of painted wood that served to mark the whereabouts of her various troops of warriors.

The all-too-apparent antagonism between the two men required that their beds be placed at opposite ends of the chamber, as far apart as could be managed. Even then, glowering looks and muttered vindicatives shot back and forth the length of the sickroom, Foulkes blaming Benoit for the wanton destruction of a horse, and Benoit blaming the elder for killing *his* boar and robbing his glory.

Sophia called for a large quantity of the strongest wine to be found in the storerooms and encouraged Benoit to drink as much as possible. Then, when the youth was grinning and rolling his eyes at Lucie, who stood pensively behind Sophia, the astrologer proceeded to set his broken leg. Sophia winced at the noise of bone grinding against bone; Benoit, no longer grinning, bit a sheet and held his breath. Even Sir Foulkes admitted later that the boy made no cries but took the pain like a man. When it was over, he obligingly turned his face to the wall and passed out.

Sophia, proud of her treatment of Benoit's wound, took a deep breath and approached Sir Foulkes. Lucie, more timid than before, was now four steps behind, not two. Sir Foulkes frightened her. He was legally yet her master and she tended to hang her head in his presence. Sophia pinched her to give her courage and then pinched herself. She was frightened of Foulkes, too.

Foulkes glowered. He was not used to being fussed over by

168

women and did not welcome the attention. But he was too weak to protest when Sophia ripped open the seams of his blood-soaked chainse to expose the wound.

Lucie, a good ways behind her, gasped at the sight of the ragged flaps of skin that bordered a gruesome landscape of red blood and white bone. Sophia calmly sent her to fetch a sewing kit. She chose her finest needle and silk threads and repaired the damage with delicate, ladylike stitches. Foulkes, like Benoit, ground his teeth and made no sound of protest or pain as she worked.

Lucie, peering at Sophia's handiwork through the fingers of her hand which covered her eyes—it was less fearsome seen in pieces through the slats of her fingers—knew she would have howled with pain.

Admiration overcame her fear and revulsion. When she had been a child, men had simply been "other." Not her. Not her mother. Now, each day, they acquired new qualities in her mind.

She thought of Godfrey and saw for the first time that love can be separated into small pieces that are all part of the whole, like a wooden puzzle. She had loved Godfrey immediately and unquestioningly, as if there had been no choice in the matter. It occurred to Lucie, looking at the sleeping Benoit, that love should involve a choice.

Sophia, now exhausted from her work, cast a satisfied glance over her two patients and signaled to Lucie they would leave them now to rest. The maid carried the heavy wooden sewing box in one hand; with the other she supported the weary but strangely exultant Sophia, whose limping gait made a step-drag, step-drag noise of weariness on the wooden floor.

The corpse of the boar lay forgotten in the emerald glade. The scavengers of the woods did their work and soon she was nothing more than a delicate, even pretty, sculpture of white bone resting against green and brown.

And as Sir Foulkes and Sir Benoit suffered Sophia's demanding ministrations over their wounds, summer made her stately, lush progress over the land.

169

The second flush of roses covered the Queen's garden with red, white and pink blossoms, and still there was no word of battle, no word from Richard. The new flowers pushed aside the wilted blooms of the first flowering and filled the air with aching sweetness. Eager new tendrils of ivy climbed ambitiously farther up the stone walls of the castle, and the sheep and cows in the fields fattened on summer's green richness.

As roses bloomed and corn grew toward the sky, the awaited battles of summer remained chessboard strategy, not reality. Louis, the Young King, Richard and Geoffrey waited to make the first strike. Henry waited, still not believing the reports of the gathered armies.

Eleanor waited. It seemed, sometimes, the whole world was waiting, holding its breath. She grew restless, and paced for hours at a time in her rooms.

Sophia was busy in the sickroom, and Lucie was left free to wander through the castle and its gardens at will. Never had she known such a glorious freedom. The hard life of a villein, the less hard but still strenuous life on the road with Godfrey, and the fright of the bishop's jail and the dunking pond were becoming memory. She dressed in fine gowns and ate her fill at the Queen's own table. With Soiette and her troublemakers gone, the other ladies of the castle smiled pleasantly, if still distantly, at her, and the pages openly adored her.

She spent long hours with Benoit, teasing him by tracing the lines of his palms till he turned red with restrained emotion. And then, surfeited with his besotted, loving glances and words, she would go watch the building of Eleanor's new chapel, and torture Godfrey by being in sight but out of reach. That was where his work as a carter had led him—to the Lady Chapel, and Lucie considered it a fitting penance for a lover who had put his own lady—herself—in such low regard.

Lucie's steps were light and her spirits high.

Sophia, caught between Lucie's open delight in her two suitors, and Eleanor's bitter war dreams of vanquishing Henry, had not such an easy time of it. In the convent, love had been the highest emotion in a whole arsenal of weapons aimed at gaining heaven.

170

In Eleanor's court of love, it was one of many mysterious emotions at play—at war, really—between men and heaven. Of that love she had no knowledge. That lack of knowledge preyed on her, made her restless and given to futile speculation.

In her library, dry summer dust gathered on her translation of Boethius. She could make no progress with it. His insistence that the sins of the flesh were to be subdued and overwhelmed at any expense only made her increasingly aware of her lack of knowledge of fleshly sins. To vanquish the enemy, you must know him. And Sophia and the sins of the flesh were strangers to each other.

She tried to imagine the kind of passion that had brought Eleanor to childbed so many times. Surely it was more than a need for heirs that had produced such an abundance of royal infants? But she could not picture her regal Queen sighing and panting in Henry's arms; she must have, of course. But how did people cross that borderline from their familiar day-to-day self to that other, secret and unimaginable state of lustful abandon?

She began to avoid the library and kept busy elsewhere, usually in the sickroom.

Benoit was healing well, with much credit due Lucie, who had innumerable ways of keeping the youth amused and patient with the stiff, biting splints on his leg. He spent most of his day composing poems for her. In the evening, when she brought his bread and broth, he would recite them for her, and the broth would grow cold as they laughed and blushed.

Yes, Benoit was young and filled with hope and expectation. For him, Sophia had no fear.

But Sir Foulkes was a different matter entirely. He was old, as old as her father had been when she had last seen him and, therefore, liable to be touched by the bony finger of death, as her father had been. He had lost much blood, and an old body takes time to refresh its humors. His foul mood did not help matters. As ill as he was, he hated lying in bed, not being able to exercise his horse or polish his armor or ride forth into battle. His dysentery did not help his mood.

Sophia had discovered it; he had not informed her of it. Soon after the battle with the boar had brought him to sickbed, he had

171

asked for a fresh change of sheeting. He had been sheepish, his cheeks red with embarrassment over his now-matted black beard. The old sheets, she saw, were stained with watery excrement and blood. Ayeeee, no wonder he was so grey in the face!

The bed remade and Sir Foulkes' ruffled pride somewhat restored with a skin of wine, Sophia hurried off to consult her copy of The Arab's "Of Perfection." Abou Moussah Djafar recommended a tea of finely sieved gold leaf for dysentery.

It was a costly illness. She consulted with Eleanor.

"That, too?" was the Queen's first comment. She drummed her fingers with annoyance on the table where her maps were spread open.

Sophia looked over Eleanor's shoulder. Aumale, north of Rouen, Driencourt Castle at Neufchâtel, and Verneuil, Henry's castle on the Norman-French border were ringed by miniature wooden knights. So those were the battles that would be waged soon, if they weren't already taking place.

Sophia had a sudden vision of men—bleeding, missing arms and legs, impaled on lances—littering a blood-soaked field. Women and children cried within the castle, mourning the deaths of husbands, brothers, and their own probable death to come. Riderless horses wandered through the carnage, vultures circled overhead in the sooty smoke of burning wood, burning flesh. It was her home, burning again.

She shook her head and looked again at the map. How cold, how clean, the map was. How strange to think that the innocent-looking piece of paper with its squiggly lines marking rivers and crosshatching marking forests, its pretty symbols of castles and roads, was a map of death and destruction, an outline of hell itself.

It suddenly seemed very important to save that one old warrior, Sir Foulkes.

"They are using gold leaf in the chapel on the new statue of the Madonna. Go, and tell them you are to have as much as you need," Eleanor replied, preoccupied.

The goldsmith had a small knowledge of alchemy; he did not protest when Sophia requested that four small leaves, ground to a powder, be sent her. But he was plainly resentful that gold that should have been used in the service of beauty was to be used to heal a man's bowels.

"I won't be able to gild the flowers at the feet of Ste. Radegonde," he warned her, making it clear that she would be held responsible for this to Ste. Radegonde herself.

Two other men stood with him; the mention of gold for a tea lifted their eyebrows into their hairlines.

The first, Godfrey, no longer wore the plain grey hose and tunic of a carter but a saffron chainse and hose with a red and blue overtunic. These were paid for by the castle's seneschal, Raoul de Faye, who had heard his voice and found it pleasing. Like Lucie, Godfrey had found himself a niche in the court of love.

Chabert, the master builder in charge of Eleanor's new chapel, had discovered that the lad was both educated and of gentle birth. He was too valuable to be used as a carter. His new duties included painting the features on the newly made wooden statues that would line the alcoves of the Lady Chapel. Godfrey was excellent at this work, finding that the life-sized statues were infinitely easier to finish than the small, delicate pages of illumination he had created for Robert.

That afternoon his cheek and hands were smudged with black, used to line the eyes, and a rosy pink seashell color used for the cheeks of the Madonnas—for most of the statues were of Mary, by Eleanor's request.

"Good day, Lady. God be with you," he greeted Sophia solemnly.

"And with you," she answered. Curiosity rose in her. She recognized the carter who had helped save Lucie, who, according to the girl, was really an educated youth, and an actor. "You seem to change occupations with some speed," she remarked.

"Thanks be to God," he answered, grinning. She saw the sparkle in his eye and the fineness of his hands, which were long and slim, and understood the appeal he held for Lucie. He was taller than most, straight as a measuring rod, fair and with a look of intelligence.

"It is some days since you came to visit the Lady Lucie," Sophia remarked.

So they call her "Lady"? he wondered to himself. Lady Lucie. The title seemed to put even more distance between him and his lost love. He liked it better when she had been a mere runaway, dependent on him for safety, for everything. They would be putting ideas into her head. And how injust it was that he, who had conceived the idea of coming to Eleanor's court, who was truly worthy of it, should be kept in the outbuildings, while Lucie, a peasant, reveled at Eleanor's own table!

"Lady Lucie did not welcome my visits." His voice had a hard edge to it. "And as I recall, Lady, you yourself turned me away when I was still dressed as a carter."

She flinched at the bitterness in his voice and eyes. This youth could hold a grudge. She had been comparing him to Benoit, and Godfrey was coming out ahead. He was intelligent, he had none of the flighty silliness that Benoit suffered. But now Sophia saw that he could be hard and filled with rancor.

"If I was rude, I ask your forgiveness." She turned to leave, but the other man standing with Chabert pulled at her sleeve, asking her to delay a moment.

It was William Maingot de Sugeres. Why is it this man seems to be everywhere? Sophia wondered. At each feast, each chapel congregation, at any event that involved the life and residents of Eleanor's castle, Maingot was present. And why hadn't he ridden off with the other knights?

"You say there is an illness in the castle? Who is ill?"

Sophia felt Godfrey staring at her; it made her uncomfortable. "Sir Foulkes and Sir Benoit," she answered. Surely that was common knowledge already?

"Ill beyond their injuries?" Maingot persisted. He had a sharply pointed nose and close-set eyes. Sophia didn't like the look of him. In fact, with Godfrey's bitterness, Chabert's annoyance over the gold, and Maingot's persistent questions, she was finding the chapel uncomfortable and was eager to be gone.

"All injuries bring the risk of fever and illness," she said, purposely vague. She turned to leave, hoping that they would not watch the ungainly step-drag, step-drag of her hobbled gait. They did.

Chabert watched, thinking of the wooden flowers that would go ungilded, Godfrey thought of Lucie's high seat next to Eleanor and did not know which he missed more, Lucie or that seat that would let him whisper into the Queen's ear and thus earn his fortune and reputation. It had not yet occurred to him that he might gain both, that, indeed, the two were inseparable.

Maingot thought of the injured knights and wondered which of them held the smallest feelings for Eleanor; which might yet be turned against her and towards Henry. Any day he expected the Queen to look at him through narrow eyes; she was not a fool. Any day rooms would grow quiet as he entered. He would need an ally who would be admitted where he was not.

Sir Foulkes, he decided, had reason to dislike, even hate, Eleanor. She had laughed at him openly—subtly of course, in the sly southern way. He had lost his wench to the Queen's protection, and much of his wealth to traveling back and forth in the Queen's service. Yes, when the time came, Sir Foulkes would do nicely. Maingot smiled to himself and hurried off to his room, where he kept parchment, inks, and sealing wax.

"He was overly curious," Sophia reported to Eleanor.

"Maingot. Yes, it is possible. I have always suspected that his dislike for Henry was more charade than reality." Eleanor rose from the map table, where the wooden knights—hers painted blue, Henry's a dull brown—postured in lifeless, therefore deathless, battle.

Her eyes were red, her forehead creased. She had been pondering campaigns and skirmishes since the sun sent its first warm rays through her casement. Now the sun was sinking in the west, and the room was lit with lamps.

"He should be sent away. Immediately," Sophia said. "He is the traitor you have feared, the one you said Henry would send to keep watch."

"Perhaps. But think, Sophia. What will happen if we send

Maingot away, or as he more rightly deserves, give him a traitor's death?"

Sophia thought. And frowned. "Henry will send a different man."

"Exactly. And then we must discover him all over again. No. We will let Maingot stay. We will use him. Tell the seneschal that Maingot is to be seated next to me at the table tonight."

Sophia returned willingly to the sickroom, to the things she knew, the mundane events of changing poultices and mixing medicines, which made her feel adroit. But there was so much she did not know.

While her convalescents dreamed of hunting boars and missed battles, she peered into the star-shot night sky, looking for the answers that the philosophers had not given. She was born in the season of Capricorn, the goat—a sad time of year, when all the land lies under a chill blanket of snow, and the sheep and other animals are slaughtered as their feed bins grow empty. Pan was the pagan deity the zodiac month honored—a god so ugly, even his mother ran from him.

"I am not *that* ugly," she told herself, leaning on the casement. A chord deep within struck a bitter note. She wanted to say, as Lucie could, "I am *that* beautiful." Or, at least for one moment, to feel desirable.

She was undersized, with a lame leg, but she was a maiden for all that, and her youth was passing, day by day, in a lackluster haze. Before it passed completely, before she truly had to resign herself to being the sexless, ageless prey of crooked old age, before then, she wanted to learn the wisdom that Eve had bought so dearly. She wanted the wisdom of the flesh.

Overhead in the night sky the Water Serpent wended its length along the southern horizon. Alphard, The Lonely One, winked at her, knowing and secret.

Just as Sophia, the sleepless one, was finally finding rest in her bed, Godfrey was rising from his. The sleeping closet off the chapel he had been given faced the church of Notre Dame; he

176

could hear the monks chanting the first service of the day. Their voices, deep and melodious in simple harmony, sought him in the small room, disturbing and rousing him.

It seemed all his days had been pursued by the song of God. In retaliation, he gave full voice to one of his own songs: a lively rondelet written in honor of Belle-Assez, the popular Parisian whore of his student days.

He was pulling on his cloth boots and still singing when a furious pounding brought him to the door. Chabert, the top half of him partially hidden by the sacks and tools that were suspended from the beams in Godfrey's closet-storage room, stood there.

"Cease your racket! Have you no reverence?" he demanded with stormy voice.

"It's only a song. What's wrong with a little music to start the day?" Godfrey said with a shrug.

"It's a song that mocks purity. It paints women in their worst colors. It glorifies vileness."

"Is that your complaint! I was afraid you disliked my voice." Godfrey grinned, but out of consideration for Chabert, did not resume the bawdy song. The man had been good to him, recognizing his worth and taking him out of the anonymous rank of carter so that he might enjoy the greater advantages of an artisan.

Chabert was an avowed Mary-worshipper. He prayed solely to her, excluding the Holy Trinity and whole litany of saints that were also available to supplicants. He called her Lady and often tilted his head in midsentence or midbite, as if listening to a voice no one else heard. Indeed, he claimed to take his direction from the Virgin, who talked to him frequently, describing her favorite colors, how light should be used to illuminate her chapels, and whether or not the arches in her home should be pointed or arched.

He had spent the past twenty years traveling the land and leaving a trail of Lady Chapels in his wake. He had studied architecture in Rome, glassmaking in Constantinople, metalwork and gem setting in Paris, all so that he could devote himself to creating the most beautiful edifices possible in honor of the Queen of Heaven, as she bid. All this he did for just enough payment to keep his body clothed and his stomach from hunger.

This, Godfrey did not understand. Chabert could have had fame and riches. Yet he chose poverty and refrained from signing even the best of his works. Chabert spoke only when necessary; he stood aloof from the workers and artisans. There was no woman—no earthly woman—to soften his nights, no children to ease his future. Yet he did not enter a monastery, where he might build a career for himself, instead of wandering the land, an anonymous face on the pilgrimage roads, a name known only to those who desired a Lady Chapel.

That morning, as the two men walked together to Eleanor's chapel, Amaria, the pretty serving woman of the Queen, strode by. She did not stop to greet them, but Godfrey's eyes followed her till she disappeared around a corner.

"Now, that would be a soft pillow to lay your head on at night," he said with appreciation.

Chabert merely cleared his throat. His sallow, long-nosed face, with its high, sunburnt forehead topped by a shock of white hair, was a mask. He looked like the stern and unforgiving statue of St. Peter that stood over the western portal of the cathedral.

"Don't you like women?" Godfrey asked, irked by his absolute lack of response and the self-righteous stiffness of his spine. "Have you never been tempted?"

Chabert's face did move, then. All the features slid downward, as if the force that clasps all things to earth's bosom grew suddenly stronger under this one man's feet. His voice, when he spoke, was weary and heavy and sad beyond any sadness Godfrey had felt before.

"You have so much to learn, Godfrey. Do you think I could love the Virgin of Heaven so well, had I not loved her handmaids first? Loved . . . and sinned against them."

"You call them Mary's handmaidens. Some others might call them the Daughters of Eve," the youth said.

"They would be wrong. The rule of Eve is over. The sin in the garden was man's fault, not woman's."

"It was Eve plucked the apple, bit it, and then gave it to Adam."

"Yes. And it was Adam, the stronger one, who should have prevented that fall, Adam who should have protected his lady but instead was led by her. That was the sin, to put aside the rule of love, that requires a knight to protect his lady from evil, even when she herself seeks it. It was Adam's sin, not Eve's."

"I am not convinced. But is that the reason you have devoted your life to Mary?"

"That. And as penance for my sins, which broke every rule of love created by God and man."

Godfrey, sensing a good story to come, grinned.

Chabert sighed. "You are so young. So green and callow. Yes, I will tell you my story. But not to amuse. To instruct. Today we set the pearls into the crown of the Madonna. Work with me. And listen and learn." With a voice heavy with remorse, Chabert began his story.

The Story of Sir Chabert of Avranches

I was born in the holy city of Avranches, in sight of the sea and the glorious Mont-Saint-Michel. The archangel overlooked all the days of my youth, which were blessed, indeed.

My mother was the fair Eustachie of Vezelay, and she was much beloved by my father, Bertran of Avranches. Never were man and wife more loving, more devoted to each other. For Bertran, the day did not begin till Eustachie had opened her eyes upon it. For Eustachie, there was no night, no rest, if Bertran be not there to share it with her. Together, they spent their days and nights like enchanted golden coins, always growing richer, never poorer.

In addition to love, they were both blessed with strength and health. And this strength they gave to their children. Many were born. Fifteen. And only three died. I had seven sisters and four brothers. My father's castle was loud with song and laughter and hurtless quarrels in those early years.

In addition to my brothers and sisters, my mother, Lady Eustachie,

179

also filled a dorter with daughters of neighboring lords. She was known for her goodness and learning, and many young damsels came to us for her instruction.

Damietta was one of these. She was my playmate, my constant shadow, for even when she was but five and I was seven, we loved each other, and thought that if God were merciful, we would spend our lives together.

But when I was eight, we were separated. I was sent to be a page at the castle of Sir Raimon of Granville. I returned home every year for Christmas, and every year Damietta was closer to grown, closer to being a woman who could love me in all ways, not just with childish adoration. "I am growing just for you," she would tell me, laughing. "So that, when you are ready, I can be your lady, not just your little damsel."

She grew tall and fair and wise. My head and heart were taken over by her, I could think of nothing else. Avranches was a night's ride away. I could steal past the sentry at dusk and be back in my bed by dawn. Damietta found ways to leave her dorter without being seen, and meet me in the castle pleasance. Those nights smelled of roses and of Damietta. We were still innocent, but quickly reaching a point where we knew innocence would have to be cast aside for a more complete love. I desired her above all things, even above redemption. She vowed to journey to hell and back before she would ever give herself to another.

One morning after one of those nights with Damietta, I was caught trying to steal into Granville by the postern. Sir Raimon was not surprised or angry. I knew then that he had known for a long time, and had just been awaiting the moment when a decision must be made. This was the moment.

"You will go to my sister's household in Paris." he said. "You may come back next spring."

When I came back, Damietta was wed to my eldest brother, Ebles. The month after I had left for Paris, they had spread the wedding carpet, prepared the wedding feast. When I came back, Damietta was already big-bellied with Ebles' first child. She could not look into my eyes.

I blamed her. I should not have. I had forgotten that Damietta was not only beautiful, she was also an heiress. Of course my mother and father would want her for Ebles, not me. Ebles was the heir of our

180

family; with their fortunes combined, they would be one of the most powerful families of Normandy.

I blamed her. I should not have. She was thin and pale, and her movements, which had been filled with grace and life, were vague and slow.

I forgot that there are ways to make a young damsel wed against her own wishes. She could have been cast in the oubliette with only black bread and brackish water, or whipped in front of the household for disobedience. She could have been forced into a convent filled with former whores and coarse nuns of low birth and no education, if she did not marry where her father wished her to marry.

Lady Eustachie would not do such things. She would seek a more willing heiress rather than cause such unhappiness. But Damietta's mother would, to see that her daughter married into the old and respected house of Bertran of Avranches. My poor Damietta, she made her journey to hell and back. And in the end she gave in and wed Ebles. She had no choice.

That was my first sin. I should have seen her suffering and tried to protect her from more, not make her dish more bitter. Instead, I could only think of the injustice done me. I was a middle son, I could expect no more from life than to journey from battle to battle, trying to enrich myself through the losses of others. Never could I wed. I had no mesne of my own, no right to claim a wife.

Knowing that, I accepted with bitter abandon the life of a jeunnesse—a bachelor. For two years, every whore in Paris and Lyon knew my name. No virgin was safe alone with me, no wedded woman could keep a good name once she had been in my company. Denied the one woman I loved, I determined to love all women, whether they would or not.

I returned to Avranches frequently, to recuperate from my debauches and to torment Damietta with my presence. Left to herself, she might eventually have learned to love Ebles, or at least live at peace with him. I was determined that should not happen. She still loved me; I twisted that love and turned it into something evil.

Two children were born to her in those two years, but she had grown too thin, too listless. They both died. Ebles, I know, beat her more than once for her failure to produce a healthy son. In addition to those sorrows, she grieved over me, over my wasted life.

That was my second sin. I took advantage of her grief. I convinced

181

her that if, just once more, she would meet me in the pleasance when all others were asleep, I would put aside my prodigal ways and return to righteousness.

Thinking to save my soul, if she could not heal my heart, she agreed. She was good, Damietta, too good for this earth, for me, for Ebles. Between us, we stamped out that innocence and killed it.

In just a matter of weeks, I had made her my mistress. I knew how to do such things, how to turn a woman's feelings around on themselves till she doesn't know good from evil, for love holds both. I had thought I would be happy and at peace once that was accomplished. But it wasn't to be. Instead of being satisfied with the dangerous hours she gave me, I wanted her always with me. I pushed her to deeper and deeper risks, making her meet me at noon when the others were at chapel, forcing her to lie naked with me in daylight by the river, knowing there was a chance one of the servants might discover us.

Damietta, in the end, did all I required of her. She denied me nothing, even when she saw it meant her own destruction. In those weeks when Damietta was truly mine, only mine, seed quickened and took hold again in her womb, and I knew the child was mine.

I begged her to run away with me. This she did refuse me, saying she would be content to give her life for me, but she could not let me ruin my own. Saddled with a runaway wife and a bastard child, I would never again be received at court or in the home of any nobleman. I would be an outlaw, a useless thing. And eventually I would hate her for it. Poor Damietta. I don't know if it's a curse or a blessing to see with such clarity as she saw.

She told me I must go away. Forever. The damage was done, she would try to make things right with Ebles. But I must leave, for the sake of the child she carried. The child was our only future; we must be parted for all time.

I left and returned to Granville. Sir Raimon was not pleased to see me, nor did he turn me away. I was a good fighter and warrior, and while he would not trust me to sit with his wife or daughters, he let me take up residence with his other men-at-arms.

Evil draws evil. Quickly I discovered a group of men who had made a secret brotherhood among themselves, and the vow we in the brotherhood made was this: For us, there would be no Peace of God. We would respect no property and no person. My bitterness at being parted from Damietta made me approve of such vows, such ungodly ways. We would meet in a secret place in the woods and drink till our vision blurred and our speech was incomprehensible. Then we would take to the roads, waylaying whatever unfortunate people crossed our path.

The men we robbed. The women we raped. Their cries meant nothing to us.

Soon it was common knowledge that the roads leading in and out of Sir Raimon's demesnes were unsafe for travel. People began to go abroad only under escort, or in large groups. We laughed at their fears.

One night some of these brothers in evil came to me and woke me from my sleep, which had been filled with dreams of Damietta.

"Come," they said. "We have found a maid who was traveling alone, through the woods. She is comely and now quite submissive, although we had to do some convincing, of course. Come, take your pleasure with us."

I dressed quickly and followed them into the forest, anxious for some sport to clear my head of those sad dreams of my lost love.

There I saw Damietta again, and for the last time.

She was lying on her back, her skirts pulled up to her hips, her legs twisted like branches caught by a storm. Her face was bloodied. A hard blow to the head had blinded her. God was merciful in that. She could not see me and the terrible companions I had befriended.

Ebles, suspecting that he was not the father of the child she carried, wearied of her inability to love him, had cast her out. My mother, Lady Eustachie, was dead by then. There was no one to protect Damietta, no one to soothe her sorrow or cherish her tears. She had left Avranches to seek me. She had found me.

I pulled down her skirt and shed tears over the way it draped her rounded belly, the belly that carried my child, the child that would never be born. I held her in my arms until dawn, that last dawn, when, like so many other dawns, we were forced to part. I buried her in the green forest.

A sparrow circled overhead. It had flown in through the large, ragged hole in the chapel's western wall, where the new altar was being built. Godfrey fixedly watched the bird's flight. Like the newly wed Damietta, he could not look Chabert in the eyes, nor could he despise the man.

The truth was that while most of Godfrey's conquests had been easy and willing, one or two had been forced, if not by violence, then by lying sweet words. Evil is not a question of degree, and Chabert's sins were all too common.

And how much choice had Lucie had? None, really. Circumstances, her mother, Sir Foulkes, and then he, had made her choices.

"Since that day I have been a homeless man, a wanderer who seeks only a penance strong enough to wash away the sin," Chabert said. His voice was unsteady. A thin film covered his eyes, although no tears had been shed. That was part of his penance, the inability to wash away grief with tears.

"After I left that forest, with her blood on my hands, I became a carter, hauling rocks and dirt in the service of Our Lady, whom Damietta had loved greatly. I have labored for her in Paris and Chartres, Amiens and Rouen, Laon and Troyes, and along the way studied those sciences required to build a harmonious and beautiful church." Chabert stopped suddenly and sighed, striking his fist to his forehead.

"Mea culpa. Even now the sin of pride swells up. Pride, my undoing. It was pride that made me covet that which belonged rightly to Ebles, the eldest. I thought Damietta was my birthright, just because I loved her. When she was given to him, my spirit rebelled . . .

"And now I am guilty of another, greater sin than my pride, which made me treasure my own delight over the weal of Damietta . . . the sin of despair. For I know forgiveness is impossible. There is no penance great enough for me."

Godfrey, who was by nature more buoyant than the world-weary Chabert, thought the man was perhaps as prodigal in his penitence as he had been in his sinning. But his story touched the youth. Pride, bitterness over a loss of birthright, the sins of the flesh and ungodliness . . . of all those, Godfrey, too, had tasted. Not as riotously, of course, or with such disastrous result, but there it was. Godfrey could not cast the first stone.

They worked in silence for the rest of the morning, speaking only when Chabert needed to ask things of Godfrey relevant to setting the pearls and beads of lapis in the Virgin's crown. Godfrey, in a meditative mood, tried to rhyme the story of Chabert in his head, and set it to music. The story would make a splendid lament. He sorely missed his lute, which, along with his purse and leather doublet, had been stolen by Rouge-Raoul and his partner-bandit. The rules of the cult of the cart decreed he could not be paid for his work. Maybe, though, Chabert could borrow an instrument for his use?

Thinking of the many new songs he could compose, and speculating that while adventures could be trying at the time they were useful for poetic purposes, the hours passed quickly for Godfrey. If his work became a little more thoughtful, his cynicism a little less strident, then the purposeful arrow of Chabert's tale had found its mark.

The sun was already sinking low in the west when Queen Eleanor came into the chapel for her daily inspection of its progress, followed by her Lady Sophia. And Lucie.

Godfrey had, so far, only seen the Queen from a distance. Close up, he realized that many of the new statues for her chapel bore more than a close resemblance to her. They were tall, almost exaggerated in their graceful length, and instead of standing stiffly upright, they swayed and bent in sinuous movement, like young saplings in the wind. The Queen herself was like that, always in soft, rippling movement, yet giving a sense of repose.

In painting these polychromed statues, Godfrey had, out of a desire to make the work easy and with a touch of mischief, painted them with Lucie's coloring. Now he saw that the Queen and Lucie shared the same high, broad forehead, wide-set eyes under gently curving brows and rounded chin with the hint of a dimple in it. It humbled him.

Lucie stood behind Lady Sophia, eyes downcast, unwilling to look at him.

"God be with you, Chabert," Eleanor said in her musical voice. "How is the work coming? Is Sainte Radegonde finished?" She stepped lightly over a pile of mortar and brick, to examine more closely the crown upon which he worked. Eleanor, exceedingly proud of her own high rank, insisted that all her saints be crowned, likewise.

As Chabert and Godfrey hastened to bow, she picked up the golden bauble and, holding it at arm's length, squinted to catch the details of the gold and silver chasing inlaid with brightest blue lapis.

"Splendid," she congratulated Chabert, handing the crown to Sophia for her admiration. Sophia, having no taste for decoration, merely speculated on its cost and then passed it to Lucie.

She had never handled anything so exquisite in her life. Had she been alone, or less shy, Lucie would have tried it on her own head, for the crown was large enough to adorn a life-sized statue. Then she blushed, because she realized Godfrey was watching her, and had read her thoughts.

Odd that he could still do that, read her mind. In all other ways, they had become like strangers to each other. So much had happened, it seemed like years, not weeks, since they had first followed the Clain into Poitiers, to find Eleanor's court of love.

Now something kept her from reaching out to touch his arm, from smiling up at him. There was that other one, Benoit. He smiled at her the way she imagined she used to smile at Godfrey, softly, full of pleading and yearning.

He asked nothing of her, demanded nothing, whereas Godfrey had been all "Do this, don't do that, come here, go away" with her.

His eyes were still on her. She handed him the crown and then turned quickly away, pretending to examine the jagged hole in the wall as if it held some extraordinary significance. Eleanor and Chabert were discussing possible designs for the new columns that were to be added. Her voice was high and animated, his low and monotonous; they melded together in songlike harmony. Lucie was aware of Godfrey standing behind her, moving closer.

"Lady Lucie," he whispered. Sophia had called her lady. So be it, if that was what she wished. It cost nothing to use a pleasant word.

The title, coming from proud Godfrey, he who knew her for what she was, only a runaway peasant girl, brought a flush to her cheeks. She was aware of nothing but the closeness of him standing at her back, the heat of him that was like the warmth of the sun, his breath on her neck like a summer breeze.

He reached out to touch her hands, which she had clasped behind her back. The touch burnt her skin. She bit her lip to keep from crying out, to keep herself from going into his arms, there, right there in the chapel, in front of Lady Sophia and the Queen and everyone else. Her joy in her new life fled; she remembered the warmth of his arms. They had been her only home for such a long time. She was an outlander, a foreigner, everywhere but here, near him. She wanted him. But she wanted more, too, things she couldn't yet name, things that had to do with the gentleness of Benoit's glances and his almost holy respect for her.

Sophia saw her confusion and discomfort and pitied her. Then, too, Lucie made a good helper in the sickroom and she did not want the maid's brains addled. Between Godfrey, who was all stiff pride and heat, and Benoit, who was all sweet yearning and cool virtue, the damsel didn't know if she was coming or going.

"Lady Lucie. Be so good as to check the hyssop syrup I left boiling in the stillroom," Sophia asked gently.

Grateful, Lucie fled the chapel.

Do you want to live forever? As a matter of fact, I do. At least, by Christ's wounds, I don't intend to die today.

Richard felt the battle fever rising in him, like love, like spring sap invigorating the greening trees, like the knowledge of death that colors our most vibrant moments of life.

> Let love quicken in my veins
> And make of the day a victory song.

The rhyme came quickly and naturally. He had inherited a gift for poetry from his Lady Mother. Not bad, he thought. When the battle is over, I will add more lines and set it to my harp.

He squinted up at the bald, hook-clawed vultures that circled in the new azure morning. They flew at such a height, they were mere black dots against the infinite sky. It was evil, the way the carrion-eaters could always sense a battle to come, the way they waited for their meal of human flesh. For each vulture overhead, a man would die that day. Richard counted the circling black specks. There were fourteen. Don't let one of them feast on me, Richard thought, and each man in the dew-sparkling meadow, each man in the vigilant castle, had the same thought.

Driencourt Castle was a strong one, and he had only a small body of men, no more than one hundred knights, archers and foot soldiers. Most of the main force had ridden with Flanders to the northernmost borders of Henry's domain.

They would sweep Normandy clean, while Scotland moved south, and Earl Hugh of Chester marched eastward from Brittany. Between them, Henry would be caught in a vise. There would be no escape for him, once his castles and strongholds had been vanquished.

"Destroy the countryside first, and then when your enemy is weakened, attack his castles," Flanders had told him. And so, the countryside around Driencourt had been ravaged. It was a side of warfare that left an evil taste in Richard's mouth. Villagers had their huts burned over their heads; their crops were trampled, their wells poisoned. The skies of Normandy were grey with smoke, and at night, when all should have been quiet, women could be heard keening.

So that the Young King could take the throne.

And so that I can keep Aquitaine, Richard reminded himself. What Henry gives, he takes back. And I will keep Aquitaine.

First, though, I must take Driencourt, he thought ruefully. No easy task. He eyed the walls, which were thirty feet high and ten feet thick. He had set sappers at them to dig under those daunting foundations. Four days of work had effectively weakened the north wall, where his men would momentarily be setting scaling ladders and siege engines.

And for several weeks, no food or other supplies had made their way into the castle. The inhabitants by now were hungry, although nowhere near starving, and frightened. He did not let himself think of the children and women in the castle, who were hungrier and more frightened than their men.

He would spare as many of them as possible, and make the misery of battle last as briefly as possible. That could be the only mercy in warfare. Death was not the purpose of this attack; to render one of Henry's castles useless, to subdue his vassals, to enrich his own men with loot and ransom money—that was the point.

There was a quick movement behind him, and black-haired Alberic of Percherain was grinning at him over his shoulder. He was full-suited in armor, all except his head, which was still bare of the visored helmet. This, because of its weight and heat, would be laced on at the last moment.

Richard, startled, reached out and tousled Alberic's springy hair. There was such a clanking and clatter of knights in chain mail, such a restless stirring of battle-anxious destriers, also protected with chain mail coats and breastplates, he hadn't heard the young knight approach.

The clearing around the castle was littered with scores of brightly striped tents and the remnants of last night's campfires. The archers, legs free of armor so they could move quickly and freely, were strapping on quivers and stretching bows. Wheeled, scaffolded siege engines were placed at intervals around the waiting castle, and the long, tarred battering ram lay in readiness in front of the gated drawbridge. Foot soldiers, armed with newly sharpened axes and the deadly morning stars, steel-thorned balls swung on long chains, stamped impatiently, eager to get the day's work under way. The sooner the battle started, the sooner they'd know if they would live or die that day.

From inside the castle wall, shouts and commands could be heard, and the fretful wailing of children and the softer, bitter crying of women. Every so often a bold archer would take aim through one of the crenellations and a flaming arrow would hiss through the morning air, setting afire one of the flapping tents. The leaden roof of the great hall had been dismantled and melted down in great kettles, ready to pour over the invaders when they approached the walls. The air was hot and heavy with the smell of it.

The warm breezes were already thick with sooty smoke; the dawn was alive with battle fever. Even the trees skirting the meadow seemed to sway restively.

Alberic gripped Richard's hand. The silence between them was filled with the words knights do not voice: Stay out of the line of fire. Stay out of danger. Let others take the first, most dangerous volley of arrows, be the first to mount the ladders and suffer the bath of scalding lead. Unvoiceable words, dishonoring instructions no true knight would give another.

Instead: "Are the ladders ready to be put against the walls?" Richard's voice was gruff, the voice of a commander, of one who might someday be King.

He could see they were, it was just something to say. Alberic, naturally spare with words, did not answer.

"Assemble the men, then. We will pray."

They knelt in the green meadow, the knights in armor, the leather-shielded footsoldiers, the lithe archers, while Richard addressed the Queen of Heaven, she whose face—in Poitiers at least—resembled that of Eleanor the Queen. They crossed themselves with reverence and reminded the Virgin of the vigils and pilgrimages they had made in her name and of their trust in her.

And then one of the castle archers, whose arms were stronger and his bow, therefore, more powerfully strung, let loose an arrow that downed one of Richard's soldiers even as he knelt in prayer. The battle was begun.

"Notre Dame Poitiers! Notre Dame Poitiers!" Richard rose to his feet and gave the battle cry at the top of his voice. The songbirds of the forest were silenced; the vultures flew lower to watch more closely.

Those around Richard reached for their shields, their weapons, their horses, and took up the cry. Then, there was no consciousness, only the raging, instinctive battle fever.

The foot soldiers ran to place the scaling ladders against the walls as the archers at their back fitted straight shafts into waiting bows and took aim. A dense rain of arrows flew through the air,

190

lodging in the leather shields and chin mail. Cries of pain, of shock, went up to the smoke-filled sky. A ladder was overturned and ten men dislodged and pinned by the fall; twice as many ran to take their place and reposition the ladder. A lethal wash of molten lead was poured over the ladder and men jumped aside to avoid the scalding bath. Finally, the fourth ladder with its load of men was successfully positioned and scaled.

With a yell of jubilation, one of Richard's men achieved the winch that held the drawbridge. Even as the drawbridge grated down, the battering ram, creaking in its leather harness, thumped and splintered the gate. The first knights, Alberic among them, stormed the bailey on their turf-breaking, fierce war-horses.

The clank of sword against sword, of axe and lance against armor, filled the air. The metallic din was punctuated with the softer, sickening sound of tearing flesh and the startled gasps of men knocked to the ground by the heavy blow of a broadsword. Most of the downed fighters were wounded, not killed: a dead warrior brought no ransom money. The horses didn't fare as well. The knights' first line of defense, they were the first to be hacked at, with legs broken by the hacking broadswords. Their screams filled the air as the battle raged like a fire that must consume every straw before it will be sated.

Later—a short time later or an eternity later, Richard could not decide if battle-time ran faster or slower or even existed within the confines of time—quiet returned to the trampled green meadow, to the ruined castle. The last of Henry's vassals quitted the vanquished castle, throwing down their swords and daggers.

They left the bailey in a streaming, ragged line, the men dirtied and slumped from the fatigue of battle, their women and children clinging to their arms and legs, wailing.

Richard had lost six of his men, but gained six times six more, for the knights and warriors of the vanquished castle agreed to pay homage to the Young King rather than be cast in a dungeon. After their ransom price was paid, they would fight for Hal and for Eleanor; they were no longer Henry's vassals.

The castle had lost eight of its defenders; the vultures had prophesied correctly. Now they preened and peered from the nearby trees, waiting for nightfall and the opportunity to collect their prizes.

The knights and varlets of the castle bent their knees and raised their hands with little show of emotion. They were alive, and Richard had taken the castle honorably. Who was to say that his cause was not just, that heaven was not on his side? The women showed greater emotion, rushing out willingly to bathe and bind the wounded of both sides, once they knew their men would neither be put to the sword nor chained and led away.

The sounds of battle gave way to the moaning of the wounded and the anxious reprimands of the women. Richard picked his way through the bailey, pausing at each felled warrior he knew to be his own, stooping by the slain ones to close eyelids and fold arms over the chest in the guise of prayer. Only six were dead, but dozens were wounded, some of them barely alive. They twitched in blind, agonizing convulsions, and Richard remarked again on the difference between death as it truly happens, and death as the poets report it.

None of the slain or wounded was Alberic. Only when he was certain of that did Richard kneel in prayers of thanksgiving. Under the thanksgiving lay a feeling that both distressed and relieved him.

Death was here and destruction was here; he was their instrument. And instead of feeling grief or awe, he felt only joy. This was victory.

"Send a message to Queen Eleanor," he said to one of his men, rising from his knees for the second time that day. "Tell her that victory is ours."

He shouted the message twice, thrice, and yelled with glee.

Eleanor, never one to overlook a gainful moment, made her announcement in the great hall, after the benediction and before the roasts. For days the castle gossip had revolved entirely around the wounded Sir Foulkes and Sir Benoit. She thought their escapade foolish and petty, and was glad to introduce weightier matters. Glad to have such good tidings from Richard, the beloved, who had not, could never, disappoint her.

"Yesterday Driencourt was taken. *Deo gratias.*" Her musical voice sang with triumph through the half-empty hall. She was dressed in blue, the color of night, the color of mystery, and had spared no effort with her appearance. Diamonds blazed in her hair and at her ears; cloth of gold girdled her waist and hips. Sitting on her high dais, she blazed with all the fiery glory of a Byzantine Madonna.

The assembled host, made up mainly now of ladies and servants left behind by knights gone off to battle, looked at each other in silence.

But quickly, quickly, the Queen was watching: *"Deo gratias!"* they repeated as one, and then began laughing and congratulating each other with much clapping of hands and lifting of goblets. They who sat feasting in her hall had thrown their destinies into the caldron of Eleanor's ambition. Richard's victory was Eleanor's, her victory was theirs.

Henry, who had learned some of cynicism—what King could reach his age and not?—might have been amused to see how quickly those who had sworn lifelong fealty to him would laugh and toast to his downfall. But it would not have been a lighthearted amusement.

"There were some injuries, of course," Eleanor said. "Not many from the houses of those with me tonight, fortunately. After the meal I will speak separately with you." Goblets were set back on the table, trembling fingers played with the rich food as maidens and mothers sat back, dreading the long hours to be sat through before they would learn the fate of their men. They smiled bravely with chins tilted high, and feigned indifference to fear. This was their part in the battle.

"The losses were much heavier on the King's side. He himself remains uninjured. He was hunting in Rouen at the time of the battle."

Eleanor blushed for Henry as she spoke the words. Hunting, when his throne and castles were at stake. The disgrace of it should make him realize how unfit he was to remain on the throne. There was no way Henry could hold out against them, he had surely lost his wits. Hunting, when the kingdom had risen against him!

His tarnished honor consoled her. That, and the fact that he had left his Rosamonde behind, finally. Unwillingly, the messenger had reported. But Rosamonde, more aware of the import of the now-declared war, had refused to travel with him, saying that he needed the company of his loyal vassals more than her companionship. Too late, too late. It was too late for Henry.

Yes, the end of the summer should see the Young King safely on the throne. But where would Henry be?

I will be merciful, Eleanor thought, a crooked smile turning up her rose-paste-tinted lips. House arrest for the rest of his life. He shall be dependent on me for everything, from his ale to his underlinen. The errant husband will be returned to his loving wife's hearth. Her heart felt hard and small as an autumn-dried blackberry. Emptiness echoed in the pauses between heartbeats.

The cool late-afternoon air that blew in from the casements stung with the knowledge of betrayal, first Henry's and now hers.

"*Bene merenti!* Victory to those who deserve it!" exclaimed a young page who all but dropped his heavy platter of lentils and lamb in his enthusiasm, eliciting a round of laughter from those gathered at Eleanor's feasting tables.

"*Bene merenti!*" Eleanor shouted too loudly.

Sophia watched her with a speculating frown, and thought of Sir Foulkes. He would be disappointed that he had not been with Richard at Driencourt. Or with Hal in Aumale. And the angry disappointment would further delay his recovery.

He was recovering slowly, much too slowly. He was losing appetite and weight. The gash in the arm had closed shut underneath her poultices, but it was shot through with red streaks, puffed and painful. Sophia watched daily for telltale signs of gangrene, the foul odor and black, dead skin, dreading the amputation that must follow. He was no fool. He was watching and waiting, too. And she knew what he was thinking: A warrior without a right arm is no warrior at all.

Sir Foulkes was learning of the betrayal of the body. Like Sophia, whose ungainly stature and deformed leg separated her from the knowledge of love, Sir Foulkes was being instructed in the ways of the greatest traitor of all—the flesh.

Henry knew that Eleanor, at this moment, must be filled with scorn for him. Eleanor, and many other people, besides. Here he sat at his hunting lodge in Rouen, while Louis and his sons laid waste to his kingdom.

But unknown to his enemies, Henry had made a secret trip to England, and returned just as secretly . . . but many chests of gold richer. With the wealth of the royal treasury of Winchester, he would buy the army he needed. And with monies borrowed from the moneylenders of London. Isaac of York had been particularly generous, putting a substantial fortune at Henry's disposal and at an interest rate so low, it would win royal favor for his household for many generations to come—or at least provide his family with many more years of royal protection, which was of greater concern to Isaac.

Isaac the Moneylender was a man who could be trusted, because his motives were clear. Loyalty in exchange for life. That was his bargain. And what of the southern barons, who could not be trusted? What of Eleanor, who could not be trusted? They were too complex, their thoughts twisted and turned like paths in a maze.

Damn the vassals who have betrayed me, Henry thought. Damn the knights who had gone to the Young King's camp.

Henry reined in his horse tightly, and coaxed him quiet. Other horses were approaching. A messenger, dressed in greens and browns to meld into the forest, rode into the glade. His lathered horse frosted the morning air with its breath and stamped impatiently. His soft whinnying drowned the rustling noise as Henry, still mounted, entered the forest trysting place.

They greeted each other in low voices. Henry took the sealed message gingerly, not removing his hunting gloves. He knew already who had sent it, and he disliked traitors. Even those who aided him. Maingot's seal, pressed into the heavy red wax, showed red as blood against the white parchment.

"Driencourt has been taken. Eleanor rejoices," Henry told his companions who had arrived quickly behind him. His voice was flat. His companions, too, showed no surprise. This loss had been anticipated; they had known that Driencourt would be one of the first castles to be taken.

Henry tore the message into shreds that snowed on the forest floor and turned from his companions, hiding his face in the crook of an arm.

He remembered her as he had first seen her, the beautiful, famous wife of Louis of France, dressed in white silk embroidered in silver, leaning out a casement to toss a rose to a troubadour who had serenaded her, much to the dismay of her monkish husband, Louis. Paris had been enchanted with this beautiful Queen and her scandalous southern ways. Paris, and Henry, who had been a youth of sixteen. Pausing under her window as his father stopped to greet a friend, he marked her then and there for his own. His Queen, his Eleanor, who had turned from that window with a blush on her cheeks. And now she was against him.

It was a man's right, King's right, to take pleasure where he found it. The years of their marriage, good years, happy years, had been strewn with hasty affairs, and rarely had she protested. But Rosamonde had been different from the other women he had taken in impetuous haste and abandoned just as hastily when the first flush of lust was over.

Had Rosamonde been heiress of Aquitaine, and not Eleanor . . . perhaps a woman of that beauty, combined with that power, could have held him before the home hearth. But why ponder what never had been? Eleanor was Queen, and he had loved the Queen, and Rosamonde was but his *amica*, and he had loved her, too.

And now Rosamonde insisted she must return to her convent . . . Their sins weighed heavily on her. And Eleanor had joined his long list of enemies eager to see him dead, or at least powerless. The world was against him.

Henry banged his gloved fist into the nearest oak; his anger reached all the way to the topmost branches, where squirrels chattered, stirring the leaves.

"We are not in a good position," said Charles, his voice heavy with understatement. "France, Scotland, and some of your own vassals are in this, too. Their armies are large, and growing larger every day. There are not enough left to come to your call."

Henry waited until the messenger had left the clearing before answering.

"Not enough sworn vassals and knights, no," he admitted. "But there are others who will fight under my banner, if not for loyalty and righteousness, then for riches."

"Brabantines," Charles said. He hated even the word. They were the scum of the earth, these men who lived and died according to the law of Mammon, fighting for whatever side would pay them the most. They were the worst of the godless, these mercenaries with no sense of honor or valor. They followed no rules, not of knighthood or the Mother Church. Victory in battle was their only calling, the gathering of coins their only reason.

Charles, who would have followed his liege lord into the mouth of hell itself, knew he would fight alongside Brabantines, if his lord wished it so. But his heart was heavy. There would be no honor in this war, not for either side.

"Brabantines, and any mercenary who will ride with us," Henry answered. "Don't look away from me, my old friend. I know your thoughts. But I will vanquish these armies, using any means. You know I must do this.

"And now we begin our real hunt. Let Eleanor think it is the wild boar that drew me to Rouen. While she celebrates, we will search out every outlaw, every mercenary within the confines of the two kingdoms, and from them make our army. God made Adam from mud; I will make soldiers from dregs."

Woman he had made from Adam's rib, so that she could stand at his side and support him in time of need. Eleanor had forgotten that, it seemed, that and the many vows she had made to Henry her lover, Henry her lord husband, Henry her King.

For a moment, a brief moment no longer than it takes to crush a wild daisy in the fist, Henry pitied her. He knew this setting of sons against the father was Eleanor's revenge, and he knew why she wanted revenge. Philandering and dalliance she could have accepted. What she could not forgive was that he truly loved Rosamonde.

The pity was replaced by anger.

"By God! She'll be sorry!" he roared to the green, fluttering treetops.

4

Abbot Robert cursed for the first time since last Christmastide, when a mule had stepped on his foot and crushed one of his toes. For a moment he bitterly regretted he had assisted Godfrey in his stealthy escape from the ill-tempered Udele. When Godfrey had been around, she had at least smiled occasionally and walked with a softer tread, hoping to ingratiate herself with her increasingly indifferent lover.

Now, she was all harsh, loud words and thudding footsteps that rattled the wooden floors of the hostelry.

For a time, a much too brief time, she had been all rolling eyes and coy smiles. That was in the days right after Godfrey's escape, when she had been unsure of Jacobus. They had begun sharing a bed the same day Godfrey left. But Jacobus was a man of few words, and such men often leave women guessing about where they stand. Uncertainty suited Udele, made her softer and quieter.

Marriage, on the other hand, suited her not at all. The uncertainty gone, Jacobus' questionable devotion now sealed by law,

Udele ruled Jacobus and the hostelry cookhouse, and none too gently.

"I know that fornication is a sin in your eyes, and only marriage can rectify that sin. But I think that for our sake, you could have made an exception for Udele," Robert addressed the sky. No answering voice came to reassure him. Robert sighed. He would have to solve this one himself. A firm hand was needed.

He trudged back to the bakehouse. He entered without knocking, his sandals slapping the bare floor as he walked.

"I tell you, there will be no additional loaves baked in my ovens. Do you think I have nothing to do but knead extra dough for all the peasants who stop in asking for alms?" Udele did not interrupt her work to speak to him. She was baking a pigeon pie. Just one, Robert noticed. For her own dinner. Flour covered her arms up to the elbows and there was a smudge on her nose, making her face comical. Robert was not fooled by this momentary aberration: Udele was not a jovial person.

"They are not peasants begging alms," he corrected her. His mouth watered as he watched her dice the boiled bird flesh and roll it in cinnamon.

"No, that they are not," she agreed, stopping the rolling motion of her muscular arms long enough to shake a finger in his face. "They are peasants seeking to avoid their honest duty to their lord."

Ah, so that was what being killed or mutilated was. Honest duty. Enlightening.

Robert had spent some time in his liege lord's service before answering the call of Him who was Lord of all, and he had seen war firsthand. The piercing arrows, the hacking, stabbing swords, the trampling steeds and baths of molten lead, the dungeons where prisoners suffered starvation waiting to be ransomed. This woman who yowled with pain when she had a stomach cramp was lecturing him about the honest duty of war. Robert sighed again and wrung his hands, more than half wishing that Udele's neck were between them, and for that he asked his Lady Mary's pardon. But he needed Udele's cooperation and was finding it impossible to obtain.

Through the unglazed window he could see the row of new lay servants the monastery had accepted in the past week. There were enough servants there to meet the need of every King, Queen, Prince and Princess in Christendom, he thought, watching the long, straggling line. And all of them were youths of military age.

According to the Peace of God, as long as they were lay servants within the monastery, they were exempt from their lord's battle duty. As soon as news of Driencourt reached this remote spot, they had begun appearing, looking sheepish and more than a little frightened, as they stood knocking at the monastery gate. A few had been accompanied by weeping mothers.

"He is my only son. Take him," they pleaded. Often the youth was not, but who am I to question a mother's love? Robert asked himself, taking in as many of the boys and young men as the monastery lay dorter would hold.

They were sleeping five to a bed, and without complaint. But there wasn't enough bread. Udele had refused to start baking more. He knew she suspected him of assisting Godfrey's sly departure; this was her revenge. Robert decided he must appeal to the one emotion that had once softened her.

"If it were Godfrey who were feeling hungry, wouldn't you be willing to work an extra hour to feed him?"

She turned on him then, rolling pin in hand, her eyes red with rage. He had made a severe tactical blunder in bringing up Godfrey. He put up his arms to defend himself, yelling "Help!" Jacobus, who had been chopping wood for the ovens, came in and wrestled the pin from his wife.

"Calm yourself, woman! That's no way to treat Abbot Robert!"

"I will not bake extra loaves," Udele repeated, sitting on her stool, putting down the pin, and folding her arms over her chest. Robert and Jacobus went outside for hasty consultation.

"Her mind's made up," the husband said.

"We must have more bread," the monk said.

They sighed in unison, squinting up at the noonday sun. War had come to the monastery.

*　　*　　*

Lucie laughed and covered her face with her long fingers. Her hair was loose and flowing over her shoulders and back. Daisies and violets were strewn through it, and a pink rose peeked out of the front of her bliaut.

"Don't laugh at me," Benoit said with great earnestness. He shifted closer to her with some difficulty. The splints on his leg made movement slow and painful. She saw the pain on his face and reached out with a gentle hand to touch his cheek in encouragement. He took the hand, touching only the fingertips, and put there a kiss so light, Lucie barely felt it.

"But you say strange things," Lucie said, closing her eyes and tilting her face up to catch the sun. Crickets chirped in the meadow where they sat, shyly distant and upright, on the cloak that Benoit had spread for her. His splinted leg stuck straight out like a beam, and ants tickled the toes he could not stretch to scratch.

It was not going as Benoit had expected. To begin with, he had not expected Lucie to accept his offer of a walk—alone, with only him for escort—with such alacrity. He thought she would protest, at least for a moment, and that he would have to persuade her with fair words. But no . . .

"Yes, please take me out of here!" she had quickly replied, not knowing that some pretty hesitation was expected. Excursions outside of the castle and congested village were becoming rare. The roads were no longer safe and the woods never had been, but Lucie, unused to being indoors for days at a time, was chafing at the confinement.

And now, alone for the first time, in a place where Lady Sophia was not likely to find and interrupt them, Lucie was laughing at him. Again.

"Lady Love . . . May I call you that?"

"You already have. Several times," she pointed out.

"My Lady Love. Humor is not my intent. I tell you that I love you, more than life itself. Your every wish is my heart's desire. Please me by giving me a command." Benoit would have gone on his knees, as good form required, but the splints made that impossible. Instead, he placed both hands over his heart.

"A command?" Lucie frowned, thinking. "I would like an apple." She pointed to a distant apple tree.

"It is done." Benoit, pleased, rose painfully to his feet and, crutches in place under his armpits, hobbled off at breakneck pace.

She opened her mouth to call him back, concerned about his wounded leg, and then thought better of it. It pleased him to do things for her. Her eyes narrowed with a new sense of power. When he returned, sweating with his efforts, she bit into the green apple. It was sour. She cast it away and sent him back for another, to please him.

They were not so far from the castle that Godfrey, with his keen sight, could not also observe this game. He sat, morose and heavyhearted, on a high parapet, watching from afar the wooing of Lucie by Benoit.

The warm summer wind, which carried the scent of ripening grapes and olives in its twining fingers, ruffled the pages of a volume lying loose and forgotten in his lap.

Godfrey's rise within the castle hierarchy had been rapid. He was educated, and charming when needed, and such men fared well in Poitiers, where intelligence and charm were highly esteemed. From carter he had progressed to laborer, and then assistant to Chabert, and now was free to roam the castle at will. He no longer wore dirty grey homespun, but finely woven and dyed linen. A sword, the emblem of a free man, was once again belted over his hips, a gift of Eleanor, who approved his painting of the new chapel Madonna.

Yet he was as discontent as any young man on a journey who finds the destination is unattainable.

There, on the other side of the silver Clain, sat Lucie, the maid he had come to rescue, giving sidelong glances to another. Yesterday, when they had passed each other coming out of chapel, she had smiled and given him good day . . . and then continued on her way without another word. That had been even worse than the times when she had ignored him, unable to look into his eyes.

He preferred the Lucie who had been unsure of herself, shy and obedient, her downcast eyes informed with the knowledge of her own inferiority.

This new Lucie walked with head high and eyes straight ahead, not down. Even in his thoughts he gave her the title of "Lady," as if she were not the same wench who had pretended to drown herself in a pond so she might escape her master.

He had taken on Lucie because her mother wept and the night was wild and stormy as a woman in heat, and because Lucie was so comely there in the moonlight.

Did she remember that night? He would have yelled the question across the expanse that divided them, except he knew she would only turn deep, unreadable eyes to him, and then look away. What good to love a maid who sits across the river, eating apples from another man's hands?

For all the good it did him, his ambition might be sitting on the other side of the river, too, and with no bridge for him to cross to it. He had been saved from common toil and disgrace, but his love songs were still unsung, his name and poems unknown.

"A pox on woman," he muttered, turning back to the volume. Eleanor had decided her new Lady Chapel should also be a Victory Chapel, so sure was she of the outcome of the war. There was to be yet another new altar, and a statue dedicated to St. Agatha. He had been assigned the task of verifying the attributes of this saint, so that her statue might include those symbols most important to her.

Trying to forget Lucie and ambition, he read the history of Agatha and soon was lost in the grisly tale of the highborn beauty from Catania who was coveted by the cruel and lustful Quintianus, consul of Sicily. Of low birth, he sought to wed Agatha for her beauty and position. Any knight would wish the same, Godfrey reflected, for it was common, indeed expected, that knights wed above themselves, using marriage to add to their family honor.

As for his lustful disposition, any man not yet descended into old age who beholds a beautiful maid feels those stirrings, doesn't he? thought Godfrey. Like other lusty young men who scorned celibacy, he thought the Church pointed its accusing finger too hastily and too forcefully at the natural inclinations of men wanting to be with women.

But chaste Agatha would have nothing to do with Quintianus. She refused him on the grounds that he worshipped idols. They were perfectly true and valid grounds, but ones that roused little sympathy from her rejected suitor. Neither did her virgin coldness kill his lust. The more she refused him, the more avidly did he burn, till he was maddened with lust and her denials. He sold her into prostitution; she so wearied her procuress with her prayers that she was returned to Quintianus. He put her on the rack; she preferred martyrdom to surrendering herself to his coarse hands. His patience at an end, Quintianus ordered the torturers to cut off her breasts. If he could not be the one to enjoy her beauty, no one would. It was done.

But St. Peter came to her in the night, where she wept in her cell in pain and sorrow, and healed her, even returning her severed breasts to her chest.

When she was brought before her persecutor the next day, she was more beautiful than ever. And more determined to die rather than share his bed, or any man's, for that matter. Quintianus had her dragged naked over burning coals. But even as this was being done, the city was shaken by a great earthquake and the people turned on Quintianus, blaming him for the disaster. He was forced to release the maiden, who was already being called the savior of her people. She was finally allowed to die peacefully in her cell, and when she was laid in her tomb, a hundred angels in white silk tunics came and bore her away.

When her emptied tomb was closed, Mt. Aetna erupted and spilled fiery tongues toward the town of Catania. The people, terrified for their lives, reopened the martyr's tomb and found there only her veil. That they carried on a spear toward the volcano. The virgin's veil repelled the lava and saved the town.

Godfrey was impressed. But he thought that Chabert's story of his fair Damietta was more heartrending. That was his kind of damsel—the type who would seek her man even in the dangerous woods, who would risk all for the comfort of his arms.

The history of Agatha, thought Godfrey, was the kind of story that a woman at war with her husband would enjoy; it was the kind of legend that a wife, once happy in wedded passion but now exiled from her lord's love, would prefer.

Well then, he thought, picking up quill and parchment. At the base of the statue we shall inscribe these words: "Saintly and generous soul, an honor to God and the savior of her country," for those were the words put on Agatha's tomb.

With cautious, even strokes, he began designing the posture and movement of the statue, which the carver would then translate into stone. Agatha stood on long, slender legs, one knee slightly bent to achieve the curving, resonant form to which the draperies of her modest gown would cling. Her hair flowed loose over her back, as befits a maiden; her eyes looked up to heaven, as befits a martyr.

In her left hand she carried a reliquary in the shape of a bell, for Agatha was the patron saint of bell-founders, who often called their shapely bell molds "Agatha's breast." This would house the relic Queen Eleanor had recently bought for her new chapel—one of the saint's own fingernails. In her right hand, she carried a dish in which rested her severed breasts.

"It is well drawn. Is it a likeness of anyone I would know?" a woman's soft voice asked from over his shoulder.

Godfrey, not knowing that his work had been observed, jumped to his feet. The volume fell from his lap. He bent to retrieve it and saw just beyond the book a pair of small, shapely feet encased in green satin slippers. As he straightened, he saw a pale green bliaut over a dark blue tunic, a golden girdle entwined with a rope of pearls, long, elegant hands clasped at a slender waist. She was tall and fair, and laughter was buried in the deep blue ocean of her eyes.

"No one, Lady," he said, although the statue had, like the new statue of the Madonna, a certain resemblance to Lucie. He felt suddenly as if he had been running for a great distance. She was stunningly beautiful; and she was obviously a lady of great rank. In this his heart echoed Eleanor's: Power was the greatest love potion.

As she bent sideways to examine more closely the drawing, one of her golden brown plaits brushed against his wrist. Impulsively he closed his fingers on the end of it and the silken strand tickled his palm. She smelled of roses and costly spices. Pearls were twined in her hair. He could not determine her age, but she was certainly no green maiden, like Lucie.

She looked at where his hand held her long braid and turned mocking eyes to him. "You have captured something that is not yours, sir," she said.

Godfrey leaned closer to her. "Yes. And I would hold it ransom . . . within my heart."

"Indeed. And what is the ransom price?" She turned her face aside, but her rosy lips were curled in a restrained smile.

"A kiss," he said.

"Now that I look at your drawing more closely, I see that it lacks educated perspective. The dimensions aren't correct. But perhaps that is a fault of impetuousness that time . . . and determination . . . may correct." He knew she wasn't talking about his artistic skill. He had been too swift, too bold. He released the captive braid.

"Your name?" she asked, smiling again, and stepping back out of his reach.

"Godfrey."

"And what do you here, sir? I have not seen you before."

"Assistant to Chabert, the Lady Chapel builder. Scholar, jongleur, and poet."

"Welcome, then, Godfrey. And a good day." She turned to leave with a soft whispering of the silk bliaut.

"Wait. Please." He took a step after her. She hesitated, but kept her back turned to him. "I have given you my name. What is yours, Fairest of Ladies?"

"I am Marie of Champagne, daughter of Eleanor," she said over her shoulder. "Tonight you may recite some of your poems for me." And then she was gone.

Godfrey stared after her for a very long time.

5

"He will sing tonight. Countess Marie invited him," Sophia said. She was starting to feel like Dame Alicia's spaniel, who had fetched shoes from nowhere and brought them to her mistress. A damsel to drown, a carter to sing . . . anything, anyone, to help Eleanor through her malaise.

It was clear that the victories of the early summer had not eased Eleanor's spirits. She celebrated her sons' prowess. But her heart was not in celebration.

"He is comely. But his voice won't be as resonant as Bernart's was," Eleanor answered. "Send him a small token, only a small one, to thank him. And tell him that I, too, will be pleased to listen to his music tonight. But it won't be as skilled as was Bernart de Ventadour's," Eleanor repeated, shaking her head.

"Yes. I'll tell him," Sophia said. "Your exact words. They are sure to prod him into a good voice." Her sarcasm was lost on Eleanor, who was deep in thought.

How good it would be to hear Bernart sing again. To hear the old love songs that had been written for her, songs that had made her famous through the land. How many years ago? Don't think of the years, Eleanor told herself.

She was lonely. And bored. Louis and young Henry made a great point of not answering her correspondence, of not keeping her abreast of the movement of the armies. They kept her messengers and couriers waiting, and if they did answer her letters, it was with a galling condescension that more than hinted she should refrain from mixing in men's affairs. As if she were no more than a country wife, or serving girl.

Henry had not treated her so. Henry had made her ruler in all but name when he went on his campaigns, leaving his kingdom willingly in her hands. He had not patted her on the back and told her to stay in the weaving room. No, Henry had assessed and recognized her competency . . . and then used it to gain what he wanted.

And Henry no longer wanted her.

A great longing to be loved again washed over her till she feared she would weep with the longing, and the name of her old lover, Bernart, sang in the dark corners of her thoughts.

Sophia thought it would be better not to carry Eleanor's message to Godfrey, else he might lose heart entirely.

Instead, she would look in on Sir Foulkes. He was still weak, and liable to hemorrhage with the rising of the full moon that evening. With a natal day in the sign of Scorpio, his body was ruled by violent passions that needed frequent purging.

Sophia consulted her volume of the *Tetrabiblos*, and fixed a drink of broom and hops. She carried it in to him on a wooden tray, trying vainly not to spill any of it, but her hobbled gait made her clumsy. By the time she arrived at his bedside, half the drink was sloshing around the tray.

This he noticed, but said nothing. He remembered the evening of many weeks ago when he had made fun of the damsel's crippled gait, and he felt shame. She had been a good nurse to him, never weeping and carrying on as most women do, but staunch and strong-stomached as a soldier.

"I thank you," he muttered stiffly, accepting the drink.

"You must sleep deeply tonight," she explained in her quiet, patient voice. "If you toss too much, you will reopen the wound and lose more blood."

"How do you know these things?"

"I read of them," she said.

"It is the devil's own doing, a woman who reads," he muttered.

"Not the devil's, but our savior's Blessed Mother, who would have some in this world not be uninstructed dolts." His words did not offend her. His attitude was a common one. Her own father had not been happy about her penchant for study.

The more time she spent with this old warrior, the more he reminded her of her father. They were of an age, or would be, if her father still lived, and of similar builds, with strong barrel chests, and muscular legs bowed from years of riding. Her father had been of a better disposition, but perhaps that was just because of the gentling love he shared with her mother. Once she died, he certainly became fierce enough, putting aside family and vassals to ride off towards Jerusalem. She wondered if he ever reached his journey's end, or had died or been murdered en route.

Either way, the ultimate destination—death—had been reached, or would be, in due time, so why pine over minor details like where and when? It was her prideful curiosity that kept her trying to see in her mind's eye some distant grave marked with a wooden cross in a foreign, dusty field.

"Today I will trim your beard," she said when Foulkes finished the drink.

"My beard is fine as it is," he said, his eyes wide with offense. Never had a woman taken razor to hair or beard of his. Did she think he was a fool such as Samson?

"It is fine," she agreed patiently, "if you desire to look like a wildman of the forest." But when she approached with the razor, he pulled the covers up to his eyes and would not release them until she convinced him that a haircut would help him heal that

210

much sooner. Overlong hair, left to itself, drew the strength from invalids. Of course, she did not call Foulkes an invalid—prideful curiosity was not his failing, as it was hers. His was pride in his great, robust strength. Strength that seemed to decrease each morn, since the boar-battle that had torn his arm and poisoned his blood.

"How fares the maid, Lucie?" he asked, watching with alarm as long, oily locks of black hair fell to the floor.

"How she fares depends on why you ask," Sophia said testily. "If you are concerned for her health, she has long since healed of her chill and fever. If you ask for the condition of your slave, then she is not doing well at all."

"Why not?" He was equally peevish.

"Because she is no longer slave but free woman, and will be much upset if she is to consider you as master, still."

"Who says she is free? Eleanor?"

"Eleanor. And the law, which states that a runaway serf earns freedom if he or she is off the owner's mesne for a year and a day. Lucie left your lands more than fourteen months ago."

"You may slyly call me an uninstructed dolt, but I know the law as well as you, Lady. And the law says that the serf must be living in another lord's court for that year and a day. Much of that time Lucie spent on the road with her charlatan jongleur. Ouch, that was my ear you trimmed, woman!"

"A fine point, and one that ignores the essence of the law, which is to provide escape for men and women mistreated by their lords." Sophia dabbed at the nicked and bloodied ear with a cloth.

"How did I ever mistreat her?" He was growing sulky and mean. Sophia handled the razor more gingerly.

"You cruelly used her mother, and then had her cast out of her cottage. And when the girl was grown, you would have done the same with her." Lucie had finally revealed those things to Sophia.

"As lord, I have rights," he said.

"The right to bed female serfs, if you must," she admitted. Even the laws of chivalry, even Mother Church, granted him that

211

right. "But you had no right to cast the woman and Lucie out of their home."

"I had no hand in that. My wife, Lady Maria, did that."

Sophia bit her lip in frustration. He was twisting it around, trying to get free from the charge and her anger. And he had. Lady Maria did have the right to do as she pleased with female serfs. The lord was King of the castle, but his lady was Queen and reigned over the domain of the hall and kitchen and servants.

"Even so, it is foul to bring so much misery upon a woman, through your own lust."

"I don't remember your being there at the time. Are you so certain my lust gave her nothing but misery?" He was smiling wickedly. With his hair shorn and combed, he looked a little younger and not as fierce. She hadn't expected the hair to feel silky between her fingers, nor his face to be soft and white where the beard was trimmed away.

"What else could you give, other than misery?" she asked in an acid voice. And then, tongue-tied and shy, she fled the room.

"Much more. Think about it, Lady," he called after her. His laughter pursued her down the hall till she reached her own chamber door. She drew the bolt and leaned there, gasping and furious.

Godfrey thrust the drawing of Agatha under Chabert's red nose and then dashed out of the chapel before the man could comment on it. If he was to sing his songs and poems for Marie tonight, then much preparation was needed. He would bathe, have his clothing brushed and cleaned of grease spots, and maybe Lady Sophia, who was both physician and barber, it seemed, would trim his hair. And the poems. The poems. He had been confident of their power and beauty just a few short hours ago. Now he worried that they would be found caviling, clichéd, lacking in the ability to stir the listener. My God! What if she didn't like his poetry? What if she found his voice off-key and lacking?

Many, too many it seemed now, of his songs and poems were in

212

the Goliard tradition, full of bitterness and rage, and not gentle enough in their sentiments. Why hadn't he listened to Robert?

Marie would expect poems that glorified women, that praised their values and beauty. And what had he wasted his time on, this spring, but bawdy tavern songs that poked fun at women! He could kick himself, but he didn't have time.

It was more than the beauty of Marie that filled and frenzied his heart. It was her power. Next to Eleanor, no woman in the land had more influence . . . more ability to raise a poor and unknown poet to the ranks of the wealthy and the famous. This was the chance he had hoped for, the thing that had drawn him to Eleanor's court of love in the first place. If he sang sweetly enough tonight, his future was made. He would have a velvet cape lined with vair for the winter, and his name would be known for many generations to come.

He spent the afternoon searching through his papers and memories. Then, when the sun began its downward climb, he dressed with infinite care, brushing his hair till it gleamed. Hopefully, he plucked at the borrowed lute to gauge its tuning, and strode to the great hall. He could barely feel the gravelly paths beneath his feet.

He thought all eyes would turn to him when he entered; surely the whole world knew what this night meant to him. But they did not. Indeed, except for Chabert, who nodded morosely, Benoit, who smiled scornfully, and Lady Sophia, who watched him with a certain wary pity, no eyes turned to him at all. Lucie pretended to be busy with a speck of something on her sleeve and did not look up.

The hall was crowded with women, as halls are wont to be when their men are busy at battle. But these women weren't country clods who would openly cast longing eyes on a handsome youth. They feigned indifference and only stole long looks under lowered lashes. They hid any pleasure they took in the sight of him. And that, for many of them, especially the younger wives still unused to spending long nights without their lords, was hiding much.

213

Lady Marie was not there.

His heart felt stony, till he remembered that Lady Marie liked to arrive after the others were already assembled. Perhaps even now she was peeking from behind the curtains at the end of the hall, waiting for the correct moment to enter. He forced a casual smile to his lips as he took his accustomed place next to Chabert. He was exactly opposite the great salt cellar; it was a precarious position. One slip, and he would be seated below the cellar and disgraced. He could also, if proven worthy, be moved above the salt cellar and thus be held publicly in great esteem.

Lucie, thanks to the high position of her companion, Sir Benoit, sat well above the cellar, just a few places away from Lady Sophia, who, in turn, was just an arm's length from the Queen's place.

The knowledge that he had found favor with one of the most beautiful and powerful women in the world flavored Godfrey's meal. Never had roast lamb been so succulent, wine so heady, the perfume of a myriad women clothed in every color of the rainbow so enchanting.

Godfrey ate and drank with great appetite, his senses inflamed by the promise of greater pleasure to come. A beauty with eyes as bold as Marie's could make even the longest night of summer too short by many hours. When his songs were finished, perhaps she would let him come to her that very night. Stray, unbidden memories of Lucie sometimes intruded into his thoughts, but he pushed that awareness away, bidding it go elsewhere.

Lucie, for her part, had noticed how splendid Godfrey looked once again, with the dirt and coarse homespun of the carter banished from his person, and wished Benoit wouldn't chatter so much. He had a way of leaning close to her face and thus blocking her view of her Godfrey. When she could, she studied Godfrey's face with great intensity. As soon as he looked in her direction, she looked away.

He, in turn, often found his eyes on Lucie. How different she looked with that silver and amber fillet hung over her white forehead! She ate with delicate style, being careful not to soil her gown or leave grease in the corners of her mouth. This was a

Lucie he did not know. She was more comely than before. Ah, but so young, so naive, compared to Lady Marie's mature and worldly wisdom!

Sophia watched them, a bitter smile playing on her pale lips. They were young and handsome and fools, the pair of them, she thought, to place such an importance on love. If they had any sense at all, they would leave this court and go about their lives, before it was too late. Too late for what? she wondered. She wrapped some quail baked in pastry in her napkin; she would bring it to Sir Foulkes. He had mentioned a fondness for quail.

Two courses were already removed and replaced by a third when Marie, Countess of Champagne, finally arrived. She entered with stately slowness, holding her skirts high enough to reveal slender ankles and satin-shod feet. The points of her sleeves trailed all the way to the floor, and strings of garnet were twined in the plaits that cascaded over each shoulder. The stocky, shorter figure of Chrétien de Troyes shuffled behind her, a clumsy foil to her grace.

Rather than being seated instantly, she cleared her throat and stood waiting. The whole assembly looked up expectantly.

"I beg your forgiveness for my tardiness. Please, please, continue . . ." And only then, when she had gained the whole hall's attention and disrupted all conversation, did she take her seat and permit the waiting pages to serve her and Chrétien. Not once did she look at Godfrey.

The food that had tasted so sweet now tasted of sawdust. He had expected a gentle glance, a promising smile, perhaps even a kiss blown from the fingertips. But she gave him no sign at all. He frowned and Lucie frowned, too, because she had followed his eyes and seen the way they had widened when Lady Marie entered.

Lady Marie ate but lightly, spending most of her time chatting gaily with her poet, or asking riddles of the ladies seated near her. Godfrey was not close enough to hear her conversation, but the frequency of her laughter made him morose. She appeared to have forgotten him.

He was in despair. Even Chabert, who paid attention only to

215

the commands of his lady and good dishes of roast lamb, noticed. "Are you not well?" he asked, pushing a trencher piled with meat towards him. Godfrey pushed it away and took a long swallow from his goblet of wine.

He looked up and saw pity now not only on Lady Sophia's face, but in Lucie's eyes, too. That was more than he could bare. He must do something quickly, before he was unmanned and forced to flee this battlefield in disgrace.

Standing so abruptly the trestle almost overturned, he raised his goblet towards the high head of the long table. It was a great distance away. Even so, his voice was louder than need be; it betrayed him. "My Lady Marie. I ask a favor." Marie turned and gave him a cold look. Her ladies tittered.

"Yes?" she asked, and her glance showed displeasure.

"I ask . . . humbly ask . . . permission to sweeten your meal with my songs."

After a long pretense at consideration, she nodded permission, and then turned to resume her conversation.

Now Godfrey was glad that she did not study him. He was trembling. In Paris he had once, on a dare, sung at a sailors' tavern where they enjoyed cutting off the performer's little finger if his songs were not pleasing. He wanted to hold up his fingers, which were all intact, and say, "Look! I have won even cutthroats with my songs!" but he did not. He was more afraid of Marie than he had been of the sailors. Much more was at stake than a fingertip.

Her poet, Chrétien, grinned and tapped his fingers on the trestle as Godfrey began to play. He had spied their encounter earlier that day—what poet worth his salt would not lurk behind a parapet seeking a tale worth telling?—and had looked forward to this evening's entertainment. The youth was overeager, and the lady not easily impressed. It was a situation worth observing.

During Godfrey's first songs, conversation in the hall continued apace, marred with the clanking of knives and rustling of napkins. It was as if he weren't there, as if his songs had no meaning. He sang softer, not louder, and chose new verses with unfamiliar refrains and lyrics to capture their attention.

216

He sang of love and desire and the mercy of ladies; he sang of golden ripe wheat fields which tumble between mountains, and golden plaits tumbling down a slender back; of heaven, which is never farther way than the beloved's smile. He sang with the passion of a sinner and the subtlety of an Arab mystic. Slowly, like the creeping veil of restful night which, hand's length by hand's length, covers over the colors of day, his voice covered the other, lessening sounds in the hall.

Then, when he was singing the tale of Chabert, which he had rhymed and supplied with a happy rather than tragic ending, with the two lovers escaping together into the night, conversation and other noises in the hall ceased. They were his. Only then did he strengthen his voice so that it reached from the rushes underfoot to the rafters overhead, swelling and billowing like sails catching the wind, carrying them to lands they had never before visited, lands of love and enchantment and great sorrow and even greater pleasure.

When he sang of the death of Havrise, he heard weeping, and when he sang of the elopement of Isolde and Tristram, he heard sighs of joy and envy. Once, he dared look up at Marie. She did not look at him, but there was a smile on her lips and her eyes were soft with dreams.

Forgetting their estrangement, he also looked at Lucie. Her cheeks were wet with tears; she pressed her hand to her trembling mouth. He smiled at her, letting the music heal their rift for a moment. Then, remembering that he sang for Lady Marie's favor and not Lucie's love, he lowered his eyes again.

When he had finished, he put down the lute and stood, prepared to receive Marie's thanks, and the promise of her eyes and smile.

She was not at her place. He scanned the long hall, seeking her, but she was gone.

First came the anger. She made made a fool of him in this assembly, used and humiliated him. Then came curiosity. What had he done wrong? And then sorrow. All his love, all his fine ambition; what was to come of it? Naught? Could he no longer even please a woman with song?

217

Later, when Godfrey had drunk enough wine that he saw two of everything and his thoughts leapt frantically as salmon going upstream, Chrétien de Troyes searched him out in the courtyard, where he sat in the dust under an open casement.

They shared a skin or two of more wine; they sang comradely duets under the shimmering moon. Godfrey taught Chrétien a heathen dance that he had learned from Haram, and they danced till they fell in a sodden heap. Godfrey began to cry, and Chrétien put his arm about him.

"There, there," he said, enjoying himself tremendously. What a fine night it was! How soft the air, how large was the rounded moon, milky as a woman's breast!

"She didn't like my songs," Godfrey said into Chrétien's shoulder. He saw that his leg was twisted in a funny way and reached down to straighten it. It wouldn't straighten right.

"Let go of my leg, there, man!" Chrétien protested. "No, I wouldn't say she didn't like them. But you . . . you discomfited her."

"How so?" Godfrey reached for the wineskin. It was empty. He tossed it aside.

"You compromised her by saying her name in public, for one thing. You cannot pronounce her name in public till she has given you a token and permission. You will bring dishonor to her."

Godfrey giggled. "Am I to call our Lady Marie, Lady Jehanne?" he asked, punching Chrétien playfully in the arm.

Chrétien lightly punched him back. "You must learn discretion. And patience. You must learn the rules of this game, my young fellow. There are many. And it is a twisting path."

Godfrey rolled on his back and stared up at the sky. "I will," he said with drunken conviction, no longer crying but filled again with hope. "I will learn everything." And then, he was asleep.

Chrétien yawned and stumbled to his feet. It was gratitude as well as fondness that made him spread his own mantle over the unconscious youth. Godfrey had told him everything in the course of their frolic, about his now disbanded traveling troupe, and Udele, how he had come here to find Lucie, entering the castle secretly in a cart, and then met Lady Marie. Interesting, that. Not the falling in love with his patroness. Everyone did. But the cart. Could make a good story, with a little dressing up. Scratching his ribs and head, Chrétien made his way to the scriptorium. There, he lit a lamp, sharpened a quill, and put some tentative words on paper. *"Lancelot: Le Chevalier de la Charrette."* Lancelot: the Knight of the Cart.

Since my Lady of Champagne wants me to take up romance-writing, I will do it gladly, as a liege man who will serve her to the limit of his ability, without wasting time on flattery, he wrote, pausing only when the quill needed to be refreshed in the inkpot. *A writer who wanted to flatter her might say—and I would back him up—that this lady surpasses all other ladies alive as the May zephyr surpasses all other winds . . . This I will say: Her command does more for this story than any thought or labor of mine.*

Of The Knight of the Cart Chrétien here begins his book.

Quickly he was lost in the twisting paths of the story and forgot the youth.

Godfrey slept on, his arm around a large stone, which, in his dreams, he alternately called Marie and Lucie.

Lady Sophia found him there and left him there, rolled in a ball under the scriptorium casement, when she went to Sir Foulkes. The quail she had saved from dinner made her pocket hang heavy, and it swung as she hobbled.

The old and grizzled warrior, no longer quite so old nor quite so grizzled since Sophia took razor and comb to him, was sleeping on his side. His bandaged arm was crumpled under him.

Sophia shrieked with alarm and jostled him.

"What is it? Attack?" He was awake and sitting up instantly, reaching for his sword.

"You were sleeping on your wounded arm. You will rupture the stitching," she said in an accusing voice.

"Christ's balls! You woke me to tell me I'm sleeping wrong?" he roared. But he let her take the arm for an inspection. Her touch was gentle.

The bandages were intact. Sophia stroked his arm, relieved.

"I brought you some roasted quail," she said in a lowered

voice. It could have waited till morning, she knew. But she was sleepless and lonely. She took the quails out of her pocket and spread them on a napkin over his lap. He ate hungrily, tired of the invalid sops and stews of the sickroom and glad for the game. She watched, and smiled, taking pleasure in his appetite though she had none herself.

Lucie, who was also sleepless and lonely, could see Godfrey from her casement. Scorn mixed with softening pity showed in the turned-down corners of her mouth. Marie had wounded him mortally. No woman knew Godfrey's pride better than she, and the greatness of the wound when that pride was insulted. But what did he expect from a great lady like Marie?

And what do I expect? she asked herself. Sir Benoit had come to her last night, and begged to lie naked beside her. "It is a test of my purity," he told her, blushing. "Let us lie together, and I will prove my worth. I shall not touch you."

And he hadn't. They had lain together naked and the test had been hers, not his, for even without love between them, she ached for a man's touch . . . not his purity. She ached for Godfrey, and what had been between them in the orchard-scented spring nights.

The summer had gone wrong. The days and nights were hot now, no longer pleasant, and they brought the kind of lethargy that encourages regret and backward glances. She missed Godfrey with all her heart. She hadn't known how much she missed him till she saw the way he had looked at Lady Marie that night.

One other presence disturbed the peaceful night. William Maingot, as sleepless as Lucie, as drunk as Chrétien, as hungry with unsatisfied appetite as Godfrey, leaned out his casement. Eleanor had refused to see him that night.

The message had been courteous enough. "The Queen is not feeling well. Perhaps tomorrow the game may be continued." The game referred to was an ebony and ivory set of chessmen set up in Eleanor's receiving chamber. They played in the new manner, using two Kings and two Queens, rather than four Kings. It was said that Eleanor herself helped start this vogue which amended the ancient game by making the Queen almost as powerful as the King himself, her movements so subtle, so oblique, she was all but impossible to capture.

But Maingot wasn't convinced that Eleanor wasn't aware of another, more dangerous game that was being played.

She was courteous—too courteous. Her smile was fixed, the touch of her fingers on his arm too light, as if he were loathsome to the touch.

She knows I will betray her, when the moment is ripe, he thought. Her hatred brought him no distress. He was Henry's man. Not Eleanor's. He served the King, not the Queen.

Henry, given time and loyalty, would forge an empire the world would not soon forget. A Queen's only empire building occurred in the royal nursery. Eleanor had already done her work there; she had brought four sons into the world. Let her retire now, and attend to her needlework. What was it John Chrysostom had said of women? . . . Ah, yes, that was it. They were a necessary evil . . . a desirable calamity. A domestic peril. They were Eve, poised to pluck the fruit and dishonor all of mankind.

He breathed deeply of the night air and then sat down at his writing table. In carefully memorized code he wrote of the doings of Eleanor's court of the past week. It revealed little. She hunted daily, just as she always had. She conversed at great length with her daughter, Marie of Champagne, over women's issues. She spent three hours a day instructing the noble Poitevin children who had been sent to her court for polishing. And long hours each evening, in her private rooms with her ladies. It was then, he knew, that the plotting possessed her, and the letter writing, and the waiting for letters from her sons.

What he would give to see those letters. But her staff was well paid and loyal. And cautious. They were tiptoing around him, and avoiding conversation when he was in the room. He didn't know how much longer Eleanor would be willing to play cat and mouse with him. He must find an informant in the castle quickly, someone Eleanor placed above suspicion, someone she would feel free to speak with openly—or at least with whom she would not think to be secretive. But who?

221

The Old King's days were numbered.

That was the popular consensus in Aquitaine, France and England. The barons had risen against their King, and now their King would fall. William the Lion of Scotland, Earl Hugh of Chester, Philip of Flanders, Henri of Champagne, Ralph of Fougères, the Viscount of Bayeux, the great lords of the South . . . all had answered the call to arms and now were slowly, inevitably, mercilessly, working their way to Rouen, where Henry waited and hunted.

Count Philip of Flanders took castle after castle in the name of Young King Henry. In Anjou and Brittany the Old King's castles were raided and looted, their great halls burnt. Henry's banners were cast in the dirt; Hal's were raised to the smoky sky.

The kingdoms were on fire with revolt, the countryside ravaged. Giant, grotesque siege engines, pulled from one conquered castle to another, moved over the land like tethered dragons, terrifying the populace. Peasants and townspeople alike knew that where the siege engines took up a stand, starvation soon followed. Knights and mercenaries roamed in looting bands, and neither brought joy or comfort to those whose work was merely to survive. Newly homeless peasants wandered the roads. Their arms and faces bore angry red scars where cinders of their burnt cottages had fallen on them. Their eyes were filmed with despair. Fields were untended, left to go to ruin, their crops turning to seas of greedy, overwhelming weeds.

Smoke and carrion eaters filled the skies thickly enough to blot out the sun. All over the land was heard the sound of marching armies, and a new generation of widows and orphans was born.

But while the North was devastated, the triumphant South rejoiced. Victory would go to the Queen and her sons. *Bene merenti! Victory to those who deserve!*

The Old King's losses were the Young King's gains, and generous as chivalry demanded, he freely assigned the conquered castles, fields, serfs and riches to his vassals. Poor vassals grew wealthy; those who had been well off grew richer yet. Each victory brought new wealth to the Young King's vassals and increased the war lust in their hearts.

Henry, stony-eyed and red-faced with rage and shame, bided his time in Rouen. Eleanor's name was anathema to him. This was all her doing, Hal would never have turned on him without her insistence. God, how he would make her suffer for this!

Doing nothing, as castle after castle fell and one vassal after another pledged loyalty to his son, was the most difficult thing he had ever done. But blind panic was a thing of the night, a ruse to startle away the archbishop's demon. A true King, a noble and wise one, does not jump up and slash away at everything that moves, not in the daylight hours. No, a plan was needed, a strategy. He needed time, time to test who would remain loyal, to gather his resources and wits.

He passed the long, galling mornings hunting the wild boar . . . and other game, fierce two-legged creatures who would kill for nothing more than a day's wages.

In the afternoons, wearied of the hunt and finished with the many messengers he both dispatched and received, he climbed to the top of a craggy hill where the wild broom grew. There he stared morosely at the tall, yellow-blooming stems, miniature suns in thick, green settings. His father, Geoffrey, had worn a twig of broom in his hat, earning the new name of Plantagenet, "sprig of bloom."

Henry plucked at the broom, absentmindedly sticking twigs of it in his hair as he mentally counted the numbers of Brabantines and *routiers* already in his pay, and added to that the number he must reach before he could counterattack.

His men, restive and speculative, cast sidelong glances at him. He knew he looked half-witted, lolling lazily on the sunbaked rocks with weeds stuck in his hair as his castles fell to the vengeance of Eleanor and Hal. He knew tongues were wagging. Let them look; let them gossip like old women at a well. He had learned humility in the time since the murder of Thomas, had learned to bear the discomfort of eyes peering into him with hatred and scorn.

I will look foolish, and they will think me foolish. As we are seen, so are we esteemed. But before this patch of broom is dry and stiff with winter, I will have swept the land clear of rebellion, he promised himself. The sun, low in the sky, tinted the horizon a pale red, reminding him of lines of Virgil, a poem he and his Queen had read together during one of the rare evenings they had lain quietly, at truce in each other's arms and asking for nothing more than the pleasure of their own wedded companionship.

> Who dares call Sun a liar? He it is
> Who often warns of dark revolt afoot,
> Conspiracy and cancerous growth of war.

He would wipe the cancer of Eleanor's revolt from the land.

In Aquitaine, the sun was not blotted by smoke. It shone bright and strong. The battles had not reached there, and they would not, Eleanor said. Henry would be captured any day. And it would be ended.

The meadows outside the Poitevin walls blazed with a riot of red poppies, while fully leaved oaks spread dark patches of

224

coolness in the hot noon sun. Sirius, the torrid Dogstar, cracked the dry roads into a maze of brown maps.

The freshness of the nights disappeared, to be replaced by a steaming, night-fever-carrying heat that made people toss restlessly in damp tangles of bed linen. Eleanor dreamed of a humbled Henry who begged mercy at her feet. Godfrey dreamed of a woman who was both Marie and Lucie, and Lucie dreamed of homecoming, the hope of fugitives. Sophia dreamed of the secret knowledge not yet revealed to her, the mysterious untraversed terrain of the heart and flesh.

She periodically disturbed the accumulating dust on her translation of Boethius, only to abandon it shortly thereafter for other tasks. The scriptorium was airless as a sealed vault, flies buzzed in the mildewed corners. It was the hottest summer she could remember, and that was her excuse for leaving the stifling scriptorium and spending her afternoons in the cooler, breeze-pampered room where Sir Foulkes rested.

They passed long hours playing chess. He was surprisingly adept; she hadn't guessed that he could be thoughtful, when needed. He was also gentler, rarely showing his famous temper and displaying a patience with his own illness that a monk would have praised.

Part of Sophia liked the softer Sir Foulkes; another part of her wanted the old knight back.

She was frightened. A flux of the bowels, a rend in the arm, should not take so long to heal. Yet his body resisted every remedy she could devise. The long illness and the new heat were draining from him the strength he needed to burn out the dark secret that was gnawing inside. She guessed that the superficial symptoms she had been treating were only hints of the true illness, which, even as she watched him contemplate her black bishop, was hollowing his cheeks.

He was dying, and there was nothing she could do.

There were good days when he insisted on leaving his rooms and exercising his charger, who grew fat and lazy in the stables. He would roar commands and stomp through the halls, tear through the courtyard and the town and terrify the washerwomen by the Clain. He would come back, sodden with sweat, calling for wine and roast meat. He would disappear into the brothels of Poitiers and days would pass like that, with Sophia both fretful and exultant. And he came back, more tired, more drawn.

And there were bitter days. He would kick at the sheets, yell at Sophia, refuse the food she brought him. He would threaten to ride off in the morning, with his serf, Lucie, tied on the horse behind him.

On those days, Sophia retreated back to her scriptorium and drew aimless designs in the dust. The heat made her lethargic and dreamy, restless with needs she couldn't name because they had never been fulfilled. She grew more waspish and short-tempered, and Lucie, who had problems of her own, avoided her.

The heat affected Eleanor, too. Even her maps could no longer hold her attention for long, and often her mind wandered to times long past, happier times. Why did Henry not fight back? She was almost sore at heart for him, for this disaster that was his coming downfall, for his aloneness and shame. But he would have put her aside for Rosamonde. That hardened her heart against him each time she thought of it.

"The cubs shall awake and shall roar aloud and, leaving the woods, shall seek their prey within the walls of the cities; among those who shall be in their way they shall make great carnage and shall tear out the tongues of bulls. The necks of them as they roar aloud they shall load with chains and shall thus renew the times of their forefathers."

Eleanor recited Merlin's ancient prophecy in a monotone.

"I was a child when I first read those words. Little did I think that the cubs would be my own sons, and that their prey would be my husband, the King."

Eleanor and Sophia and Lucie were sitting in the Queen's private chamber, cooling themselves with peacock fans bought by Eleanor in Constantinople many years before. Lucie liked this room, which had the zodiac painted on the ceiling and a colorful map of the world, replete with sea monsters and dragons, painted on the floor. Heaven was above, all the world below, in this cool, pleasant chamber. Her foot rested on Asia, and a long, green sea serpent lurked underneath her abandoned slippers.

"You will be victorious," Sophia pointed out, a hard edge in her voice. "That should make you content."

"Content? I know of no such thing," Eleanor said. She sighed. "Where is Marie?"

"With your new troubadour, Godfrey," Sophia replied.

Lucie flinched as if someone had poked her. Unhappily she twisted the ring Sir Benoit had given her. It was a small garnet surrounded by seed pearls, set in silver. He had shown her how it was to be worn: on the little finger, because it is said that a knight's life and death resides in the little finger, and on the left hand, which is a less shameful hand than the right. It was to be turned around so that only she could see the stones, to symbolize the secret of their love.

But Lucie had had enough of courtesy. She wanted love, the kind that she had known with Godfrey, in the sweet meadows under the stars. Sir Benoit had kissed her on the mouth, but chastely, with closed lips and sleeping tongue. When she had opened her own mouth and tried to pry open the fortress of his with her own tongue, he had drawn back, reproach in his eyes.

"We need distraction," Eleanor announced gravely. "There will be a court of love. It will amuse the court and keep our minds off gloomy topics."

It was a long time since she had held a court. Too long. In her youth—in her father's chateau of L'Ombriere, in Louis' castle in Paris, in the many palaces she had shared with Henry . . . Chinon, Woodstock—she had delighted in the courts, inviting the best poets and troubadours in the land to come and argue some fine point of chivalry and love. They had been great festivals, hectic with feasts and song and debate over fine points of courtesy.

The courts of love had made her famous: when Raymond had first sought her in Antioch, he had greeted her as "The Queen of love." Raymond, she reflected, what if I had stayed there with you, in that courtyard with its playing fountains and noisy peacocks, and not attended my husband, Louis, on his wasteful Crusade? The secretive East would have thought nothing of one more errant wife seeking shelter and abandon in its walled gardens, even if that wife be Queen of France and Duchess of Aquitaine.

But she had no choice in that matter. Louis, aware that he was quickly losing his young wife to a more pleasant passion, a more ingratiating life than he could provide, had kidnapped Eleanor and smuggled her, bound and humiliated, away from Raymond.

Her never-forgotten anger and frustration with the monkish Louis who had loved her too much merged with the fresh, burning anger at Henry, the second husband, who had loved her not enough.

It was Henry who had sent Bernart de Ventadour away from her, in a jealous rage. She was no longer Queen of France and not yet Queen of England, for her new husband, Henry, had not yet claimed his throne, he was mere duke, not yet King. And his ambition—or so he said then—was to keep her for himself. He knew she had been unfaithful to Louis. She freely admitted it. She had been young and unhappy and unfulfilled. What Henry did not know was that she was deeply in love with him. Their marriage was not just a political arrangement, not for her. She married her flame-haired suitor believing she would need no other for the rest of her life.

But his fine words and promises had turned out to be the vows of a suitor with an eye for gain, not a husband whose heart could be faithful. It was her wealth, her lands, that Henry wanted. And her body. From this vessel will come a great line of Kings, he had said, stroking her belly. And so it was. And no more.

Their great love turned to mundane purpose. Poetry fled before his horrible pragmatism. He was a mere youth, ambitious and ruthless and often cruel. She was older by eleven years, a woman who had found the one thing she wanted from life, which was to rest in his arms and heart, safe and beloved. With Henry, there was no safety, no rest. She was not beloved.

She buried her disappointment in busy routine. She had a talent for administration and Henry took advantage of it, sending her from one neglected castle to another. When she left, all was in order and Henry was richer, not poorer, for her accountings. She counted tithes, taxes and war-horses, while he conquered new lands . . . and new mistresses.

She was not yet swollen with Henry's first son when he sent her to the Limousin well in advance of him . . . well enough for Eleanor to put all in order for his arrival, which was delayed by "foul weather" with the name of Isabella. Bernart de Ventadour was waiting for her there. It was Bernart who kept her company and sang her praises while Henry delayed elsewhere.

> When the sweet breeze
> Blows hither from your dwelling
> Methinks I feel
> A breath of paradise.

Bernart wished to be the lover Henry had not been. He played her heart as skillfully as he played the lute, but it was his music she had loved, not his body. Henry filled her life, leaving no room for anyone else. All she gave Bernart was what she had been born with: a deep love of music and beauty.

And Henry had spoiled it all. In a fit of possessiveness he exiled Bernart to England, well away from Eleanor.

Poor Bernart. How he hated cold, damp England. How he pleaded to come back to her. But what could she do? She was pregnant and by then she was Queen, and there were other demands for her consideration. Her troubadour was lost to her.

For that, too, I can blame Henry, Eleanor thought bitterly. Bernart de Ventadour had greatly enjoyed and approved the courts of love. She would sponsor a court of love now, for amusement. It was time to renew herself with her first love, the one that never betrayed her, the love of poetry and music.

And she would invite her old friend, Bernart.

There was a quick flutter of pleasure in her chest. Yes. This very afternoon she would send a message, inviting him to her court. It would please her greatly to see him once again.

And it would infuriate Henry. A second flutter of pleasure was made stronger by a hint of fear. To invite Bernart while at war with Henry . . . That was dangerous. She could imagine how red-faced and temporarily speechless Henry would be when he heard of it. And perhaps Rosamonde would be there, at his side, when he heard.

Yes. Most definitely, she would invite Bernart.

Lucie and Sophia watched the Queen warily: Lucie because she didn't know what a court of love was, Sophia because she did. It meant hours of sometimes good, sometimes abominable poetry; days of ritual and formality; noise, confusion and living in a world where everyone's emotions were taut to the point of breaking. Inevitably there would be at least one fight, one knight with a broken nose or worse. Sophia, who preferred a quieter life, sighed.

Eleanor, though, happy to be caught up in something other than war plans, paused to consider the men available for such a court. The contestants must be comely and full of courtesy, and there were few promising men in her war-emptied court. Chrétien, the clerk-poet, was cynical, Sir Foulkes was old, the pages were too young, and Maingot . . . Maingot was a wolf in sheep's clothing. That left the new troubadour, Godfrey, and young Sir Benoit.

"The question shall be put to Godfrey and Sir Benoit," Eleanor decided.

"Then who will be the Queen, and what is the question?" Sophia asked; every court of love must have a Queen of love and a question to be answered.

Eleanor considered. "Lucie shall be Queen. Yes, yes, Lucie." She drummed her fingertips on the side of her chair, not in impatience but in eagerness. Lucie, tall and fair and young as spring itself, was as Eleanor herself had once been. "And the question is this: Once love has died, can it be rekindled?"

Sophia blinked. Still Eleanor thought of Henry. Did she hope to win him back to her arms after toppling him from the throne? Yet it was a worthwhile question. To answer it would take hours of tensons and poems, quotes and references. It was a suitable question.

Lucie frowned. What did it mean, to be Queen of a court of

230

love? She remembered her first task in the court of love, the ordeal by water, and hoped this one would be less dangerous.

Godfrey was amending his neglected sketch of St. Agatha when the news of the court was carried to him by a tow-haired page. The virgin martyr now smiled, and in her smile could be seen all the haughty splendor of the Countess of Champagne.

"You're to go to Lady Sophia. She will explain it to you," the page said, turning on his heel to next find Sir Benoit.

A court of love? With Lucie as Queen, and a foolish question of rekindling dead love? At first he was dismayed. And then, elated. This would be his proving ground. If his words were sweet enough, his voice true, his arguments convincing, perhaps he could win Marie's favor and patronage.

He had kept his vow to Chrétien, learning all he could of courtesy by scouring the few manuscripts in the scriptorium devoted to love, by watching Marie and learning to read the subtle clues of her eyes, by listening avidly to Chrétien. The older poet was a cynic, not a lover, yet he had a good mind for scholarship and could recite without stumbling or need of prompting all thirty-two rules of courtly love.

Godfrey could not, but he knew their essence. Service, prowess, moderation, long expectation, chastity, secrecy and pity . . . Those were the qualities a Queen of love looked for in her knight. He must be willing to admire her above all others, yet do what is expected to keep his love secret; to serve her faithfully day and night; to die for her, if called upon, without even asking why. Worse than death, Godfrey thought, he must be chaste until the Lady indicates, with no persuasion on his part, that she is willing. She was allowed to be whimsical, showing friendship one day and scorn the next; he was to be constant as the North Star, never veering from his only goal, which was to win her approval. He was to treat her as a Madonna, not Eve.

The wooing was marked by severely ritualized stages, wherein the lover was allowed to sit next to the beloved only in secret, and then, when his discretion was assured, in public. If she permitted, he could kiss her glove, then her hand with the glove removed. He could give gifts: rings, girdles, gloves, but they must in no way compromise the lady. He could sing love songs, but never use her name.

This kind of love required more patience than Godfrey had. Did Marie truly expect him to wait the required seven years before receiving the gift of her love?

Yet he had already learned that the more distant, the more unattainable the goal, the more desirable it often becomes. A mere glance from Marie could make him happy for hours. It was as if his very senses were being purified and heightened in the fire of restraint.

Once again he hastily finished the sketch of Agatha, thrust it under Chabert's nose, and was off. Four days till the court of love; four days to compose his arguments and songs. He must do well in this.

Sir Benoit was seated in the Queen's rose garden when the same panting, tow-haired page brought him news of the contest. The young knight would have fallen to his knees to thank heaven, had it not been for the splints that still bound his leg. He still was sore at heart that his beloved had been rescued from the ordeal by water by one other than himself, and by Sir Foulkes' killing of the boar he had meant for her. He was filled with shame and failure. Now, he thought, can I prove my love and win my lady.

He was to argue that a finished love could never be rekindled, while Godfrey took the opposite viewpoint. His arguments would prove to Lucie once and for all that the saints had destined her for him, and no one else. She would be his.

It occurred to him that the fair Lucie could have been his in every way weeks ago, but he pushed the unworthy thought aside.

The next few days were ominously serene. Benoit and Godfrey had hied themselves off to secret nooks to compose their lyrics and practice their instruments. Lucie and Marie were totally forgotten by their lovers, who were so eager to prove themselves publicly, they abandoned their private wooing.

Even the war seemed to abate. No messengers arrived with news, good or bad, and for hours at a time Eleanor was able to forget the rending that had divided her family, and the battles that stormed too close to her lands. Henry's silence no longer puzzled her. He was old and beaten. What message could he have sent? The first stirrings of pity turned to thoughts of mercy. When Hal was safely on the throne—with his brother Richard at his side to share the power—she would do what she could to restore Henry's peace of mind. He would be her captive, but she would not be heartless. She would give him what consolation she could.

In time, he would forget Rosamonde. And if he did not, he would learn to hide the remembrance of her.

Eleanor's headaches were at an end. She hummed as she folded away her maps and returned to their brass coffer the small soldiers that had marked her victories and Henry's defeats. She awaited only one last final message to arrive: that announcing Henry's absolute surrender.

Sophia fared not as well. It was as if Sirius, the Dogstar that brought summer's humid heat, had seeped into her head and skin, making her limpid and fretful. She was filled with restlessness and yet could find no activities that kept her attention. She was tired, yet could not sleep. She was hungry, but no food pleased her.

She studied Sir Foulkes with a frowning avidity that puzzled him. Often, he would find her placid brown eyes on him, studying him as if he were a strange herb she couldn't identify. Such intense scrutiny made him nervous and irritable. He didn't know that her eyes and, by now, a good deal of her heart searched for missing signs that he might yet grow well and strong.

She would turn away and grow philosophical. We are all dying, she told herself. Some are closer to it than others. The ailment in his guts may not take him for many years; I may die of the side-rupture tomorrow. Or maybe of a bad fish that poisons me, or of a little sliver that carries the lockjaw. Then, only partially consoled, she would study her tables and charts as intently as Eleanor had studied her maps.

She could make no sense of them. She, who had been known to predict quarrels between people who hadn't yet even met, who could tell from the stars when a village should prepare for famine or enjoy feast, and when a troublesome boy-child was most liable to break his arm, could no longer read the stars.

The stars were contradicting each other. In the midnight sky Mars could be seen glowing red near the western border of Capricornus, an event that augured well for Eleanor's battles with Henry. Yet the moon and Saturn were in disharmonious positions, signifying difficult times ahead for the Queen.

It worried her, this contradiction. After consulting her ephemeris many times and redoing calculations and observations, she came to the same nonanswer. Mars was victorious, yet Eleanor and her court were entering perilous times.

Frustrated, she leaned out her casement to study the Serpent, where it curved southeastward under the Northern Crown. The bright star Ras Alhague, the "head of the Serpent holder," glowed beyond it. The ancients believed this star represented Aesculpius, a physician so great that when he died, the gods placed him in the firmament. It was said of him that he could bring the dead back to life.

She envied Ras Alhague his wisdom and skill. She who had devoted her life to the search for wisdom found it as far from her reach as the stars themselves. Might as well try to grasp a star in the palm as try to contain knowledge in an addled head like mine, she reprimanded herself. How disappointed with her Sister Alicia would be.

"You are jealous of the maid, Lucie," Sir Foulkes told her with rare insight. "That she is to be fought over like a meaty bone between two curs." He chuckled with mean glee and raised his eyebrows at her.

"I am not. To be jealous of such a ridiculous thing, Queen of a court of love."

234

"It is a ridiculous thing," he agreed. "But you are jealous all the same." The chessboard was between them. He pretended to study his Queen, avoiding Sophia's eyes. "But tell me. Which of them would you choose for yourself, Lady Sophia?" There was an edge to his voice she had not heard before. He was teasing her. The pain hadn't been there to rouse him awake this morning and he was in a good humor. Good for Sir Foulkes, at least.

"Which? You mean which of Sir Benoit or Godfrey?" She was surprised by the question. "I have given the matter no thought." Her voice was waspish.

But she wondered what it would feel like to have Sir Benoit fetching her fragrant fruits and special dishes from the kitchen, and to have Godfrey singing under her open casement when the moon came out. Not that the two had exactly forgotten her existence. On the contrary, they came to her with annoying frequency, asking her opinion of the tensons and arguments they were preparing for the court. They came to her to learn how to win other women's love. She was not as other women.

They begged her wisdom and discernment; she, on the other hand, plied them with questions she had not yet answered. How did desire for a person differ from a preference for roast lamb over oxtail?

Godfrey, pale and glassy-eyed with fatigue, for he burnt midnight oil every night at his thoughtful chores, bit his lip. "Desire," he told Sophia, "feels like the summer sun shining on the back of your neck. But it is the beloved that gives the warmth. Desire is color. When she is near, the world is flooded with color. When she leaves, the world turns grey and filled with shadow." Lucie's bright face crossed his inner vision.

"Desire, then, is heat and light," Sophia repeated.

"Yes. The same thing that makes twigs grow in the spring makes men to grow, too," laughed Godfrey.

Sir Benoit, when quizzed, blushed and looked at the ground. "To love is to care for the lady above all other things and all other people, to spend your life in service to her, to value her good name and chastity." Desire, he said, fed the flame of love. But to accomplish desire was to kill the flame.

Sophia did not envy Lucie her choice. Both men were comely and strong, if still sometimes clumsy in the fullness of their youth. Both had received some education and could use a quill as well as a lance. But Godfrey, who had great charm, could also be coarse and selfish. Benoit, who was never coarse and buried his own self under a litany of courtesy laws, was lacking in imagination.

Sophia sighed, and was not amazed that the maid in question, Lucie, was looking wan, as if she wished it to be over already.

There was that matter of Godfrey and Marie. Did the youth really think Marie would take him as lover? Marie, like Eleanor, differentiated between true desire and the courtly manifestation of it. This was a ruse, a game, a distraction for her. Godfrey had much to learn.

"Your mind wanders, Lady Sophia. Don't you want to play the game?" Sir Foulkes' voice was taunting.

"No. Not now." She rose to leave. When she passed by the stool where he sat, he reached out a hand and slapped her on the backside. There was affection in the gesture, but she knew only the insult of it. She slapped him on the face, hard as she could, and left a red palm mark under his startled eyes.

In the scriptorium she gnawed at already ragged fingernails, and planned to return to Paraclete as soon as this disastrous summer was over and the roads safe for travel. The court of love was no place for such as she. The convent had better suited her. That wasn't true, she knew, but there was no third choice and Poitiers had grown intolerable.

She feel asleep at the large, cluttered writing table, her head cradled in her thin arms and Boethius under her cheek. In the uncomfortable sleep, her crippled leg grew prickly and numb.

When she awoke the sun was gone and the moon was hidden by thick clouds that churned muddy brown against the dark blue sky. A storm was coming. She could feel the heavy, charged air as it plundered papers and tapestries in the chamber. In the distance, but coming closer every moment, a large rumbling rode the horizon like a frenzied herd of war-horses, coming to trample and destroy.

Sophia was afraid of thunder. The noise and confusion of its accompanying jagged lances of lightning reminded her of the siege of her father's castle, of the burning, and the puddles of blood, and the death of her mother.

She ran into the corridor and lit a lamp from a jumping-flamed wall torch. Her breath came in gasps. Her hands trembled, making the flickering flames of her lamp cast weird, live shadows against the stone walls. She must not be alone. At Paraclete, when still a child, she had clambered into Sister Anne-Marie's bed, along with five or so of the smaller children, and they had held hands and told each other stories to stave off the fear of the stormy nights. When she was grown, it was her bed the little ones had clambered to, and in comforting them, she had conquered her own fear.

Blind with fear, thinking only of the need to be with another person, she made her way to Sir Foulkes' chamber. She could pretend she was worried about his wound opening. Storms were perilous; they could cause rupture.

She swung the heavy wooden door to and saw that he was awake, sitting at his casement.

"Lady Sophia," he said, and there was surprise but not displeasure in his voice when he turned to her. He modestly pulled a sheet about his nakedness, and the gesture reassured her.

"The storm," she said. She was already calmer and stood, hesitating, in the doorway.

"The storm," he repeated with unaccustomed gentleness. "It will be here a good deal of the night, I think. Come in. We'll set up the chessboard." But he made no move to fetch the ivory and ebony pieces.

There was only one stool and he occupied it, so she sat on the bed. She was so small that her legs did not even reach the floor.

The wind grew chill. At least she thought it had; something was raising the goose pimples on her arms. She drew the coarse, grimy woolen coverlet about her shoulders and sat there, quaking.

She realized it was more than the storm that brought her to this man, at this moment. She wanted to be as other women, to know

237

what they know. She wanted to know the promise of the flesh, and that final intimacy between two very different bodies. She sat on his bed, visibly trembling when the thunder rattled the beams overhead, and looking at him out of the corners of her eyes.

Sir Foulkes saw how one of her feet hung lower than the other by the span of two fingers. It was such a small defect, when she was sitting like that. Yet it had tainted her whole life. He knew of knights missing arms, legs, eyes and other even more elemental parts, but they all had ladies. It was different with damsels, who were rendered worthless by even a small imperfection. Pity, a new feeling that reminded him of heartburn, rose in his chest.

"What happened?" he asked gently, looking at the misshapen leg and feeling an impulse to touch it. He remembered the afternoon slap, and held back.

"A fever. When I was a baby. It left the muscles in one leg weakened. For many years I could not walk at all. My sire believed me backwards, till he learned I could read his Latin breviary when I was but four."

A flash of lightning lit the room and made her jump.

"Why were you awake?" she asked a bit shrilly, trying to hide her fear.

"Because I wasn't asleep." He grinned. For what seemed a very long time only the rumbling across the heavenly bridle paths could be heard as the thunder horses stampeded overhead.

"You are afraid of the storm," Sir Foulkes said finally, the warrior in him recognizing the terror she choked down. He had seen storm-fear before. His own lady mother, he remembered, ran shrieking through the great hall when a storm came to the marshes, believing that the lightning was pursuing her. They had to soothe her with a strong, large draft of wine.

He handed Sophia his wineskin and indicated she was to drink. She took a small sip, but he tilted it closer to her mouth and pressed her to take several large mouthfuls.

He wasn't grinning anymore. There was purpose in his expression, which was almost stern.

Rising from the stool, the sheet still clutched around his middle, he put his free arm about her shoulders. He sat next to her, closely holding her, and pressed her sleek little head against his shoulder. Her smallness was pleasing.

Sophia breathed more steadily, relaxing as she leaned against him. He smelled of wine and horses. Fear and sadness were both gone, now. She trembled with curiosity. Never had she been held so. It was time, she knew, to learn of things not found in the scriptorium. It could well be her only time. Never would there be another night such as this, wild and terrible with storm, shared with a man who, unknown to her, had achieved the right, the need, to share an intimacy she herself now desired.

When he took her chin in his hand and turned her face to his, she did not try to turn away. The kiss was long. His lips were moist and surprisingly soft, like a very ripe fruit wet with its own juices.

She waited for repugnance, for the revolt of her untried senses, but it did not come. Instead, the curiosity became greater. A warmth grew in the pit of her stomach, small at first, like a fire banked for the night, and then greater and greater as each fueling kiss and caress fed it to greater strength.

With unusual tenderness, the grizzled old knight removed her overmantle, her bliaut and tunic. She felt like a child being undressed for a bath, but there was a glint in his eyes that made her shiver. They did not speak, but his fingers were coaxing and knowledgeable against her flesh.

Sir Foulkes was no stranger to deflowering virgins. But this night's work came as a surprise to him. The waspish Sophia was tamed and waiting softly on his bed. He felt flattered that she had come to him for this. His pride, which had been injured by the long and wearying illness, swelled, and so did his manhood. He chortled, rubbed his beard against her shoulder, and hugged her tightly.

Sophia was no beauty. But he couldn't deny that she was appealing. Her skin glowed ivory in the darkness, her loosened hair, brown and sleek as a woodland creature's, was soft as shadow. What had started as a gift of mercy to a lonely damsel was resulting in emotions he hadn't expected. Her dark eyes were large and luminous, her thin, pale arms clung to him with tenacity.

Thinking that she would yet pull away from him, he tentatively tickled the insides of her thighs. Her legs parted of their own free will, welcoming. He tossed aside the sheet and drew Sophia on top of him. The sudden impact of flesh on flesh made them both gasp.

She reached down and touched him where all of his energy, all of his need, seemed to have gathered. This piece of flesh was to be the instrument of her education and initiation into all that the philosophers could not explain. He moaned as she stroked the satiny skin. She kissed him, using her tongue as Ovid recommended, and he crushed her to him happily.

Exultant voices in her head yelled songs of thanksgiving as Sophia was made as other women.

7

It was hot and muggy. A relentless sun beat down on the tops of the tents, making the knights and foot soldiers inside them irritable and quick-tempered. Dust hung in the thick air, and insects filled the atmosphere with an ominous, irritating buzzing.

The first flush of victory had abated. Now, with victory behind them and a summer of battles to come still ahead of them, the men were silent and grim.

Richard, still wet and refreshed from a swim in the river, did not speak to the soldiers milling near the flap of the tent as he entered. Nor did lines of poetry spring into his thoughts, making them lighter and larger than life. It was too hot. The heat drove away all but those thoughts, those movements, that were needed to get through the day.

The air in the tent was suffocating and filled with a sickening, sweet smell. Richard resisted the urge to hold a cloth over his nostrils and forced his features into a smooth mask.

In the dim light, he saw Matthew, Count of Boulogne, lying on his cot.

"I would rise to greet you, but I am having some difficulty standing," Matthew said.

"So I have heard." Richard forced a lightness he did not feel into his voice.

Matthew was covered with furs, rugs and blankets. Yet he shivered. The knight was dying. He had been wounded by an arrow in the knee at Driencourt. Such wounds were common. But Matthew's refused to heal.

Richard went to the cot and lifted the layers of cloth covering Matthew's leg. He looked for the knee, but at first could not find it. Instead, he saw a huge, swollen mound of flesh where the knee should have been. The flesh was black. From that deadly crater it sent out red streaks that ran into Matthew's belly and chest. Gangrene. Soon it would reach the heart, and then Matthew of Boulogne would be no more.

"Hal's own physician will be here tonight. He'll set this to rights," Richard said.

"Better to send for a priest," Matthew said.

Two days later the still thick air was rent with the screams of Philip, Count of Flanders. Matthew had died in his arms, and Philip, his elder brother, was inconsolable. He wept openly, like a woman. He screamed and ranted, and cursed Louis and the Young King, who had started the rebellion that had killed his brother. Philip was without children; Matthew was to have been his heir. Now their bloodline would come to an end.

"It is God's punishment," he stormed at Richard. "God is punishing me by taking my brother, Matthew."

"Why would God punish a knight devout as yourself?" Richard was losing patience with the man's grief.

"For warring against my liege lord, Henry of England. This is a cursed war. I'll have no more to do with it. God has shown me the error of this. To rebel against Henry is as black a sin as rebelling against God Himself; that is what the death of Matthew has shown me. No more."

And Philip of Flanders tenderly wrapped his brother's stiff body in a fur rug, strapped it over the young knight's horse, and rode away. He took his knights with him, for if Philip abandoned the war, then they must, too. No promises, no entreaties, no threats, could force him to stay.

With Philip gone and that army considerably reduced, the immediate threat to Henry in Rouen collapsed.

Henry was now free to put his own plans into action.

The sun rose in red-gold splendor, casting strong shadows in the town of Poitiers even in early morn. The dragon wove in and out of those shadows, bumping over apple carts and pushing aside pasty vendors as it made its way through the town.

Lucie screamed with delight as the dragon approached, and hurriedly fetched a copper penny from her pocket in offering.

"Here, good dragon. Don't harm me, I beg you," she told the monster, laughing.

From underneath the painted cloth she heard the giggling of a dozen children. A small, grimy hand reached out from under the fabric and accepted her coin. With an ungainly dip, the head of the dragon curtseyed, then turned away in search of new victims.

"Harrumph," said Sophia, watching it weave and sway down the narrow road in the direction of Saint Pierre's Cathedral. "Their families should not let them go out a-begging."

"They're not begging. They're playing a game," Lucie protested, still laughing.

"There are better ways to honor St. Udele's feast day," Sophia insisted. She hadn't had enough sleep the night before—Sir Foulke was responsible for that—and was feeling irritable.

As St. Udele was famed for killing a dragon, Lucie thought the children's game was very suitable for her feast day. What she couldn't understand was how the Udele she knew could have anything in common with the saint for whom she'd been named. Oh, well. There were more pressing matters to ponder. The court of love, for one.

It was to be held in three short hours, and Lucie, nervous, had decided to amuse herself in town for the morning, rather than sit and wait. Her instinct was to run and hide, but she could not. Instead, she went to mass at Saint Pierre's. It was outside this

243

cathedral that she and Godfrey had been separated. She knelt and offered prayers that they might yet be reunited. Then, buoyed with hope, she dragged Sophia to Saint Hilaire's Church, to gawk at the pilgrims. The nave was so thick with them, their straw hats were brim to brim; Sophia and Lucie couldn't get through to admire the magnificent mosaics.

The streets were equally crowded, but not just with pilgrims and townspeople. Many villages to the north had been burned to the ground, and Poitiers was filled with the newly homeless. They had thin faces and empty eyes; strangely silent children dragged listlessly at their mother's skirts. They, too, held their hands out for coins, but did not laugh as had the children in the dragon. Lucie soon emptied her pocket of the pennies Sophia had given her, and was grateful that the war was far from Poitiers.

Too quickly, it was time to return to the castle. Time for the court of love. She must give judgement on Godfrey and Benoit, before Eleanor and Sophia and all of the court, choosing one over the other.

She must judge their poetry and courtesy, but she must also judge the past and the future, and their hearts, for the one she chose could then claim her. He would sit next to her at the feast and she would have to accept food from his hands, drink from his goblet. She wished Eleanor had chosen someone else for this playacting.

What she wanted was a cross between the two young men, some new Benoit-Godfrey animal, like the kind of larger milk cow farmers produced when they bred wild kine with German bulls. Or like a gilled Amphibia, which can walk on land and swim in water, as it chooses.

But why waste time on such thoughts? She sighed and began to neatly plait her hair, wishing the day were already done.

When the sun was past its zenith and the enervating heat of the day was lessening, the court of love assembled with much fuss and fanfare in Eleanor's great hall. The great horns were blown and fifty ladies, gathered from all corners of Poitou, entered with a great rustling of silk. Tittering and exclaiming in eager merriness, they took their places in a tapestry-draped gallery.

Next came Lucie, led in more solemn procession by Amaria. Lucie was pale and had a stricken look in her eyes. To keep her nerve, she pretended she was acting one of Godfrey's mimes—Cleopatra's forced appearance before Caesar. Sophia was on her right side, and the three had to walk quite slowly to keep pace with her. Sophia was as discomfited as Lucie; she hated spectacles . . . especially spectacles that required her participation.

After what seemed a very long time, they had traversed the length of the great hall. Then Sophia and Amaria took their places in the galleries, while Lucie walked alone up the seven steps to the high dais. She forced herself to look straight ahead, but she had the fugitive's fear of public display, and was trembling from head to foot.

Lastly, when all others were at their places, Eleanor and Marie of Champagne arrived. Eleanor's silver silk cast glints of light. Marie was all in white, and veiled.

She is very beautiful, Lucie thought in despair as she watched Marie.

She looks like a sheep being led to the slaughter, Sophia thought, looking at Lucie. She would have pitied her if she were not herself still reeling from the trial of her long walk down the galleries. Had her hobbled gait been very pronounced? Had Sir Foulkes watched? Watched, and then averted his eyes from the sight? She did not want to be ugly in his eyes. In that she wished to be as other women, too, finding favor in their lovers' eyes.

Unbidden, a passage of Plato flashed in her mind. *The soul traverses the whole heaven in divers forms appearing—when perfect and fully winged she soars upward, and orders the whole world.*

They had soared fully upward, she and Foulkes. The storm had come and gone, and many other long nights, too. She had learned what the body had to teach. It had been a pleasant education. And in learning the limits of the flesh, she had begun to suspect the limits of philosophy. They had soared upward. But they certainly hadn't ordered the whole world. What she had always suspected was proven true: passion was a much overesteemed condition.

And now, here they were, toppled to earth again. He wouldn't look at her, indeed made a point of sheepishly studying the rafters and wall hangings rather than the gathered assembly, as if he were the only person in the room. He had dressed in his best tunic, one worn so infrequently that it no longer fit properly. Where he had once been full and muscled, he was now thin, even gaunt. Sophia watched him, and felt great pity, and gratitude, and some anger, too.

Lucie, painfully aware of the many eyes turned her way, looked over to where Eleanor sat. The Queen smiled encouragingly, but so far Lucie preferred the ordeal by water to the court of love. Let it begin, she prayed. Let it begin, and then let it be quickly over. A restless stirring filled the galleries. Pages bustled about, filling silver goblets with cool lemon-water made pink with rose petal syrup, and musicians idly strummed lutes. The sound of rustling silks, soft murmuring and buzzing flies made Lucie feel lightheaded. And then, it was begun.

They approach. Sophia gestured towards the opposite end of the hall. From now on, Lucie must watch carefully for the signals from Sophia or she would make a mistake and ruin the court. She feared Eleanor's anger, Sophia's scorn, Benoit's disappointment, and Godfrey's disdain. She feared Sir Foulkes, her master, who eyed her in a strange manner.

Lucie peered into the far corner of the great hall and saw Godfrey and Benoit, both pale under their sunburnt complexions. She remembered the words of greeting that Sophia had made her memorize—the two youths weren't the only participants who had much preparation to make for the court—and the two approached. Lucie made much fuss of smoothing the pleats of her gown, not looking up until the folds were as straight and even as those in a master plowman's fields.

"Welcome, gentle friends," she finally spoke. Her voice quavered. And then she remembered how Godfrey had made her put pebbles in her mouth to strengthen her voice. They had tasted of mud and coldness. "Please approach. And solve for me this question, if you will. Once love has died, can it be rekindled?"

Relieved, she sat back. Her part, for the next two hours, was done. Now she had only to listen and look attentive.

The gallery of ladies and their attendants sighed with expectation. Their colorful veil-tipped headpieces wagged and tilted like a field of banners as they imparted opinions back and forth amongst themselves.

Godfrey allowed Sir Benoit to approach first, as any unknighted man must allow a dubbed one to do, by rule of courtesy. This gave Benoit a tremendous advantage in the contest. He would be the first speaker, the one to set the pace, the verse form, the rhythm that Godfrey must follow. The old bitter wound burnt in Godfrey's chest. It was the loss of his patrimony that gave Benoit the advantage on this important day.

A storm of flowers was strewn in Benoit's direction from the galleries. He was the favorite, because of his high birth and gentleness. Godfrey was the more handsome of the two, but his outspokenness had not won him many friends. Benoit knelt to Eleanor and then Lucie, to whom he made his dedication.

"Who can judge the beauty of a summer day?
My heart knows such perfection,
And it is only found in the fair face of my lady
Who sits on high. For her do I live,
For her will I strive."

Eleanor leaned forward. The youth spoke too softly. And his poem lacked originality. Could the young men of the day do no better than this? She was already disappointed, and bored.

Bernart de Ventadour had ignored her invitation. He had not come. The day seemed lackluster, the court of love a waste of time. Her poet no longer came to her call. She had planned this court as a distraction, but a hollow feeling in her stomach argued that this amusement had turned on her, betrayed her, as had everything else, and her mouth filled with a bitter taste.

247

Her headache returned, along with a numbing tingling in her hands and feet. She had dreamed of Henry last night, and now her thoughts were of the King, and they were not pleasant. For the first time, his silence, his persistent, stubborn silence, frightened her. His silence, and the fact that Richard had not sent a message for more than a week now. The quietness of her court now no longer spoke of serenity but of isolation . . . and vulnerability.

Henry was up to something, and she did not know what.

Benoit bowed to the gallery, where his poem was enthusiastically applauded. Lucie sat unmoving, and now Godfrey knelt to her. Fewer posies were thrown his way; he had made too evident his infatuation with Marie. Godfrey pulled a stub of something green from his pocket. He held it in one hand and continued pulling; as the court watched, it grew taller and taller and exploded into a handful of yellow silk flowers.

Lucie applauded with delight. She had seen the trick before, but never tired of it.

Eleanor accepted the silk roses with quiet, distracted dignity, but Marie gave him an icy frown.

"Sleight of hand is not suitable in a supplicant lover," she instructed him. Her voice was strong. All heard the reprimand. Godfrey turned red. He hesitated, then offered his dedication:

> To youth, gentleness, and generosity
> Do I offer this love's labor.
> Beauty is but a coffer that shelters all
> Tender fine things of womanhood
> And makes men to sing.

Eleanor forced a smile for Godfrey's quick-minded effort. Had it scanned properly? She had forgotten to tap out the measure; she must try to concentrate. Lucie thought Godfrey by far had the better voice, but she wished he had made more of her comeliness, as Benoit had. The gallery was pleased greatly, though, and offered loud applause. Benoit, slightly flushed, stepped forward to offer his second rhymed tenson of the debate.

She has wounded my heart
And her own. She whom I thought
Never to be parted from
Loves me not, nor never did.
For love that changes its mind
Never love has been.

He played the part of a wounded lover well, sighing and letting his voice give full vent to the imagined sorrow. Lucie avoided meeting his eyes.

Godfrey countered with cunning simplicity, when it was again his turn.

If I have displeased her, it is correct
That she turn away from me. But again
Will I win the love of my lady.
Love once given can never be returned.

He looked at Marie as he sang. Lucie leaned back in her flower-decked chair and tried to look undisturbed, but she more than half wished that Godfrey would choke on his own tongue. He should look at her, not the countess.

The afternoon wore on as Benoit and Godfrey argued in rhyme back and forth. Lucie found her thoughts wondering constantly and once even nodded in half-sleep. Sophia pinched her awake.

Sophia was not sleepy; she had been studying Sir Foulkes, who had been studying Lucie. He desired the girl, if Sophia was any judge of the different kinds of glints that appear in men's eyes. The way he looked at her, from under knitted brows where his brown eyes glowered like coal, made Sophia's stomach queasy.

Did she love him, or detest him? Perhaps a little of both. If he were thirsty, she would give him her last drop of water; if he insulted her in any way, she would be his enemy for life.

A realization dawned on her. This was what had led to war between Eleanor and Henry, this same binding between men and women that could be twisted into love or hate. That a creature such as this, a snoring, bass-voiced knave prone to temper tantrums and fits of sulk—and make no doubt about it, King Henry himself was no better—could so easily affect the matters of the world, through one woman's heart! Sophia enumerated Foulkes' many faults over and over again, and all the while her skin was remembering other things about him, and she was wanting to be in his arms again.

And there he sat, glowering at Lucie. And Lucie glowered at Godfrey, while Benoit made sheep's eyes at her, and Godfrey kept looking to Marie for approval he found a long time in coming. Eleanor, who had ordered this court of love, sat smiling stiffly, her thoughts turned inward to a man who was not amongst them, a man who had once loved her and no longer did. Ayyyyye, what a coil!

Sir Foulkes was completely unaware of the storm flooding Sophia's heart. He looked at Lucie because she was an easy focal point for his tired eyes. But he thought of Sophia. He was impressed by her generosity and bravery, knowing it had been no easy thing for a woman of her years to go to a man for the first time. She was a plucky damsel, for all her book learning and that waspish temper of hers.

I'm getting soft, the old warrior upbraided himself, letting a woman take up so much room in my head.

Women. For all their softness and sweet voices, they were a pain in the ass most of the time. He had more important things to consider. The war was one. And the twisting ache in his gut was another. One was going on without him. And the other refused to leave. The war promised to be successfully over any day now, and not once had he donned armor and joined a fray. Because of that stinking, fucking, twisting pain in the gut. No more. Sophia had cozened him, convincing him to stay in bed long past the time when a good warrior knew he should leave it.

He would leave it now. What was going to heal had long since healed. What was not healed would maybe never heal. And never was a long time to avoid battle. Tomorrow, before he missed the whole fracas, he would ride off and join his knights and soldiery. Whether Sophia willed it or not.

He looked at her from across the room. She met his gaze with her steady eyes. A moment of hesitation, a flicker of shared memory passing between them, and then came the smile that would haunt Sophia's memories. He smiled at her, did not grin or leer or glower, but smiled, openly and with affection. Tonight, he was thinking, I won't wait for her to come to me. I will go to her and save her pride.

The Queen's water clock, copied from a design she had first seen in Constantinople, dripped away the hours. Benoit and Godfrey fell into a sturdy pace, like racehorses, saving their voices, their sentiments, for the last, for the final judgement. Lucie daydreamed. The hall droned with lyre music and voices, and the gentle whispering of the ladies in the galleries, who alternately discussed love and the new cut of sleeves.

Eleanor, disappointed, stifled yawns and thought of the war. It was all but won. Soon the Young King would be on his throne, and Richard and Geoffrey would also gain the power and wealth that should have been theirs several years ago. But what of her, Eleanor? What of the Queen? Henry would be her captive, her prisoner, but this time it would be bolted doors that kept him by her side, not desire or any tender feeling. The victory had a sour taste to it.

But a victory is a victory, she reminded herself. With this victory achieved, she would pack Rosamonde permanently off to a convent, seal her in if it must be, so the harlot could spend the rest of her days repenting the harm she had done her. Rosamonde would grow thin and ugly on a diet of bread and water. And all those who said the Queen was old and no longer powerful could go to hell.

And one day, she was certain, her beloved Richard would sit on the throne, and she would show all of Christendom and the pagan East how powerful, how beloved, a Queen could be.

One last time she tried to pay attention again to the court. Strange, the poetry that had so enchanted her in her youth no longer had such power over her mind and heart. She was only mildly curious to see which one would receive the winner's ring from Lucie.

Godfrey did not have to be told that Eleanor's attention was

251

lagging. Her expression was frozen, her eyes distant. And Marie had not looked at him once; she paid great attention to Benoit, but when Godfrey sang, she busied herself in conversation with her women. She carries it too far, he thought. This secrecy. This coyness.

Chrétien was right. He had taken Godfrey aside the night before, and given him a final lesson in the rules of love. "Countess Marie wishes for a young and comely troubadour who will dedicate himself to her, and make her famous through song and poetry. She has no need for a bed partner," the older, worldly poet had explained.

"Then why does she look at me like that?" Godfrey had protested, confused.

"To inspire love, which inspires poetry. But Countess Marie is chaste. Perforce, she must be. Her husband is a jealous one and would lock her in a tower if she took to bedding her poets. And he would beat the poet within an inch of his life for dishonoring his name." Godfrey wondered if Chrétien spoke from personal experience, but respectfully did not put the question to him.

"Sing well and hope for her favor. But not her bed," Chrétien had warned him. And he had been right, if her behavior during the court of love spoke of her true feelings for him. She wanted admiration. Not sport.

Godfrey was disappointed. His vanity was wounded, for Marie had not found him irresistible. But he was also relieved. There was Lucie, also coyly avoiding his eyes, but she blushed bright red each time he approached. She was not indifferent.

His pride was battered, his throat sore, his repertoire exhausted. And he had discovered a truth about himself that required thought and reflection away from this crowd. He had come here for Lucie, and it was still Lucie he desired. More than ever. She looked beautiful and queenly, sitting on her dais. She looked distant and unattainable, and that distance between them was one he could abide no longer.

His songs and poems had argued that love once given could not be taken back, and he judged from a new lightness in his own heart that it was so. He had convinced himself, if no one else.

Love could be changed, transformed, but never completely ended. He felt a new protectiveness for Lucie. He had a responsibility to her; she had been given into his keeping.

Godfrey decided that his next verse would be his last. He had given it his best. Benoit, he admitted unwillingly, had acquitted himself well. He could have done what most knights did, hired a singer with a stronger, more melodic voice to present his songs, but he had courageously sung them himself. Now Benoit was pale and strained from the effort, and his voice faltered.

It was time to end this contest. More than anything, he wanted a full wineskin and the feel of Lucie's hand in his.

But what if she chose Benoit? He could not think about that. He bowed deeply to indicate he was finished. Benoit, obviously relieved, also bowed, and the two young men sat and accepted large goblets of cool wine and waited for the decision.

Lucie, aware that it would be unseemly to give too hasty a judgement, delayed the moment by pretending to consider. She waited and watched for Sophia's signal from the corner of her eye. The galleries were again filled with restless murmuring when the signal—hands turned palm up to the ceiling—came for her to rise and give the decision.

And what was she to say? There was Sir Benoit, ready to adore and love and protect. And there was Godfrey, who had taught her all she knew of love so far, except for the thirty-two rules of it, with which Benoit had confused her. Benoit's love was made of commands and words and all sorts of things that must not be done. Godfrey's love was as selfish as a child's, but it had the wind of freedom in it, and the smell of the meadow. Which was the more perfect love?

Lucie rose. Well, it must be said, and aloud, before all these people. She would give her judgement. And she prayed the rejected one would forgive her, but knew he would not.

A clarion blast announced the moment. Lucie waited for the final notes to fade away and then opened her mouth to speak.

But just as she would have named Godfrey, a new figure entered the hall and won the attention that should have been hers.

He was covered with the dirt of the road, and it was quickly

253

apparent that he had ridden for many long hours nonstop to reach the court. An arrow wound in his thigh bled profusely. As he stumbled towards Eleanor, he trailed droplets of red on the grey stone floor. He clutched his stomach in pain and had barely enough strength to give his message:

"Henry Fitz-Empress has entered the war with an army of mercenaries. The North is routed, madame. There is fierce fighting and great trouble. Henry has razed the castle of Breteuil and his army is moving south."

Eleanor sat still as a statue for a very long while. All eyes turned to her, and a deathly quiet had strangled the court of love into a gathering of fear.

"Henry has an army?" Eleanor repeated, shocked out of her lethargy.

Her voice was almost exultant. Here was the news she had been awaiting, here was the message from Henry. He would try to destroy her, as she had tried to destroy him.

Henry. It is you and I, again. As it should be. As it will be, till death do us part.

Lucie, not understanding the meaning of the message, or the danger it brought, closed her mouth on the judgement she no longer had to pronounce, and felt relief, rather than fear.

Sophia's mouth dropped open and then closed again around this news. She remembered the contradictions of the stars and her inability to read them of recent weeks. How blind she had been! She had seen victory. But not for Eleanor. Victory would go to the King. That was the knowledge that had been concealed, and was now revealed in the serpentine splatter of blood drops on the palace floor.

BOOK THREE

Eleanor: The Eagle's Lament

Autumn 1173

There is always someone to carry news, the bad faster than the good. The rumor came to Lancelot that his lady and beloved was dead. Never doubt his distress: everyone could see he was upset and grieved. Indeed, he was so sad, if you want to know, that he despised his own life and was on the point of killing himself; but first he made a lament. He knotted one end of his belt into a noose, and weeping said to himself, "Oh, Death! How you have entrapped me, making of my very health a sickness. I am sick, yet I feel no pain but the sorrow descending on my heart, and that pain is grievous, even mortal."

—Lancelot: The Knight of the Cart

Pembroke. Mandeville. Arundel.

Louis, King of France, recited the three names over and over, like a litany. His supper lay before him, untouched. Gauzy circles of fat grew cold and congealed on the mutton stew. His wine was untouched. Pembroke. Mandeville. Arundel. Those three had joined with Henry Fitz-Empress, and razed Breteuil. He added a fourth name to the litany. Leicester. Leicester had watched from the tower and seen the dust raised by Henry's army. Terrified, he had abandoned this strategic castle and fled. Like a raw boy who has never tasted battle.

Louis pushed the plate aside, repeated the names, and added a fifth. Philip. His son. It was not for his own glory that Louis had warred against Henry, but for Philip, who would inherit the kingdom. And its problems. Henry Fitz-Empress was a problem. He had dreams of empire that, if realized, would surround France with knights loyal to Henry and lands owned by Henry. France would suffocate under Henry's dreamed-of empire. It was to prevent that that Louis had gone to war.

And now Pembroke, Mandeville and Arundel had taken Breteuil for Henry, and Henry's army of mercenaries was on the march. Gall rose into Louis' throat. He hated Henry with a passion greater than he had ever felt for a woman. He rejoiced in this passion, for it would give him strength.

Rising from the trestle table his pages had set up under a large, sheltering oak tree, Louis looked at the vista before him. Verneuil, the walled city, lay before him in peaceful splendor. The war had moved south. And Louis would crush this city, knowing that in doing so he would crush Henry Fitz-Empress. Finally.

The sun had abandoned them. The huge, vaulted hall was cold and dusky with afternoon shadow. The members of her court of love huddled and shivered together like sparrows on a winter day. From Eleanor's throne, they seemed small and insignificant. Henry, even when absent, had been larger than life itself. It was, as usual, Henry she thought of.

Her strange exultation was passing; now she felt fear, and something else. She felt old.

She shivered and wished she had thought to bring her yellow silk mantle. How cold these stone chambers could be, not at all like the golden warm rooms of Constantinople and Antioch. How she had loved the fiery East, those many long years ago when she and Louis had gone on Crusade. She had even loved the grit-laden *Samiel*, the breeze the Arabs called "poison wind," because of the heat it brought. She had brought back silk tapestries and bronze urns and heathen paintings of sensual love for her castle in Poitiers, but she could not bring back the vivifying, comforting warmth of the East.

When all was said and done, one had what one had. No more, no less.

Something must be said. Something must be done. She rose to her feet.

Her people, those frightened winter sparrows, had broken up into disheveled groups of weeping women and stamping, protesting men. Eleanor stared at them, disappointed. How ugly an emotion fear was. It made highborn ladies seem commonplace; it made the bravest knights seem like pigeon-toed boys. They had gathered to celebrate love. Now they wailed at the prospect of death or dungeons. Their innocence appalled her. Hadn't they yet learned how closely allied were love and war?

Of the women, only Sophia and Lucie waited, composed and silent. Eleanor felt a sudden thrust of kinship with them. They were queenly in their bravery, those two. But how young they were. How young they all were, these smooth-skinned ladies with their high breasts and slender waists. No wonder they feared death, they who knew so little of life.

She must say something. She could not abandon them to their fears and despair. She was still the Queen, still Eleanor of Aquitaine. Henry could take much from her, but never that.

"See to the messenger, Lady Sophia," Eleanor ordered. He looked as if each breath would be his last; his face was as pale as his blood-soaked thigh was red.

Sophia, nodding, pushed three pages toward the messenger, using the same gestures she had once used to herd her father's geese, and instructed them to carry the man to the infirmary. Judging from the looks of him, there would not be much work there, she thought. He was already half-dead from loss of blood and his heart-bursting ride to carry the news to Poitiers. He would be made comfortable, and then probably buried. She would try dosing him with witch's-thimble, but the greyish blue color of his lips and fingers told her he was past benefiting from even that strongest of herbs.

He was too large for the young boys to carry. They half dragged, half supported him out of the hall and down the steps. A thin, wavering line of red marked the path they took. Amaria followed a few steps after, wiping at this omen of defeat with her veil. She thought of the valiant Richard, who must surely now be in danger, if he hadn't been before, and wept.

Eleanor lifted her hands, palms upward, in the familiar gesture of the Holy Virgin known as "Our Lady Protects and Preserves Us." It was the same gesture a mother uses with frightened children. Motherhood had taught her much of queenship; weren't the two roles often identical? That was why she had dedicated her life to furthering the cult of Mary, Queen of Heaven.

Henry had never been sympathetic to her Lady Chapels; he had merely tolerated them. And now he would come to defeat her.

"My friends. Don't fear. The King's army cannot march all the way to Aquitaine. You are safe." Her voice was strong and confident. But the words were the meaningless, soothing chatter a mother makes to comfort a child afraid of the dark.

Henry had made an army out of nothing. He had appeared out of nowhere. Henry, wily, unpredictable Henry, had done the impossible. His enemies had always rumored that he traveled by wing, like the devil himself. He moved fast as the wind, restless and unerring and unmindful of all in his path, listening not to his own aching bones or the discomfort of his retinue, who slept in the saddle and ate while standing.

When he moved, Henry moved so quickly that the wits of England and France had amended the Biblical proverb of the things that are too wonderful to know and discern: the way of an eagle in the air; the way of a serpent upon a rock; the way of a ship in the midst of the sea; the way of a man with a maid . . . and the way of King Henry on his journeyings.

Part of her, the part that did not fear death or even dishonor, was proud of this resourceful and wrathful husband of hers.

The ladies, who had been so gay, so bright, just moments before, stared pale and trembling at her and then, in small groups of twos and threes, left the court of love and returned to their dorter. The youngest of them, the small damsels of twelve and thirteen years, wept openly.

The older ones, grown damsels who had husbands and lovers on the battlefield, held back their tears, saving their strength for practical matters. They would have to send servants to see who lived and who had died, or been taken prisoner. Ransoms would have to be raised, arrangements made, for their men. The children comforted themselves with dolls, and some stuck thumbs into trembling mouths. The women sat with quill and parchment, deciding what properties could be sold or mortgaged, what mon-

eylenders would offer the lowest rate. The dorter was grim with
fear and misgivings.

In the great hall, Eleanor was alone. The candles burned
down, the musicians dispersed. Already-withered roses cast in
the aisle for the poets sent up a scent of decay. She sat for a very
long time. When she finally walked the length of the hall, her
steps were slow and heavy.

She went to her rooms and closed thick, dusty curtains against
those who would disturb her. I must have Amaria take these down
and air them, she thought, grimacing at the curtains. I must make
plans to leave Poitiers before Henry arrives. She let each thought
carry the same weight, refusing to panic. Plans must be made.
But first she must rest. She lay down on her silk-cushioned bed
and closed her eyes.

She had imagined she would feel despair; she did not. Her
thoughts were flooded with gold; the sun of Antioch was still em-
blazoned on her eyelids. She felt as if she were flying high above
the earth, searching, but there was no firm land in sight where
she might rest.

Lucie went from the hall to the open, flower-carpeted meadow
where Benoit had once picked still green apples to please her.
The castle was unbearable, the very walls seemed atremble with
fear. She needed sun on her face, the green grass under her feet.
If war was coming, then soon the sun would be obscured by
smoke, the grass brown with trampling and fire. She remembered
that much of war . . . that, and the hunger that soon followed, the
unloved and fatherless babes born in the spring to the village and
castle women who had been raped the summer before.

She had been a child then. She was one no longer. If Sir
Foulkes' fief were taken, and she still there, it would be her turn
to spend the winter swollen with what the women called battle
bastards. No shame came to the women, no more than shame
came to the apple orchard when evil winds felled premature fruit,
or to the kin in the field that dropped calves of unknown siring.

Sometimes the babes were even welcomed, if they were healthy and whole. It was bitter humor that soldiers and knights seeking to ruin a castle and its fields would leave behind fruit that, in years to come, would help rebuild them.

She was light-headed with fear, as she thought those things. And with a homesickness that made the fear that much greater. She longed to see her mother and even Black Oaks itself, the prison that even a month ago she had hoped never to see again. She longed for the wild cry of the marsh hawks overhead, the salty breeze that stung the eyelids, the yellow lady-slippers that grew in the spongy fields.

She had once thought of it as a prison. But now she thought that a prison did not consist of walls that shut you in, nor a lord that bids you come and go at his will. The soul itself can be a prison, if it is too long homeless.

A dream. The summer has been a strange, sometimes sweet dream, and now it is over, she thought. The playacting is done.

She knew what would happen if Henry's army took Godfrey. If they moved south and entered Poitiers, they would take the men. And those not rich enough to ransom themselves would be sold as slaves.

She once had seen a long line of slaves, roped together and pulled behind a knight's horse on the way to market. Godfrey could not take such treatment. He was proud. It would destroy him.

Lucie dropped to her knees, put her hands together and pointed them to heaven. Me, instead, she told God. If this is punishment for what I did, take me instead.

She had stolen herself from her rightful owner, removed herself from the only home and society in which she could claim an honest identity and purpose of being. And now, as punishment, she was no one and no thing. And Godfrey was in danger.

She steeled herself, and made the pact with God. When Sir Foulkes returns North, she told him, I will go with him. He may beat me and bind and make me walk behind his horse. But it will be my duty and there will be an end to this. I don't want freedom, if Godfrey is in danger.

The decision eased her heart. She lay back and looked at the sky, trying to enjoy the few moments of freedom still left to her. Foulkes would want to return North immediately, now that Henry was marching.

She thought of Broderick, whom she had not thought of for some time, and wondered if he was well. She thought of Udele and in her numbed thoughts asked Udele to forgive her. Slowly she picked from her hair the flowers that Amaria had twined in the braids. Sitting up again, she removed the gilt crown from her head and left it there, in the meadow.

She returned to the castle, and sought out Sophia.

"Let me be of service," she said. "I have had enough of playing the lady."

"There is nothing to be done," Sophia replied. Her hands still bore rusty smears from removing the arrowhead that had been lodged in the messenger. It had been deep, and left a ragged hole through which the lifeblood still flowed, even as he slept in his cot. "Yet. We must all sit and wait."

Sophia saw change in the maiden. The girl had a new quietness to her, a sad serenity, and the astrologer's analytical mind quickly determined this alchemy. The fickleness, the newly learned pride, was gone. Here was a grown woman, free of vanity and illusion, who bore all the marks of the truly loving woman that troubadours prized . . . the generosity, the forgiveness, the depth of feeling that showed that love had burned through all the trials and produced that most Christian and perfect of deeds—sacrifice.

"Then I will wait with you." Lucie sat next to Sophia. There was no summons from Eleanor to feast in the great hall that night.

Marie had sent for him. She who had given him neither glance nor smile for weeks had sent for him to come to her. Quickly. When he arrived, candles had been lit, sweetmeats and wine set out in silver plates and pitchers. Her handmaidens stirred outside in the hall, leaving them to shadowed privacy.

He had wanted to follow Lucie out of the hall, but could not ignore Marie's summons. Godfrey sat at her small, intricately carved table and waited, knowing he was not to speak first.

"You sang well today," she told him from behind her silk veil.

"My Lady is kind and generous," he answered in a formal tone.

Marie poured a goblet of wine for him, and indicated he might sit. The bench at which she nodded her chin was a low one; he would be looking up at her. Godfrey, who had learned that humility was one of the most pleasing qualities to women of the court of love, accepted the bench, and the wine. He hid his curiosity and kept his face blank. Marie spent some moments arranging her skirts and veil, opening the latter so that he might fully see her face. She watched him, intent and unsmiling.

"I would be pleased to hear you sing often."

"My Lady. I am at your command."

"Are you? Would you dedicate yourself to my service?"

Godfrey hesitated, as this ritual required. He pretended to give it thought, just as she pretended to make the offer spontaneously. He knew now this was a ritual, not an invitation to seduction. And what she offered was more than he had hoped to accomplish even months before, when he first made his clumsy way into Poitiers with false magic tricks. She was asking him to be her troubadour. She had entrusted her body to her husband, her soul to her chaplain, and now she would give her reputation into his keeping. He was to be her Lancelot, but he must not make the mistake that knight had made, which had brought dishonor to Guinevere and sorrow to the King.

"I would gladly serve you, and defend your honor with my life," he answered.

"Then I accept your service. You will, of course, follow the rules." There was a question in her voice. He was not of the court, and he was new to the thirty-two rules of love. She did not yet fully trust him. A knave would misinterpret her wishes and bring her dishonor. He would try to achieve possession of her body, not her heart.

"It will be said, in years to come, that never was a woman better loved or better served than was Marie of Champagne, by her troubadour, Godfrey," he promised.

"Kneel, then, friend, and make that vow before God and your lady." Godfrey knelt and repeated his vow. When he had finished, Marie took a small ring from off her own finger and placed it on one of his. "I accept you," she said.

She smiled for the first time, and the smile made her eyes glow with pleasure. She extended her hand. It was small and white and Godfrey kissed it with delicacy and gratitude. He felt a great tenderness for her, and pride that she had chosen him. This tenderness and pride had nothing to do with passion or possession in the carnal sense. Their love would be one of the spirit.

"You are already friendly with Chrétien, I understand," she said, relaxing now and leaning against the pillows of her couch. "That is good. He is a great poet, and will teach you much. He speaks highly of you."

"Then I am doubly blessed."

"Understand, my friend, that I have accepted you in haste. But these are unsettled times. Tomorrow is not to be counted on." A flicker crossed her face. She was thinking of the messenger, and of Henry's army.

Godfrey thought of them, too. His first impulse had been to take Lucie by the hand and flee the approaching danger. Now he could not. He must go where Marie went, and stay where Marie stayed.

"Are you frightened, my lady?" he asked.

"Fear is an unworthy emotion. But I grow cold at the thought of being taken by Henry's mercenaries. He would be merciless. I am his enemy twice over, being both daughter of Eleanor, and of Louis, who have warred against him."

"Nothing evil will happen to you while I still live," he spoke, even though he knew such a promise could not be enforced. Yet such things had to be said. They were like prayers which, though often unanswered, still lighten the heart.

She trembled, and he saw her fear was great even if she was too proud to voice it. He moved close to her and embraced her chastely, trying to still her trembling. She did not push him away. He pressed his lips to her forehead and, testing himself, tried to feel passion. There was none. There was only warmth, and a desire to protect.

He thought then that all the rules of love could be summed up as the reverse of Chabert's sins against Damietta: to make the loved one's suffering less, not greater; to put aside pride in order to give solace; and to protect the lady against evil, even the evil she is willing herself to commit.

"Lady, in truth, I love you dearly. Let me be your servant."

He held her a moment longer, then released her. She was composed again, no longer trembling. He saw the gentleness of his embrace had strengthened her and he thought he would burst with pride.

His heart was light with new knowledge and firmness of intent when he left. He would serve Marie chastely, bringing her great honor. But the very chasteness of that service gave him freedom to love Lucie. Marie would command him. But Lucie would have all that Marie did not want . . . and that was much.

Godfrey strode quickly through the courtyard, searching for Lucie. He hoped he would find her with Sophia. If she was with Benoit . . . if she was with Benoit, then he must separate them. The court of love was over and Lucie must be his, as she had been before.

Would Benoit be foolish enough to fight him? He thought not. Godfrey was a freeman, but Benoit was a knight, and a haughty one at that, who would not care to dirty his hands on a common man. He also suspected that Benoit had little taste for battle, either on the battlefield or in a bedchamber. No, Benoit would be no problem.

What if Benoit learned the truth of Lucie, that she was a runaway serf? Would he be so gentle, so wooing, then? He doubted it. In fact, he himself had scorned Lucie even as he loved her, thinking her less than himself. No more. He had learned humility and tenderness and the generosity and vulnerability of woman, and Lucie would benefit in the future from his lessons.

What a coil the girl had gotten herself into. She had help with that, his conscience told him. You brought her here, when she would have been content sleeping in the meadows, staying in the small, lackluster villages where love was a rowdy and satisfying Saturday night embrace, not an obsession.

Lucie must come to him now or there would be no chance for peace between them. And if she hesitates, he thought, if she hesitates, I will convince her. For Lucie he would use all the loving, cajoling words he had not used this night with Marie. Love, real love, the kind that uses the appetites of the body to bring two souls closer, gives license.

No light burned forth from the chamber she still shared with Sophia, although the coming night already chased away day and the castle rooms were in full darkness. Yet he felt she was there. Perhaps they were already hoarding candles, in case of siege?

He threw a handful of pebbles against the wall, and then loudly hummed the song that had been the old sign between them. A stirring, a murmuring of voices from within. Godfrey smoothed back his hair and pulled tight his hose, bagging with the exertions of the day, which had required much kneeling.

Lucie appeared at the window, her tawny hair giving off glints like starlight in the dark. His own Queen of love. She looked sad. Was it the coming war that made her so pensive, or something else? His heart, already light, grew lighter with hope that she missed him.

"Come out," he said. "We must talk." He held his hands out, palm up, the way lovers do to invite the beloved into their arms.

She hesitated a moment, and then turned to Sophia. They had been about to go to the infirmary to begin the routine of all women preparing for war—to tear bed linen into bandages, bandages, and more bandages.

"May I leave for a moment, Lady Sophia?" she asked.

"Lucie, you are no servant here, but a free woman. Do as you please." There was no emotion in Sophia's voice, but she smiled with satisfaction. Mayhaps something yet would turn out right, this day.

Lucie and Godfrey greeted each other stiffly, keeping a wary distance.

"There are things I must say to you," he said, hopping a little with excitement.

"Then I must listen. But not here."

"We will walk. Will you come with me to the meadow? No one has come this way but the messenger; it will be safe."

He took her hand, and they walked companionably together in the old way, matching stride for stride, and he admired again the length of her slender legs.

"Remember the day we came to Poitiers, when you did not wish to wear the boy's clothes, and I forced you?"

"How could I forget? It gave me a stay in the bishop's prison."

"For that, I am sorry, and for many things. Were they cruel? I spent sleepless nights worrying about you."

"It was merely uncomfortable. I had a small revenge, though, when I thought you had abandoned me. I named a rat after you, and railed against you to the rat for days."

"A worthy revenge, if not great enough. Lucie . . . I was afraid to come back. I was cowardly."

"I know."

"I failed you."

"I know."

"What I want to say is this: If you will come with me when we leave here, then I will never fail you again."

"Never is a long time, Godfrey." She kept her face turned away.

"I will not make you wear boy's clothes, or act in mimes, or do anything against your will. I will care for you and protect you, as your mother wished me to, when she gave you to me."

"I was not my mother's to give, Godfrey."

"No, you were not." She has changed, he thought. The childish way of following anyone who promised to show a path had disappeared. Gone, too, was much of her easy openness. She had not answered his question: Will you come with me?

He has changed, Lucie thought. He gives no commands, but asks gently.

They arrived at the meadow. A soft wind waved the tall grasses, and an owl made mournful calls.

"I love you, Lucie." Her face shone pale. He took it between his hands, enjoying the cool smoothness of her skin.

"What of Marie?"

"I have sworn myself into her service. As troubadour. Do you know what that means, Lucie? I will bring her fame and honor. But not love, not love as we know it."

"I am happy for you. You achieved all that you wanted." Her voice was distant. She pulled away from him. His empty hands retained the lovely feel of her skin even after she had turned away from him.

"Not all, Lucie. What of Benoit?"

She sighed and then, finally, turned back to him and threw herself into his open arms.

"I tried to love Benoit. But he is not you."

He turned in a circle, holding her, letting the meaning of her words settle in slowly and happily. Then he fell into the grass and pulled her down to him. She returned his kisses with all the passion Marie had not shown.

He held back, letting her shower kisses on his face and neck, waiting for the kiss to grow just a little desperate and urgent. Rule number six. Thou shalt not exceed the desires of the beloved, but let her guide you into passion. He had had enough of forcing damsels, of using their innate generosity to quell his own needs. By restraining himself, he learned that the fires burn fiercer when they are first fed with a little hesitancy. And his hesitation was bringing out a fiercer fire in Lucie.

He wanted to please her, to melt her with his love, to win her once and for all. He went on his knee to her, and took her hand in his.

"My Lady," he said, gallantly covering the small hand with kisses.

"Ah, my good knight," she whispered. "Are you using on me the lessons you learned from Marie?"

269

He laughed at her quick insight. "No, I learned more from old Chabert, the Lady Chapel builder, who burned my ears with his holy complaints of my wantonness. Don't you wish me to be your sworn knight?" The knowledge that he would never be knight, that his patrimony was lost for all time, rose to the surface of his thoughts, but there was no more bitterness, there was only desire for this golden damsel who had once been his and might be his again.

"I would have you be Godfrey, just as I desire to be only Lucie," she answered softly.

"Then listen, and listen well. You are all I desire in this world. I pledge to love you and serve you all my life."

"You have used those words to Lady Marie, I'm sure."

"Just as Benoit has spoken them to you. But there is a difference, Lucie. Don't you see there is a difference? There are those who love only love, it is a word among many, it is their grail, their quest, and their quest never ends. And there are those who see love looking at them from one maid's eyes, and know the journey ends there, with that maiden."

"And with that man. I know the difference, Godfrey. And now, if you would please stop talking and get off your knees, we have other matters to attend to this night. I will wait no longer."

She did not wait, but herself pulled the bliaut and tunic over her head, revealing to the soft, moonlit night skin white and soft as a Queen's. He held back from her for a long moment, thinking that he had never seen anything as perfect as this woman before him. Her eyes were filled with the perfect patience and sadness of Chabert's Madonna in the still-unfinished Lady Chapel.

The loving was slow and long. He made sure she was with him every step of this path they took to delight. He would not lose her again, even for a moment.

Benoit knelt in the chapel. He had lit a dozen candles to the Virgin Mary in thanksgiving. The decision had been interrupted, but he had won the contest, and its Queen. Surely he had won.

Who could choose Godfrey over him? A common, landless man over a knight? Never. She had not said so, but so must it be.

He had a pang of regret. The goal, he feared, would not be as glorious as the quest. But she was his, he had won her, and the rules of love themselves decreed the next step. Praise the Virgin, that Lucie herself was so virginal. Else . . . and this he could not admit, but only feel within himself as a lurking suspicion . . . else he would be frightened. But she was as spotless, as inexperienced, as worthy, as he. He would use her gently, doing only that which is required to seal the bond between them. Her great love for him would be frosted with a sweet layer of gratitude.

Of the war, he tried not to think. He had been eager, even desperate, to ride off to honor and victory. But now that donning armor meant perhaps defeat or even death, he was not so eager.

And where was Lucie? He had meant to comfort her. Surely the damsel must be quaking with terror, but she had disappeared. She seemed to have a habit of disporting alone in the wild woods and meadows.

I'll have to put a stop to that, Benoit thought. My Lady must understand that it is not safe to wander alone. It will harm her reputation. And he waited.

"You have not answered my question," Godfrey said, helping her adjust her clothing and hair. She was as graceful as Marie, more so, and his heart exulted in the graceful arcs her pale arms made as she plaited the long, brown locks that had recently lain in wanton disarray over his chest.

"Will you come with me, when it is time for us to leave?" he repeated. She must say it aloud; no more would he take for granted the gift of her love.

Her arms dropped and she looked away. He swallowed and felt a tenseness in his stomach. Did she still doubt him?

"I cannot," she said in a low, sorrowful voice.

"You cannot? Why? Does what has happened between us mean nothing?"

"It means everything. But listen, Godfrey. I can no longer be what I am not. Not a minstrel, not a lady, not a Queen." She looked away, to hide her face. "I love you, and will never love another as I love you. But I cannot give myself to you . . . except in this way. I still belong to Sir Foulkes, to Black Oaks, and I will not hide away from what God himself has made me. And," she added, "I worry about my mother. She may be in need of me."

"Your mother has lived her life. And you cannot, must not, go back with Foulkes. I forbid it."

She looked at him pityingly.

"I must have a place where I belong. And that place is Black Oaks," she said.

"Your place is with me," Godfrey insisted.

"No. Our love began with sin, so it could never bring us happiness or peace."

"I don't want peace and happiness. I want you," Godfrey argued.

"And how long before you tire of me, again? I am nothing, Godfrey."

"I regret the day I brought you here, Lucie. You have grown philosophical and developed a conscience. I liked you better without one."

But she would not laugh, no matter how he teased her.

They walked back to the castle in silence. Lucie thought her heart would break, but she had made her bargain, and God was already keeping His end of it. Godfrey would be safe with Countess Marie, he would prosper. And she would keep her bargain in exchange.

He had failed her. She had sent for him, and he had failed her.

Bernart de Ventadour groaned in anguish, both because he had failed the lady he had promised never to fail, and because each bouncing footfall of his plodding donkey shot pains up and down his spine.

The abbot of Dalton had warned him that he would overdo it, that he was no longer a young man and should practice moderation in his labor. But Bernart found true pleasure in tending the monastery's herb garden. And that new stone wall should have been completed weeks ago. At the end of a long day of labor the largest stone still waited to be moved. Bernart lifted it alone and found, after he set it in place, he could no longer straighten his back.

For the price of a stone wall, he had failed Eleanor.

The infirmarer had massaged him and bound him and soothed him with poppy tea, but, he warned, a week in bed, at the least, was needed to prevent permanent injury. Bernart, stiff with pain, had obeyed not his Queen but his infirmarer.

The court of love must be over by several days, Bernart reckoned. But perhaps his Queen would yet be glad to see him. Grimacing because any strenuous movement of the arms caused more pain, he signaled to his menservants, following behind on foot, to sprint in faster fashion, and urged his donkey to a quicker pace over the dusty road to Poitiers.

He hated donkeys. They were stubborn, ungainly animals, but the monastery could afford no richer mount for him. The horses were needed to cart in the harvest. Christ himself rode on a donkey, he told himself. But this reprimand to his pride did not erase his longing for a fine, high-spirited destrier with which to make his entrance.

Donkeys reminded him of his early years, at the court of the viscount of Ventadour. He, bastard son of the lord, had been given a donkey to ride, while the legitimate heirs preened on expensive stallions. And it was expected that he would be grateful for the donkey, for many bastards rode never at all, but walked barefoot through life.

It is just, he told himself. I began on a donkey, and will end on a donkey.

But in between those years . . . yes, in between, he had ridden some of the finest horses in France and Poitou. Had called them his own, and adorned them in silks and jewels only slightly less resplendent than those on his own person. The viscount's bastard had done well for himself as a poet and troubadour, winning praises and purses from the highest lords and ladies of the land.

Then he grew too bold with his serenas and aubades for Margarida, his lord's new and comely wife. Bernart called her Bel Vezer, Beautiful to Behold, and let it be known that Bel Vezer and Bernart, her troubadour, were sick with love for each other. Young men often make such mistakes, letting pride overwhelm caution and modesty. Poor Margarida was imprisoned in a tower and he, Bernart, sent packing.

Wiser from that experience, he was a more accomplished, and more cautious, troubadour when he first landed in Eleanor's court. He and Eleanor were the same age. They both had been past the first flush of youth . . . but blessed with knowledge of the

274

world that youth often lacks. And the sincerity that youth often lacks.

While his love for Bel Vezer had been only a motive for his love songs, his love for Eleanor had been sincere. And while Bel Vezer had fallen in love with him and opened her bedroom door to him, Eleanor remained aloof, though he knew she loved him, too. That, the older and now even wiser Bernart reflected, grimacing, probably had much to do with his passion for Eleanor. Love, once consummated, too often ceases to be love.

Those had been the years in which Eleanor, who married Henry for love as much as ambition, was preoccupied with the queenly duties of begetting and being delivered of Henry's heirs to the throne. She loved Bernart's music and fine sentiments. But it was Henry who ruled her body.

No one knew better than Bernart of her fidelity to the English King. He had paid the price of that fidelity, the years of wanting and not having.

And now, fifteen years later, she and Henry were at war. And she had sent for him.

Nothing was as it had been the day before, the day they met to discuss love and departed thinking of war. The schoolrooms were closed and Amaria told the children and older ladies and pages they must amuse themselves. There would be no lessons in dancing or rhyming that day. Nor perhaps for many days to come.

The littlest girls played at skipping stones over the small pond in the Queen's pleasance, and whispered in low voices. The older girls sat upright on stone benches, needlepoint poised precariously in their laps.

It would be a pleasant scene to behold, could I not see their eyes, Eleanor thought, watching them from her casement over the garden. They look like rabbits already in the trapper's bag. They irritated her.

"The demoiselles should be sent home to their families," she said to Marie, who sat with her.

275

"What of you, Lady Mother?" Marie looked up expectantly from her tapestry.

"I will make my plans. But I cannot speak for their safety. Nor yours. You should leave Poitiers."

"Not unless you also leave. I will not abandon you." Marie knelt and put her head in her mother's lap.

"You have been my comfort," Eleanor whispered. She kissed her daughter's forehead. But she felt strangely uncomforted. "Leave me, now. I must think."

Alone, Eleanor paced the length of the chamber several times over. She must make decisions. But she could not. She had wanted to question the messenger further, but he had died in the night. His heart had given out, Sophia said. All she could do now was wait for more messengers, more news. Oh, the gall of being a woman who must always wait, wait, wait. Surely pain during childbirth was the lesser evil that women endured; it was this useless waiting that was their hardest penance for original sin.

"Amaria! Amaria! I'm suffocating in here. Ready my things. I will hunt."

It was better, more bearable, in the green and fragrant woods, with the horse moving beneath her and starlings chattering above and the great hooded eagle perched on her shoulder. Occasionally the eagle, Miribile, would make her high-pitched cry and Eleanor would answer back, humming the song that she had used to teach the bird to come to her shoulder.

Eleanor trained her own hunting hawks, and she would hunt with nothing less than an eagle, the emperor of birds. Very few lords, much less ladies, hunted with such hawks. They were cumbersome and heavy. Mirabile weighed eleven pounds and perched as heavily on her shoulder as a stone. To fly her, Eleanor must lure the bird down the length of her arm and then use her free hand to support the fist from which Miribile would take wing.

Eagles were also the most difficult of birds to train, being temperamental, unpredictable and fiercely independent. And they were dangerous. Through the specially made leather vest she wore, Eleanor felt the menacing, lethal talons that could crush a fox's skull in the blink of an eye, and had been known to blind falconers in a whim of anger or frustration. Even Henry chose the more amenable goshawk over the eagle. The sense of leashed danger thrilled Eleanor, and she was fully aware of the awed looks her own men and the townspeople gave her when she rode by with Miribile on her shoulder.

Such regal, fierce birds were never truly trained, but a patient and skilled person could eventually convince the eagle to participate in a kind of partnership of man and bird. And once won over, they were the most superb of predators, killing with a cold and beautiful efficiency.

"My eagle, my own," Henry had once said to her, years ago. "Be flown by me, and see to what heights we will climb, together." With such sweet words had he wooed her when she had left Louis' cold, monkish bed and put aside the crown of France. She was the eagle then, the free and untamed thing that could bring crowning joy by returning to the fist, or supreme disappointment by rejecting it.

"To see to it that an eagle returns to the fist after the kill, if such is your desire, then train the bird with a lure of still-beating heart," the great Armenian book of falconry recommended. Henry had lured her with his own heart and she had taken the bait.

Miribile was growing restless. Eleanor winced as she felt the talons creep closer to her flesh through the thick leather vest. "To fly a hawk well, you must be light of heart," the book also said. Hawks and falcons were intelligent; a distressed or preoccupied falconer made them distressed and preoccupied, and an eagle in such a state was a great danger.

She began to hum again to quiet the great bird, for eagles love music, and tried to put Henry out of her thoughts.

The sweet-smelling forest reminded her that she must soon leave the Poitiers castle for sanitary and aesthetic reasons, if nothing else. No castle could be steadily inhabited for long months at a time without soon smelling like an overflowing cesspool, and she had stayed overlong in Poitiers.

But where to go? Straight north to Henry, to beg his clemency.

Or northeast, to Louis, for his protection. To her wrathful husband, the King of England, or her bitter first husband, the King of France? Those were the choices. Neither was a welcome one. Henry would imprison her and divorce her; Louis would patronize and reprimand her. Henry would roar and rage. Louis would sulk and chastise.

She longed for a third choice, but there was none. She was a woman, so to a man she must go. To the devil she would go. And what of her sons, should the war be lost?

The hunting party reached a large open glade and Eleanor was glad of it, for her shoulder ached with the weight of Miribile.

When I was young I could ride with an eagle on my shoulder all morning, she thought ruefully. Now, one hour's ride tires me. What a thief time is, to rob us of our very strength.

"There will be game here," she called to the men who rode with her. They were all of the castle, subordinates who would accompany her but make no demands on her mood, for she was not feeling generous or sociable. Unquestioning, they dismounted while her falconer set the hawk's perch and lure in the field.

The falconer, a reticent man with eyes turned red and watery from the darkness of the mews, set beside the perch a bag that contained a live rabbit . . . the still-beating heart that would be used as a bribe to win back Miribile from her free flight. The leather bag squirmed and gave off small squeals of distress.

Eleanor stayed on her horse and scanned the horizon for signs of movement. There was a time when Eleanor would see the quarry as soon as her bird. But now her eyes were growing dim. Age made her see only that which was close at hand. After a suitable time—a time in which her men would think she had taken her bearings, not that the distant forest was a blur of indistinct green—she extended her arm and stroked Miribile's bright plumage. The eagle, tense now with expectation, lurched down her arm to the waiting fist. Once there, Eleanor used her other hand to remove the leather and chased silver hood that covered the bird's eyes. She made certain the jesses were not tangled and undid the glinting swivel from the leash.

For one glorious moment Miribile sat contented on Eleanor's

fist, peering around, choosing between this strange companionship and the freedom of the sky. Then she grew tense and Eleanor knew she had spied her quarry. With both hands, one fist supporting the other, she raised up the eagle in an invitation to flight; with a flurry of golden brown wings and a great ringing of the gold bells that were tied to her jesses, Miribile rose and wheeled above them in free flight; Eleanor's heart rose with her, exulting. Ah, the freedom of the eagle in flight!

Soon the golden brown bird was a mere dark spot in the distant blue heavens. No bird flew as high as the eagle, nor had vision as sharp, nor plummeted as quickly, when she had sighted her prey. It was those qualities that made Miribile Empress of the skies. Vision, cunning, speed. And Henry, admiring and half-envious, had called her "The Eagle," for he knew his wife had those very qualities, and he could use them to further his own ambitions.

And my ambition, Eleanor admitted, watching the eagle. I wore the crown of France and England; who else can boast of that? I helped Henry win and keep his crown, and I gave him many sons to wear the crown after him. And now if he doesn't murder me outright, he will put me aside, because I am no longer young, nor necessary to him. But that is where he is wrong.

A vague stirring in the long grasses ahead indicated that the eagle had chosen her prey and was circling lower, ready to descend on it like the wrath of God. A red plumed tail straightened in a fearful, streaking flight through the green grasses. The fox had spied the eagle and was running into the forest, trying to lose itself in a tangle of roots and felled trees that would protect it from otherwise certain death.

But Miribile would not be cheated of her prize. The dark spot grew larger as the bird plummeted to earth, her wings stretched back behind her, talons already reaching. The fox quickened speed and was only an oak's length from the forest, and then no more than the length of a man; the fox was feeling the first sense of safety achieved, when the eagle struck.

Even at a distance Eleanor could hear the blow as the talons drove into the small skull, and then it was a fox no longer but only a small and bloodied thing that made Miribile preen with satisfaction.

With such ease Henry should have been taken, Eleanor thought. Her mind filled with anger . . . anger at Louis of France, and her own sons, Hal, Richard and Geoffrey, who had so botched things that Henry, a King half-vanquished even before the war began, should now be marching toward her own domains.

Still on her horse, Eleanor rode to where the great bird waited. Her men followed discreetly behind, running as quietly as possible, for they must follow their Queen, yet not frighten the bird.

Miribile looked up at her rebelliously. The kill is mine. What right have you to it? her dark eyes asked. Her talons were grasped round the fox's skull the way a King grasps a scepter.

Eleanor dismounted with forced slowness and grace. The eagle must not be startled or threatened, or she would take to the sky again, or bate at Eleanor, striking out with her huge and dangerous wings.

The kill was the easy part. Any unlearned savage can kill. But to leave the bounty behind, to choose loyalty over greed, that was the difficult test. For eagles, and men. This moment was the true test of her training, her months of work. Would Miribile return to the fist and give up the fox, simply because she, Eleanor, required it of her?

Sacrifice was called for now. Without a word Eleanor reached back to where the falconer stood. He, canny man that he was, had read her thoughts . . . no, not her thoughts, but the eagle's wishes . . . and had already slain the rabbit and drawn forth its beating heart. Eleanor took it in her gloved hand and attached it to the lure. Miribile watched all this with a skeptical and haughty look, her talons still fiercely imbedded in the fox's skull.

Eleanor, holding her breath, held out the lure. Miribile, after a moment's hesitation, abandoned the fox and flew to the lure and to her reward. Eleanor signaled to a page to fetch the fox; she would have it made into a lining for her green velvet sleeves.

"Well done! Well done!" her men called, stomping their feet and applauding.

She accepted their compliments, knowing all the while that

their admiration would not be half so strong were she a man, not a woman. A man is expected to be masterful and confident; were Henry to fly an eagle, they would only smile and say, "Of course." But women, even Queens, were expected to be mastered, not masterful. They should fly merlins, the smallest and easiest of the hawks.

Her men flattered her, but in their hearts they called her bold and arrogant.

And I am, she admitted. When I rode to Crusade with my ladies, we wore breeches and called ourselves Amazons. I rode my mare and would not hide myself in a curtained litter, as Louis wished. As the French wished. I will not make less of myself, nor be hidden away. I will not fly a lady's hawk to suit them. I will not let Henry put me aside to suit himself.

"Leave me awhile," she said, weary of them. "Hood Miribile and then fly the goshawks so that we may have game for tonight's table. Affairs are not so bad that we must serve Lenten meals to those who remain with me." They bowed away and Eleanor walked into the rustling forest, her tall figure quickly slipping into the dappled shadows.

"You stared at the maiden all the morning long," Sophia accused, trying to keep her voice light.

"She is comely. Why not? Or you think I should have eyes only for you, now that I have bedded you? You are not half so pleasing to the eyes." Sir Foulkes doubled over in pain and bit his lip to keep from groaning.

"The pain is back," said Sophia with some satisfaction, for his words had cut her to the quick. She moved to his side and helped him to sit on his cot, knowing that those were the very actions most likely to wound him.

"Begone! Begone! I'm not so old that I must be led on a woman's arm!" He pushed her away, but she would not go. She clung to his arm. The anger was already passing and something else stirred within her. He sensed it and no longer pushed at her, but pulled her close.

281

"Sophia," he said. "You must not be jealous of other women. They are not as you; you are not as they."

"I know that well," she said with rancor, but allowed him to press her head to his chest.

"You are so small. Fragile. Like a bird in the hand." He smoothed her hair. "But I will be honest with you. If I stared at the maiden, it was not her I was seeing. There were other matters in my thoughts."

"Other matters? Such as?"

He made a growl deep in his throat, and she knew that with him, that passed as mirth. "Maids and ladies. Love is all their concern and naught else. Even with you, Lady Sophia, once you are trapped in the lime like any other dove."

"I am not trapped. Certainly not by a lout like you," she protested, burying her head deeper into his surcoat.

"I thought of Eleanor, and this war of hers. It is a sorry affair. I didn't need that poor devil of a messenger to tell me things would go badly. Don't look at me so. I don't read the stars, like you, nor have portents in my dreams. My dreams are of a randy nature that would offend you, My Lady." He pinched her thin flank; she slapped his hand, but did not remove her head from his chest. "But I am an old soldier and have seen many things, and I saw that this war could not go well for Eleanor. Her sons are young and untried, and her main ally was the King of France, her ex-husband. What man will fight well for a woman who has scorned and mocked him?"

"You speak convincingly. I have never favored this war. But now what? Will you leave Poitiers?"

"I will. But to march with Eleanor's men."

At that, Sophia moved away from him, startled.

"And just as I thought you were wiser than I had first accounted, you prove me wrong. What point to fight a losing war?" she asked, dismayed.

"That is the point. I will not abandon her now because it is convenient. There is more glory to aid the distressed than to run, tail between my legs, to the victor."

"Glory. If women make fools of themselves for love, then men wear the dunce's cap for glory." She was angry. His face was still white and pinched from the pain, and he spoke of going willingly to a battle he would lose. He would die, on that battlefield.

"You must not," she said.

He turned away after a moment.

"You overreach yourself, Lady Sophia. It is not your place to say what I must or must not do. And you think me overly stupid, to think I cannot read the look in your eyes. There are moments when you look at me, and I think you are already seeing a dead man."

"You know the truth, then," she said. "It need not be so. If you would rest, not test your body so, nor require so much of it . . ." she began, but did not finish. He had turned back to look at her, and was smiling ruefully.

"You ask me to live death in my life. And you know I will not."

"Yes. I know."

She put her head back on his chest. They stood quietly together, at peace.

"How soon will you depart?"

"Soon."

"Stay a bit. I can make you stronger," she promised. "For a time."

"For a short time, my limed dove. Since you ask so sweetly, like any complaisant maid." He laughed aloud and lifted her up in his arms to show that he was already strong, still strong, but the pain lurked like a thief and stole the mirth from his laugh.

Soft moss pillowed her head. A chattering red squirrel jumped from branch to branch overhead, and green leaves filtered the late summer sun, giving the glade an otherworldly quality. Below, far below and in the distance, she could see the silver river circling Poitiers and the tall spires of the churches and the cathedral hovering over the red-roofed town like watchful mothers.

Behind her, hidden by a large cluster of white wildflowers, lay the even whiter bones of the boar that Benoit and Sir Foulkes had slain in the spring, picked clean by scavengers of the two- and four-footed kind both, a sharp testament to the power and futility of love. She was unaware of the boar, of her proximity to death. She looked before her, to the beloved city of Poitiers, and thought of nothing. Soon she fell into a light sleep, wearied by the weight of Miribile on her shoulder during the long ride, and by her many cares and worries.

In her sleep, music played. A piper blew his merry, floating notes and she recognized the tune. Her grandfather, William the Troubadour, had composed it. *All joys give ground before her, all arrogance is obedient by reason of her soft mien, by reason of her soft glance. He who has joy of her will last a hundred years at least.*

The light-hearted melody gave way to a sadder one. In her sleep, the world became a dolorous place, filled with complaints of the heart. *When I see the lark stir her wings for joy against the sunlight, forgetting herself, letting herself fall with the sweetness that comes into her heart, AIE! so great an envy comes on me to see her rejoicing I wonder that my heart does not melt with desiring.*

The music slipped in and out of her sleep, entangling itself in her memories, making her restless and sad with longing. It was a long time since a lover had sung his complaints to her; it was an even longer time since her Bernart, her sunray whom she called *Rai*, had composed his music for his Queen, Eleanor, whom he called *La Lauzeta*, the lark. The music suddenly ceased, and the silence of its absence proved the reality of its former presence.

Eleanor's eyes opened. This was no dream. She had clearly heard that music, those words. But how could it be? Rai had written that lovely, love-sick poem, and for her, and Rai had left her more decades ago than she wished to remember. Not left. He had been driven away, by Henry, who could not bear that his wife would look with favor on another man. And he had not come when she sent for him.

Last year's fallen leaves snapped and rustled behind her. Before she could sit up, or make a noise, two hands clapped over her mouth and eyes.

"Don't scream, *Lauzeta*, my beauteous lark. I mean you no

harm. Quite the opposite. I would solace you, if you find me worthy."

By the Virgin, it was Bernart, her Rai. She would know his voice anywhere. And he had called her by her *Senhal*. To all others she was the eagle: proud, imperious, dangerous. But to Rai, she had been the lark: sweet and filled with rejoicing and love.

The confining, secret-keeping hands, after a moment, released her. She sat up and looked over her shoulder.

It was truly Bernart, smiling at her, looking deep into her eyes, and the brightness of his eyes obscured the sun. She threw her arms around his neck and kissed him more times than he could count, like any glad maid. But then she drew back, as angry now as joyful she had been a moment before.

"Why did you not come soon as I sent for you?" she asked. The message had gone out weeks ago. She had not counted on delay, and it had wounded her.

"I could not," he said ruefully, taking her face between his hands and kissing her lips to silence them. Her mouth was cold. He sat next to her and would explain no further. He would not admit to his beloved that he was an old man who had spent a week on his cot because he had lifted a stone too large.

Eleanor now noticed his travel-stained mantle, which was nowhere near as rich or flattering as the clothes he had worn fifteen years before, and then peered more closely at the still bright face of her troubadour. There were thick lines about his eyes, and his hair, which once had been raven, was white. When last they met, he had been a man rich with years ahead of him. Now he was aged. And he was dressed like a lay brother, in weary browns and rough cloth, not the bright colors and silken garments of a troubadour.

"You frown, my Queen," Bernart whispered, taking her hand. "Am I so displeasing to look upon?" He was like a wild thing of the forest in that moment, ready to take flight, and her heart opened to him, as it had years before. With one great sigh she admitted the longing that had been buried in her breast these many long years.

She leaned into his arms again, resting her face against his shoulder, in the old manner that was familiar between them, and the years melted away. She had a strange sensation: She had thought that, once together again, it would seem as if they were moving backward in time, back to earlier years. But it was not like that. Instead, she felt as if they were truly young again but had full knowledge of what the future was to bring them . . . the sending away by Henry, the long separation, the many problems that beset lives. They wore their years like an outer layer of garments.

"No. Not displeasing," she whispered, pressing closer to him. "There is no face in the world I would rather see right now. And you have kept your litheness and brightness of eye. Indeed, if I hadn't known you in your youth, I would think the man before me to be the most fair I have known, just as you are now. But seeing the changes that time has wrought in you, it makes my heart tremble to think what you must see in me. Have I changed, Rai?" Her voice asked him to lie.

Bernart hugged her close and rocked her in his arms.

"What could I ever see in your face but all that is beautiful, all that is good and worthy? You are golden; time cannot tarnish you."

"And you are as big a flatterer as ever. But I thank you for it."

They rose and stood together. The day was waning and the ground felt cold and damp beneath them. Eleanor stumbled slightly as she got to her feet. She had forgotten: rising too quickly now sometimes made her dizzy. Bernart reached out to steady her. She pushed him away. "I don't yet need a nursemaid," she chastised.

"I don't yet mean to be one," he answered, stepping back. He watched as she straightened her veil and mantle. She, too, was still slender, but there was a stiffness that rendered her less graceful, and she frowned and squinted so that there were lines between her eyes. Her hands, which once had been white and with fingers slender as church tapers, had grown fleshy. All these changes he saw, and they grieved him. And yet at the same time they made him love her even more.

Seeing her now, like this, with her star in the descendant and her youth gone, he loved her even more than he had those years before, when she had been perfect and brittle with power and self-confidence. He looked away from her eyes, not wanting to reveal too much of this at once. Larks frighten easily; she would take to wing and evade him again, as she had before.

It was Henry who had ordered him away. But he would never have left, had not Eleanor given the same silent order with her eyes. She loved him, but she loved power more, and power rested in Henry's bed, not his.

"Tell me of yourself, and how you came here," she ordered, "even if you won't say why you were delayed. Those garments are not attractive. When last we met you were wealthy as a prince and as brightly dressed as a cardinal. Now you are dressed like a monk. You smell of ashes and repentance."

She gave him her hand that they might walk together as friends. He kissed each finger of her hand before answering.

"I wear these clothes and smell of ashes because I have spent the last years in the monastery of Dalton."

"So I had heard. The famous Bernart closeted himself in a monk's cell."

"The infamous Bernart. Has it ever occurred to you, Lauzeta, that we mortals always seek that which is most elusive? I think this is God's plan for keeping us humble and worthy of heaven. I sought love. Only that. My whole life was an arrow aimed at that one target. And yet, despite that direct flight, I missed the target. It eluded me, would not be felled by my longing." He stopped walking and, still holding Eleanor's hand, forced her to stand still and look up at him. "You eluded me."

Hawks and eagles dislike close scrutiny. When stared at, they bate their wings and try to fly away. So did Eleanor begin to fidget when confronted with the open gaze of her troubadour. She found a pebble in her shoe which must be released, and a small tear in her veil. She sighed and coughed and tried to turn away, till her Rai took her chin in his hand and made her look at him.

"I, too, had a goal," she whispered.

"Yes. To be Queen. You had already been Queen once; wasn't that enough?"

"No."

"After you allowed Henry to send me away . . ."

"I had nothing to do with that."

"After you allowed Henry to send me away, I used to pray that he would beat you and treat you in all ways like a common wench. Of course, much of my bitterness was due to the English climate itself. Henry exiled me in London. It is a cold city, well designed to dampen a young man's ardor. But it could not extinguish mine, Lauzeta. Instead, it gave me a frightening truth about myself."

He released her chin, but she did not look away.

"And the truth?" she asked.

"That my love songs were not just songs good for passing an evening or winning a reluctant maiden. They were the truth. I loved you, Eleanor. My God. Can you think of anything more frightening to a man than to discover all his words of love are sincere?"

"But a monastery, Rai? Having loved once, couldn't you love again?"

"I could, in fact. If the Queen of England closed her heart to me, then I would spend the rest of my life asking love of the Queen of Heaven. On your knees, Eleanor. That is the best place to learn of love."

"And vengeance. Henry will see me on my knees if he has his way."

Bernart smiled, but bitterness pulled down the corners of his mouth. So had it always been. He spoke of his love for her, and she spoke of Henry. They walked in silence for some moments, and the years that had divided them disappeared like morning mist being burned away by the noon sun.

"That is why I have come," he said, knowing she still thought of Henry, and his wrath. "You are in danger, my Lauzeta, and I vowed once to serve you always."

They had reached the clearing, where Eleanor's men were impatiently stomping their feet and muttering at the lengthy delay.

The game bags were filled and the goshawks hooded again. Miribile waited, regal and silent, on her perch. Bernart's two men also waited next to the donkey, their austere, brown monastery garments contrasting sadly with the rich clothing of Eleanor's men.

"Will you offer me the hospitality of your castle?" Bernart asked softly. "Even though my arrival was delayed?"

"I will," she answered, smiling.

"Because it pleases me to be here, or because it will displease Henry, when he learns I am here?"

The sharpness of the question startled her into answering honestly, without forethought.

"For both reasons, I welcome you, Bernart."

The royal hunting party and Bernart's small group kept much space between themselves as they rode through Poitiers. They entered the castle separately, Eleanor riding proudly at the head of her retinue, and Bernart following some minutes after, on his plodding donkey, his two men running behind.

Maingot was in the courtyard when they entered. He who made it his business to observe everything also observed this forced lack of connection between the two parties, and was not fooled. The Queen's eyes were bright, she looked feverish. He recognized de Ventadour immediately, albeit the troubadour was now dressed in dour colors and had aged considerably. Eleanor and Bernart. Together. He grew light-headed with pleasure.

Now, not only would Henry win the war. He would have ample reason to repudiate Eleanor, once he heard of this further betrayal. Eleanor must be befuddled with fear and confusion, to commit such an indiscretion at this stage of the game. Why, then, that impervious tilt of the chin, the gleam in her eye?

The game was not finished yet, the Queen not yet taken. To best serve his lord, Henry, he, Maingot, would deliver the Queen to him, a humbled captive.

But how? The Lady Sophia was increasingly wary of him, and Eleanor smiled beneficently at him, which meant, of course, that she suspected him. He was surprised that no "accident" had yet befallen him . . . no deadly sickness brought by poison, no midnight assassin with a rope for the neck. He and Eleanor, the two of them, were both biding their time.

Perhaps it was time to leave Poitiers, and ride north to Henry. No. He would do this last thing, he would deliver Eleanor. He must find a small-brained, openmouthed lout who would assist him in this, some innocent who had not yet tipped Eleanor's suspicion.

Benoit. Benoit and innocence went hand in hand. But how to convince Benoit his best interest was in serving Henry, not the Queen?

Maingot scratched his head and then stroked his chin, deep in thought, searching for the one impulse, the one emotion, that would deflate a young knight puffed with mistaken ideals. The hand stroking the chin froze in midaction.

Jealousy. That would do it. Make him hate one woman, and he would hate all of them, at least long enough to betray Eleanor. There was that strange, shy damsel Lucie. Whenever she was near, Benoit could not take his eyes from her. And she could not take her eyes from that other, Godfrey.

How easily all the pieces would fit together. He must move quickly. There was work to be done.

Rumor, aided by Maingot's wagging tongue, spread quickly through the lanes of Poitiers and the chambers of the ducal palace that Eleanor's court was adorned with the brightest of the bright gems of troubadours in the land, the famous Bernart de Ventadour himself. But there was no public feast in the great hall that night. The Queen wanted Bernart, and his voice and music, to herself. And there was rumor about that, too.

Lucie noticed the newly arrived knight . . . he looked quite old, she thought . . . who was unceremoniously ushered past the public hall and into Eleanor's private chambers. She also noticed the way Raoul de Faye looked at the man with open disapproval, saw the platters of meat filled with the best cuts carried to those chambers, and knew something was afoot.

"He is Bernart de Ventadour," Sophia said gruffly as she pushed tiny wads of white bread into her pursed mouth. Moments before, the astrologer had been ravenous for meat; now the greasy smell of the passing platters turned her stomach. It was a queasiness past others she had suffered. It dismayed her and made her answers brief and sharp.

"Who is Bernart de Ventadour?" Lucie asked, not enlightened by the mere name.

"A troubadour. The Queen's friend."

"Friend?"

Sophia raised one thin eyebrow, and Lucie knew what was implied by that term, "friend." She, too, lost her appetite.

Here, then, was an end to peace. Lucie had hoped that in time, living without Godfrey, she might forget him. Even if she never found again that particular happiness she found in Godfrey's arms, she might learn to live without it, in some semblance of peace. But even a Queen, even a woman with grey in her hair, remembered old friends and wanted their company. Then how could she bear to be parted again, and this time for all time, from Godfrey?

She repented of her vow to return north with Foulkes. But it was a vow nonetheless, and she would have to keep it, or lose her immortal soul . . . and Godfrey would be in danger. That had been part of the bargain, Godfrey's safety for her obedience.

Lucie pushed away the quail and ginger pie she'd been eating.

"Your appetite is dulled by something. Is the pie gone off?" Sophia asked hopefully, as her stomach railed and roiled. Whatever it was that had momentarily subdued her stormy retorts and threatening frowns had lost its sway over her. She no longer grew soft and dreamy thinking of the love-play in Sir Foulkes' chamber. His bed was covered with leather vests and armor needing to be cleaned; the warrior was brusque and bristling with thoughts of war, not love. And she herself was preparing medicines that would be needed after battle, not love potions.

The fear of death softens some, sends them to their knees in quaking piety. The closeness of death made Sophia shrewish, as if she would give the Reaper himself a piece of her mind.

"The pie is tasty. But I have no appetite for food," said Lucie. "Can't you just eat your meal and let me be? You talk too much," she protested to the shocked woman who had said little for the past hour.

Lucie had made her vow and the sacrifice. Did God also require her to be meek, a ready object for everyone else's wrath and frustration? She tore little pills of bread from her pushed-aside trencher and refused to look at Sophia.

"You're angry. But I don't think you're afraid. You don't think of the war, and the danger, as the others do." Indeed, the great hall was half-filled with subdued ladies, young and old knights not in the strength of their combative years, and softly treading servants. There was no bustle, no music, and little chatter. "Why are you not afraid?" Sophia asked, now genuinely curious. The girl was changed, and she would know why.

"There are worse things than sleeping in the earth," Lucie said gently, repenting of her rudeness to Lady Sophia. "To be tormented forever in hellfire. That would be worse."

To live with the image of Godfrey always before her eyes, and never hear his voice, never feel his hand on her shoulder, that was worse. To live, when he might die, that was worse.

Hellfire, Sophia mused. Could hellfire truly be worse than the siege and burning of a castle and its village? The smell of flesh burning on still-living animals, babes crying in the dirt of the road, the thatched huts afire like torches . . . and confusion, everywhere confusion, the devil's own madness.

Sophia heard again the sound of the arrow that had pierced her mother's breast, the hissing and the deadly thudding of it, the roar of her father's grief and anger, the weeping and screaming of the people.

"Aye," she said. "There are worse things than sleeping in the earth. I have already seen some of them." She put her head in her hands.

Tears came. Even as she wiped at them, hoping that none saw

293

this weakness, the part of her that studied Aristotle and faulted the logic of the Epicureans looked down on the other self that was soft woman, and sneered.

Something is amiss here, Sophia told Sophia. I weep for next to naught and all too readily, like a maid with the cramps. But I have no cramps. And my courses have been frightened off their schedule by the news of the war.

Lucie put an arm around her shoulders. "Lady. Drink your wine. It will strengthen you."

"Yes." She took up her goblet and gulped down a large quantity so quickly, she choked and sputtered a little after. "And tell me a tale," she ordered Lucie. "Distract me from this morbid mood."

"A tale. Let me see now . . ." Lucie searched her memory. "I'll tell you a tale that Godfrey once told me."

"Godfrey. It's sure to be overladen with tall, boasting youths and buxom maidens, if it's a tale of Godfrey's making," Sophia said, glancing sideways at Lucie.

"No, no," she protested, smiling. "It is about animals, nothing lewd at all.

"A long, very long time ago," she began in a soft voice, "when the Garden of Eden was just completed, Adam decided that he had better give a name to all the strange creatures he saw sharing the garden with him. So that he could call them, and speak to them, for this was before Eve made him to eat of the apple, before he lost that ability to commune with all living things . . ."

"Are you so certain it was Eve made Adam eat of the apple, and not the other way around?" Sophia asked, cantankerous. "It has always sounded like a man's trick to me."

"The Bible tells us it was Eve," Lucie said. "But, Lady, I have sometimes wondered about that, too. For one thing, men are taller and more apt to go apple picking than females." Benoit had picked sour, green apples for her, trying to win her pleasure by willing the fruit to be ready before its time. The memory of that fair afternoon left Lucie unmoved. He himself was like one of those apples, it seemed to her. Hard and too shiny, better left yet on the bough, but once plucked and bitten into . . . leaving a bad

294

taste in the mouth. The thought of Benoit and the sin she had almost committed with him was like the stomachache.

"And as Godfrey told it, it must be Eve gave the apple to Adam," Lucie continued. "But that happens after this tale because, as I said, Adam could still speak with all the animals. So he called them to come to him and they came, some galloping, some creeping and crawling, some fluttering in the treetops. All except one animal, which was perverse by nature, because it had been touched by Lucifer's wing when he fell from heaven to hell.

"Now, this animal did not like to come when called by man or God and had the great sin of restlessness and discontent, never being able to stay in one place for more than a moment at a time. It was a strange-looking creature, with a nose like an arm, and a head like a foot, and legs like skinny fingers, and hair in some places but not in others, and parti-colored it was, too. All because when God had made the animals, this one had been restless and charged about the creation field, taking for itself parts of other animals, rather than wait to be assigned its own appearance.

"It was an unhappy animal," Lucie continued. "Being neither this nor that, nor indeed anything that could be named. It desperately wanted a name it could be called by, a thing it could be known as. But because of its patchwork body, it didn't know when to come when called by Adam, not when the horses came, nor the monkeys nor the griffins, for it was a little of everything and a lot of nothing. It waited and waited, and never was a name called out by which it could go, and never did it then gain a name for itself. It lived all its life in solitude, being scorned by all who saw it, and knowing that at death it would only receive more scorn and hatred, for without a name, it could not enter heaven."

Lucie, finished, bowed her head and folded her hands in her lap. Night was stealing into the room, and pages were busily lighting oil lamps and the wall torches. A platter of ripe pears, her favorite fruit, had been set before them for dessert, but she had no appetite. She waited for Sophia to understand, and to say something.

Sophia, who usually hated fresh fruit, took a pear and bit into it with relish. She then cleared her throat and fidgeted.

"That is a most strange tale," she began, slowly. "And it seems to me there was another layer of meaning in your words, and why you chose that particular tale."

Lucie bowed her head yet more deeply, so that her small, pointed chin rested on her chest.

"Yes, Lady. I have vowed to go back to St. Servan, with Sir Foulkes."

"With Foulkes?" Sophia was incredulous.

"Yes. With Foulkes. My rightful lord. I don't wish to be a nameless outcast without place or position."

"Ayee, my aching back," said Sophia, putting her hands to her head. "I won't ask you to explain. That would mean I credit you with logic. No, you are a crazed woman; there isn't an ounce of logic in you," she protested, shaking her head. "A year you have been away. More than a year, isn't it? And now you think you will return?"

"I know this law, Lady Sophia. I have not found sanctuary with another lord . . . or lady. The law says that I am not free, but still bound to Foulkes. It was a sin to run away from my rightful lord, and a greater sin to stay away. I will be punished for it, and I fear that those I love will be punished also."

"Oh, my stupid girl," said Sophia. "You think to right the world by sacrificing yourself? It will do no good. The war will still come to Poitiers. Or perhaps you sincerely wish to return to St. Servan?" To Sir Foulkes, she meant but could not say, thereby feeling a twinge of jealousy.

"No, I have no wish for it. It is only my conscience that calls me to it. I have a great fear that Godfrey will be punished for my wrongdoing. I would die if anything happened to him." Lucie hung her head in misery.

Sophia finished the pear and began another. She was angry. Not with Lucie. But with God Himself, who seemed determined to make a mess of things. Would it have been so terrible for the maid to have been born a free woman, instead of a bonded peasant? What pleasure did He take in giving the girl desires, and the

296

intelligence to match, that best suited a free heart? For that matter, why did He make her, Sophia, so ugly that every maid better formed—and that was almost all—stirred the great sin of jealousy in her own breast? And for that matter, why had He made Eleanor so possessive, and Henry so greedy and randy, that nothing less than war could come from their personal strife?

Yes, God was having a laugh on all of them. From now on, Sophia would read only the pagan philosophers. Meanwhile, how to right some of these wrongs?

"Ayeee, my back," moaned Sophia. "You say you have made a vow? Well, we will find a way out of it. God made lawyers; He appreciates a bargain. Let me think . . . only stop crying, you're giving me a headache. Hush, hush, and talk no more of death. Eleanor may lose this war, but not even Henry would raze a castle filled with terrified young maids and harmless pages. I don't think."

The pages had finished lighting the lamps, and the hall flickered with strong light and deep shadows. It was the time of day when Eleanor would challenge them to debate fine points of music and poetry, or ask the court troubadours to play for their pleasure. But Eleanor was not with them. The people in the hall, lacking focus, broke into small groups. Many used this opportunity to seal friendships and pledges between families and then say farewell, for the court of Aquitaine was no longer such a pleasant place to be.

"Stop weeping and let me think," Sophia insisted.

Benoit made a smelly paste of vinegar and sand and then rubbed it into his armor, till it shone bright as new silver. Finally he would taste battle. Real battle. Eleanor could not deny him this honor now, with the enemy at their very door. Well, not quite at the door. But close enough. All able-bodied men would be required to fight, and that well suited him.

He could not believe that for a moment, even for that brief moment, he had doubted Lucie. What harm that she walked side by side with Godfrey? She had a kindly nature, she would not

297

disdain to speak to her inferiors. It was only kindness that had prompted her to smile on the rude fellow. Only kindness.

Too bad the court of love had been interrupted, just as she was about to name him the victor of the day, and her heart. But perhaps it was a blessing in disguise. No one could deny the perfection of his poetry. But now he could prove himself on the battlefield. As a true and loyal knight.

He rubbed harder, glad at heart as only the young and untested can be when danger peers over the shoulder. He worked with such concentration that he was not aware of that other looking over his shoulder, till the man spoke.

"It is a handsome piece of work," Maingot said admiringly, tracing a pattern of twining laurel on the chased metal breastpiece.

"It was my father's," Benoit said. "He brought it great honor. I will bring it more."

"I have no doubt of that. Never have I seen a more able-looking knight." Flattery was the surest way to the youth's heart, of that he felt certain. Young men such as this were usually much taken with themselves, and pleased when others also were.

"Too bad you will win honor for yourself in a dishonorable cause." Maingot sighed heavily.

"What do you mean?" Benoit looked up, puzzled.

"This war of the Queen's. Think you not that, well, perhaps her cause is not just? That honor might be better earned by defending the true King?"

"Young Henry is the true King. And I have sworn loyalty to Eleanor. I am not a man to take vows lightly," said Benoit, greatly offended.

"I see you are a man of great virtue. A knight of great loyalty." Maingot's voice was oily with flattery. "As was Adam, the first knight. And see how he was led astray by a lady. The devil is clever in his disguises. That maid, Lucie, for instance. She seems pure and simple as the dawn. But there are rumors . . ."

"I will not have my ears tainted by gossip of Lady Lucie," Benoit protested, rising from his scouring and raising a sand-

298

covered hand. Maingot caught Benoit's fist in his own and warded off the blow.

". . . rumors that she is Sir Foulkes' leman. And that lowborn fellow, Godfrey, too . . ." Maingot finished. The two men glared at each other. Benoit blanched; Maingot grinned.

"You have not lost your gifts for pleasure," Bernart said, leaning back into a pile of silk cushions. They had feasted on roast quail and white cheese; the wine and the fruit had been sweet and golden. Her conversation had been light and merry, designed to put him at ease and heal the traveler's aches and the man's worries.

"Rai, Rai, why did you stay away such a very long while?" Eleanor turned in his arms and kissed his chin. From where they lay twined together, she could see the sun setting over a meadow, turning the green grass to gold and lavender, and a little shepherd girl with her crook who led her sheep up the path to Poitiers town. The tower was high up, and everything in the world seemed below them, as if they were gods.

How quickly, how easily, her arms and lips had remembered him. It was as if he had been gone only a day, not many years. The flesh has memory, too. Memory and will of its own. His kisses and poetry had not been enough this afternoon. Her troubadour had waited for fifteen years; she had made him wait no more. Indeed, what was there left to wait for?

"I stayed away because you were a Queen, and I was naught. Then, too, you were a Queen with a strangely jealous King for a husband," Bernart answered, returning her kiss. His bare arms, strong and brown from working in the fields, surrounded her waist.

"Still lithe as a maid," he said, pulling her closer.

"As a maid who has had nine children," she retorted, pleased by his flattery but not taken in by it. Could he span her waist with his two hands? No more, nor could she run playful fingers through his thick, black hair, for much of it was missing, and what was left was

299

the color of shining metal. They lived in different bodies, and their futures were no longer the shining morns that youth look onto; more of the road was behind them than before them.

But he was Rai nonetheless, with or without thick black locks, and her heart rejoiced each time she looked at him. It was a miracle, this reunion, that he came to her at this time and place. With Rai to hold her, there was no war, no Henry, no sons. Only the moment. It was like living in a never-before-inhabited castle, one built solely for her, with room after room awaiting her new discoveries.

"You feared Henry, then?" she asked, rolling away from the casement to look up into his eyes.

"Aye, any man with even half the wit normally supplied to us would fear Henry," Bernart answered, tracing a pattern on her bare chest with his finger. He bent over and kissed each berry-small nipple. "And, my Lauzeta, I feared you."

"Me? How so?"

"You can't deny your ambition." His voice was mocking, but there were depths to it that made her frown.

"How could my ambition hurt you?"

"I had a nightmare. The same nightmare, over and over. Henry found us together. As we are now. But he did not curse nor draw sword. He stood over us and laughed. And then he turned to you and said, 'Well, Eleanor. You chose to play the slut over being Queen of England. It is your choice, I'll leave it to you.' And each time in the dream when Henry said that, you pulled a knife out from under the pillow, and you yourself stabbed me to the heart."

They were silent for a long time.

"You cannot deny the crown meant more to you than I did," Bernart said finally.

"No. I cannot deny it. I loved as a Queen must love. And you cannot deny that had I loved as a maid and not a Queen, your love for me would have been lessened. I gave you the part of me that was free to give. The rest belonged to Aquitaine, and to Henry. A Queen has less freedom than a dairy maid, Rai. My

300

youth and health, my womb, my fate . . . they were not mine to bestow."

"You bestowed them on Henry. You chose Henry, not he you." There was no anger. But there was the green, stinging taste of bitterness in his mouth that love, the subject to which he had devoted his own youth and fate, was such a worthless one, in the long run. The troubadour realized what the monk had been learning: love was lies and vanity. He would not have loved Eleanor as he had, had she not been Queen. She had seen that, and dared say it, and it made a lie of all his songs and poems.

"Yes. I chose Henry. Because I saw in his youth the King he would be. I wanted him as the lord of my lands, and the father of my children. Land and children. It is all I have truly loved. And now, I have lost both."

A young maid would have wept bitterly for what had been and what never was. Eleanor rolled over and peered out the casement. The shepherd girl was gone and the waving grasses had turned grey with twilight. Somewhere to the North those grasses were red with fire, the sky dark with smoke; somewhere in the North the war crept on its foul belly, closer, closer.

"You will never lose Henry," Bernart told her. Other things he had told her that day had been words of love, whispered into her ear. This was a pronouncement, spoken loudly and with force. She looked up at him in surprise. Bernart was still jealous? After all these years?

"But I already have. He is with Rosamonde even now, and has turned his back on my sons," Eleanor insisted.

"No. He is not with Rosamonde. She has gone back into her convent." He had not meant to tell her that. Had not meant to give her hope. But she had given him truth, that love is not an ideal, that it can't be separated from people, and all their imperfections. He looked away from the sudden shining joy in Eleanor's eyes. This, too, was part of love, this delight in a rival's affliction.

"Back to her convent? Truly? How do you know this?"

"Through a message brought to the monastery last week, that

301

would have us pray for her soul. Our chaplain is cousin four times removed from the abbess of Rosamonde's convent. Rosamonde is dangerously ill, Eleanor. She will not be much longer on this earth."

"Rosamonde. Ill. Dying. Henry's leman is dying. Why, she is a full fifteen years younger than I, and she is dying."

"Let that be a lesson in mortality, Eleanor. It is time to forgive those who have trespassed against you, and to beg forgiveness for yourself."

"Rai. Do not preach at me. Do not play the monk. Rather, play the troubadour. Sing to me again. Hold me, again."

"Am I to sing you love songs, while you sit and gloat over the illness of your husband's leman? Does that not seem perverse to you, Lauzeta, little lark? There is more you must know. They say Rosamonde is dying slowly. Of poisoning. Poison that you have paid her servants to administer to her. You are being accused of her death, Eleanor."

"You look at me so strangely. Do you believe those rumors, my Rai? You think me a murderess?" She moved away from him and stared meditatively at an icon of the Virgin that hung on the wall opposite them.

Did Henry believe she was murdering his mistress? She smiled, and then shivered. She had suckled infants at her bosom, her breasts had flowed with life and mercy and love, and now how easily did the world accuse her of murder.

"This is not to be borne," she said aloud. "For the sins I have committed, I will admit guilt. But not for ones I have not committed. I knew nothing of Rosamonde's illness till you yourself told me of it. I won't feign grief, but neither will I be accused of her murder."

"Then the wife must pray that the mistress will regain her health, or be named guilty of murder in the eyes of her husband," Rai said lowly. "Henry, it is said, believes this gossip."

He picked up his lute and began plucking at the strings, feeling them quiver and move beneath his hand sweet as womanflesh. She put her head in his lap, and the loosened hair of his Queen flowed over his thighs.

"Sing to me of the eagle, who conquers," Eleanor whispered.

Verneuil was a dying city.

Henry Fitz-Empress, astride his war-horse in a green glade opposite the walled town, crossed himself thrice as he looked at it, and smelled it on the wind, and listened to it. From this distance, Louis' foot soldiers trying to scale the walls were like ants scurrying over some fallen creature. Immensely tall wooden siege engines hovered at the walls like giant vultures. The odor was foul; the noise was of weeping. The city was like some giant creature in its death throes. It had the scent and the sound and the appearance of ruination.

July had shed its skin and metamorphosed into August. It was time for labor to be rewarded. Townspeople should have been coming and going through the city gates, noisily returning home with carts and baskets filled with the glories of the harvest countryside. But no one came out of this city. No one went in.

Verneuil was a city under seige. There was no harvest, no reward, only fear.

Henry wondered if the townspeople had slighted their town yet . . . gone through the ritual of burning the guild halls, salting the wells and razing the marketplace so that the taking of the town would be a bitter and useless victory for the conquerer.

He hoped not. He hoped they had the grace of faith and optimism to wait for him, for rescue them he would. By his oath as King, he would save this town.

He ground his teeth as he paused there, in the sweet, green glade, and he wished Louis were prone on the ground before him, with the hoofs of Henry's war-horse grinding the French King's face to pulp.

It was weeks now since Louis had drawn up the hellish war engines and positioned the sappers to take this city. Only now, after more than a month of siege, had Henry been able to march south with his mercenaries to this place. The fighting in the North delayed him, yet surely the people knew their King would not abandon them. They had faith. They trusted. As Eleanor did not. As his sons did not.

Verneuil had held out during the long summer. No amount of digging had felled its walls. No battering rams had yet caved its gates. The townspeople, loyal to Henry, had ignored bribes, demands, promises and threats. They would die for him, if it came to that.

Henry knew full well what it meant for a city to be under siege for as long as this one had been. He could see in his mind's eye the city wells gone dry, the empty-eyed maids who leaned against them, dreaming of the forest and its cool, endless streams. He could see the warehouses, with their emptied wheat and pease barrels. Very few of the townspeople would have food left by now . . . only the rich and the prudent. The rest would be thin with hunger, but hunger was nothing like the pain of thirsting and not being able to quench that thirst. That was hell itself.

The beggars always died first. The evil odor carried to him on the wind was from smoldering pyres, for no one dared to transport the dead ones outside the city walls. The gates couldn't be opened to serve life; they certainly wouldn't be opened to serve death.

This was Verneuil. Beautiful, loyal, strong Verneuil. Of course this was where Louis would prepare his fiercest attack. This would be where Louis would take his vengeance. Louis, who pretended to be saintly as a monk but had the soul of a demon. Damn him to hell.

How long since Louis had first tried to take Verneuil? Twenty years? That much water under the bridge, truly? Henry reflected, grimacing. What a whore time was, always making promises and never keeping them. Twenty years. So be it. He had been a young man then. Now . . . well, now he was not old. Neither was he young.

He crossed himself again. The fear of death was nothing when stood next to the fear of simply growing old. Of losing his strength. His power. Of seeing the bright morn grow dim through thickened eyes, of dreading the stairwell that would make him pant with fatigue, and the women who would be all sly smile to his face and then laugh behind his back. Of growing defeated and useless and helpless, of having his own person become like this city under siege.

Rosamonde, he thought, and the name brought a thrill of grief. If you were here with me, the pain would be lessened just by the touch of your hand on my shoulder, in that old way that felt like an angel had just blessed me.

Never would Rosamonde laugh at him, not even if he should take to crawling in the dirt and wearing ashes on his face. She would smear her own face and crawl with him. She was a good woman. Too good.

"I don't repent of loving you," she had told him, unsmiling. She had looked down at the floor, so that the curtain of her flaxen hair had fallen forward and hidden her face from him. "My soul is small and insignificant and unworthy of even the grace of repentance. But I repent of having led you from the path of righteousness."

He, standing at the washbasin with his chest and loins all alather, had laughed at first, thinking she jested. Righteousness. Did she think he had been a virgin, or even a faithful husband, before he took her to bed? he asked. She did not laugh.

305

He toweled himself quickly and returned to their bed, taking her small, delicate face between his two hands. She looked at him solemnly.

"Not the bedding, Henry," she said gently. "That is but a small thing. But . . ."

"But what?" He had roared at her. She put a tentative hand on his shoulder. Her fingers burned his naked skin like coals.

Rosamonde was the only woman who had no fear of him. Eleanor hid the fear very cleverly, but Eleanor felt fear. Rosamonde did not. It was as if she took the arrow of his own anger and directed it back toward him. He feared Rosamonde. There was too much depth in her large, grey eyes, too much fire in her touch, too much meaning in her words. She was incapable of being frivolous or light-hearted, and Henry found that a fearsome quality in a woman. He feared losing her. With her, he was all things; without her he would be the sky emptied of its sun and moon.

Repenting of his anger, he turned his head to kiss the small hand resting on his shoulder. Rosamonde was not wearing the rings he had given her. The room felt cold.

"I fear I have led you away from your sons," she said lowly, and her voice could not have been more terrible if she had announced the end of the world. "I have separated father and son. That is the true sin. That is why I must leave."

Was she witch or saint, that she knew his heart so well? The man feared she would leave. The King hoped she would. With her, he was torn in twain between reason and desire.

In her solemn grey eyes he saw reflected the dangerous dream that had haunted him since the murder of Becket. The dream of sharing his throne with Rosamonde.

Becket had cursed him. Becket had cursed his sons, saying never more would Henry have pleasure or joy of them. And it had been Becket's death that started the turning away. He, the King, would enter a room and his sons would cease talking and grow thin-lipped and hold their heads with infuriating superior tilts. Eleanor would stop her songs and avoid looking at him, as if the sight of him were offensive.

It was this coldness, this silence, that had hurtled him to Ireland as much as the political problems of that island. Henry could no longer stand to be with his family, nor his family with him, it would seem. He needed to be loved, and he was not.

And the dream had begun then; it took root in his mind and grew daily, hourly, like some fantastic flower, blossoming with neither sun nor water to strengthen it. The dream of seeing Rosamonde thicken and ripen with his fruit . . . his sons. She had given him two. Two bonny, loving boys whom he could not own, because he could not own their mother.

Or could he? He need only do what Louis had already done. Declare the marriage with Eleanor to be sinful in the eyes of God because of their blood relationship, and the marriage would be no more. The Church was used to such coils; it would be as routine as an Easter confession.

And as for Hal, Richard, Geoffrey and John Lackland . . . There the dream ended. They would never stand to have their mother put aside and their own claims reduced to ashes. It would mean war with them, and that had made him reconsider, fool that he was. He was at war with them anyway.

And now she was saying she must leave him. She had read this dream in his eyes and deemed it sinful, and she must leave. As if he were no mighty King but a simple peasant who had cast covetous eyes at his neighbor's wife.

With a blasphemous oath and a roar of anger, he leaped from bed and threw back the coverlets, revealing to the harshness of day her sleep-stark nakedness, to humiliate her. She hated to be seen so. She cowered before him.

"You will not!" he screamed. "You will not leave your King!"

But her implacable eyes said a yet mightier King called her to different duties and a different loyalty and she would leave.

"I have come between you and your heirs," she insisted quietly.

My sons. Henry cursed loudly, disturbing the quiet morning and making his charger rear up. Sons of the jackal. But a pain like a green youth's lovesickness shot through him as he thought

307

of those boys, who had once been his babes and were now his avowed enemies.

Eleanor! he called out to the morning, to the dying city of Verneuil. How has this come to be, Eleanor?

If William, that first son born to them, had not died . . . perhaps William would have grown up to be the son he deserved . . . the brave, loyal knight who would serve his father and grow in wisdom to take the throne when . . . when Henry could no longer serve the land. Which is not for some time, he told William, who was dead.

Vernueil was William's city. It was here that Louis had first tried to take his vengeance when Eleanor had given Henry his first son. Louis was prepared to forgive Eleanor and Henry for marrying without his consent. Henry had been duke, not King, when he took Eleanor. As such, he needed his overlord's, the King of France's, permission. Instead, he and Eleanor had married secretly, and in great haste.

Louis had not gone to war over this, as was his right, but had forgiven them. Perhaps he believed that Henry would have as little joy of Eleanor as he had, in the final bitter years of marriage. Eleanor had given Louis only those two daughters, and much trouble.

She gave Henry her true love and a son, and quickly. The babe, William, had been the final insult to Louis' devastated pride. In blind fury Louis had roused his soldiers and war machines and sought to destroy Verneuil.

He hadn't been able to do it then. Nor would he do it now, its King promised. And damn Louis for trying.

Henry heard footsteps approaching. He composed his face to hide all feeling and turned.

"My Lord. The sun grows high. Louis awaits us." Charles was leading his horse behind; his armor clanked mightily as he walked. His dark face was perplexed. Louis had agreed to meet with Henry, indeed, had insisted on it, outside of this doomed city of Verneuil, and Charles' stomach was churning only as it did when something foul was afoot.

"You are prepared for battle," Henry said, frowning. Louis had

308

said he would treat with them; there was to be no battle between them.

"Aye, My Lord. I have little cause to trust the French."

"They sent us fair warning, did they not?"

Fair. And explicit. If Henry did not come to Verneuil by the third sunset of receiving the message, then Verneuil would be sacked and destroyed. It would be given no mercy.

"Fair if you look at it one way. A trap, if you look at it another," Charles insisted. "Since when do the French invite us to come stop them from sacking a city?" He plucked reflectively at his beard and would not look his King in the eye.

"Louis tires of the war," Henry insisted. "The expense proves greater than he had considered, and his men are nearing the end of their forty days' service. They want to return to hearth and woman."

But his own heart was far from being light. Henry's warrior's instinct told him Louis was not to be trusted. There was too much ill between them; life, in fact, had conspired to make them enemies, and enemies they were. But as King, Henry's reason told him he must believe in Louis' word of truce.

"We will treat with the French. They will go back across the Seine. It will be quickly over and then I will be free to march on Eleanor. That is the day I long for. I will march into Poitiers and the Eagle will become a frightened sparrow that I will crush in my hand." Henry grabbed at empty air and crushed it in his fist with great relish. But the gesture gave him no satisfaction. With Rosamonde he was torn in twain between pleasure, which bid him linger with her, and reason, which bid him part from her.

With Eleanor, he was torn between anger, which made him grimace as fiercely as he did when thinking of Louis, and years of long habit, which made him anticipate their meeting with a kind of pleasure. He would like to discuss the battles with her, in their old way, over a good, heady claret, reenacting forays with play soldiers to perfect strategies that had been less than perfect on the battlefield. But how strange. In this war, Eleanor was the enemy.

"I will crush her," he repeated.

Charles looked sadly at Henry and said nothing more.

It was many weeks since Godfrey had donned his carter's clothes and joined Chabert in the chapel building. The shirt and breeches were stiff and grey with stone dust; the thick-soled worker's clogs thudded heavily as he walked. The clothes, and the wearing of them, were like a penance.

Like a penance, too, was Chabert's face. The old man eyed Godfrey up and down, unsmiling, querulous.

"What have you come for?" he finally asked, never putting down his chisel. The old man's face and clothes and hands were coated with stone dust; he looked as much made out of stone as the unpainted statues lined up in the workroom.

"To work," Godfrey answered. He grinned, but his face felt as stiff as the coarse work shirt, and the grin did not work. It slid from his mouth like snow tumbling from a roof.

"Huummph." But Chabert, the living statue, found a palette and clean brush and pointed to the statue of the Madonna that Godfrey had abandoned weeks before. "Go back to the work you left unfinished," he told him.

Only the top half of her face had been painted; the eyes were colorful and bright as life itself, but her mouth and chin were stone grey, lifeless. The artist in Godfrey, who could make an audience think they saw two elephants going two by two where only one Broderick had gone, who could take an empty page and turn it into a love sonnet, smiled with anticipation. He would bring this piece of masonry to life. Carefully, with pleasure, he mixed a crimson paint and began to paint the Madonna's sweet, Lucie-like lips.

"They say Henry will soon march to Poitiers, and his temper is in a fine blaze," Godfrey said after a while, when the top lip was all but finished and the bottom one outlined with a fine-tipped brush. There was a slight, delicious pout to the mouth. The carver had made the shape so lifelike that, with color added, it looked like the Madonna was about to speak. Godfrey's chest ached to behold that pout, it was so like Lucie's.

310

"I've two ears like other men," Chabert said. "I've already heard. You've wasted a morning's hour if it be only that news that brought you to the chapel."

"What will you do?" Godfrey asked after another moment.

"Do? Why, stay and finish the chapel. What else would I do?" Chabert put down the chisel. He went down on his hands and knees on the floors, searching for the fine-pointed stylus which would complete the delicate engraving of the base of the Madonna's statue. Finding it, he rose to his full height again and glared at Godfrey.

"You might consider traveling south or west, as so many others are. They say this is a fine time of year to make a pilgrimage to St. James de Compostella." Godfrey kept his voice even.

"Flee, you mean. Nay. The only things I fear are those that we can't flee," Chabert said. "Henry's wrath is naught to me. But to leave a Lady Chapel unfinished? To leave incomplete my penance? That is something I fear more than death itself, for it would mean the eternal death of my soul."

"You hope for sainthood." Godfrey grinned, and Chabert sounded one of his rare laughs.

"Sainthood? Nay. I hope only for life in the world to come."

"And what of this world?"

"This world doesn't matter, except that it be a testing place for the soul's courage." Chabert nodded again and again in the bobbing manner of one accustomed to long, one-sided talks with God.

Godfrey reflected for a moment as he continued to apply the ruby-colored paint to the Madonna's mouth. The image of the world as a giant tilting yard where young knights were tested seemed an accurate one to him at that time. And what of woman? How was she tested? She did not tilt with lance nor strike with mace; her body did battle only in childbed. Her heart, then, was her testing ground. Choosing righteousness over the pleasure of the moment was her test.

Lucie had been on that testing ground. She had gone to it a young maid who dreamed of lovers and wresting what joy she could from this life. She had returned from it greatly changed.

What vision had she seen there to change her heart so? What terrible angel had appeared with what awesome demand to turn his coltish, young Lucie into a lady who walked with slow stride and always looked straight ahead, as if some unseen herald beckoned? She had seen Godfrey's death brought about by her own sin, but that Godfrey could not know, for she would not tell him. That, too, was part of the penance.

Penance, he knew, was the food Lucie craved. But to make up for her sins by returning to Foulkes' mesne, where she would doubtless be beaten and then quickly wedded to some villein and bear a brat a year to labor in Foulkes' fields . . . No, that seemed too hard. He could not imagine such a life for Lucie. Worse, he could imagine it. And it filled him with fear. She, bright thing that she was, fresh as violets in April, would shrivel up and die, day by day, till she was empty and lifeless as the painted statue of the Madonna.

His hand slipped. A thin, crimson line snaked from the Madonna's mouth down her chin, like blood. Godfrey stared at it, thinking of Lucie, till Chabert handed him a resin-soaked rag with which to clean away the mistake.

"You are greatly altered," Chabert finally said to the younger man. "You've not told one bawdy joke all morning, nor sung your lewd lyrics. What's amiss?" He turned away to work at something behind Godfrey's back, knowing that confession is easier when eyes cannot meet.

"I have been thinking about the story you told me. About Damietta," Godfrey said. The workroom grew silent except for a slight rustle of cloth. Chabert had stopped his work and blessed himself at the pronouncing of his private saint's name.

"And?" Chabert asked, not trusting his voice to say more. He thumped his chest, mea culpa, mea culpa, and a bubble of despair welled up as the dead Damietta's face filled his mind's eye. She would never forgive him, never would he find peace. He remembered with longing the day he had tied a stone around his neck and stood by a bracken pond. But such an easy path was not for him. He took off the stone halter and continued on his way. Then Chabert's heart floated with joy, for he knew the despair was

312

part of the penance and he must embrace it joyfully and then do battle with it.

"And just this. If it could be done again, how could it be done differently, to keep harm from coming to your lady?"

Chabert sat down heavily and put his head in his hands.

"Many times I have asked myself just that," he sighed. "And this is what I think. Sin was inescapable, for me. I should never have loved her. She was not mine to love. Yet God gave me my heart, and my heart was hers, so I could not help but love. This, I think, is what the monks preach of as original sin. But having loved her, sinful or not as that love was, I should never have left her. I should not have let them take her from me. Giving your heart against your father's permission is a small sin compared to stealing away again the heart of a wedded wife. I should have kept her safe at my side for all her life, and not torn her heart in twain. I failed in courage and loyalty."

The western wall of the chapel had been open to day when Chabert first told Godfrey of Damietta. A bird had flown in and circled over them, mocking. Now the wall was complete. The stained-glass window was in place, and light shone through the rainbow-hued segments of the portrait of St. Eugenia. In one hand the saint held the man's clothes with which she had disguised herself; in the other she held the twine-tied stone with which the Romans had tried to drown her. Her smile was of incomparable beauty.

As he considered the portrait of Eugenia and Chabert's words, new purpose filled Godfrey. He would not let Lucie leave him. He would not. If need be, he would leave Marie's court, give up his ambitions, and follow Lucie to St. Servan itself. But he hoped it would not come to that.

Sophia stuck a cautious finger into the brewing vat of lady's-milk thistle and tasted the greyish mess that stuck to her fingertip. It was known to be sweet and soothing; this batch had an off smell and an evil taste to it. She tried it again to be certain, and almost gagged.

No, it hadn't been her imagination. It was foul. She searched the crannies of her knowledge to find the cause for this spoilt brew. She knew the meadow whence they had been gathered, and the hour and method of their gathering; the water that had been mixed with them was sweet and untainted; the pot was whole and clean. Still, the batch was ruined.

It is me, she told herself, aware that it was the month of Leo and she had Leo in the ascendant. Perhaps this double dose of Leo's prudence had made her mouth overcautious. She tried one more time and one more time her mouth pursed and rebelled and her throat all but refused to swallow.

Angry, she knelt and doused the fire in the hearth. No sense finishing the potion. It would do no one any good. As she rose, dusting her sooty hands, the bile leapt again in her throat. Crablike because of her great hurry, she hobbled to a nearby basin and emptied the morning's bread and weak ale into it from her heaving stomach.

Then, exhausted, she sat on the floor and moaned.

It was thus that Eleanor found her, crumpled and pale and furious.

"What ails you?" the Queen asked with great solicitude, stooping to scoop the tiny woman into her embrace. "You look like . . . like I have never seen you before." Lady Sophia, at her best, was pale and wan and lackluster; today, indeed for many days past, she had looked all that and worse.

"My stomach rebels against me," Sophia muttered, letting Eleanor help her to her feet. "That is all. No need for concern . . ."

"Come. Sit here, on the bench." Eleanor led her to a window seat with much fussing and fawning. She had ignored Sophia of late, and it rankled in her conscience. She had been ignoring much of late. With Bernart here, the days and nights had grown too short to accommodate her needs and duties.

"What ails your stomach?" Eleanor asked, her voice sweetened with repentance for her neglect. Sophia, she saw now, was thinner, too. It was already days past the time when someone should have stopped Sophia and said, "Lady, what's amiss? To bed with you!"

"Ayeeii. It has turned on me and become mine own worst enemy," Sophia answered, gladly leaning against Eleanor for support. "I do not know what is causing this."

Eleanor smiled gently, remembering the many times that she had felt her own stomach seemingly turn against her. It was thus that her babes had first made themselves known, by a queasiness that felt as if fish swam within.

Then she stopped smiling. She looked harder at Sophia. The lady was thinner and green in the face, but other things were also remarkable. The brown hair, just barely visible under the strict wimple the astrologer wore, had more sheen to it than normal; her brown eyes were large and more brilliant. Holy Virgin Mother.

"Does this ailment disappear by afternoon, and return again the next morning?" Eleanor asked.

"Exactly like that."

"And your bleeding cycle, is it also askew, perhaps quite late?"

"By several weeks," Sophia added.

"Truly, you have no name to give this ailment?"

"None."

"Then I will name it, dear friend. You are with child," Eleanor announced, bemused.

"That is impossible!" Sophia jumped up. She sat back down and put her hands over her face. "No. It is not impossible," she whispered through her fingers.

She felt no emotion. Or she felt them all at once. She couldn't tell. It was as if a million candles had been lit inside her, obscuring all shadow and definition with blinding light.

Henry stayed mounted as the three emissaries approached. He turned and looked at Charles, who rode always at his back.

"You were wrong. Louis did not await," he said, and there was dark anger in his voice. They were back at Breteuil, seven miles from Verneuil, at the place where Henry and Louis were to meet.

Louis had not come. Instead, he had sent his brother, Robert, Theobald of Blois, and the archbishop of Sens.

315

Henry looked past Charles, at row after row of Brabantine mercenary flanking the meadow. Their iron-studded shields glinted in the morning light; the soldiers' eyes were hard. As the three emissaries approached, Henry could see anger and disappointment in the faces of his mercenaries. Not that Louis hadn't come in person, which was the reason for Henry's anger, but that Louis had sent an embassy and not soldiers. Without a battle pending, their day's wages would be lower. They had come for blood and silver, not words and papers. A restlessness went through the ranks, and Henry, also restless, turned back to the approaching emissaries.

"Where is Louis?" he called soon as they were in hearing distance. "The King of England will treat with the King of France, not his lackeys."

Robert and Theobold, knights taught in courtesy, had the sense to blush. The archbishop, who was a haughty man, did not.

"Louis bids you welcome and asks your patience," he called back in a mincing, preoccupied voice. The ground was still wet and soft with dew. The cleric seemed more concerned with keeping his red satin slippers out of the mud than with the greeting of Henry. Behind him, Henry could hear some of the mercenaries snigger.

As the archbishop came closer, the sniggers turned to speculating mutters. The cleric wore a ring on each finger, and the rubies and sapphires in those rings were large as turtle eggs. His vestments, all of silk and embroidered with gold threads and pearls, were also worth much money. In this way did mercenaries assess the worth of a man, and the archbishop, wearing his wealth for all to see, was like a sparrow dust-bathing before hungry cats. Henry hoped the archbishop would have the sense not to go abroad alone after dark this night, now that the Brabantines had weighed his jewels with their hard eyes.

"Where is Louis?" Henry called down to him, for by now the man was standing, panting from exertion, at his feet. It was not his rings that Henry assessed, but his face and particularly his eyes. They were open to the day, yet closed to Henry. Those eyes were shielding secrets; the mouth was prepared to speak falsehood.

316

"Delayed" was all the archbishop would say. It was what Louis had instructed him to say. Robert and Theobald said not a word, but stared intently at their feet. "The King asks that there be a truce today, and on the morrow he will meet with you to discuss the peace terms."

Henry was seething with anger, but he kept his face smooth and emotionless. Louis had written that he would burn Verneuil if Henry did not come to its defense by the ninth of August. It was the eighth, and he was here. Where was Louis?

"I do not like this," Charles said in answer to Henry's thoughts.

"Nor I," Henry answered. "But I won't go hunting from tent to tent to search the French King out. We must wait."

The archbishop of Sens smiled up at them benignly.

Eleanor returned to Bernart in an unpleasant state of mind.

"What is wrong, Lauzeta?" he asked, rising from her writing table and putting his arms around her shoulder. There was a spot of ink on his cheek. He had been writing a new aubade for her, resting his chin in his writing hand when deep in thought, and leaving behind on his cheek the smudge. Eleanor did not notice it. Nor did she notice the paper he put in her hand, the new love words he had written for her. She accepted them with as little interest as if they were a tax roll.

"My astrologer is with child," she answered, preoccupied, twisting the paper.

"That is indeed strange. How came he to this wondrous plight?" Bernart smiled tightly.

"Not so wondrous, my Rai. The astrologer is a woman. Yet . . . such a woman that I am caught in deep confusion by this news." She stood near, leaning against him, yet her thoughts were miles from him, still not glancing at the ink-covered parchment.

It was as it had always been. He felt anger and then the

awakening of the old wound. She had been everything to him; he had been only a small part of her life, and easily put aside.

"A nun, then?" he asked, trying to feign interest.

"Not a nun. But almost. And with no knight offering homage, that I can see."

"Well, one at least has been worshipping at the temple, unless she claims that it be no man but an angel or incubus that has done this."

"She is no fool. Of course it was a man. But who?"

Bernart took the parchment from Eleanor's hands, fearful that her preoccupied twisting of it would soon render it unreadable. He laid it carefully on the writing table, trying to smooth out the new wrinkles and creases.

"What is that, my Rai?" she finally asked, putting aside her thoughts of Sophia.

"A new aubade," he said lightly. He turned to her and was happy to see that she was smiling at him, her thoughts were again aimed at him. "Shall I play it for you?" The lute was already in his hands.

"Perhaps later, my darling. I must look into this matter." She moved away from him, preoccupied once again.

Bernart blocked the door. He would not let her leave. He would not let her put him aside this easily. What of their love?

"Eleanor. My Queen." He took her face in his hands and pulled it towards his own, wanting to awaken the passion that had flared so brightly the night before.

Only if caught in those flames would she be truly his. She was not a parchment that could be satisfied with mere words, nor a bird that loves only music. She was flesh and blood and only through that flesh and blood would her heart be captured. He knew that now. He must take her into that flame of passion, where they would both be purified and made new. Their love would rise stronger from the ashes, like a phoenix.

He held her tightly, feeling her warmth and substance. He kissed her brow and each closed eyelid and then her mouth. His hands moved knowingly under the silk of her garments.

Eleanor, relaxed in his embrace, felt her legs weaken and begin to tremble. The weakness was sweet and still familiar, although no man had awakened it in her for years. She had lived chaste as a sanctified nun, and now her limbs, grown weak, her skin, burning where he touched, rebelled again against its enforced celibacy.

It was more than two years since she and Henry had embraced.

It had been Christmas; they were at Bur-le-Roi. The air smelled of frost and holly, and she and Henry, together for Christmas as they had been for so many years before, avoided each other. They sat next to each other at meals, slept next to each other in the great oak bed, attended chapel together. But they did not look at each other, nor speak to each other.

Rosamonde was there, too. She kept to the shadows like the sly, predatory creature Eleanor thought her to be, but she was there. All the court whispered and laughed of how King Henry brought his paramour with him for the Christmas celebration. Eleanor, furious, sent away any serving maid or page or stableboy who dared whisper as she approached or laughed too loud over an unheard jest. She kept her mouth forced into a thin smile that never reached her eyes.

Rosamonde, she was pleased to note, fared no better. Indeed, she looked so pale and wan, she was more spirit than whore. Like all idiots who put their faith into stolen love, she was suffering because Henry paid no attention to her.

Henry wore a long face that Christmas. He was possessed by Becket. That monk turned viper had finally returned to England from France, where he had hid from Henry behind Louis' crown and spite. Returned at Henry's invitation, after promising not to excommunicate the bishops who had crowned Hal when Becket had refused to do so.

And what a disaster that coronation had turned out to be. Eleanor was not there; she was in Caen seeing to problems that Henry had no time for. And she was still glowing from a different coronation in Poitiers, where her beloved Richard had been installed as Duke of Aquitaine.

Nor was Margaret, Hal's bride, at the coronation. And Louis of France, her father, was furious that his royal daughter had not been crowned.

The Young King himself was furious because Henry had given him a crown and none of the accoutrements that should go with it. No power. And no more money than he already had from an allowance.

And Becket. Becket was livid. As archbishop, only he had the power to crown Hal. And when he refused to do so till Henry and he straightened out their differences—which to Becket meant Henry must kneel in submission to him—Henry promptly paid poor, used Archbishop Roger to bless and place the crown on Hal's eager head. It was said that Archbishop Roger's hands trembled so at the coronation that he almost dropped the crown.

In such easy manner are the seeds of revolt sown . . . a wrathful archbishop who has won the fickle heart of the populace, a sulking daughter-in-law with a powerful and vengeful father, a petulant son with devoted followers, an absent wife who shares a dream different from her spouse.

Even then Eleanor dreamed of seeing Richard, her favorite, on the throne. Even then she and Raoul de Faye were saying, "What if Henry were no longer king?" And Louis and Hal were playing the same "what if" game and making plans.

When Becket returned to England, he promptly excommunicated Archbishop Roger and a dozen others who had a hand in the coronation. Did just what he had promised Henry he would not do.

It was Christmas. Henry was at Bur-le-Roi; Becket at Canterbury. And neither could eat, nor sleep, nor enjoy the Christmas celebrations, for thinking of the other.

Eleanor's heart burst with the need to berate Henry for his stupidity, his callousness. He most somehow make amends with Becket. He must placate Louis. That was what she had meant to tell him. But there was Rosamonde, cringing in the dark corners of the castle, and Eleanor hardened her heart and said nothing to Henry. Let the sky fall on him. It was nothing to her now.

Till one night he came to their chamber. Drunk as she hadn't seen him in many a year. And weeping like a child. Declaring that all had turned their backs on him, no one loved him anymore. Eleanor knew how much blustery, bullying Henry desired to be loved. Knew how much Hal's petulant silence hurt him, how much Louis' cold demands hurt him; how much Becket's ill will hurt him. And she could not keep her heart closed to him that night.

It was Christmas, the time when most of their children had been conceived, and though she was past bearing, it was still Christmas, she was still Eleanor, he was still Henry.

She helped him undress. He fell, unable to balance on one foot as she pulled his leggings off. He cried, and then he laughed, and she laughed with him. The laughter started as a small and foolish thing, then grew large and demanding till they were both holding their sides. It was, she knew even then, a release of other, less pleasant emotions disguised as mirth. But it was release. They laughed and shushed at each other and pointed fingers at the door where sentries stood, probably listening, on the other side.

And they loved each other that night. He held his arms open to her and called, "My Queen." It was the one gesture of his she could not refuse. They were like gods to each other, outside of time and place, and not even Rosamonde or Becket could matter to them.

How short that time lasted.

The next night the messengers came announcing that Becket was murdered in his cathedral. The announcement split time in two like lightning rending the summer sky: then, and now.

"Now," Bernart whispered in her ear, clasping her more urgently. "My Queen."

"No. Don't call me that," she said. He did not say it properly, not as Henry did, Henry who was her peer, her husband. Her troubadour said "My Queen" in a different manner, and it jarred.

"Lauzeta," Bernart whispered, bending her backward in his arms and brushing his mouth against the whiteness of her throat. "Beloved Lauzeta. Come away with me, away from this place. Be only mine."

It was the plaint of a shepherd for his shepherdess. It was sweet and coaxing. It pushed Henry not out of her thoughts but deep into their darkest corners, out of her mind's eye.

"We will sleep in the fragrant forest and live on berries and spring water, like Lancelot and Guinevere," he continued. "I will spend my days declaring my love, and my nights worshipping you with my body."

She sighed, thinking of a green glade far removed from Henry and the war, a green glade where Rai made his sweet music for her alone.

The scriptorium smelled of mildew and disuse. How long since Sophia had spent those peaceful mornings and afternoons here, working at the Boethius translation? Weeks. She couldn't remember how many. So many things had interrupted. Lucie. The court of love and the training of Godfrey. The arrival of the messenger. The turning of the war against Eleanor. The still room, where medicines and unguents must be prepared for the knights. For one knight in particular.

Sir Foulkes. The candles illuminating the dark recesses of her mind and heart grew brighter as she thought his name. Not that she loved him that greatly. She didn't. Such love . . . the love of a Lucie for a Godfrey, of an Eleanor for a Henry . . . such love had naught to do with her nature. She, born under the sign of Capricorn, was prudent and cool-headed in such matters.

Sir Foulkes was a friend, nothing more. A friend who had instructed her in matters of the flesh.

She pulled back the dusty, yellow silk cloth covering the casement; sunlight flooded into the scriptorium. Sophia stood in its path, bathing in it, and feeling that the light inside her was yet stronger than this imitative Aquitaine sun.

It was love she felt.

But not for Sir Foulkes. For him she felt pity first, and then a kind of scorn at all his rough edges second, and jealousy, yes there was jealousy, for even a woman who does not love herself seeks to be loved by the other. The love was for that light inside her. The light that would form itself from chaos into another human being.

She hugged her thin arms about her belly, cradling what was not yet fullness but only promise. A child. A child. She, Sophia, was to have a child. She chuckled and hopped a few steps of a country dance a maid had once taught her, not minding that she looked like a toad when she tried to dance. She, Sophia, was to be as other women. From her womb would issue a child.

The bright candles inside her went out one by one as shock gave way to joy, and that in turn gave way to fear. Should she tell Foulkes?

No. Good Christ, he might well laugh at her. Whatever it was he had expected of her, it most certainly wasn't a child. There had been too much pity in his love for her to trust him. No. He was friend now, not lover. The child had naught to do with him.

But with whom, then? She could not go into the forest and raise it on berries and water. They, the two of them, must live somewhere. But where? Poitiers was pleasant, but Sophia was clearseeing enough to know that this capital might soon be dangerous. Henry was pushing south. Henry was greatly displeased with Eleanor and her followers, and with good reason.

The convent? It was not unheard-of for a lady to go out of the convent flat-stomached and come back from a journey with a babe-in-arms. A little cousin or baby brother who could not be cared for at home, was how they explained it. And the child was put to crawl on the kitchen floor and drool and dirty himself with the cook's children, and no more thought was given it.

The grille. Sophia remembered the grille in the chapter house door through which visitors were greeted. The world was divided

324

into two parts, the outside and the inside, and for the nuns and lay sisters, all was on the inside. She hated that grille.

And the bells. The merciless bells that divided each day and night into four-hour segments, the bells that ruled time and all activities that take place in time.

No. Not the convent. That was for a different Sophia, not for this new one who had the future of another human being to consider.

Then where?

Home. Where she hadn't been in eighteen years, since the day her father turned his face to Jerusalem and never returned.

Would Berengar, her brother, welcome her? Not in his heart, perhaps. But he would make outward show of it, to preserve his own honor. And when the babe came, he and his lady would make up some story that no one would believe but all would accept. Berengar had six children as far as she recalled; they might have had another two since their last letters to each other. What difference would one more make?

Home, then. She would write the letter announcing her plans now. But first, there was another matter to attend to.

Remembering the convent had made her think of Lucie, and her problem. If she, Sophia, dreaded an imprisonment where she was well fed, well housed and much liked, how much more must Lucie dread an imprisonment where she would be meanly housed and fed, and treated with contempt.

She, Sophia, had changed. And so had Lucie. Neither could go back to what had been. Lucie was serf once, but no longer. She was a free woman who knew of will and self-determination. She had the appearance and the manners of a lady. She had suffered much and learned much and for what, to now go thresh wheat and sweep floors? That could not be what God intended. It would be cruel beyond words. She, Sophia, would take this matter in hand and do what Lucie and Godfrey could not.

She found Sir Foulkes in the stable. He was dressed for travel, in thick leather hose and quilted shirt, and with his breastpiece on but not secured so that it flapped a little as he worked. His heavy black cape was thrown hastily over the back of his restless stallion. The horse pawed the ground and rolled his eyes in anticipation of battle.

Sophia eyed his armor, which was bundled into gleaming heaps on his mule, his thick leather traveling clothes, his set face.

She stood in his path, immovable as the granite mounting block, breathing in the stable smell of horses. They stared at each other angrily for a long moment. He was the first to drop his eyes.

"Do you expect me to sit by the hearth doing nothing while my castle is burned to the ground by Henry's Brabantines?" he roared at her, looking at his boots. Then, in a meeker voice, "The message came this morning. The Brabantines are but a day's ride from St. Servan. Henry is wroth with me for my loyalty to Eleanor."

The Brabantines. Unless they were hindered by some force more powerful than their own greed, St. Servan would soon be leveled to the ground. The men would be spitted like cattle; the Brabantines took no prisoners when set loose on their own. They would kill a man for the half-eaten apple in his purse. The woman would be raped. Lucie. Thank God Lucie was here, in Poitiers. She must not go north.

Her fear changed to sorrow. Because Foulkes must not remain here. He was right. It would be shameful for him to remain idle in Poitiers. Even the canker that ate at his insides was not excuse enough to leave abandoned in war a castle and the people who belonged to it. They served him; he, in turn, owed them protection. Even . . . especially . . . if it meant exchanging his life for theirs. Foulkes was not a graceful man, nor one given to bouts of poetry and moon fever. But he understood duty and obligation.

She pitied him, then, that he must face death from both inside and out. Her pity gave expression in the lightness of her voice as she teased him. "I would expect no such common sense from you, Sir Foulkes." There was hidden meaning in her voice that reminded him of his own Lady Marie, his wife, and he peered sharply at Sophia.

"Weren't you going to give me the opportunity to pray you a good journey?" she asked, unsmiling.

326

Dutifully he leaned against the mounting block the leather shield he had been grasping, and went to Sophia's side. He put his arms around her and hugged her close, rubbing his chin against the top of her head.

"I carry your babe."

The words blurted themselves out. She hadn't said them, some demon inside her whispered them aloud.

When she heard them, she knew that some of the fear she felt when she looked at Sir Foulkes was fear for her own self. Her own small, ill-prepared, thin-hipped self who must carry and deliver this burden. She was trembling.

He did not move, but stood, frozen, with his arms about her.

He repeated her words. "You carry my babe." There was an almost imperceptible change in the way he held her; he shifted her lightly in his arms so that her heart beat closer to his own. He sighed, and she sighed, too.

There was a new covenant between them. He would never truly leave her, no matter how far he rode. She could never be a maiden again, but in her heart would know herself as Foulkes' woman.

"Still, I must leave," he said after a while, pushing her away.

"I did not tell you of this to bind you."

She was glad he knew. The knowledge of a new life would ease the pains of his old and dying one. Already his movements seemed more energetic, more confident. Cock of the walk. That was what he must have been as a young man: arrogant, brash, loud. She smiled and patted the horse's smooth, velvety black flank.

"You will see to your own safety," he mumbled. It was a command, not a suggestion. "You are a capable woman, Lady Sophia. You will see that you are well attended when . . . when the time comes." He coughed a little, hiding emotion.

"I will, Sir Foulkes. And you will see to your safety. God protect you and go with you."

He stepped onto the mounting block but she knew he would not yet leave. There were too many things yet unsaid.

"Perhaps next spring I will come south again. Would you welcome me?" he asked, fussing with the stallion's saddle and not looking at her.

"I would. But before then, there is another matter we must settle."

There was that tone, again, in her voice. She sounded like wife, not maid. The authority of it suited her, he thought. If he were a more powerful man he could wed her to one of his young knights and be godfather to the child he could not claim. Was that the other matter to be settled? But he was not powerful or rich to so freely arrange such binds. Nor did he think that Sophia, meek where other women were bold and bold where others were meek, would accept such a marriage.

For the second time, he stepped off the mounting block, perplexed, and confronted her. "What matter?"

"Lucie."

The one word was enough. His gruff gentleness fled, he grew taut with the knowledge of a coming demand. "What of Lucie?" he asked peevishly.

"She must be given her freedom." Sophia stood, stern and unflinching.

"Now you go too far, Lady!" Foulkes roared, putting hand to sword in a threatening gesture. She did not flinch nor waver.

"It is not that I go too far, Sir Foulkes. It is that you haven't gone far enough. For months now you have known of her presence here, yet you did nothing. You neither ordered her back to St. Servan, nor acknowledged her freedom. For she has been free, for a year now, and by law she is no longer yours."

"I know the law as well as you, Lady Sophia." He spit the words through clenched teeth. "She has not been in one court for a year, as the law requires, but has lived as a vagabond . . ."

"More as a pilgrim, journeying from shrine to shrine . . ."

"As a thief, more likely, slinking away in the night. She has not earned her freedom, and to give freedom to her would endanger her immortal soul." He finished on a note of self-righteousness: the concerned lord caring for his people.

"Yes. Now I understand. It is for her own good that you would let her journey north again to St. Servan." Sophia's voice began sweet as honey but grew more acid with each word. "For her own good that you would send her into the midst of the Brabantines, to be raped and murdered. Yes, I see all the good that will do the child." She ended on a high, vinegary crescendo.

They glared at each other again, chins jutting forward, hands on hips.

"I am not a rich man, Lady Sophia, to give freedom to all who ask," he finally insisted, wavering.

"We are not concerned with all. Only with one. She is not yours, Foulkes. Let her go."

He paced in angry circles, thinking.

Only last year he had planned to bed the wench. When he beheld her he beheld all that was seductive and desirable and sinful in women. She was the moist earth ready for plowing, the dark night that hides man's secrets, the hot sun that awakens the senses . . . the Woman, holding forth the apple of forbidden knowledge.

Now, when he beheld her, he saw other things. Gentleness. A look of suffering about the delicate mouth. Love, there in the brilliant dark eyes. Youth. Innocence. The delicateness of her form made his heart ache, not with lust but with amazement for God's artistry. He no longer envisioned her under him, naked and pressed flat and panting. He thought of the way she looked, kneeling at Mass in Queen Eleanor's chapel, her slender back and limbs as graceful and pure as the Virgin's. The sinner was saint.

What had happened in this twelvemonth to change his vision so? He continued to pace his angry circles, knowing it was more than the freedom of a runaway serf-maid that he must consider.

I have fought for a lost cause, he thought. The Queen's war may well cost me St. Servan, and even if I don't lose my holdings, I may well lose my liberty. Or my life. That would give any man pause for thought. Battle has never before worried me. But never before was I also battling my own flesh.

The knowledge of death lurked like a serpent ready to spring. Man must do good deeds before his death.

329

He looked at Sophia, the healer who had not been able to heal him. The pity in her eyes angered him. The anger slithered down his gullet and into his stomach, causing a spasm of pain so sharp it stole his breath. He braced against it, refusing to bend.

"She's free. My present to you, Lady Sophia," he said when his breath returned.

Freedom. The wish for it was like a canker in the stomach, eating one from the inside out. How often had he wished to be free of this burden of kingship, this drive for empire.

But freedom was for others, not such as he. He was chained to his ambition, wed to it. It, more than womanflesh, warmed him at night and prodded him alert in the morn. This love for land and power, this need to conquer and erase borders, was the most demanding love of all. It did not let go, not for a moment. Becket had understood. Becket had felt it himself. Had surpassed even Henry's ambition, because Becket's love for power reached to the heavens themselves. And so they became mortal enemies; power had been the seductive mistress that came between them.

And what would Becket think now of these sleekly fat, sly emissaries of Louis? Henry Fitz-Empress wondered. He would sneer at them. And pronounce anathema against Louis, who kept him waiting and then would not condescend to come in person to discuss the peace. Except Louis and Becket had been allies. Thomas had fled to Louis, for safety and succor, and spent long months at his court in Paris.

"Tomorrow, we beg of you," the wheezing archbishop of Sens repeated. "There will be a truce as of today, and on the morrow the King will meet with you to discuss the peace."

Henry heard Charles behind him curse and then spit on the ground.

But Henry, still thinking of Becket, raised his gloved right hand in acceptance. "Tomorrow," he said, frowning. He wanted to slash at these three with the broadaxe, separate their ears from their heads and send them back to Louis howling. But he was two days' ride ahead of the greater portion of his army; he hadn't the means to stage a pitched battle. And Verneuil must be saved at all cost. Even his pride. To save Verneuil, he would even delay his vengeance against his Queen, Eleanor.

To save Verneuil, he must abide these fools and wait upon Louis' will.

"Food will be brought into the city today. And water." He spoke this as a demand, not a question, to the emissaries.

"It will be done," they agreed, "now that Henry Fitz-Empress is here." There was something sniveling and sly in their tones. Something beyond the overly refined Parisian accent which had started to grate on Henry's nerves in these past years.

Henry turned his horse toward Verneuil, which was seven miles distant. He thought of his city, how in the still misty dawning it had been strangely quiet, too quiet. He wanted to ride up to the city gate, order them to throw the doors open, and ride in triumph to his people, yelling that their King was here, he had not abandoned them, not forgotten them.

He wanted to hear them shout back with joy. Long live Henry! Long live the King! Wanted the children to throw flowers at him, the young and fair maidens to extend their white arms as he passed, trying to touch his tunic for luck.

It was a while since he had felt that love, which was like fresh air and sweet water to him.

Tomorrow.

"We will ride back to the encampment," he told Charles. They left without exchanging further words with Louis' emissaries. The air was thick with ill will.

*   *   *

"What are you doing?"

Rai stole quietly into the chamber where Eleanor sat. Years in the monastery had taught him to be stealthy as a cat, when he wished to be. It was that potential for silence that had first eased his time in the monastery, when he could think of nowhere else to be, when it seemed that everything but silence had deserted him. Silence is the nothingness from which poetry is born.

He knew much of silence. Had, in fact, written aubades and philosophical letters about it. There were, Rai estimated, nine categories of silence, ranging from the ineffectual silence of the sleeping dog, which twitches and yips in dream-chase, to the complete silence of nonbeing.

Eleanor, he saw now, was at the fourth category of silence, where daydream begins to merge into action. She made no noise as she sat at her writing table, but her dark eyes were lively with thought and her mouth alternated between frowns and smiles.

"Penning a letter," she answered, slowly turning to him. She tried to clear her mind of thoughts to make room for her lover there. Rai was never satisfied with a small corner; he must have the whole chamber of her concentration.

"To the Young King," he guessed, kneeling before her and surrounding her knees with his arms. He laid his cheek against her thigh. It was a young man's gesture. It was strangely unsuitable for a man who was past fifty, she thought. But its very unsuitability touched her. It was as if Rai acknowledged no time that passed when they were separated. She twined her fingers into the steely grey hair at the nape of his neck, where it still grew bountiful.

"Not Hal. Richard," she corrected, growing agitated. She released her fingers from his hair and tapped them nervously against the writing table. "Hal is slow to write. It is always more informative to keep in touch with Richard."

"And what does Richard write, my love?" He gazed up at her, aware that his expression of love, his submissive stance, was the same attitude with which he adored the statue of the Virgin in its

333

little niche at the monastery. This is appropriate, he thought. Eleanor is Queen of my heart, ruler of my life.

"That Paris is losing enthusiasm for warfare, now that Matthew of Boulogne has been killed." Eleanor tried to smile, but her lips twisted with bitterness. That moment of ugliness pleased Rai, for it tested his love. Even when caught in imperfection, the beloved was adorable. He reached up and kissed her. She kissed him back, but in a preoccupied manner. She pulled away from him after a moment, rose, and walked to the casement. The breeze that came in there was as hot as a draft from the kitchen bread ovens. It made her thin silken veil cling wetly to her forehead, and she wondered for a moment what it must be like to dress in full suits of armor in this heat. No wonder men wearied of war in August.

Rai rose from his knees, where he had knelt before her, and claimed her deserted bench, grateful for its comfort . . . The dampness of the monastery had robbed his knees of their strength. He considered what he knew of this dead man, Matthew, who preoccupied his mistress.

Matthew, Count of Boulogne, had fought for the Young King and Eleanor against Henry. He caught an arrow in the knee when he fought the Old King's troops at Aumale. It was a simple and common enough wound, one that most knights quickly recovered from, even if they did retain a limp and no longer made a fine figure at the May fair dances. Yet Matthew's knee had not healed. It had festered and poisoned the whole of the body. Matthew had died of that simple, common wound.

Matthew's brother, the Count of Flanders, grieved strongly and loudly. Convinced that the death was a punishment for sin, he went to church and publicly repented of rebelling against his lord, King Henry Fitz-Empress. For that surely, he said, had caused his brother's death. A vassal must be loyal to his sovereign lord; to rebel against the true King was to repeat Lucifer's sin of pride, and be cast from heaven.

And now others were saying the same.

That the war was not a just one. That Henry had justice and God on his side.

Henry had taken Breteuil, and razed the castle there, Henry

was loosing his Brabantines on the countryside and all would be destroyed. Surely God was nodding his head in Henry's direction, they whispered.

What they meant was that they wearied of battle, Eleanor knew and Bernart suspected. They, all those clamorous knights boasting of brave deeds, wished to return to welcoming hearth and soft feather mattresses and gentler pastimes. In the stimulating morns of spring men dreamed of fine and glorious deeds. But in the breathless, hotter morns of late summer, ambition turned overripe and yellowed like hay ready for the scythe, waiting to be brought home to the barn.

And Louis. King Louis of France, who had once been Eleanor's husband but had lost her. He had been born a fool and hadn't changed his colors, it seemed. Louis could think of nothing but taking Verneuil.

"And what does Richard say of this?" Bernart asked. Richard. How could the name of the son stir the jealousy that did not come when he named either of the two men who had been, were, husband to his lady?

"That I must pray. And be patient." Pray. And be patient. Oh, God. When what she wanted to do was put on armor and breeches, as she had when she rode to Crusade, mount a horse in knightly style and lead the laggard troops herself. Richard would have her meekly on her knees, beseeching God.

"We are on the verge of taking Verneuil. Aumale has fallen, Brittany and Normandy are ours. We have lost Breteuil. Yet we could easily lose all, if we aren't very careful. And Richard tells me to pray and be patient."

Bernart of Ventadour stared at his beloved, feeling and suffering her impatience. She paced the chamber and beads of sweat appeared on her forehead from her great agitation. He had no words to give her. His songs were of love and her thoughts were of war. He was helpless.

At that same moment as his mother paced angrily in her chamber, Richard knelt submissively in prayer in the ruined castle of Breteuil.

His father, Henry, had been here before him. Henry had taken the castle, and then left it to his mercenaries. They had looted and razed it. All the coffers had been thrown open and emptied. The walls of the castle had been pulled down, salt thrown into the wells. The silk wall hangings were slashed and charred and trampled into the dirt. There wasn't a living soul about. All were either dead or in captivity.

Life had been extinguished in this spot, all beauty returned to the earth from which it had come.

Smoke and dust hung heavy in the air, obscuring distant fields where brown-clad peasants mourned their trampled crops and stolen cows and chickens. Their wailing merged with the calling of the magpies overhead. The chapel where Richard knelt was open to the day, its roof and walls gaped with jagged holes. The altar was stripped bare of its relics and icons, the walls were blackened from smoke and flame.

Richard had never before experienced destruction on this huge scale. Nor on such an intimate one.

It was a warm day, but his hands felt cold. They trembled as he prayed for the soul of the archer, Alberic. Yesterday Alberic had been full of life and laughter and bravery. Today he was underground, cold and lifeless and as distant from Richard as a soul can be.

He had fallen bravely in battle. Richard smiled and his lips twisted in the same way Eleanor's had when forced to say aloud that Paris might yet lose her war.

Battle. It had really been no more than a skirmish, one of those stupid things that sometimes happens but would not, were the world a well-ordered place. Richard's guard had come across some mercenaries camping in the forest. It was a small, ragged band, caught by surprise; they were tired and hungry and thinking only of the pungent chunks of meat sizzling over the fire and the night's sleep that awaited them.

Richard's guard, too, was tired from an all-day ride and not enough sleep or food for many nights before. There they were, Richard's men on horseback, the mercenaries gathered around the fire, both groups yawning and stretching, suddenly spying each other. The startled silence that immediately followed this unfortunate encounter lasted a long time, but not long enough. One of the mercenaries sighed and then cursed, and before Richard's sword could be unsheathed, the mercenary had taken a dagger from his belt and aimed it at the man closest him.

Alberic. He was stabbed to the heart and dead almost before his body hit the ground. Richard's guard quickly made carcasses of what had been men and they took revenge for Alberic. But revenge was cold comfort.

Richard, who was later to be called the Lion-Hearted, was sixteen and his hands trembled because they were cold from having been bathed in Alberic's blood, and then laying his friend in the earth.

Shame tainted his grief. He had watched Alberic's eyes open wide in surprise as he slipped and fell to the ground. Had watched the blood spurt as if from a fountain and then stop as the heart lost its pulse. Had thought, There but for God, and felt the fear of his own death long before he felt grief for his friend's death.

He was young enough that he did not yet know that it was so with all men, when death brushes so closely. And he felt shame.

He tried to harden his heart. A knight must conquer fear. As for the shame, two weeks of sleep in a hairshirt would be penance enough to wash away the guilt for his relief when Alberic fell and not he.

His hands, which had been folded for prayer, dropped to his sides, for no prayers had come. Then the left hand reached up to his right forearm and felt, under the cloth of his shirt, the ribbon studded with rubies tied there. The battle gift from his dame, Eleanor.

It was four months since she had first tied it around his arm. Four months since he had marched from Poitiers, a knight untried and inexperienced. It was a very short time. It was a very long time.

He knew now what battle was. One by one all his young man's questions were being answered, except for the most important. Why?

Did Alberic's death really have anything to do with putting Hal on the throne? Hal and Alberic had never even met, that Richard could recall. Yet Alberic had died for him. And what did it matter whether Hal sat on the throne, or Henry? What did it matter to Alberic, who was dead, or the peasants who had lost their huts and livestock and all the others who had, this summer, seen death and destruction come for them?

You are weary. You must sleep, he told himself sternly. These thoughts are not fitting. You have sworn your sword to a cause and you must not abandon it, or you will be dishonored in heaven and earth.

Why? that part of him that was still young cried out again.

I am free, Lucie thought, and the words made her dizzy. Free to go where I please, to stay where I please, to leave if I please. No one may say to me, "Come here" or "Go there."

The parchment said she was free. For this, she took Sophia's word. Lucie could no more read than Foulkes could write. Sophia had written the declaration for Foulkes, and read it to Lucie.

Lucie opened the paper and peered at the black marks on it, but no matter how hard she studied, they had no meaning for her. But deep in those black, curling insect legs of script was the message: Lucie of St. Servan was a free woman, bound to no one. She folded the paper into neat little squares and tucked it into her girdle, content that Sophia would not deceive her, especially about a matter as serious as freedom.

Free. As if to test this new theory, she plucked a rose from the overhead arbor. No thorn pierced her thumb; no gardener came to berate her for being where she should not be. She breathed deeply of the flower's perfume and caught within its green muskiness the very scent of freedom.

Sir Foulkes had left to go north, and she, Lucie, had not gone with him. She, Lucie, was no longer bound to the dreary marshes and stubborn fields of St. Servan, or to their lord, Sir Foulkes. She no longer must hide when sheriff's men approached, nor abstain from communicating at mass because of the sin on her soul.

She was a free woman with a clear conscience, innocent of sin against man or God.

She had sworn to return to St. Servan if God required it of her, to keep Godfrey safe. He had not required it of her.

Free. She was faint with joy and relief. Only now did she admit how much she had dreaded that return to St. Servan, the shame and beating that would follow. The long years without Godfrey.

Godfrey wore a sword now and knelt gracefully before great ladies and the Queen herself; Godfrey was all but a knight. He would not follow a serf-woman to her disgrace. She would have gone alone to St. Servan; alone she would have followed back into bondage the route that a year before had led her to freedom.

Alone. She was free. And alone. The day should have been golden with joy, but it was not. The rose fell into her lap. She stood, and the rose fell into the summer dust at her feet, and her own heart felt filled with that same dust, because of that word, alone.

There was a noise behind her, on the other side of the trellis that separated the pleasure garden from the more public gardens of the castle. Lucie shrank against the trellis, trying to become invisible. Benoit had been following her about for days, keeping a respectful distance but rarely letting her out of his sight. She felt she knew how the hart feels when the hunter is hot on its trail.

Since the court of love, when news of war had prevented her from naming the lord of her heart, he had been persistent in his pursuit of her. She tried to indicate by stern looks and gentle words of dissuasion that her heart was not his. The more she protested, the more enamored Sir Benoit became of what he thought was maidenly virtue. It was disdain and scorn he mistook for modesty, but he had not the schooling to know this.

Lucie pressed flatter against the trellis, hoping the white of the roses would meld in with the white of her bliaut. She wanted to relish the knowledge of new and honest freedom. But with Benoit she could not; he did not know she had once been bound. He knew naught of her. It was Godfrey who knew her as well as her own mother did. Indeed, better. He knew her as a man knows a woman when they take true pleasure in each other, opening one to the other every secret of flesh and spirit. That day in the meadow, after the court of love, after her vow to God, when they had joined again, had ended all dissemblance between them.

The intruder was near, just inches from her, hidden only by a thin screen of leaves. She held her breath. He began to talk to himself, practicing a speech not yet ripe for human ears, as men do when they are distracted and think themselves to be alone. She released her captive breath in a sigh of relief.

It was not Benoit. It was Godfrey.

"You waste your words on these shrubs. Speak them to me," she said, peering out at him from behind the trellis. The day grew glad again for having Godfrey in the midst of it, but she made her voice solemn, to match the tone of his.

"Lucie? Is it you?" He looked up, startled. "Yes, it is. Come then, and hear the words, for they were meant for your ears at any rate."

She came out from behind the trellis and took the hand he held out to her.

"I have been thinking, Lucie," he said without smiling.

"Me, too." She was eager to tell him her news, that she was no longer bound to St. Servan or Sir Foulkes. But instinct . . . and Godfrey's impatience to say his own speech first . . . made her hold her tongue.

"This vow you have made. It cannot be amended?" he asked. They had walked from the rose garden to a small flight of steps, sheltered by the tall wall of the Maubergeonne Tower. He sat on a damp stone, then rose again, took off his vest and spread it on the stone for Lucie to sit upon.

She blushed for joy at this new thoughtfulness. But she kept her face stern. "No vow can be amended once it is made."

They sat side by side on the step.

"I knew you would say that," he answered with a deep sigh. They sat in silence, listening to magpies and rooks scream in the sky overhead. Away from the coolness of the garden, the day was hot and breathless. Lucie watched as little crystals of sweat appeared on Godfrey's sunburnt forehead.

"Then this is what I have to say. I was the one who took you away from St. Servan . . ."

"At my behest . . ." she corrected.

"But I did the deed. I will return you to St. Servan, if you are determined to go back."

"And then what?" she asked, not looking at him.

"I don't know." There was pain in his voice. "I failed you twice. I cannot thrice."

"If you go north with me, then Marie may well forget about you. Another troubadour will come and take your place, and this summer's adventures will have been for naught. If you stay, you will have all you desire, I think. If you return with me, you will lose all you desire."

He hesitated. He was about to say a proposal fit for only a true saint or knight, he thought, and he was neither. Squaring his shoulders and taking a deep breath of resolve, he plunged into the midst of the speech he had been preparing.

"I cannot let you go again, Lucie. I will go with you because we belong together. Whatever it costs me."

"It will cost you a place at court."

"I know." He was growing angry. "Woman, why do you keep reminding me of what I would forget?"

"Because I would have you be certain in this. No looking over the shoulder once we have left."

"I am certain. We will stay together, come what may. There is no choice in this." The words were said. He felt relief. And great pride in his sacrifice. But he seemed to have lost stature; his shoulders slumped and the top of his head did not brush the sky, as it had a moment before. Lucie's heart thrilled to this sacrifice of the proud Godfrey. For her.

"Then I choose to stay here. At least for the time, till Marie decides to go elsewhere. It will be pleasant to be woman to a court troubadour. I want a dress of blue silk. And red leather slippers." Still sitting on the stone step, she stuck her legs straight out and pointed at her clumsy thick sandals as if to say, "See how unsuitable they are, if I am to be your woman again."

341

"You mock me," he said, glaring at her from under stormy, knit brows. "This is cruel, Lucie. I did not take you for a cruel woman."

"What is cruel here?" Feigned innocence left her voice. "Read this, Godfrey. I cannot amend my vow. But others can amend it for me, and Sir Foulkes has done that." Smiling now, she took the paper from the thick sash that tied her tunic close to her hips, and handed it to Godfrey.

"This says you are a free woman," he said after a long while. He reread it three times to be certain.

"So I am told," Lucie agreed. "Free to come and go as I please."

He read again the words on the paper and knew them, but did not comprehend them. Lucie free? Then an evil suspicion jumped into his jumbled thoughts.

"How did you come by this? What did you sell or promise to Sir Foulkes, to receive in turn such a pledge from him?" He had a sudden vision of Lucie's long, white legs captured within the hoary trap of the knight's old, gnarled ones. Jealousy and failure . . . once again he had failed to protect the choice of his heart . . . made him leap up in anger, the emotion that is a mask for all our others, when we wish them to be masked.

Lucie tugged at his shirt and smiled at him. "Nothing. I promised and gave nothing. Lady Sophia has arranged this."

Now he could understand. He had suspected all along that Sophia was a magician, that she had the skills he pretended to have when he heard thunder before all others and claimed to pull the rain from the clouds. Sophia had pulled a miracle from thin air, the miracle of Lucie's freedom. No longer was she a refugee, a creature who belonged to secret night shadows. She belonged to the day as well as the night. She could choose the road she would trod, say yes or no to all questions, rather than nod meekly and obey.

He looked at her and saw the tawny hair, the dark eyes, the mouth where he, disinherited son of a free knight, had placed his kisses to a serf maid. Now she was a free woman; she was the same, but not the same at all. He beheld a stranger.

"Godfrey, I thought this would be glad tidings for you, as it is for me," Lucie said, now worried. His expression was as unreadable to her as the spider leg markings on the paper he still held. She ceased pulling at his shirt and looked down at her feet in confusion, and that gesture took the veil from his eyes. It was no stranger, but his own beloved.

He knelt before her. He took her hands between his own and pressed them to his heart, so that she looked into his eyes and the flush came to her face.

"Now you are free, you must choose who will be your friend," he told her solemnly.

"Your brains are addled," she answered, equally solemn. "Who else but you?" They kissed, and sealed anew the pledge.

"We are free, Lucie," Godfrey said then, throwing his head back with a loud whoop of joy that echoed in the quiet bailey. No northern trek for them, no years of penance in Sir Foulkes' salt marshes. They could go where fancy took them, and he had a fancy to follow Lady Marie and see how far his songs could take him in this life. He pulled Lucie to her feet and, lifting her easily in his arms, swung her around and around in circles.

The next morning a thick mist covered the land. Henry, newly awakened from troubled dreams, leapt from his bed, believing the tents of the encampment had caught fire and they were enveloped in smoke.

"Nay, nay," Charles told him. "It is not fire but merely a strange fog that arose in the night and has not yet been dispersed by the laggard sun." Charles was already clothed in glistening mail, fierce and stubborn as the archangel Michael himself.

"It is an evil sign," Henry muttered. In the predawn darkness, made even darker by the fog, the camp had an otherworldly quality to it, as if, sometime in the night, a secret door had been opened and they had disappeared into the fairy mountain. Or purgatory. Warriors moved about, but all was strangely silent.

Henry, sleep-naked, his body cutting through the darkness like a silver blade, picked up a ewer of cold water and poured it over his head. The coldness of it made him gasp, and he threw his head and red hair back so that the water ran down his back and loins, driving from them all traces of sleep.

Just minutes later, he was dressed and mounted. His black charger picked his way over the cobbled road of Conches leading to the church. He rode with a small force of men. The mercenaries had been left behind at the village gate. He had come to treat for peace; no need to unleash the greed of the Brabantines on these people. He was weary of the war, and of the misery it brought.

The village was still shadowed in predawn darkness; no colors gleamed, everything was clothed in greyness. The mist was thinning, yet it still seemed to Henry that they moved unnaturally slowly, as in a nightmare when one is pursued by an enemy one can't outrun.

"I dreamed of fire last night," he told Charles.

"I dreamed of water. The one conquers the other. That is a good omen," Charles said.

Henry snorted and was unconvinced. Something was amiss.

The church doors were bolted shut from the inside when they arrived. Charles, dismounting, pounded on them till they boomed like thunder. In the silence between the great thumps, the village grew even quieter. Henry felt eyes, many of them, blazing into his back. He knew that if he turned to look, no one would be there. He felt the fear of the hiding villagers.

After a long while an ashen-faced, trembling priest opened the doors. He made the sign of the cross and then turned to flee within to the safety of the vestibule, but Charles caught him by his sleeve and would not let go. "Speak," he commanded. "Where is Louis of France, who was to meet us here?"

"M-M-My lords . . ." The priest stammered so thickly, he could barely be understood. "L-L-Louis is not within . . ."

Charles released the man so quickly, he almost fell. The priest made the sign of the cross again and fled.

"The French bastards are late," Charles muttered, turning to Henry.

Under his quilted warrior's vest, Henry felt his heart pounding, faster and faster like a runaway horse. It was the start of battle fever. He knew it well. But when had battle fever begun to leave him dizzy and blurry-visioned?

That was easy to answer. When everything else starting going bad, too. When Becket died. That night when the news was brought to him that Becket was murdered, when the Christmas holly still adorned the great hall and the wassail bowl was not yet empty, he had first felt this curious sensation of falling but not falling. As if his heart would jump out of his very chest.

He put his hand to his chest and pressed, as if such soothing could calm his frenzied heart.

"No. Not late. They aren't coming," he answered. "They have deceived us. We must ride to Verneuil. Now." The meaning of his dream of fire came to him, and his face was whiter than the priest's had been.

Verneuil was ablaze. The flames rose tall and wavering from the roofs, licking at the sky, coloring the grey dawn with rose tints.

Strange. He had expected to feel . . . triumphant. He did not. Louis had thought this act would finally lay to rest an old ghost. It did not. The flames were to have cleansed his soul, once and for all, of the bitter dregs of the already drunk past. They did not.

Louis of France, clothed in silk and silver garments adorned with the royal fleur-de-lis, stared down at burning Verneuil and felt . . . nothing. Except regret. Always regret.

He, who feared for his immortal soul, had risked it for one moment of sly cunning, for one moment of deceit. He who most prized his knightly honor had thrown it away for this one cunning moment.

His whole life had led to this one moment, and it was a moment of regret. Regret. That he had been born second son and therefore fit only for the Church. They taught him to love God and prayer above all else. Regret when that elder brother died and he, Louis, was pulled out of his meditative life to prepare for the kingship. He was taught to love glory and action above God. And being a King, he would need a Queen, and so the celibate, reflective young man was wed to the most beautiful lady of the land, Eleanor.

He had agreed to wed out of duty. If he was to be King, then he must produce heirs. But then he had met Eleanor, seen her for the first time, and everything was changed for him. She glowed like the moon, danced like a willow sapling in a breeze, she was all gay smiles and midnight whispers, perfume and poetry. He had not known that such beauty existed in this world. And it was for him. Or so he had thought.

Regret. He had loved her. Regret. She had not loved him.

He had tried to change that. Tried so hard to win his wedded lady's heart that he had been laughed at. There were the bedtime potions to increase his ardor and produce the son that did not come. The Paris barbers and sewers and gem-cutters who adorned his person. The physicians who recommended he beat Eleanor to make her pliable, and the poets who recommended he take a concubine to make her jealous. How he had degraded himself, all in the name of love.

And there was Vitry. Vitry-the-Burned, and as it was now known. Vitry, the town that had burned as easily as this Verneuil burned now. Vitry, the first blackbird sin on his pristine soul. For Eleanor.

All these many years ago, when he and Eleanor were still youthful bride and groom, she had decided that her sister, Petronilla, must marry Count Raoul of Vermandois. This man was a frequent visitor to their court, and a favorite with the ladies. He had broad shoulders, shapely legs, long-fingered hands and a silvered tongue given to poetry and flattery. It was rumored that he wooed at no less a love-shrine than the Queen's own.

Louis was beside himself with love. But he was not a stupid man. He saw the yearning looks that flowed between Eleanor and Raoul. He knew that, so far at least, his bride was still faithful. But her heart was under siege. If she wanted Raoul to bed and wed her sister so that she could, in some mysterious feminine way, take pleasure in the thought without actually committing the sin, he would help her in that. The wedding would kill three birds with one stone. It would please Eleanor, it would remove Raoul from court, and it would settle Petronilla's future.

There was but one problem. Raoul of Vermandois was already married, and to the daughter of the mighty house of Champagne.

Louis took the well-worn path used by all those who wished to dissolve a marriage . . . the same path Eleanor would later take to end their marriage. He found three bishops who "discovered" a degree of consanguinity that prohibited marriage between Raoul and his wife; thus the marriage was annulled.

Eleanor and Petronilla were pleased. Rome, Raoul's wife, and Thibault of Champagne, the put-aside wife's uncle, were not. Raoul was ordered back home to his wife; he refused. His new wife suited him better.

Champagne swore to avenge the dishonor to his family. Louis swore to defend his sister-in-law and her husband. Louis the Pious, the protector of the faith, the oblate of Notre Dame, found himself excommunicated from the Church, his soul in mortal peril. To please Eleanor.

Oaths were sworn, swords drawn, sides taken. Louis himself led his invading army into Champagne, to chastise its overly proud count. To please Eleanor. He had donned armor and weapon, not thinking of the blood that would be shed, but wondering if Eleanor would call him her fair knight and give him her colors to wear.

Vitry. A sleepy town like hundreds of others, except it was in his army's path. It was an ill-defended town, vulnerable, quick to be taken. And so Louis' army had taken it. Vitry blazed like a pile of kindling. The people of Vitry fled their burning homes and sought sanctuary in the church. That, also made of wood, caught fire as easily as the rest of Vitry.

Women and children. He heard their screams and wailings as the church caught fire and filled with smoke. He watched and listened, his heart racing. This was battle. This was war. The screams of women and children being burnt, being suffocated. The church roof collapsed, sending a shower of burning wood onto them. It took a long time for all the screams to finally die away, for silence to come. And when it was finally over, Louis was pale and shaking and feverish.

He fell sick after Vitry, with a sickness that robbed his body and soul of the desire to live. He could not eat or pray. Nor sleep, because when he closed his eyes, he heard all over again the screams of the women and children of Vitry.

Nor could he die. Not while Eleanor lived. He could not bear to be parted from her, to leave her widowed and vulnerable. Many would seek to console her. And Louis knew that it would not take Eleanor long to be consoled for losing him. He did not die. Nor did he live, not in any real sense, for many long months, except for those rare moments when his Queen would take his hand and smile at him.

Vitry-the-Burned, the place was called now. And now Verneuil was ablaze.

He had expected to feel triumphant. He did not. Watching the flames of burning Vernueil lick at the grey sky, he felt a sickness like the one that had come over him at Vitry.

He had set fire to Verneuil to avenge himself against Henry, who had stolen Eleanor from him. But that was a lie. Eleanor had never really been his. He had set fire to Verneuil to topple Henry from his precarious throne and set the Young King, and therefore Louis' daughter, who was Hal's wife, on that throne, finally. And that was a lie, too.

This was Eleanor's war. Verneuil burned for the same reason Vitry had.

To please Eleanor.

Louis turned away from burning Verneuil, sick at heart, defeated.

7

As soon as Rai picked up his lute and began strumming it, that curious sense of lethargy came over her. As if she had no will of her own. As if her destiny were written in the music, in the words, of his love song. She could not live outside of his singing. Eleanor nestled deeper into the gold-threaded silken cushions of her couch, and listened.

> And in this My Lady appears very much a woman
>   for which I reproach her.
> She thinks one should not want what is forbidden him.
>   It happens. And here
>   I have fallen in bad grace.

I have fallen in bad grace. This was one of the old songs. Bernart wrote it when they first realized that Henry was watching them out of the corner of his eyes, growing suspicious. Fifteen years before this moment, it had still been Henry and Rai and Eleanor.

This was the strange thing. She hadn't seen Rai for fifteen

years. Yet when he came to her in the meadow and put his hands over her eyes, it was as if they had parted just the day before. Whereas with Henry . . . her separation from him was measured in months, not years. Yet it seemed an eternity. Which separation—the long one which seemed short, or the short one which seemed eternal—bespoke of the better love?

And what was happening at Verneuil? Had Henry broken Louis' siege? How irksome to play the part of the woman, to sit on soft cushions and merely imagine the happenings in the larger world, happenings achieved and decreed by men.

She tried to summon up the hatred, to remember that Henry was foe now, her worst enemy. But her memory tricked her, or maybe it was Rai's song, which called back earlier, sweeter times. She remembered Henry, not as he had been at Christmas past, cold-eyed and crazed with the knowledge of his own mortality, the realization that even he, Henry Fitz-Empress, could not go on forever, could not wear the crown forever, no matter how much he wanted to.

She remembered him as he had been twenty years before. Slender in his youth, and so confident of his ability to mold men and lands that he was generous, not grasping. Life and power and love he held lightly in his opened palm. Now his hand was closed in a grasping fist and the things he most desired were escaping his grasp like water.

Henry had regained the North; but if Louis won Verneuil, victory would yet be hers. And how would Henry be comforted?

She was watching Rai, smiling at him, listening to his song, but her love for Henry was like a bird beating its wings against a cage, trying to be free. It would not be silent and still, as she bid it.

They rode like demons, driving cruel spurs into their horses' flanks, not caring that soon the army of foot soldiers was far behind them and then the mounted mercenaries were also left behind and it was just Charles and Henry fleeing, not from death, but to it, to Verneuil.

Henry tried not to think. It was painful to think. But some stupid, barely remembered song in his head kept time with the pounding horse hoofs.

> I have fallen in bad grace . . .
> The chance for grace has been lost, I shall not taste it,
> for she who should have it most has hardly any, and
>   where else shall I seek it?
> It is bitter for me to look on her
> who lets a helpless wretch die of his desire
>   and will not aid him.
> He will have nothing without her.

He will have nothing without her. Eleanor. Bernart of Ventadour, that star-gazing fool, had written the song for Eleanor. Eleanor, when she was Henry's young wife and rounded with his second son, Hal. Being with child suited Eleanor, made her flesh soft and yielding and her mind quick and ambitious. William's birth had been a hard one; Henry could have guessed from the trouble the boy-infant gave that he was not long for this world. But that second son, Hal, had been born even before Henry knew the birthing had begun. He had come willingly and joyfully into the world with a great wail and flailing of arms.

What a pretty babe he had been. Henry, proud as any father, dangled the bald, toothless Prince Henry on his knee, fed him ale from his fingertip, which the angel-faced boy sucked at greedily. It was the same babe grown to manhood who now warred against his own father and King. Eleanor had brought this about.

Henry, with the bitterly recalled words of a love canso written by a troubadour for his Queen ringing through his thoughts, rode harder till even the faithful Charles was left behind, choking and muttering in the dust.

The sun was high in the sky when he arrived at Verneuil, the mist long since burned off the land. But over Verneuil, the sun was a vague, thin silver disc, almost obscured by smoke.

The siege was over. Verneuil was taken. The gates were now thrown open. A few villagers milled out of them, quick or slow, depending on their ability, with cloth bundles thrown over their shoulders. A lifetime of striving was hastily scooped up into a rag and thrown over the shoulder as they fled their burning huts or town houses, the once wealthy with the once poor brought to new equality by fire and war.

Henry pulled his charger to a stop outside the gate. Or what had been the gate. Pieces of splintered wood lay all about. The gatekeepers were nowhere to be seen.

The city was devastated. It had been vanquished and then set ablaze. The cruder wood and thatch huts had burnt to the ground. Only charred squares indicated where they had once been. The grander buildings of wood and stone had been burnt and razed, the brick guild halls of the market square turned to piles of rubble. The air was thick with smoke and dust and weeping.

Henry was awed that Louis had been able to wreak this much destruction in a mere twenty-four hours.

The people of Verneuil did not look up as their King rode into the city. They did not cheer. They were like sleep walkers, dazed with grief and shock. This day they were to have been rescued by Henry. Instead, Louis' army had ridden boldly into the city, denying the three-day truce, and devastated it.

Henry heard another rider approaching behind. He looked only briefly, and that out of the corners of his eyes, so that the arrival would not see the traitorous liquid that seeped from behind his eyelids.

It was Charles. He said nothing. His stern warrior's face, as he pulled his horse abreast of Henry's, was pale and frozen. This was infamy as he had never before witnessed. Louis, who had arranged the three-day truce, had given his pledge as knight and Christian and King. And then broken that pledge. Chivalry that day had been trampled into the dust.

Charles and Henry rode without speaking to that part of Verneuil known as the Great Burgh, the fortress that crouched behind the last moat and wall of the castle of Verneuil. The destruction was just as great here. Greater. The villagers, the merchants and tailors and fishmongers, had the right to flee when threatened with death, and flee many had. Thank God, Henry

thought. But here, in the Great Burgh, here was where the
knights and foot soldiers and archers had gathered for the last
brave defense of Verneuil. From here, no man fled. The stone
walks and balustrades were stained with blood. Everywhere the
shocked eye turned there was a corpse waiting to be discovered.

"We will need gravediggers," Charles said, finally.

"Yes. Find who you can, and tell them they will be paid well.
And have word sent to my army now approaching. They are to
camp outside of the walls tonight. I will sleep here. Alone."

Charles nodded grimly, and turned to leave. His horse clopped
over the bloodstained paving stones of the Great Burgh. Overhead, vultures circled in the smoky sky.

> But I have no right, and no pity or prayer
> can avail me with My Lady:
> since my loving does not please her, I shall
> speak no more to her of it,
> so take my leave, sever myself from her, she
> has killed me,
> answer her like a corpse, she
> does not keep me,
> go away into exile, I
> don't even know where.

For such a lady's man, Bernart had an accurate sense of the
macabre aspects of loving, Henry thought. He stretched his bare
feet closer to the fire he had built. It was only a little blaze giving
only a little warmth, but its dancing light kept the night darkness
at bay. The darkness, and the ghosts—the old familiar ones and
the new ones made that terrible day.

Outside that weak circle of light lay dead Verneuil. Henry,
alone, camped in the midst of the destruction, surrounded by the
razed and burned homes, the pile of rubbish that had once been
the Great Burgh.

He had not bathed, nor supped, not taken wine. This fire was
his only consolation for the labor of the day, and that was as it
should be. A man with as much hate in his heart, as much thirst

353

for revenge as Henry had at that moment, was better off with an empty stomach; it made more room for the hate.

> . . . she has killed me,
>   answer her like a corpse, she
>   does not keep me,
>   go away into exile, I
>   don't even know where.

Yes, fine words from a lover to his beloved. If that beloved be Eleanor. She was a viper, a harlot. A traitor. Men died for lesser crimes. The hatred swelled his gut like an undigested meal, sending acid and poison into his veins, into his brains. Louis had done this. But he had done it for Eleanor.

"Eleanor, make thyself invisible," Henry told the surrounding night. "Hide thyself under a rock from the searching light of day, for wherever thou art, I will search thee out. And if I find thee, I will murder thee."

He felt better then, almost able to sleep. Eleanor, his Queen, the traitor, would die.

First, Henry would chase the craven Louis to France, to the very gates of Paris; if he caught Louis, then France would be without a King and better off for the loss. And then, when Louis was dead or shown for the coward that he was, then Henry would go for Eleanor.

He smiled, imagining his wife's face and the fear in her eyes as he, Henry, burst into her sleeping chamber and, dagger drawn, put it to her breast. Smiling, with the ghosts of Becket and the newly murdered villagers of Verneuil dancing and calling to him from outside the little blaze of his bonfire, he fell asleep finally. He was unaware that this was the first day in many years when he had not thought of Rosamonde, but only of Eleanor. Eleanor had two victories that day.

She climbed up from the depths of a dream, a dream of being buried alive, cut off from all light, all gaiety, all happiness and music. At the top of that climb, peering at her as if over the sides of a deep well, was Henry. He was laughing. He held a dagger.

354

She wanted to scream but could not; all she could do was climb, climb and struggle up out of the dream.

She sat up, eyes open, awake. Her skin was damp with sweat, her heart pounding. Bernart, sleeping next to her, woke up instantly.

"What is it, beloved?" he asked in a gentle voice. He reached across the bed and pulled Eleanor to him. The night was hot and humid, the air had a stifling, underwater quality. Salty perspiration covered his chest and shoulders. When she leaned against him, she had the slippery, wet sensation of being submerged. She could not breathe. Gasping, she pulled away. His hand pursued her in the moon-shot darkness, captured her shoulder once again and she remembered, yes, love was this, too, a prison one could not escape. Did not wish to escape.

"A dream. Only a dream," she whispered, sighing and leaning against him in surrender. She closed her eyes, forced her breathing to become leisured and easy, forced her arms and legs, still tensed for flight from the nightmare, to relax. They rested companionably against each other in silence, watching the patterns the moonlight made on the stone walls of Eleanor's chamber. Outside, an owl hooted, and from far across the bailey they heard the yapping and howling of the kenneled hunting mastiffs.

"I wonder sometimes . . ." Bernart began, reaching for a silk cushion to support her shoulders. The silk was cool against her skin as he slid it in place, but in seconds it, too, felt hot as noon sun.

"What do you wonder?" she replied, concentrating on his voice, putting aside the dream, the heat, Henry.

"What our lives could have been. Had you not been Queen. Had you been just another lady seeking love as the greatest goal." His hand brushed against her bare neck and breast, light as a breeze. His voice was light, but she knew the words came from a dark and deep place, the land of what-might-have-been. It was a dangerous place.

"But I was not just another lady. Nor did I wish to be. For a Queen, love cannot be a goal, but merely a reward."

"Or a pastime," he added, and there was bitterness in his voice.

She turned in his arms and looked up at him. His profile, in the moonlight, was still beautiful as a well-sculpted statue. Age had changed him, had made his once raven locks grey and thin, and etched deep lines in his brow. But it had not touched the profile, had not weakened the jaw or lengthened the nose. He had been, and still was, the fairest man she had ever met, even at this more dangerous age when beauty easily slips into a caricature of what it had once been.

"Bernart of Ventadour. You were never my pastime. You were more. Much more. Too much more. That is why I let Henry send you away from me."

"Thank you," he whispered after a long while. "That is the closest you have ever come to saying you love me, Eleanor."

Her words awoke his passion, stirred his hands to more zealous activity than teasing her earlobe. They wandered down the inside of her thigh and then up again, circling the center of her pleasure as if it were a town under siege but not yet taken. Her knees, the gates of that town, opened willingly and he entered in triumph, setting fire to her senses. They rocked together and filled the chamber with sighs and pants and groans till the night was alive with their love and even the noisy owl stopped to listen.

"Come away with me, Eleanor," he said afterwards.

"Away, where?"

"Wherever you wish. Wherever you will be safe. Constantinople, if you like. Paris. Campostela, Sicily. The world is filled with places where a knight and his lady can live in privacy and peace."

"Flee, you mean. Hide. Are you so certain I will lose this war, Bernart?" She answered lightly, but there was ice in her voice. He ignored it and continued, carefully picking words thorned as roses, not for their poetry but for their finality. Once said, these words could never be unsaid.

"It will be better if you do lose. It will avail you nothing to win this war, except more war. All I care for is that we should not be separated again. I lost you once for fifteen long years. If we lose each other again, there will be no more reunions. Eleanor, let us live out together what remains of our lives."

She rolled away from him and sat up. His words upset her; he had meant to upset her. Not because what he suggested was impossible. But because it was possible. And it frightened her. She had spent her life becoming what she was at this moment, Henry's wife, for better or for worse. Henry's Queen. Mother of a new King. And a simple nod of her head could destroy all that. In a moment. She could leave this life as easily as she could leave Poitiers, leave here a Queen, and enter another city as just lady. She had easily and without regret given up the crown of France when she divorced Louis. This second crown, the crown of England, could also be discarded.

Despite the heat, she now felt cold.

"I must think of my sons. Of Hal. He needs me. He needs guidance," she stalled.

"No. The Young King does not need you. Nor do the others. No more will they come to you to heal their little wounds and tell them tales of Arthur. They are grown men all, and must do grown men's work."

He wanted her, what was left of her life, so desperately, he was willing to be cruel. "Nor does Henry want you anymore. Many years ago you gave him all he wanted from you—the richest lands on the continent, and sons. He wants nothing more of you. He has the fair Rosamonde. You have served your purpose, Eleanor. All your purposes. Now serve yourself. Let love be your purpose."

"Rosamonde. Hah! That white-faced little nun. He'll tire of her . . ." She grabbed at arguments. There must be a reason why Eleanor of Aquitaine, Queen of France, should continue to be all she had become. Or all her striving had been for naught.

"He will tire of her," Bernart agreed. "And then find another. As he always has. His heart was never yours, Eleanor. Mine has always been. Let me love you. Let me give you peace and pleasure. And safety."

To go away with Rai. To Constantinople. To see again the turrets and minarets, to taste the sweets sold by black-veiled women in the bazaar, to hear the musical fountains that adorned each city square, chasing away the eastern heat. She could buy a marbled pleasure house in the royal city and wear strings of amber, and trousers and tunics. She could veil herself and go into the secret parts of the city where men trained serpents to dance, and every pleasure, every amusing oddity, could be seen and even purchased. She could live for pleasure, far from duty, far from memory, far from her sons. Children brought pleasure, but they were also a burden, they never turned out as one expected. Their failures were daggers in her heart.

She would be with her Rai, who would sing for her and make love the sum meaning of existence. She could be young again, for a little while, before age robbed and cheated her of all possibilities.

It was possible.

Let it be possible.

The owl called again, bringing her thoughts back to Poitiers.

"Come away with me, Eleanor," he repeated. She frowned, deep in thought, and did not answer.

The next morning, news came that Verneuil had been betrayed and burned by Louis.

Eleanor, pale and with deep shadows around her eyes, sipped at a mug of weak morning ale while Amaria helped her dress in her riding habit, fetching thick leather boots and red, flowing mantle.

Bernart was already dressed for the hunt in glowing green tunic and hose and stood impatiently nearby. Rather, he feigned impatience, sensing that Eleanor expected it. In reality, he loved watching this morning ritual of his beloved, the brushing of the long hair till it crackled and then the plaiting of it, the bathing of the face and bare chest in rosewater, the womanish donning of the morning's costume.

Amaria stood, comb in hand, teasing one last snarl from the end of Eleanor's ribbon-twined plait. Amaria saw the open desire on Bernart's face and thought of Richard, whose eyes would one day burn just that way for her. Please God. She blushed and backed out of the room, almost bumping into Raoul de Faye, who was just entering.

"You are hunting today?" he asked, eyeing with obvious satisfaction Eleanor's choice of costume. "It is well for a Queen to hunt. Henry was at fault when he discouraged you from joining him in the chase." As always, his voice was heavy with hatred for the King. Eleanor heard it and wondered for the hundredth time whence originated this hatred. Probably in some long-ago deed, some imagined slight, that had naught to do with her.

"Fair uncle, the King has many faults as we all proclaim, but never did he exclude me from the chase. Only when I was large with child did he encourage me to take my ease."

"As any husband should," de Faye insisted, refusing to acknowledge any virtue in the King.

De Faye did not look at or greet Bernart de Ventadour. The troubadour was, by his thinking, no more than Eleanor's plaything, certainly not a peer worthy of courtesy and consideration.

Bernart, irritated, pointedly sat at Eleanor's desk in the middle of the chamber, where only a blind man could not see him. Still de Faye did not offer him a greeting. Bernart's fine mouth turned up in a twisted smile. Thus had men always treated him, when they weren't treating him to harsher measures such as bodily eviction. In the silence of his monastery cell he had often wondered if he would have had more and better male companions if he had not been so comely and sought by women. But that had not been God's intention, it seemed. And if this disdain from men resulted in a larger share of Eleanor's love, then it was as it should be.

"A message," de Faye said, solemn. "That is what prompts me to disturb you at this early hour, my child."

"Uncle, well you know that I have been up for many hours already, and a message at this time is not disruption but possible purpose for the day's activities." She spoke through clenched teeth, angered by his lack of courtesy to Bernart and his condescending manner to her.

De Faye, conscious that he had successfully angered the Queen, handed her the parchment, then hastily retreated back out the door, glad that Eleanor's displeasure provided a ready excuse to cut short the interview. He was already well aware of its content, as was all of Poitiers. News, especially bad news, raced over the land like wind before a storm. And the sacking of Verneuil, no matter how it furthered the war, would not please her. Not the way Louis achieved it.

Eleanor did not tear it open till de Faye had gone, but her heart was pounding. The red sealing wax bore the Young King's signet.

Her son had written curtly and to the point. "The siege is over. Verneuil is burned. We ride ahead of Henry to Paris."

She sat on a bench and let the parchment drop to the floor.

"They have sacked and burned Verneuil," she told Bernart, white-faced.

"I thought Verneuil was under a three-day truce, till Henry and Louis could treat," he said, confused by this news. Since when was a city under truce openly sacked and burned?

"It was. Louis and Hal broke the truce. They deceived Henry, and burned the city while he was camped at Breteuil."

"My God. That was not well done." He looked away from Eleanor. Her expression was terrible.

"No. It was not well done." The chamber was empty except for Eleanor and Bernart. But it felt crowded, very crowded; she wanted to go to Rai but could not find the strength to move through the thick air. Instead, she leaned against the casement and peered out, squinting. The sun was getting high in the sky, casting a yellow glow over still sleepy Poitiers, which lay at her feet like an obedient, loyal mastiff. In the far-off golden fields, farmers, always early risers, flashed scythes in swinging arcs as they cut rows of wheat. She could see the sun glinting on the scythes.

"He delayed coming to my bed as long as possible. Oh, the hours he spent on his knees." She spoke as if from a great distance, softly, her voice low with remembrance. "Louis has always had a reputation for monkliness. That, I suppose, is my fault. When I was young and foolish, I confused his lack of skill as a lover with saintliness. For a saint, he has a terrible penchant for burning villages. And to have done it in this way. By deception, instead of open battle. He has shamed me forever." She kept her face turned away from her lover, and squinted harder into the distance.

"You are not shamed, for you are not the agent of this evil deed," Bernart said softly. He did not go to her side. There are times when everyone, warrior, lover, saint and noble, must stand alone. To try to embrace her now would be as distasteful, as condescending, as de Faye's tone of superiority.

"No, Rai. They will say it was done for me. All of history will name me as the destroyer of Verneuil." She laughed bitterly. "I think I liked it better when I was known as harlot."

The laughter, harsh as it was, woke her from her reverie. "Too late for regret," she said. "Now there are other matters to consider. Hal and Louis ride ahead of Henry to Paris. They are fleeing, is what Hal meant. Henry is pursuing them for revenge, and they are fleeing like rabbits before the hounds. And when Henry catches them, he will come to Poitiers. For me. And he will not be forgiving. He will not be gentle."

They went hunting as planned. Eleanor insisted upon it. "Else I will sit and pine in my rooms," she said. "There is naught I can do. And that is the hardest thing to do, nothing."

She insisted that the entire household ride with her, all those ladies and knights still encamped in the many chambers of the ducal palace of Poitiers. Some dozen ladies and two dozen knights, dressed in hunting greens and browns and reds, accompanied by pages and trumpeters and all the falconers and hunting dogs of the Queen's stable, rode in double file through the streets of Poitiers and out into the fields, and then into the wild, wooded countryside. Only Sophia was excused. Sophia was afraid of horses and she was always sick to her stomach these days.

Eleanor's retinue smiled frozenly and made light conversation, but their eyes were never still, always darting to see ahead, behind, in case Henry's mercenaries should be lurking behind a peasant's hut or in a green copse. Benoit, the youth who had never seen battle, rode boldly with outdrawn sword. The sly, beady-eyed Maingot rode close to him, praising Benoit's comeliness and bravery till the youth blushed from all the honeyed flattery. Lucie, lately Free-Woman Lucie, rode at the end of them, bravely clenching reins and muttering sweet bribes of after-hunt carrots to her horse, if only he wouldn't toss her.

Godfrey rode farther up the column, next to Countess Marie, but he spent more time looking back to see if Lucie was still mounted or fallen into the mud than he did conversing with his lady. Marie looked a little put out at this discourteous behavior, but she could hardly command her troubadour to ignore the maid. She knew there was a friendship between the two, and she, the superior being of the three, would have to be patient. He had sworn his love and honor to her; if he also maintained a little *amica*, as did most knights, then she was more than willing to overlook that slight fault. Men, after all, were corporeal beings with certain appetites that must not be sated within the chivalric love pact. Yet she could almost be jealous of the way he regarded Lucie so frequently and with such obvious tenderness . . .

At the head of them all rode Eleanor, straight-backed and proud, with Miribile, the eagle, on her right shoulder. The raptor's plumed and jeweled hood glinted in the sun, and the golden bells on her jesses rang with authority.

Bernart, who carried only a small goshawk, knew Eleanor's back was rigid with pain from the weight of the eagle. But Eleanor would never show the pain except for a certain tightness in her lips, nor relinquish the eagle to her falconer, who rode behind. Eleanor was no less proud than Miribile; this was the woman whose memory he had carried in his heart for fifteen years. There was no more worthy woman in Christendom, and his heart swelled with pride.

But her temper was short that morning. She felt him staring at her and turned to him with a look of great scorn.

"You are not so steady in your seat that you can afford to leave the way entirely to your horse," she reprimanded. "Pray, pay some attention to the path before you injure the beast."

Fifteen years before, his cheeks would have blazed with fury for being so addressed in public. But the silence of the monastery had taught him the futility of anger; besides, he knew she was not truly angry with him but with the situation that Louis had created.

"I forgot, My Lady. Eagles must never be stared at. I beg your pardon." She smiled then, as he had intended. It pleased her to be reminded that more than one knight, more than one chronicler who records great deeds, had nicknamed her "the Eagle," for her braveness and boldness.

"But Lauzeta, your lark, is happy if she pleases you. I beg your pardon, Bernart de Ventadour," Eleanor replied, and there was peace between them again.

They dismounted in the same fringe of meadow outside the great forest where she and Bernart had been reunited just weeks before. He wished she chose this place for sentimental purposes, but he knew she chose it because the hunting was good here.

In the short span of time it took the sun to move from the fringed green treetops to the heat-whitened sky directly overhead, Eleanor flew Miribile at three pheasants and two rabbits. Miribile hunted with calm, efficient deadliness. For each kill, she wheeled and soared up to the nether part of the deep sky till she was a mere black speck, then, raising her wings above her, she dove with lightning speed, catching her prey by the mask and driving her inevitable talons deep into the skull.

Obediently she dropped her kill at the falconer's feet and then half flew, half hopped back to Eleanor's shoulder, landing there with an audible thud. Eleanor sat smiling, denying the weight and the pain, swaying from the force each time Miribile returned to her shoulder.

The other raptors—Marie's gentle merlin, known as the Ladyhawk, Bernart's goshawk and Chabert's kestrel—did not do half as well, but no bird can compete with an eagle for speed and determination and farsightedness. The game bags were soon filled, but mostly with Miribile's kill.

After, when the others were gathered at long trestle tables set up in an open glade, Bernart and Eleanor walked together in the forest. It was quieter away from the now relaxed and chattering retinue. A gentle green light filtered onto them, a light as comforting as that which is filtered through a cathedral's stained-glass window, and a choir of starlings sounded from high in the forest canopy.

They sat beneath a huge oak whence dripped tendrils of mistletoe. She leaned against him, no longer a proud and strong Queen, but merely a woman, and a tired, aching one at that. He massaged her shoulder, feeling through her thin gown the red welts left by Miribile's talons.

"You should hunt with a gyrfalcon, or even a merlin. Miribile is too heavy for you," he reprimanded.

"I will not hunt with anything less than an eagle," she insisted, wincing as his fingers probed a particularly painful spot. "When Henry asked me to wed with him, he said, 'Eagles are for emperors. With Eleanor as my bride, with this eagle at my side, I will rule the land.'" She plucked at a blade of grass, split it with her fingernail as if she would make a wind whistle of it, as the children did. Then, with a gesture of defeat, she tossed it aside.

"And so he did," Bernart supplied.

"Yes. He ruled. The land. His sons. He tried to rule me. I will not be ruled, Rai. I will not let him make of me a discarded wife fit only for spinning silks and tales of what-once-was."

"I have offered you a different path."

Again, she did not answer.

8

Broderick clapped his hands with pleasure when Robert told him the mercenaries were coming, because the startled monk also said that Broderick would have to leave the monastery.

"You'll have to go into the forest," Robert explained. "Play hide-and-seek, and not let the soldiers find you."

Broderick, delighted, clapped his hands again and jumped up. In doing so, he overturned the fragile trestle table in the refectory, toppling bowls of apples and baskets of bread onto the floor. The other monks—there were considerably fewer than there had been a month before—yelled with displeasure, their tempers considerably shortened by the menace that was pounding closer.

To leave the monastery would be no hardship for him, Brother Robert realized, going on hands and knees to help Broderick fetch the errant apples. The man with the child's mind had the child's sense of wrongdoing, even when no wrongdoing occurred . . . at least none that he could help.

Broderick had tried to walk quietly, to take his meals in silence as the rule required, to get up before the sun for matins and to sit alert, not yawning, for late-night compline. That he had failed in those things was not sin; God in His mercy had made Broderick as he was. Only God could answer for those faults.

But it was Broderick who knew the failure and bore the guilt. Monastery life was draining his spirit. He had become less merry of late, his huge shoulders were slumped, his mouth, turned down. In fact, he reminded Robert of that other one, Godfrey, who had also chafed and grown pale under the rule. Both men, though their intelligences were worlds apart, were of the world, and must live in it. For better or for worse.

But God made the world as well as the monastery; we must not be judgemental, Robert reminded himself. It is as easy to find salvation in the village as it is in the chapel, if the heart is pure and simple. He told himself that. But he did not believe it. He, too, had once been of the world. And he feared greatly for Broderick, who must now go back into it.

"You understand. Hide-and-seek. You must not let soldiers find you," he repeated, putting the bowl of apples back on the table and gesturing to Broderick that he should continue his meal.

"Hide-and-seek," Broderick agreed, putting a whole apple into his mouth. Indeed, Robert saw, the green apples of the monastery orchard looked like grapes in Broderick's huge hands. Mercenaries would know how to harness and use for death and destruction such largeness and strength. And if Broderick, who disliked even harming flies, refused their commands, Robert also knew how they could torture and torment him. No, Henry's mercenaries must not find Broderick.

Later, when the sun had set and the moon not yet risen and the night was a dark world unto itself surrounding the monastery, Robert showed Broderick out the gate. The giant was dressed all in browns and greens, as fitted a fugitive who must now blend into the colorings of the forest. Over his shoulder he carried a cloth sack filled with all the bread and cheese Robert thought the refectory could spare. There were tears in Broderick's eyes. His earlier joy had given way to fear and loss.

"Now, now, man. Don't weep." Robert reached up and patted Broderick's shoulder. "We'll meet again. Soon as things are

366

quiet, you can come back to the monastery. But remember. Hide-and-seek, till then."

Broderick brushed away tears that had made tracks of shining cleanliness through the soot on his cheeks and smiled feebly. "Hide-and-seek," he promised. Then, turning his huge back on the monk, he plodded down the path that led into the forest, and was gone.

His was not the only shadow to merge into darkness that night. Many of the monks also left. The monastery was quieter than Robert had ever known it. The village youths who had sought sanctuary behind its gates had departed weeks before when the crops started to ripen. They were needed back home again. As fearsome as it was to be forced into a straggling foot soldier's march, it was more fearsome to starve, and starve they would if the fields were neglected overly long.

And they knew: If the war was being fought with mercenaries, the monastery no longer offered protection. Knights would honor the ancient chivalric custom of sanctuary; Brabantines and the bloody Flemish would not.

This monastery had remained loyal to Eleanor. It had sent to fight those worldly monks who still wished to don sword, and paid scutage taxes for those who did not, for not even monks were exempt from the binds of vassalage which required them to fight when the lord, or lady, demanded.

Not that Henry himself would set torch to the monastery. The murder of Becket had put a fear of God, and religious men, into the King. But his mercenaries would have no such qualms. The gold in a chalice was as valuable and takable as the gold in a rich man's mantle brooch, to those godless warriors. And monks bled and died as easily as did other men who stood between mercenaries and gold. Hence, the creeping emptiness of the monastery, the ruling silence of the night.

Robert didn't blame the young monks; they were inexperienced enough to believe that tomorrow was important. They obeyed their instinct to try to live to see yet one more dawn. But the older ones who fled . . . he deemed that unseemly. Older men, with even a little accumulation of wisdom between their ears, must know that clinging to life is like clinging to a sinking boat in the raging storm of eternity. This body is not for immortality.

Robert sighed and stumbled his way to the refectory, for it was a dark night and his footing unsure. He poured himself a mug of flat ale from a pitcher left from supper. The taking of ale between meals was against the rules, but then, so was leaving ale on the trestle after a meal, to tempt him. He and God were even on this score.

The monastery, which had always felt small and cramped before, now felt overly large and sprawling in its new emptiness. The new ceiling, only just completed, gave off the fresh smells of tar and resin. Strange. All this fussing and worrying to get a new ceiling over their heads, when God was planning all the time to burn it down to the ground through His agents, the mercenaries.

He felt anger. Blinding, hand-trembling anger.

Then guilt. For through the pounding in his head he could hear the pounding of horses. It was as if God were an overtaxed, petulant parent. One whimper from a child and He loses temper and threatens terrible things. Robert had allowed himself to be wroth that all his work in this life would come to nothing, and soon as that sinful thought came, God saw fit to visit the mercenaries on him as if to say, "Now you'll really have something to wail over."

Robert crouched down in the dark and made his ungainly way, on hands and knees, to the open casement that looked onto the monastery courtyard. The pounding of the hooves had stopped. The horses now neighed and stamped in the courtyard, just a stone's throw from where Robert crouched. Their riders had dismounted.

There were a full dozen of them . . . laughing and drinking from leather wineskins, their crested helmets and chain mail shirts glinting in the weak light of the moon, their leather hose stained with ominous spots that had once been the blood of their enemies. They shouted back and forth to each other in a harsh tongue that sounded as if it were composed only of guttural consonants. Most of them had flaming red hair that hung in long braids down either side of the face.

One, who seemed to be the leader of this band, shouted an

368

order over the clattering and two men broke hastily away from the group. They returned a moment later with firewood. Robert saw with a heavy heart it was no tree they had sacrificed, but the monastery gate. They would build a fire, rest, fetch a bleating lamb from the pasture and slaughter it for their supper. Then, at their ease, ravage the monastery. And all left in it.

For a moment, Robert ached for the morrow he would not see as avidly as he had once ached for a laughing Greek shepherdess named Peripateia.

That is unworthy, he told himself. You have seen your portion of morrows. Better to go to the chapel. Pray. And wait. He tried to feel joy, or at least resignation, but there was more than a little self-pity revealed in his shuffling gait. Like a lover who won't believe his wearied beloved wants to part from him, he hadn't truly believed God intended to make his tonsured head a plaything for mercenaries. Yet now it would seem so. Pray God they would at least eat slowly before beginning their ravaging.

The chapel was dark except for one taper burning in the middle of the altar, before the chased gold receptacle that contained the Holy Eucharist. In that dim circle of light knelt Brother Jacobus, his ancient, toothless mouth grinding a mouthful of blessed wafers.

"Help me," he tried to speak around the large clump of bread in his mouth.

The Holy Eucharist! Jacobus was right. It could not be left in the chapel, to be desecrated. Robert patted Jacobus on the back, crossed himself, then helped himself to a handful of sanctified bread, bread that through the mystery of the priesthood was the body of his Lord. They chewed together in determined silence, and when the last of the sanctified bread had been gulped down, they knelt together to pray.

"Remember, O most gracious Virgin Mary . . ." Robert began. A sound of splintering wood and cursing sounded from the dark hall that led to the refectory. The Flemish were looking for the salt cellars to season their lamb, and the ale. ". . . that no one who fled to you for help, or sought your intercession . . ."

". . . was left unaided," Jacobus mumbled. "Brother Robert, I'm going to be sick."

Oh, Christ. Judging from the noises and smells come from him, the old man was going to let loose through both orifices the rejected foods that sought their way out of his body. Not here in the chapel, Robert thought. Jacobus would die of shame if he messed himself here in the chapel. Robert almost laughed. Here they were, about to be massacred by the Flemish, and he was worried about Jacobus' pride.

But to be a martyr is one thing, he told himself, helping Jacobus to his feet. Christ never said we had to be fools, besides.

"To the pasture, then," he told the old man. "They have already killed the fattened lamb, and will not be returning there tonight. We must make our way quietly, though, brother. They have the devil's own ears."

"The relics," Jacobus said, pulling back from Robert. "We must take the relics." Robert hesitated, torn. To leave the sacred altar relics would mean their eventual desecration when the chapel was destroyed. To take them admitted of craven flight. There would be no further pretense of returning to the chapel and kneeling serenely as death approached. Jacobus let loose a volley of belches and farts that decided Robert. There was no time to waste.

He grabbed up the sacred, mold-covered vial that contained a drop of the Virgin's milk and the small gilt box that contained St. Hilary's left forefinger, dropped them in his voluminous pocket, and then he and Jacobus, too, were shadows disappearing into the night.

Sophia could not sleep. The hot, quiet night was alive with moving shadows in the darkened halls and in the castle courtyard outside her window. She thought she heard whispering outside her door.

Frightened, she put her hands over her belly, as if to comfort both herself and the new creature that was being formed within. She hadn't imagined the whispers. They sounded again, and

370

footsteps, too. Heavy, angry footsteps that attempted stealth but did not achieve it.

Oh, God, they were going to be murdered in their beds. Who was it? Mercenaries? Angry barons? Henry himself?

She crept from bed, no longer frightened but now angry herself. This was too base for words. Murdering women in their beds as they slept—or like Sophia, suffered another night of insomnia.

Well, they wouldn't find her cowering in the bedclothes, weeping and shivering. She yearned for a weapon, but had none at hand. Instead, she pulled on her shift and picked from the floor several sheets of her translation of "Consolation of Philosophy." She was working on it again. Now, with Foulkes gone, Lucie freed, and Eleanor closeted most of the time with Bernart de Ventadour or her war barons, now with that miracle put in her womb, Sophia had grown tranquil and again prone to exercises of the mind, not the heart.

She clutched the papers to her chest and braced herself to open the door and confront her murderers. Her sheets of translation felt hot and damp with the night, feverish as an ill child's forehead. She had always wondered why the statues and portraits of the martyrs showed them clutching the things of this life—books, animals, candles, even the instruments of their death. Now she knew why. They provided a modicum of physical comfort. They were the heart's backward glance as the soul prepared for an eternity of abstraction.

One last hope made her open the door slowly and quietly before flinging it wide with challenge. She was, a moment later, glad for that precaution.

It was no murderer making his way in the night, but Eleanor's own uncle, Raoul de Faye. He poised at the top of the narrow stairwell that led down to the great hall, giving last-minute instructions to one of his men. He was dressed for travel.

Puzzled, she spied through the door's narrow opening as de Faye finished the mumbled instructions and then turned to go.

Strange. He was dressed for travel, for flight, not fighting. Strange, to leave under cover of darkness, with no farewell to Eleanor.

Not strange, she told herself with a groan as she saw, truly saw now, what had happened. De Faye was abandoning them. The baron who had done much to further this war, who had taunted Eleanor with her husband's cruelty and faithlessness, had joined the rats and was fleeing the sinking vessel. He feared Henry, whom he had greatly wronged, and would leave Eleanor to face Henry, and the mercenaries, alone. The bastard.

She couldn't resist it. She stepped forward and called down the stairwell.

"Raoul de Faye. Don't trip over your skirts . . . You are wearing women's clothes, now, aren't you?"

He did not answer. But his footsteps had paused and she knew he had heard.

From the deep shadows of the great hall, Maingot also saw de Faye leave. Saw, and knew what it meant. The Queen was abandoned. Her uncle had left, and most of the other barons who had stayed to protect the ducal palace left with him.

For a fleeting moment, he felt anger stir where before there had been only a hard coldness. He had been Henry's man from the start in this matter, had gladly spied and bribed and listened at closed doors to protect his King's interest. Eleanor took too much on herself. She was woman. Mere woman. She should not have interfered in matters of state, nor pushed her sons at her husband's expense. Maingot hated her for that, hated and feared. This was what happened when woman no longer walked behind her master, but boldly at his side, or brazenly in front of him. It destroyed the order of things, turned the world to chaos and strife . . . as Eleanor had done. But now he could almost pity her. She was valiant and fearless, and that was more than he could say for the cravens who had counseled her.

The moment of sentiment quickly passed. A sense of urgency throbbed in his brain like the beginning of a headache. There was no time to be lost. The wait was over. Henry was on his way, and Eleanor and her castle were ready for the taking.

This would force Eleanor's hand. And when she acted, Maingot would be ready. He, Maingot, must be the one to deliver the Queen and the castle to his King.

Tomorrow. He could wait no longer.

There was no need to wait longer. The young knight, Benoit, sought him out, coming in dawn's thin light to inform him that horses had been stolen from the stables and the bailey was surprisingly empty of soldiery.

"Not stolen. Taken. De Faye has gone," Maingot said, instantly awake and alert. "He has abandoned the Queen to her fate, which is Henry's vengeance."

"The knave!" Benoit spat out in outrage.

Maingot, shaking out the wool blanket that covered him in the nights of all seasons—he was always cold—stifled a smile. How young this man was. He truly hadn't realized that once Eleanor began to lose the war, she would also lose her supporters. This green youth had much to learn. He, Maingot, would begin his instruction now.

"Let us go together to the stables, and see what has been left for our use," he suggested, pulling tunic and vest on over his hose and shirt. He purposely dressed in clumsy fashion, exaggerating his sixty years and the stiffness of his joints. Benoit, watching with eyes full of a young man's pity for the old one, reached out once to steady Maingot as he pulled on his boots. Good, Maingot thought. To win trust, first show your own trustfulness.

The bailey was the quietest that Benoit had ever seen it. Charred rings of cooking-fires showed where soldiery had once rested and exchanged tales, but now that bailey was quiet as a convent's courtyard. It was an eerie quiet, like the stillness in a cemetery.

They passed the place where the loudmouthed Sir Foulkes had been wont to rest and drink from his wineskins in the evening. Benoit, feeling too alone, would have welcomed even the sight of that enemy, so frighteningly still was the bailey.

The passed the place where the harlot, Soiette, had accosted him so many nights ago when the land had been restless with spring, not exhausted with the hot, wearying end of summer.

Soiette. He remembered her thick, greasy black hair, the overripe fullness of her hips and breasts, the fish-market smell of her, with loathing. She had touched him, placed her hand on his thigh, and he had been terrified. He could never forgive the harlot for his young man's fear.

He remembered Soiette, the woman who was Eve, and thought of Lucie, she who was the Sacred Virgin. He felt his heart would burst with love.

Maingot, who had passed the summer watching and listening and waiting, did not find it difficult to read this transparent knight. He read his love of Lucie, and hardened his heart against pity for what was to follow.

They had been meeting in the stables at dawn for the past three weeks without missing a morning. Would they be there this morning, now when patient Maingot needed them? Benoit had already been in the stables; he might have frightened them away without even knowing they were there. But lovers are brazen. They probably hid in the straw and laughed at Benoit.

Horses neighed in the cool darkness of the stable as he swung the heavy gate aside. The earthy smell of horse droppings itched in their nostrils, making the stable smell fecund as a field ready for the plowing. It was, Maingot thought with a grin, a suitable place for a tryst.

"The Queen's beasts have not been removed," Benoit said. "I checked earlier. We must look in the pastures to see if the castle horses have been stolen."

"In a moment. First, I ask your patience. I dropped a mantle brooch here yesterday, and my eyes cannot find it in this poor light." Maingot whined, made himself sound older than he was.

"With pleasure. Where did you drop it?" Benoit, newly aware that Maingot was, perhaps, older even than he appeared, took the elder by the elbow and guided him deeper into the cool interior. Maingot chuckled. Benoit thought it was with gratitude. It was delight, though, delight that this was even easier than Maingot had imagined. How vain youth can be.

"I was up there," he said, pointing to where a yellow clump of

374

hay overhung from a high loft. "Napping." Quickly and with irritating agility, Benoit leapt to the loft ladder and began to climb.

"I'll have your mantle brooch in a moment," he said over his shoulder.

Even as he spoke there was a stirring overhead, the sounds of two startled voices exclaiming.

Lucie pulled her shift up on her shoulders to cover her breasts. "Hush, Godfrey. Someone is climbing the ladder!" she whispered in alarm.

"What matter?" he whispered back sleepily, trying to capture her rosy mouth again with his. She was his now, forever and in all ways, as he was hers forever and in all ways. She was a free woman and she had chosen him. What else could matter?

There was the war, of course. It was going badly and Godfrey knew they would have to leave Poitiers soon, very soon, or be in great danger. It was Lucie who held back, saying, "No, you must wait for Countess Marie to decide. You must not leave her now, or you will lose everything." And she was right, of course. Marie's poet, Chrétien, had oft repeated the same advice. If he could steel his nerves and learn patience . . . to serve a woman would require great patience, he thought . . . then there would be much profit in this. Stay with Marie, and he would be welcomed in her court, that much he already knew. It would not be Eleanor of Aquitaine's court of love, but it would be her daughter's, and that perhaps was even better. Eleanor's future, at this time, did not appear promising or long.

"It's just some raw stable boy wanting to spy on us," Godfrey whispered, now hearing the boots climbing the rungs.

"No. It is not. Something different, something dangerous," Lucie countered, sitting up. Her expression, no longer soft with lovemaking, grew tense with the urge to flee. But there was no time. Soon, in a second, whatever was going to happen would have already happened. She would not turn her back and run like a coward. She was free, no longer a creature of the shadows.

It was Benoit. First his hands, climbing rung over rung, and then his face appeared. His eyes, not yet accustomed to the darkness of the loft, peered at them without seeing. When they did focus, they stared straight into Lucie's eyes. They widened in happy greeting. He began to smile. Then he saw Godfrey reclining next to her. Saw that Lucie was partially undressed, that her hair was loose and wild and her cheeks flushed.

"Benoit!" The single word came out of her mouth more as a protest than a welcome. Frightened, she put her hands to her chest, pressing tighter to it the garment now covering her. Benoit was no longer smiling, but frowning, his eyes wide with insult. She began to tremble.

But why should she fear, she who was free? She had been Queen of a court of love and now she was a free woman, and she was Godfrey's, so the whole world should rejoice with her. Smiling, she extended one small hand to where Benoit paused, on the ladder, offering to help him clamber into the loft, if he so wished. He was green with vertigo.

Godfrey, watching wordlessly, knew that gesture was, by Benoit's thinking, unforgivable. She pitied him, and showed her pity.

Godfrey rolled onto his back and stared overhead, where pigeons roosted and cooed. This moment must be played between Lucie and Benoit.

Benoit, ignoring Godfrey as Godfrey ignored him, cringed back from Lucie, his eyes now narrowed with emotion. He stared at the hand she offered him as if it were a vile thing. Without a word, he made his way back down the ladder and out of the stable.

"He is a fool," Godfrey said, putting his head in Lucie's lap. "You are well rid of that puppy."

Lucie nodded, but was heavyhearted. Benoit hated her now; she had seen it in his eyes. And hatred can be a dangerous thing.

Maingot was waiting for him outside, in the bright sunlight. "Did you find my brooch?" he asked with great innocence.

"No." Benoit blinked and rubbed his eyes as if there were dust in them.

"Ah, well, too bad." Maingot sighed with the weight of his

loss. "It was a goodly brooch, one given me by my lady mother many years ago. I will miss it."

"The Queen's maid, Lady Lucie, was in the stable," Benoit said. The revelation was calmly made, but even as they walked, the young knight felt his heart cracking and breaking, and as it broke, some precious thing spilled out and was replaced by other feelings.

"Seeking a gentle mare for a morning ride, no doubt," Maingot said with warmth and sincerity.

"Not a gentle mare. A stallion. I discovered her with Countess Marie's new troubadour." By all the whores of Constantinople, why Lady Lucie? He had believed in her, trusted her, worshipped her. Had loved her, been prepared to suffer and die for her, to remain chaste all his days if she so required. Chaste. And all that while she had been a whore and he had been played for a fool.

The new feeling gathering in his chest took shape, grew dark and stormy like the earth on the first day of creation, before light is separated from darkness. It was chaos. It was hatred.

"A troubadour, huum? This shows the Queen's influence. But do not be so surprised, my friend. A woman is not a creature to be trusted. No matter how fair the face, how innocent the eyes, they are one and all evil. My grandfather used to tell me that wenches had no souls, they were no better than animals. I know the Church, which is fickle in many of its beliefs, would have us believe otherwise. Yet I wonder if there was not wisdom in my grandfather's words. There is, after all, the lesson of Eve to be considered and taken to heart."

Benoit thought for a long while. Yes. The lesson of Eve. The temptress waiting to lure men into eternal damnation. That was Lucie, with her fair face and comely shape and lecherous ways. A serpent in woman's form. The chaos and hatred grew stronger within and he wondered now how he could ever have knelt to such a creature.

"What did you say of the Queen?" he asked finally, after a long enough while that Maingot worried he had overplayed this scene and ruined it.

"Only that the Queen had a penchant for dallying with trou-

377

badours, too. She was sent off in disgrace when King Henry found Bernart de Ventadour too often in the Queen's bower." Maingot, feigning tiredness, sat on a mounting block. It would not do to end this conversation too soon.

"And now Bernart de Ventadour is within Poitiers," Benoit mused. At her age, still playing the whore, he thought. The Queen had been a sanctified creature in his eyes, pure and radiant. But Soiette and Lucie and Eleanor were no longer distinct; they merged into one creature, and that creature named woman was sullied forever in his eyes. His mouth tasted of dust and grit. He put one foot on the mounting block and leaned on his upraised knee.

"Yes. De Ventadour is here. Eleanor sends off her sons to free herself of male authority. Like all women, she needs guidance, and now has none. I am not so certain we are acting wisely in this quarrel between the Queen and her rightful lord."

Quarrel. Months ago it had been a war for power, for righteousness. Henry had been deemed a Nero, an old man who would not relinquish his throne to the crowned King, Young Henry. He had bled men and gold from Aquitaine so that the barons had risen against him. But now Benoit thought perhaps this was indeed merely a quarrel between husband and wife. He had wronged Henry by interfering in this family matter. Women should not be left to operate alone and unguided; they were weak and misled creatures needing a firm hand. Eleanor should be returned to Henry.

That would be Benoit's revenge on Lucie.

"May he and the others that fled with him rot in hell," Eleanor cursed. Her bower was a shambles. She had thrown all that could be thrown, from inkwells to pillows to vases, and now stood empty-handed and shaking with anger.

Her anger was not just for Raoul de Faye and the other cravens who had fled under cover of darkness. It was also for herself. Because while her uncle fled, unremarked and unhindered in the night, she had been in Bernart's arms, counting with him the many different ways that love can be enjoyed. She was no better than Henry, who flaunted a common mistress for all to see and spent his hours in dalliance, not the King's work. Henry, who had lost a kingdom while enjoying the hours with his Rosamonde. And now she was losing a war while Bernart twined her heart round his fingers and promised her the unpromisable.

A breeze stirred the tapestry on the wall as she paced. The breeze carried a warning of autumn and the winter to follow. Time passed quickly, too quickly, like water that can't be held in the hand; the tighter you grasp, the quicker it eludes you. There were so many plans she had meant to consider, so many messages and strategies that should have been conveyed to Hal . . .

And now, too late.

The forests of Poitiers turned red and gold, and then brown and grey, as their leaves fell victim to the law that all must die in its time. The seasons were merciless in their advance.

Sophia reflected on this as she scoured the forests for the last herbs, roots and flavoring berries that the growing season would provide.

Tired and queasy because she was with child, she moved slowly and carefully, like a nun who has just received the Holy Eucharist. The forest was like a cathedral, quiet and somber and filled with mystery and a promise of immortality. This year's leaves were fallen; but what fool would doubt that new leaves would burst forth in the spring to come?

Clinging balls of mistletoe were visible in the bare treetops. They were brown and ugly and threatening. They killed by clinging too tightly, by strangling the very trees that gave them sustenance.

She thought of Foulkes sometimes, knowing he was still alive but knowing, too, that in the near future, probably within the twelvemonth, there would come a dream at night, or a chill down her spine during the day, that would tell her that Foulkes walked this earth no more.

She would grieve then, but not before, for the uncouth bear

who had made her as other women. Studying the clinging mistletoe, she felt that had things been different, had Foulkes been unburdened with a wife, they still would not have stayed together. A wife she could never be. There was none of the soft yielding in her, nor the hard determination, that makes it possible for a woman to join her life with a man and take pleasure in the union. Human nature was originally one and we were a whole, and the desire and pursuit of the whole is called love. In all of its forms . . . including that of a philosopher-woman who will not give herself to a master, she told herself.

But she carried Foulkes' child and was grateful for that, and sometimes she sang to herself as she searched the forest floor and thought of father and child. Sometimes she muttered prayers as she walked and searched. The world had grown dangerous and unpredictable.

It was three weeks since Raoul de Faye had cravenly deserted Eleanor and fled north to defend his own castle. Henry, not of a mind to forgive de Faye for his role in encouraging Eleanor's war, burned de Faye's castle and manors, reducing de Faye to a cringing supplicant in Louis' court in Paris.

After Verneuil, Henry cast off any pretence of indifference or passivity to the rebellion. His goal now was to end the war he had originally tried to ignore, and as quickly as possible. He seemed to be everywhere, leading attacks on all fronts at once. Never had he traveled quicker, never had he been more decisive.

He captured the castle of Damville, enriching himself with a long, chained line of ransom hostages to help pay the mercenaries. Then Henry, cursing the rebellious knights Ralph of Fougères, Hugh of Chester and Eudo of Porhoet, who fought for the Queen, turned his army toward the castle of Dol, which overlooked the stormy sea and the stormier Norman border. Ralph, Hugh and Eudo, knowing that defeat was inevitable, trapped with their backs to the sea, surrendered before Henry's armies could even set up the siege engines alongside Dol.

When the uprising in Brittany was over, Henry was lenient with the prisoners, to show he could give forgiveness when it was asked of him . . . except in the case of his Queen, Eleanor. She would not be forgiven, Sophia knew.

Meanwhile, a lesson was made to show that Henry would not take rebellion lightly. From that granite mound of Dol Castle he loosed his mercenaries to ravage Brittany. They were merciless in their greedy rampage. Death and mutilation and hunger and poverty crept across the land. The town-dwellers and villagers and peasants who lived in the way of the bold menace grew to look upon all soldiers as imps from hell, knights as a plague, and Kings as the devil incarnate.

Louis, seeing the tide had turned, lost interest in the war. The burning of Verneuil had satisfied his old, bitter desire to revenge himself on Henry for stealing away his Queen. His feelings for Eleanor had now come full circle, traveling the great span of years from Vitry-the-Burned to Verneuil. He was not a man given to romantic reflection, but monkish Louis realized that the burning flames of his love for Eleanor had finally extinguished themselves. He no longer loved her. More, he was weary of her. And her war.

Louis abandoned the attack on Normandy and directed his knights and foot soldiers to turn their backs on the sea and follow the rising sun home, back to Paris. They were content to do so. The fighting season was over and their bags were heavy with loot, for they were no less greedy than the mercenaries. Many a peasant or newly impoverished nobleman looked up when a group of soldiers passed by, wondering whose smoked pig or silver candle sconces bounced tauntingly at the pack donkey's side.

War was, more than anything, a way to redistribute wealth. Those who had gained wealth were content, those who had lost were discontent, and the changing of borders or allegiances had less to do with them than the violent changing of hands of property.

And Louis realized now that Henry would not yet share the wealth, power and properties of his kingdom with his crowned son. The rebellion, if anything, had made Henry more determined to cling to what was his. Louis, who was of Henry's generation, not the Young King's, no longer faulted Henry for this. Death is time enough to relinquish what has taken a lifetime to achieve; why hand a lifetime's work meekly over to the young just because they whine for it? Henry's throne was Henry's. Hal would have to be content with less.

Louis, realizing he couldn't win this war, decided to do the next best thing. He would reconcile father and son and end the fighting and estrangement. It was God's will.

9

It was not Eleanor's will. The war might be over in Normandy, but it was not Eleanor's will that the war end in Aquitaine. It would not advance Richard's cause to surrender at this early date. When she heard that Louis was arranging a meeting in Gisors between Henry and his sons for the purpose of a reconciliation, Eleanor wrote furious letters to the court of Paris. Louis did not answer her letters.

She was beside herself with anger. Henry had stolen her land, her youth, her heart and her peace of mind; now he was to take her sons from her, as well. And with Louis' help. The year was closing in on her. Spring and summer had come and gone; soon it would be winter. Never had she felt so filled with despair, so helpless.

In her helplessness, she turned to an old source of solace. Sir Chabert was almost finished with the new Lady Chapel. Eleanor, who had paid scant attention to this work of devotion during the hectic days of summer, renewed her interest in the new chapel. The statue of the Madonna, with its jewel-encrusted crown, was set in the central niche; it was there that Eleanor went for reflection and guidance.

The impassive, beautiful face of the Queen of Heaven stared down at her with pitying, merciful eyes. She held the Christ child in her hands, not in the old, stiff manner that portrayed the Madonna as nursemaid to a God and no more, but in a more intimate, natural manner that showed the mother was as filled with grace as the child. The Christ child, rosy-cheeked and rounded of limb, leaned His curly head trustingly against her bosom while she, Divine Woman, smiled and clasped Him tenderly.

In just such a manner had Eleanor clasped her own infant sons to her breast. Chabert, proud of this statue, dared approach the Queen to ask her opinion of it.

"It is as I remember motherhood," Eleanor said, pleased.

"It is as motherhood should be," he answered. "Only through the mother can we come to love the father and son. Only through the Queen of Heaven can we achieve full grace." Well said, Chabert, whispered a voice in his head. He nodded happily. It was many days since Damietta had spoken to him. She, too, was pleased.

"What if the father wars with the son?" Eleanor asked him, touching with admiration the carved and painted stone roses that Chabert had placed at the Virgin's feet. Two stone pillars surrounded the Madonna; their twisting, turning lengths had been painted in bright blue and orange, exotic colors that reminded Eleanor of the bright beauty of Constantinople. The Madonna's face was serene and confident; a smile played at her lips and in her eyes.

Chabert, who had paid as little attention to the war as Eleanor had to the construction of the chapel, thought she spoke of divine matters.

"Why, the mother intercedes between father and son," he answered. "Without the Mother, none of us could come to the Father." His faith was such that her question stunned him. Did any yet doubt the power of the Virgin?

Eleanor continued to stroke the statue of the Madonna for a

moment. Then she paced away from the niche to the larger central altar, alternately staring at the tiled floor and the wood-beamed ceiling. She paced back to Chabert; she smiled at him and took his hand.

"You have done me a great good this day," she told him. He tugged happily at a forelock, abashed by the Queen's generosity, believing that she thanked him for the completion of the chapel.

As elegant and winsome as the chapel was, though, it was his words that had caused Eleanor to smile once again, and to move with her old brisk pace. Without the Mother, none of us come to the Father.

She had been in a morass of indecision and lethargy all summer. Age had tempered her fearlessness, made of her a docile, uninspired Ladyhawk ready for the hood and jesses, ready for the master's voice to instruct and liberate. She had waited. Waited for the Young King to answer her messages, for Louis to end the siege of Verneuil, waited to see what Henry would do . . . waited, waited.

It was the waiting that had made things go badly. She had left matters too long in the hands of father and son. She had abdicated . . . no, had let them push her aside . . . from her divinely appointed role as the intercedent, the mediatrix. She stood between father and son just as the eagle occupied that intermediate land between earth and heaven. She would wait no more, keep to the side no more.

Besieging castles was but one way to win a war. There were more subtle methods, methods that she must employ now. Let Henry take the castles and ruin the countryside. Let him win the battle. The victory would yet be hers.

Her solar was flooded with afternoon sun. It gilded the stone walls and wood benches. She poured herself a cup of wine and drank it quickly without savoring it, to steady her hand. Then she sat at her table, and wrote.

"To her esteemed and beloved son, Richard, Duke of Aquitaine. From Eleanor, his mother, Queen of England and Duchess of Aquitaine."

She paused. Hal was the eldest. By all rights the letter should be addressed to him. But Hal was not the choice of her heart. Hal was not the crowned Duke of Aquitaine. It was not Hal she saw during those long, sleepless nights when, behind burning lids, she envisioned her son sitting on Henry's throne. It was Richard. She twisted the pen more tightly in her grasp and continued to write.

"My son. Let there be no more enmity between father and son. It has turned against us. Louis marches back to Paris, and the Young King with him. Henry marches south. Richard, return now to Aquitaine, and keep your distance from the King's wrath. Your mother, and the saints themselves, ask this of you."

She paused again. How different was the tone of this letter from ones sent earlier. This was a letter of defeat, and just months before, they had deemed defeat unthinkable. But much had happened in those summer months of golden optimism. Verneuil had been burned, and Henry's wrath had been awakened. And Louis, who was now an old man, it would appear, had tired of war and gone back to his hearth and milksop wife. If Richard was captured now, Henry's mercy could not be counted upon.

Resolute, she heated the sealing wax and then dripped a large, red gob of it over the folded message. Richard would already know most of what she had told him. He would know of Hal's cowardice and Louis' old-mannish change of mind. He would know they were doomed to a military defeat. But would he understand her meaning? Would he return to Aquitaine, out of Henry's reach, and bide his time?

Time was what she needed now. Time for Henry's anger to cool, time for Richard to gain in strength and cunning. And she knew how she must buy that time.

"Lady Sophia, are you well enough to travel?" Eleanor asked. The Queen stood in the doorway of the scriptorium, the afternoon sun behind her, casting a long shadow of her form across the tiled floor.

Sophia eyed her with suspicion. "Travel where?" she asked,

looking up from her manuscript. Her fingers were covered with ink and there was a smudge on her nose.

"To Paris," Eleanor said. "If Louis and the Young King will not come to me, then I must go to them."

Sophia put down her pen and squinted at the Queen in surprise. To Paris? Surely by now all roads leading to that refuge would be thick with Henry's men. And dangerous.

But she agreed with Eleanor that it was time to quit Poitiers. The Flemish and Brabantines rode closer each day. Poitiers was filled with refugees from the North who had been burned out of their villages . . . men who limped or were missing hands and arms, and their blank-faced women, some of whom already showed bellies rounded with what the peasants called soldier seed. They spent their days in long lines outside the convents and monasteries awaiting the daily ration of bread, bread paid for from Eleanor's and Richard's private coffers. Their eyes were not grateful. Let them who started this war feed us, their faces said.

The streets were crowded with these dismal folk, the forests dangerous with reckless bandits. It was many days since Sophia had dared leave the safety of the ducal palace. And soon the ducal palace would be the least safe place of all, if Henry had his way.

Poitiers was a large and strong town and one that the barbarians would not take with ease, if at all. But even the mercenaries' attempts to take it could make life very uncomfortable, very dangerous. In Paris, at least, they would be safe from Henry's troops.

"When?" Sophia asked, resigning herself to another journey.

"Three days hence."

"Then I will be well enough. Two days' work will see the completion of my manuscript." It was decided.

Eleanor lingered in the scriptorium, trying to delay the afternoon hour she had come to spend with Bernart. It wasn't just the waiting, the pushing aside, that had kept her in Poitiers that summer. There was Bernart, too, Bernart who loved her as Henry hadn't in years; no, never had Henry loved her like this. How would she tell Bernart?

She peered over Sophia's shoulder, watching the words appear on the blank page as Sophia struggled with the difficulties of converting formal Latin into more conversational langue d'oc.

"Is there any true wisdom to be found in this work of yours?" Eleanor asked. "Read me a passage."

Sophia hesitated. "This treatise was written when Saint Boethius was imprisoned, awaiting death," she warned, putting down her pen again.

"And what does a man awaiting death think of?"

"If you spread your sails for the wind, you must go where the wind takes you, not where you wish to go." Sophia stared her full in the eyes, daring her to quarrel with the philosopher's opinion of fortune.

"Ah, that is where he is wrong," Eleanor said with a confident smile. "I am no small vessel guided only by fickle breeze. I am the eagle, who commands the breeze, who does with it as she will."

"So say you. And I hope you are correct, and not the philosopher," Sophia said morosely, going back to her work.

Bernart was waiting for her in the solarium, lute and soft pillows arranged at his side for her comfort and amusement. Her heart missed a beat as she looked at him. He had given her greater happiness than she had ever known. He had come to her in her middle years, when it seemed all had abandoned her, and shown her a way out of that dark forest that had threatened to swallow her. To live for love and pleasure was not a goal to be disdained. But it could not be her goal. She was the mother of Kings, and she could act as no less.

She went to Bernart, slowly, and knelt before him, as if asking benediction. Never before had she knelt to a man. It was the greatest gift she could think to give him.

He, at first startled by this deviation from the strict rules of love, soon understood her meaning.

"You asked me to go with you into a new life," she whispered, keeping her head bowed and not looking at him.

"But you cannot. You are Eleanor, Queen. Eleanor, Henry's wife." He could not keep the bitterness out of his voice or his

388

words. "No man will put asunder what God has joined. But Henry will, my eagle." His voice became strident with prophecy. "Yes, I named you my lark, my songbird, but in my heart I have always called you the eagle. Now it is Henry who will call you lark, and cage you, for his pleasure."

"Bernart," she whispered, throwing her arms around him one last time. "A great disaster will come if Henry and Hal treat for peace, and I don't guide this meeting. Henry will deny my sons all their rights and power and they will be as nothing. My sons will be as dust in the corner, powerless and scorned."

"Don't you care for your own life?" Bernart asked, pushing her away from him in anger. "You go to intercede for your sons, never realizing that Henry will have you killed on sight. You ask my blessing, my forgiveness, so you can go to your death."

"I fear death less than many things that old age can bring me. And I think Henry will not murder me. I am still Eleanor of Aquitaine, not a milkmaid that can be strangled and buried unremarked in the hillside. Don't think harshly of what I must do. If I did not do it, I would not be Eleanor."

Bernart, seeing this matter was decided in her mind and that she could not be dissuaded, put aside his anger. She had never been his; not before, in their golden youth when she gave herself to the service of a King and two countries. Not now, when queenhood and power still meant more than womanhood and love.

"You gave me a summer," he said, going to her. "How could I complain? When autumn comes, and winter, and all the winters to come, I will remember the summer, and that you let me dream for a while by your side."

They embraced then, rocking in each other's arms, but neither wept for what had been and what would not be. One summer was as good as a lifetime, if it was lived well.

"Where will you go?" she asked when finally she could bear to let go of him.

"To Dalton, again. To the monastery. I knew peace there," he answered without hesitation.

"Is that what you want, Bernart? Peace."

"It is all I can hope to obtain," he replied. "I will write poems and watch the bees dance circles in the sunlight as they collect nectar for honey. It is not a bad life."

"Bernart de Ventadour," she whispered with a hint of regret. "The fairest of his time, the man whose music challenged the seraphs themselves for its sweetness and longing. Bernart will retire to his monastery, far from love and delight."

"You are wrong, Eleanor. There is much love there. Not the kind we have known, but other forms. The love of the dark night for the dawn, of the earth for the rain, of the soul for restfulness. I will tell you something, Eleanor, something I have never said before to a woman or man. When a man loves a woman as I have loved you, it is not the woman he seeks. It is the dawn, the rain, the soul of the world itself, he seeks."

His words gave her comfort and she thought of them for a long while.

"Do you think it will be as bad as I fear?" she asked finally.

"What is it you fear?"

"Age. Creaking bones and thin hair and missing teeth. All that. And more. I fear that the less desirable life becomes, the more will I cling to it and become as foolish as any foolish old woman."

He cradled her head against his chest, trying to make her feel small and young. It would be his final gift to her. "It is no sin to cling to something you love, and that loves you. To do less would be the sin."

"Yet you do not cling. You do not protest and complain."

"Of what should I complain?" he asked in a voice she did not recognize. It was a question he asked many times in his life, especially in bitter moments when complaint would have given release of sorts.

But she still did not understand, he saw with sorrow. He was a troubadour. True, a wealthy and famous one. Yet a troubadour just the same. The kind of man whom other men shun because of his uncallused hands and winning ways with ladies. The kind of man whom ladies love . . . but only when their lords are not present. Of unknown parentage . . . or at least unclaimed by his father . . . he had walked this earth as a pilgrim, never having known home and hearth of his own. Complaint had never been his right.

"You are locked in my memories and in my heart. It is a prison you will never escape. Lauzeta, beat your wings against the bars, I hold you all the tighter in my thoughts." He sang the words to her to mask their emptiness.

When night-scented dusk crept into the castle, Eleanor called her ladies to her side: Sophia, her astrologer, Marie, her daughter, Margaret, her son's wife, Amaria, her loyal serving woman, and Lucie, who had been her maid that summer.

Eleanor's face was stony, her eyes expressionless. At that moment her lover, Rai, was leaving the ducal palace by a side portal, and he would never return. With him he took what remained of the little joy that had blessed the shortening days. Happiness, that goal of youth, was gone, replaced by stern conviction, by duty. By a sense of honor. It will have to be enough, Eleanor told herself.

"Tomorrow we leave Poitiers, for Paris," she spoke. Her ladies looked up, quick-eyed and alert, from the needlework or books they carried. Lady Lucie, who neither stitched nor read, and so was empty-handed, stood still as a statue when she heard this news. Only her eyes moved from face to face, reading them as easily as others read pages. Sophia looked both frightened and relieved. Margaret, the daughter-in-law, was terrified. Amaria, Eleanor's maid and friend, looked hopeful . . . Richard must join them there. Marie of Champagne merely looked perplexed. Her former rival was, Lucie saw and rejoiced, a cold-blooded woman.

Eleanor waited a moment before saying anything else. The silent room, in that moment, grew loud with the sound of a rider and his escort leaving the bailey. She forced herself not to go to the casement, to see if that rider was Bernart. The sad sounds of departure died away and were buried by the quiet night. Eleanor felt suddenly cold. And alone again.

"We leave when it is dark, not before," she told her ladies, making her voice loud with authority. Impose order. Give commands. It has worked before, to drive away the coldness. "It is, you understand, necessary to make our departure as surreptitious as possible." No one expressed surprise at this. Women of fortune and family, traveling at any time, thought it well to draw as little attention to themselves as possible. It wasn't the common highwayman they feared, but knights of their own ranking. Many a marriage had been forced onto a virgin heiress taken by surprise in her travels; many a married lady had been abducted and held ransom, thereby ruining her family's fortune.

Even in time of peace, it was dangerous for women to journey. Now, with war on the land, the journey from Poitiers to Paris would be strewn with opportunistic knights and even less gentle mercenaries.

"We should travel in disguise," Marie spoke up, eager. "Men's shirts and hose. A group of men would pass through the countryside with less notice then a group of veiled women riding sidesaddle."

Eleanor nodded agreement. How like her Marie was. Almost thirty years before, Eleanor had insisted her women dress and ride as men to make their way through the rough, mountainous routes of Greece toward the goal of Jerusalem. "The Amazons," the Crusaders had called them.

Lucie, who had stood quietly thus far, opened her mouth in alarm. Sophia shot her a hard look, and the maid clamped her mouth. But her eyes were wide. When Bishop Jehan had released her from the cell, he had exacted her promise that never again would she wear men's clothing.

"Speak, maid," Eleanor said, turning to her. The girl's distress was too obvious to ignore.

Lucis hesitated, thinking. It would be a sin to put on men's clothes again. It would also be a sin to disobey the Queen. And surely the Queen was right. They must go in disguise for their own safety. Yet, she had promised . . . Lucie, the freewoman, torn between two evils, had to decide which sin would best suit her conscience. She decided in favor of the Queen.

"I am already familiar with men's garb and will assist any lady unsure of its buttons and lacings," she offered.

"Then those who will may come to you for advice on their garments," Eleanor said approvingly. "Make them mean, but not beggarly, common but not offensive. Our purpose is not to draw attention. Because of that, our escort must be small. Take only what you immediately need, and as few people as possible," Eleanor instructed. "All else will be supplied us in Paris."

Sir Benoit, having learned betrayal, now learned guile and cunning.

He sought revenge for his scorned heart. Revenge was his knightly right, Maingot reassured him.

And so the fair knight, Sir Benoit, seeking his moment of revenge, just happened to be shrinking in the shadows in the stable when Lucie and her Godfrey arrived for their evening rendezvous. He just happened to hear Lucie's little gasps of pleasure as Godfrey unrobed and loved her. He drew his sword then, prepared to plunge it first into her heart, and then the troubadour's. No one, he felt, could blame him for this act.

But something stayed his hand. He thought it was pity; it was cowardice. Instead of murder, he merely eavesdropped, fascinated by the way her voice now chilled his blood, that voice that had once warmed it like sun on spring earth. He had once heard the Queen of Heaven in her voice; now he heard the harlot strains of Eve.

And so, Sir Benoit learned that the Queen would leave Poitiers on the next eve, with only a small party attending her. He went to Maingot with his news. Maingot had been waiting for him.

The black night outside the torchlit bailey was alive with the sound of wind whipping the trees and autumn leaves crackling underfoot. A group of plainly clothed knights paused briefly at the side gate of the ducal palace, hesitating, before plunging into the midnight darkness that was Poitiers. A town surrounded by soldiers and mercenaries is not much given to burning midnight oil to light the way for the marauders. The leader raised his hand as if in encouragement, and the knights, astride their palfreys, moved forward into the dark town.

Once started, they galloped hurriedly through the narrow streets of Poitiers. Cats and dogs scurried for cover out of their way. It was a night for stealth, for quick and surreptitious departures. No one questioned the knights or stopped them.

Soon they were out of the city. The fields and pastures passed in a blur. Only when they reached the forest did the group slow from a gallop to a gentler trot.

Eleanor, dressed in blue hose and brown tunic with darker brown cape over all, felt leaden with regret, now that the city had been left behind. She had been happy in Poitiers. More than any other place on this earth, this city had been her home, her comfort. Now she was leaving, and it would be a long time before she returned.

So much had happened to her there. So much of what was important had occurred within its walls. It was thick with memory, and memory always brings a certain sadness for what has been and is no more. She thought of Bernart de Ventador, who had loved her in Poitiers, and given her much happiness.

It had been springtime again, for a brief while. The world had been made new for their love. And now Bernart was gone. And now it was autumn. Paris, she told herself. Think of Paris, and what must be done there. If the war cannot be won, I must find a way to reconcile Henry and our sons so that all is not lost to them. The peace that follows must be on terms that will aid the Young King. And Richard. Do not let Henry rob them of the little they have gained. Do not let Henry render them useless. Think no more of Bernart de Ventadour, but of Henry, your husband, and Richard, your son, and the peace that must be made between them.

"Ayeeeee, my back," Sophia complained to Lucie, who rode beside her. The gallop over the cobbled street had caused her much pain. But in a way, she had enjoyed it. The night air was invigorating and brought a sense of freedom. She thought of Sir Foulkes, and felt gratitude. His love had not bound her, as Henry had bound Eleanor, but rather set her free. He had given her the knowledge she had sought, and he had made her as other women. And now, once again, she was Sophia, wife to no man.

"I will rub it for you when we stop to rest," Lucie promised. She rode near to Sophia, fearing that the frail woman might have difficulties on this journey. There was a litter waiting for them in the forest, but Sophia kept to her palfrey, refusing the easier litter. Marie of Champagne also disdained the litter, as did younger Margaret, the Young King's wife. Margaret, in fact, would have given a year of her life to abandon her unruly mare and recline during the rest of the journey. But if Eleanor rode, so must she. She cast a resentful look at her mother-in-law. It was not the first, nor would it be the last.

Behind them rode Godfrey the troubadour and Chrétien, the poet, whispering loudly back and forth in argument about plot and rhyme. These two had become thick friends in the past few weeks. Godfrey, the younger of the two, admired Chrétien's narrow-eyed, slightly jaded worldliness, and Chrétien admired Godfrey's youthful exuberance. They had even begun working on a long poem together, a piece Chrétien called "Lancelot: the Knight of the Cart." He had started it that spring, when Lucie and Godfrey had first arrived at the court, she as a prisoner and he as a common carter.

Godfrey's lady, Lucie, rode before him, and before her rode his patroness, Marie of Champagne. Let the soldiers come, Godfrey thought. Let them spit me through like a pig and roast me. I'll die happy, if I die in this moment. But he had no intention of dying. Death was for old men, not for such as he.

"I said, how does Lancelot answer the knights who wish to dissuade him from crossing the Bridge of Swords?" Chrétien hissed at him, impatient. Godfrey had a habit of daydreaming in the midst of a line or an argument, which infuriated Chrétien. He reached across the distance that separated their two horses and boxed the youth on the ear.

"Ouch!" Godfrey protested. "Let me think, let me think. I know. He says, 'Sirs, many thanks for your kindness . . . no, concern. It comes from your love. And your goodwill, he should add. But . . . but I have faith that God will guard me in all things. I'm no more afraid of this bridge or this water than of this dry land. I will risk going that way and crossing it. I'd rather die than turn back.'" Godfrey finished triumphantly, with the kind of sneer he imagined Lancelot bestowed on his less brave comrades-in-arms.

Chrétien grunted in admiration. Rather die than turn back. Those were the words of a young man. Those were the words that no longer came to him. An older man, a wiser man, would turn back rather than cross the Bridge of Swords.

"We might be able to use it. Language is rough. But we might use it," he admitted, committing the lines to memory.

Eleanor, straight and proud, thought of eagles. She had left Miribile behind, in the mews of the palace. No party of non-descript knights would have carried such a rare, telltale prize with them. Eagles were for emperors.

It would be a long time before she hunted with Miribile again, feeling her ponderous, regal weight biting into her shoulder, enjoying the triumph of working in unison with a creature known for its stubborn and temperamental nature. Eleanor smiled. So once had the young Henry who begged audience with her been described. She had bedded and wedded him, and ruled him as cunningly as she ruled her eagle. She would do so again. How to do so would come to her somewhere along the way.

It might be never, before she saw Miribile again. The eagle was growing old. It was many years since she had been brought down from Scotland, an ugly, protesting eyerer with unplumed wings and beady eyes. Eagles live longer than other birds, but even they do not live forever.

"They say that when an eagle grows old, and its eyes dim, it searches out a fountain and dips in it three times to restore its vigor." Eleanor spoke lowly to Sophia, more thinking aloud than needing conversation. The night had completely surrounded them. They rode in darkness, afraid to illumine the way with torches. The horses nickered nervously, and many of the riders fell silent. Owls and other creatures of the dark called over their heads and from the forest fringe, mocking their human suspicion of night, that frail preference for sunlight.

"I have heard that," Sophia agreed. "First, though, it must fly to the sun and singe its wings and eyes. Then it dives three times in a fountain, and its youth and strength are restored."

Eleanor rode in silence for some moments, imagining the coolness of water against her eyelids after the burning heat of the sun, longing for it. She had been filled with energy when they began this journey. Already she was growing tired and her eyes stung from trying to focus in the darkness.

Sophia could no longer see Eleanor's face, but she felt her tiredness and tried to distract her.

"Pliny, in fact, offers more information on eagles in his bestiary," she continued. "He says that the eagle tests the strength of her children by holding them up to the bright, hot sun. If they stare straight into it, then they are true-blooded eagles. If they flinch and turn away, they are not worth bothering with."

Eleanor frowned, trying to focus a memory that crouched at the edge of her thoughts, vague and indistinct as night shadows. Then it grew clear and so strong, it seemed it had always been the foremost thought in her mind.

Christmas. Chinon, just last year. Henry, red-faced and hearty from an excess of wine, announcing that John Lackland . . . Johnny, he called him with great affection . . . would wed Alice, heiress of Maurienne. Her father, Count Humbert, had no male children. For her dowry Alice would bring to the Plantagenets power over all those great and small Alpine passes that could provide so much Mediterranean wealth.

The price of those passes was high. In exchange for Alice and her lands, Count Humbert would receive the castles of Chinon, Mirebeau and Loudon.

Henry had to have been crazed with his dreams of empire to think of such a scheme. Did he forget that other men, including Count Humbert, might have similar dreams of aggrandizement? And what better place to begin than with Chinon, Mirebeau and Loudon? He would sacrifice the security of the Aquitaine for the privilege of killing horses in the wintry Alpine commerce routes.

Eleanor sat stiff and outraged and silent after the announcement of John's betrothal. Hal had jumped up from the table, pounded his fists against the wall, cursed and stormed. Geoffrey also left the table and paced the hall, watching everyone from the corner of his eye to gauge his own reactions. Of her sons, only Richard had remained seated. His eyes had narrowed with anger. But he stared his father straight in the face.

"Never will you give away Chinon, Mirebeau, and Loudon," he said quietly. "I will not permit it."

"You will not permit?" Henry roared and jumped up. It was almost funny, how alike in their temperaments Hal and his father were, Eleanor had thought. Richard looked the most like Henry, but he had her guile and calm purpose. Her pride in him was greater than usual at that moment.

"I, the Duke of Aquitaine, will not permit it," Richard repeated.

Henry had grown red-faced, had thundered and threatened, and the matter was dropped for the time being.

Richard had been held up to the sun, who was Henry, and he had not flinched.

Richard, her beloved son, would be King. Not tomorrow. Maybe not soon. But Richard would be King.

The night reached its zenith of darkness. With the dark came a cool mist that drove away the heat of the day. Eleanor lifted her face into this mist and closed her eyes, letting the coolness refresh and heal her vision.

Brother Jacobus, hungry and exhausted, watched with greedy eyes as Broderick broke off a hunk of bread from the store Robert had given him. In the darkness, his old eyes saw only the outline of the movement, but it was enough to make his mouth water. It was the last loaf.

Broderick brought the hunk to his mouth, then, seeing Jacobus' eyes on him, reluctantly offered the bread to Jacobus.

"There's a kind lad," Robert said approvingly, patting Broderick's broad back. "The Lord will reward thy generosity." Robert put down his staff and leaned wearily against the rough bark of a tree.

"When?" Broderick pouted, his stomach rattling with hunger.

"Soon. Perhaps. Try not to think of bread. Think of where we will get to tomorrow." But it was hard to ignore the smacking, pleased sounds of old Brother Jacobus as he downed the last of their bread. "God will provide," Robert promised.

It was three days since Robert and Jacobus, wandering in the large forest beyond the monastery, had stumbled into a clearing where slept the huge, childish Broderick. Their reunion had been tearful and joyous.

"I don't like the forest. I want to go back to the monastery," Broderick had protested, taking Robert's hand and trying to pull him back toward the rising sun, the direction in which he wrongly guessed the monastery lay.

"We can't. Not yet," Robert had said.

"More hide-and-seek?" Broderick stamped his feet.

"Water," Jacobus demanded now as a messy paste of chewed bread ran down the corners of his mouth. He had changed greatly in these three days of wandering, fear and his great age reducing him to a helpless child whom even Broderick, himself a child, must help care for.

"Water," Robert agreed. "We are all three parched, and I hear a stream there, beyond that hill, I think." He frowned and scratched his head. How did he come to be a fugitive, a homeless monk wondering the road like a brigand or vagabond, far from his cell, far from the orderly ways of his monkish life?

Ah well. One thing had led to another. Jacobus had made it from the chapel to the pasture. By the time he finished his business there, they both could hear that the Flemish, finished with their dinner of stolen mutton and wine, had made their way to the chapel, seeking rich vestments and gold chalices. It would have been suicide for Robert and Jacobus to return there, and suicide was a great sin, it was Judas' sin, greater even than betrayal. So they left the pasture and made their way to the orchard, and from the orchard to the road, from the road to the river, following in the wake of Louis' retreating men-at-arms, knowing only that they could not return to the monastery.

They traveled at night, when it was cool and dark and discovery less likely, moving slowly northeast, towards Fontevrault, where they would be given shelter. They stayed away from villages and isolated huts, trying to avoid the mercenaries who were now scattered over the land like hungry locusts.

"Water," he said again. "Yes. I will go fetch water. In a minute. Let me catch my breath."

A wolf howled and Broderick screamed in terror. The three men huddled together.

"Perhaps we should all go for water. Together," Robert amended.

The hairs at the back of Maingot's neck bristled as the wolf howled for the third time. Surely that was a bad omen. But what could go wrong this night? They knew exactly when Eleanor had left the palace, how many rode with her, and in what direction they had gone. Taking the Queen would be child's play. There need not even be bloodshed, as Eleanor was accompanied only by women and the kind of men who need not be counted as men.

"She won't be hurt?" Benoit hissed again, his voice frayed with worry and guilt. His betrayal already sat heavily on his conscience.

"She won't be hurt," Maingot insisted, not knowing or caring if Benoit worried about Eleanor or the Lady Lucie, who rode with her. It made no difference. He already wished this work was done.

"Easy, easy," he muttered to his horse, who stamped and snorted. The other men-at-arms took less care to keep their mounts quiet as they waited for the Queen and her escort to arrive.

That, Maingot reflected, was the beauty of the plan. All they had to do was wait. Eleanor was riding to them.

She thought no more of Bernart. He had been left behind and was no more a part of her life. But of the future, she also did not think. It was enough to exist in each brief moment of time that, strung like beads on a rosary, made up this night. To feel her horse move confidently under her, and the cool night air on her face. To not know where she would rest her head later, when they clamored for sleep, or where she would be when the dawn awakened them.

Now, not knowing seemed a treasure beyond price. Because for many years to follow this night, she would have nothing but knowledge. Her bed would be the same, her meals, her gowns, her companions. Each day would be like the day before and the day after. Henry would see to that. But for now, there was the peace of not knowing, which is, for a Queen, the only true freedom.

"Hush! Hush! There are riders ahead!" Robert whispered. They stopped and listened. Louder than the murmuring stream which beckoned, louder than the sighing of the wind in the trees, they could hear now the sounds of horses who snorted and pawed the ground with restlessness. Under that sound, softer but still distinct, the mumble of men's voices. And occasionally, the clank of metal against metal.

"They are armed." Robert pulled the other two men down to their knees and shushed them into a frightened silence. On hands and knees, trembling, they crawled up the hill and peered down into the clearing below.

There were about a dozen men-at-arms, mounted and waiting. It was dark, too dark to make out faces. But the standards they bore were large and unfurled in the strong wind. Even in darkness Robert could make out that they were the standards of Henry's men.

The men seemed impatient, eager for the night's work, whatever it was, to be finished. Robert could hear the impatience in their angry, clipped voices which the wind carried towards him. A party coming this way from the other direction would not hear them, or see them, till it was too late.

Ambuscade. These men were lying in wait for someone.

Robert's scalp crawled with fear. Henry's men. And, therefore, no friend to them. Yet not mercenaries but full-fledged knights, by the look of them. And they waited. For whom?

"We will stop here," Robert whispered to Broderick and Jacobus. "I don't like the looks of this. We dare not go forward, and will waste time if we go backward. I would see what this is about."

Just then, he heard other horses approaching from the other side. So did the waiting men-at-arms in the clearing below. They sat straight and stern on their horses, unsheathed their swords, and readied themselves for battle.

"You said no one would be injured," a voice hissed in the night. Benoit turned accusingly to Maingot. The readying of weapons for battle frightened him. Maingot ignored the young knight and kept his eyes straight before him, awaiting the arrival of Eleanor.

The Queen, riding at the head of her party, was the first to see the war party waiting in the clearing. Unsheathed swords gleamed in the moonlight, and the chain mail of the men, who had sat restlessly for too long, clanked like prison chains.

The dozen men, in one quick motion, maneuvered their horses in a circle around the Queen and her small, unarmed escort, bringing them to a quick and surprised halt.

Lucie screamed once, more in outrage than fear, and Chrétien cursed soundly. "Flee! Flee!" Godfrey yelled. "We are taken!" Eleanor only sighed. Her moment of freedom was at an end.

"We are surrounded," she called over her shoulder. "And we are not in great danger. These traitors will not dare touch us. Only do not panic and force their hand, for they are cowards, and cowards will strike without thinking."

"Cowards? Traitors? That is a harsh word. There are those who say you are the traitor, my lady." Maingot, triumphant, leaped from his horse and grabbed the reins from Eleanor's hand.

"My Queen," he said, grinning maliciously. "And with such a small escort, on such a dark and dangerous night. This is a surprise."

"Is it, sir? I think not." Eleanor looked at him coolly, and struck his knuckles with her crop. He yelped and released his hold on her horse. "Is that you, Sir Benoit? Come. Let yourself be seen." She spoke over her shoulder, sensing someone standing behind her. Benoit stepped closer, but would not raise his eyes, which stared intently at his boots.

"I pity you," she spoke in a strong and loud voice, for all to hear. "You learned nothing while you were sheltered in my court. Nothing of value, at least. You have let yourself be used, just as Judas was used by the Pharisees. Used by Maingot. And by myself. Benoit, is this any way for a knight to behave? Even one that has been scorned?"

Lucie rode closer to Eleanor and peered at Benoit as if seeing him for the first time. "You betray the Queen because of me?" she asked him. "Then I am glad I scorned you." She turned her back on him and returned to Godfrey's side.

Benoit gasped as if the Queen's words and Lucie's had been physical blows. He forgot his shame long enough to look up at the Queen. "Used by you, my lady? What do you mean? How could that be, that you have used me?"

Eleanor did not answer him, but turned to Maingot, who was stroking his beard in puzzlement. Why did the Queen not weep and wail, and beg for mercy? Why did she sit so calm and even more proud than usual and eye them as if she had ordered their presence, rather than been taken by ambuscade?

And then his puzzlement turned to fury as he saw the knowing, disdaining smile that curled on her lips. She was not surprised because she had expected this. She had used him, Maingot. He pulled off his gauntlets and threw them to the ground in anger.

"Ah. I see the light dawns in your thick skull, Maingot. I have never deemed you a clever man, and this night you have proven me right. You honor me, Maingot, for in this action you have preserved my life. I thank you." The Queen nodded her head at him, almost coyly, as if he had just offered her a tidbit of roasted pheasant from his table knife.

There was a buzzing of talk among the men-at-arms as they puzzled out the meaning of the Queen's words. One, a knight new

403

to the art of ambuscade, took off his visor and scratched his head. "What means she?" he asked in an almost petulant voice. "Is she not our captive now, and all her party with her?"

"She is just that." Maingot's words slid through clenched teeth. "Our captive. And we are duty-bound to deliver her to Henry. Alive and unharmed. She is a hostage, and must be treated according to the rules that protect them."

"I was taken fairly in war, and must be treated fairly as a hostage. And all of Aquitaine, France and England will soon know I am Henry's hostage," Eleanor added. "Why, I even brought two poets, who can spread the news in rhymed couplet, to make it that much more popular and well listened to." Eleanor laughed once, briefly, and then her voice turned to ice that was cold and sharp with cunning.

"So you see, Maingot, there can be no secret poison, no knife in the night, for me. All would know it was murder, and Henry fears the accusation of murder even more than he fears my tongue, which is saying much. Becket's murderer can't have another such stain on his conscience. My loving husband himself must now assure my safety." The ice in her voice turned to hot bitterness.

Maingot, understanding, drew a design in the air with his hands, as he had often done when he and the Queen played at chess together and she astounded him with an unexpected move. "You could not lose," he told her. "You could make it to France, and safety, or you could be captured . . . and still be safe." He shook his head in disbelief and felt a stirring of admiration for her. "You have outmaneuvered me, my lady."

"Let that be a lesson, Maingot. The most dangerous thing to do is nothing. And now, let's decide on the terms."

Eleanor dismounted and instructed her escort to do likewise. The men-at-arms also dismounted, and soon the group was gathered around a newly make bonfire where all, Queen and knave alike, spread out chilled hands to the warm flames.

Maingot himself warmed a flagon of spiced wine and carried a silver goblet of it to Eleanor.

"You should have been born a man," he told her.

"Nay, Maingot. You should have been born a woman. You would have proven right all the slanders they put out about us, that we are deceitful and slow to learn." She accepted the goblet from his hand, but passed it to her companion, Sophia.

Maingot blanched at the insult and then returned to his men, who occupied the other side of the fire. He glared at Eleanor through the flames, hating and admiring her at the same time.

"Now what, my lady?" Sophia said, gladly accepting the wine. She was exhausted and ill and wished only to spread her mantle on the ground and sleep. "I take it our journey to France has been permanently interrupted."

"Now, Lady Sophia, I go to my husband. And you to your brother. The convent will not welcome you, and Poitiers will not be safe for you. You must return to your own lands and face your brother's wrath, and find a convenient lie to cover the birth of your child."

"I don't fear my brother. He is weak-minded and would not dishonor his family by casting out his sister. As for the child . . . something will come to me. But, my lady, is it safe for me to leave you? Will they let me leave you?" Sophia finished the wine. It made her light-headed and almost gay. Now that they were captured, they were safe, it seemed.

"They will, because I will insist on it. Henry seeks revenge on me, not on the others. And he will not want the expense of feeding and sheltering two poets and two ladies, so yes, the others will be free to go. Marie must return to Champagne, and Godfrey and Lucie will go with her."

Amaria, seated on the other side of Eleanor, leaned closer to her and took her hand. "I will go with you," she said simply. Her large eyes were placid and shining.

Sophia wondered if Eleanor guessed the root of Amaria's devotion: only in service to the Queen could she hope to catch occasional glimpses of the Queen's son, Richard. But did it matter? Nay. If good comes from love, so much the better, and it was good that Eleanor had one companion who would remain with her.

"I would be pleased, Amaria, to have your companionship. Thank you. And now I will go argue these terms with Maingot."

Eleanor rose to confront her captor, realizing that this was one of the last times that she would be her own spokesperson, argue her own terms. In the future, Henry would speak for her. Henry would set the terms of her life. Her heart was heavy. But somewhere, in the back of her thoughts, an eagle soared high and free and would not return to the lure.

"They've murdered the Queen! They've murdered the Queen!" Broderick hopped up and down in fear and excitement. He had kept quiet all the night long, while the men-at-arms and their captors rested as best they could and waited for daybreak. But when dawn came and the Queen was led away from the clearing, he could keep still no longer.

"Not murdered. Only captured," Robert corrected him. But to no avail. Broderick's overheated imagination, stimulated by fear, dwelt on the way the moonlight had glinted on unsheathed swords, and the roughness with which that one man had grabbed the reins of the Queen's horse, and remained convinced that if the Queen wasn't yet murdered, she soon would be.

And so, the three resumed their journey, casting backward glances at the now empty clearing. Each time Robert and Jacobus and Broderick met another group of travelers on the road, or paused to drink at a farmer's spring, the giant with the child's eyes would shriek and wave his arm and tell all within hearing that the Queen was murdered. Rumor was set free from her cage and took to wing.

The Elm of Gisors, a huge and age-gnarled tree, fluttered occasional leaves onto Henry's head. Those brown and red envoys he casually brushed away. He was deep in thought, and had the Elm of Gisors shed its whole voluminous load of leaves at once and buried him, he would barely have noticed.

The Old King. They had called him the Old King, and within his hearing. Loudly and with love in their voices, the peasants lining the road of arrival had called for the Old King, as if it were a title of worth.

By the blood of the Virgin. I'm forty. My beard is still red and my tool rises each morn, and not just with the water it's held all night, he reassured himself. One of his hands went up to stroke the prized red beard; the other gently coddled between his legs in the soldier's after-battle gesture of insuring that all was intact. Then both hands banged on the wooden trestle before him in anger.

But by the blood of the lamb, I could swear I feel a taint of age in my bones this evening. The Elm of Gisors teasingly dropped another leaf onto his flaming hair and the Old King did not bother to remove that latest one. The negotiations had failed. Hal and Richard and Louis had refused his terms.

Refused him! Him, Henry, who had been refused nothing since Eleanor did not refuse him her hand!

Eleanor. Aye, these were her sons who had sat before him this short autumn day, her sons who had looked him coolly in the eye, fresh from warring against him, her sons who said, "Nay, King and Father, we cannot accept your peace." Louis had smiled, had given Henry that conspiratorial glance that said, "Aren't children irksome?" and under that feigned sympathy that devil of deceit, Louis, had been gloating.

Verneuil was between them. Henry could never again look at Louis and see a man. He would see a demon, a hypocrite with knees callused from kneeling, whose ears rang with the yells of the innocent of Vitry and Verneuil, who were murdered. Louis had sat with Hal and Richard, as if to protect them from the righteous and stern wrath of the father, whom they were seeing for the first time since the Queen's war began.

In reality, that seating arrangement under the Elm of Gisors had saved Louis, not Hal and Richard. All during the treating Henry's fingers had ached to close over Louis' thin neck, but he restrained himself. He must. There were things he wanted that he would not get by murdering the French King.

He wanted peace in his kingdom and his family. He wanted

things to be as they had been before: his sons content and obedient, his wife loving and wise, his lands rich with harvest, not
trampled from battle. There were times when he could even wish
that Becket, that irksome hairshirt of a priest, were still alive. He
wanted things to be simple again, and even as he thought this, a
secret panic whirred in his brain, telling him that it had never
really been simple, he had only forced himself to see it that way.
But he could not complete the expansion of his empire if he must
fight for every foot held behind, while he also fought for every
inch still ahead. Let me go forward! he wanted to scream at them.

He had stayed calm. He had himself poured out many jugs of
wine to smooth their moods and he had smiled when he offered
Richard and Henry the peace terms. They would enjoy the same
lands, the same revenues, that they had enjoyed before the war.
There would be no punishment.

He had made his sons slightly drunk, but he had not made
them pliant. Hal was the one who had surprised him. Pale and
shaken, he had risen to his feet and thrust his fist in his father's
face.

"No punishment! Sire, I remind you we are not babes in the
nursery. There was never a question of punishment. It was a
question of rights. Mine. The fact that I am anointed King yet you
sit on my lands and revenues like a knight with dysentery afraid
to leave the privy! I want what is mine!"

Louis rose between them. This meeting had been arranged by
him as a peacemaking effort, and he realized now it was pre-
maturely done. All he could do was save grace by preventing it
from becoming a rowdy free-for-all or a pitched battle.

"Henry, respect your King and father," he began, but the
Young King merely spat at Henry's feet and walked away.

"He was never so eloquent as a child. Has Eleanor been giving
him lessons in poetry?" Henry turned to Richard and tried to
make a joke of it. But his hand was on his sword, and only the
strong tie of blood preserved Hal's life at that moment.

Richard did not smile. Nor did he look away. "I am returning
to Aquitaine," he said simply. "I, too, refuse these terms. They
would leave me so impoverished, I could not even maintain an

army." Henry and Richard glared at each other, knowing that had been the purpose of the terms all along.

"Go, then, I'll offer you no more. But I warn you, Richard. Make no further trouble for me, or you will rue the day. I need Hal. He is my heir. But you are a second son and you are a luxury to me."

Richard bit his tongue, remembering Eleanor's letter. "Do not anger him, do not make yourself noticeable to him. Keep yourself safe and out of the way, and a day will come when you will have his lands as well as mine."

"Farewell then, loving father," Richard said, grinning. On an impulse, Henry came to him and threw his hands around him. He hugged him close and tight for a moment and put a loud, wet kiss on his cheek. When all was said and done, he was a fair youth and gentle, and his worst fault was that he was too easily led by his mother.

As soon as his boys were gone, Louis disappeared, too, and Henry was left alone with his restless, murmuring men at the long, goblet-strewn trestle. He called for more wine and sat brooding, trying to put off his own moment of departure. Now he must go south and confront his Queen, Eleanor. She who had caused all this to happen.

The husband in him wanted to relate to her all that had happened today, how their boys had looked and spoken. They were men, by God. Misdirected, but men for all that, and beneath his anger and discontent, Henry was proud, as he knew Eleanor, their mother, was. The husband in him wondered if the wife's head pains had grown less, or if her vision still worsened. The husband in him hoped that when they met, Eleanor would not question him too closely about Rosamonde.

But the King in him thought only of revenge. She who had been his greatest ally was now his worst enemy, and that was the unforgivable. She had turned against him.

Still he sat, and brooded. The retreating sun cast a long shadow behind the Elm of Gisors, and a twilight wind blew cold. His men had left him by ones and twos and he was alone now. Henry wrapped his mantle tightly about him and watched the night close in. He feared this time of day. The superstitious peasants of Wales and Ireland said this was the hour when spirits walked the earth, when the thin veil between life and death was rent for a time and all sorts of evil things could happen.

It was this hour when he most wanted bed sport, to jump under a warm fur coverlet with his lady love when it was still day, and rise only when night was safely arrived, with the dangerous time between spent in pleasant, worry-erasing pastime.

But Rosamonde was in her convent. Rosamonde was ill. After she had left him, he had found a handkerchief she had hidden in a jug. It had been covered with blood, coughed up one night when he had slept soundly and she, apparently, had not.

There were some ills from which the body recovered. A healthy woman, for example, could be in childbirth bed one day, and singing in the solarium the next. A sword wound to the arm, if it did not cut the sinews, tended to heal quickly, while a wound to the knee did not. And from the coughing up of blood, one might recover for a time. But one could not be healed. Rosamonde would die of it, and not a long time hence: her future was a short one. He grieved for her.

Eleanor. She, on the other hand, was strong as a horse. She would live forever. Longer than him, at least, of that he was sure, although she was older by many years. What a travesty that Rosamonde should die, and Eleanor should live.

Charles approached through the gloaming, the chain mail that always protected his chest glinting dimly in the growing dark. His face was even longer than usual.

"Sire, there is news of the Queen. More rumor than news, for it was not officially sent but overheard among the peasants."

"Then tell it quickly, and if it be but rumor, I'll take it lightly." Henry was irritated. Probably it was just more scandal about Eleanor, who had chosen this touchy time to flaunt her infidelities by welcoming Bernart de Ventadour to her court. Of that, Henry had already been enlightened several times over by knights who, while they served him, were still glad to bring bad news his way. This infidelity was one more crime for which he would soon take his revenge against his Queen.

"Sire. They say the Queen is dead. Murdered by your men." Charles kept his eyes on the ground.

Silence hung thickly between them. Then Henry, stunned and outraged, roared with anger and that feeling he had least expected to feel. Sorrow. He had been robbed of his Queen, and of his revenge.

10

Chinon. Why did it have to be Chinon? Of all the castles and fortresses held by Henry, why did Maingot have to choose Chinon for her imprisonment?

This place was thick with memory. It was crueler punishment than leg-irons would have been. The very walls smelled of Henry, of Eleanor and Henry, as they had been in earlier times. Loving. United in body and soul and purpose. Journeying together on the same path, till strife sent them separate ways.

Eleanor closed her eyes and allowed herself to remember those other times, just for a moment . . . the feel of Henry nuzzling his face in her loosened hair as he carried her to bed, the sound of a nurse's voice singing to her sleeping babes in the chamber next to them, the smell of holly and pine boughs brought in to adorn the hall for the twelve nights of Christmas . . .

It was always at Chinon that they most liked to keep Christmas. It was at Chinon that Henry, made merry by wine and the joy of Christmas, the birth of Mary's babe, most liked to narrow his eyes at his Queen over the feasting trestle and whisper, "Let's to our chamber, and make another babe! By God, it's work I relish! And we'll need a large passel of fry to hold the lands I intend to leave them."

She'd given him all the children he needed, and more. And she'd administered his governments while he warred for new lands, collected his taxes and soothed his people, and in short made it possible for Henry of England to be Henry of England, and to do the things he had done.

And now she was his prisoner.

Eleanor, eyes still closed, leaned against the casement and felt the damp chill of the stone wall seep through her clothes. Her reverie ended, to be replaced by anger. By God, this pissing spot of a prison didn't even have tapestries on the walls! Maingot had added insult to injury by confining her to an unfinished set of rooms just above the great hall, where the sounds of drunken, carousing men disturbed her sleep and the eastern light of dawn roused her much too early.

She was always tired and had no appetite, because the food brought to her was unfit for pigs. Her spirits were low. But one thought buoyed her. Richard had refused the peace terms. Richard had stood up to his father, he had stared into the sun without flinching and turning away.

But that was the last she had heard from the world outside these rooms. Maingot was careful to keep her in darkness. He knew that news meant more to her than sleep and food, and this, too, was part of her punishment for having been a bad wife.

She had laughed the first time he called her that: a bad wife. "Why, sir, if being a good mother and a better Queen requires being a bad wife, then so be it. Christ himself praised Mary, who preferred the world, over Martha, who preferred simple housekeeping." Maingot, at a loss for response, had glared at her and thundered out of the chamber. But he continued to call her a bad wife, and took care to place troubadours under her windows so she could hear the reproaching songs he paid them to write and sing.

The best of these, the one whose tune even Eleanor's discerning ear found pleasing, was about Eleanor's war against Henry. *"La Senza Sans Amur,"* the war without love, it was called. And

Eleanor found it an apt title. She had spent many hours, this past month, leaning against the damp wall and listening to an unseen troubadour sing of the war without love. She wondered if Rosamonde was still in her convent, or in her crypt.

"My Lady. The time approaches . . ." Amaria, a flash of crimson silk against the grey stones, like a winter cardinal against dirtied snow, came to Eleanor carrying her jewel case. Amaria, too, was thin and pale. To Eleanor, it seemed a year since she had news of Richard; to Amaria, it seemed five years.

Eleanor, reluctantly opening her eyes, checked the hour candle. There was a large puddle of wax on the floor under it, showing the hours that had burned away, and the flame hovered above the line indicating four in the afternoon.

"Yes," she agreed. "Help me prepare myself."

Henry at least had had the courtesy to warn her of his arrival and the hour he would come to her. For that, she was grateful.

She sat on a bench and took off her veil so that Amaria could comb and replait the long braids. While Amaria did that, Eleanor opened the jewel case and took out a strand of pearls that would be wound about the coiled braids, and two gold cuffs for her wrists. "Just those," she said aloud. "Henry never cared for an excess of jewels." For the first time in a long time, she was adorning herself to please Henry. This, too, was part of the war without love.

At the top of the case, fitted in a special drawer, were pots of creams and unguents and colorings. Eleanor studied these, frowning. If she colored her face, it would be too obvious that she wanted his admiration. If she did not, she would look pale and tired and might earn pity. Pity. I'll have none of that, she decided. She rubbed a very small amount of carmine rose cream into her cheeks and lips, just enough to make her look as though she had been in the sun for an afternoon.

Oh, God. To walk in the sun. To ride free again. Maingot had not even permitted her to walk in the gardens of Chinon. For a moment she lost courage and began to tremble. Henry might well think that Maingot had been too kind by far for keeping her out of

414

the earth-floor dungeons, for not starving her and chaining her. Henry might well wish her dead.

Amaria felt Eleanor tremble. "Courage," she whispered.

Henry of England, dressed handsomely in blue surcoat, purple bliaut and yellow-and-white-striped hose, strode boldly to the door. But as the guards made to open it for him, he turned his back on them and retreated six steps back down the hall.

One hand on hip, the other stroking his freshly trimmed and pointed beard, he paced in a circle for some minutes. There was such a war of emotion within him, he could not yet go through that doorway, to where Eleanor awaited him.

Eleanor. Too fresh in his mind was last month's grief and rage, when she had been rumored dead. He had believed his rage and the sleepless nights that followed that rumor were the result of being cheated of his revenge. How do you insult, punish and humiliate a dead Queen? Refuse to have masses said for her soul? Henry doubted that a dead Eleanor would much miss masses not said. No, death had saved her from him.

But then came the news that superseded the rumor: Eleanor was not dead, but held captive at Chinon, by his own knights. The Queen was his prisoner.

And the instant joy that had replaced the previous grief confused him. Surely this joy was too extravagant, even for a King who had regained the target of his wrath? But yet he had sung and danced for a wild moment, celebrating his Queen's resurrection.

Now he stood outside her door, uncertain, angry, confused, impatient. Loving, and hating, all at once. He strode to the door once again and, without waiting for the guards, thrust it open with a fury that made the rusted hinges complain.

Eleanor was sitting on a bench, with Amaria, still holding the hairbrush, standing behind her. Her veil was off, so he could see her hair shimmering in the dim light. She looked up at him, still and serene, and smiled, as if he had been gone for two hours, not

415

almost a year, as if he had gone to pick roses in the garden, not end the war she had begun.

Then, with downcast eyes, she picked up her veil and modestly placed it over her hair, covering its glory, making of it a secret lover's reward. Henry groaned. He knew that every nuance of her expression, every movement, was calculated to disarm. And it did. He remembered the feel of that cool, silken hair sliding over his chest and face and belly.

"I gave you ample time to veil yourself, madame," he reprimanded, yearning, not for Eleanor, but for the old feelings between them, making his voice crackle with anger.

"So you did, Sire. But as you know, I am frequently behind times." She rose, but made no movement to greet him.

"Don't play the woman with me, Eleanor," he muttered, shaking a clenched fist in her face.

"Why, I don't know what you mean. Many men run behind times, too, and as I am a woman, how then should I play one, or not play one?" Her voice was calm, her eyes serene. He knew this tone of voice, these mannerisms. He was in deep and dangerous water.

"Not a woman. A viper," he raged, shaking his fist again and roaring as loudly as he could, fire to match her water, wrath to match her feigned meekness. He picked up a goblet from her table and flung it at the wall. Amaria jumped.

"Go, my friend. I don't need you here," Eleanor told her. Quickly and gratefully Amaria bowed through a curtained arch into the next chamber.

When they were alone, Eleanor turned back to him. "Are you enjoying yourself, Henry?" she asked, smiling.

She had always found his fits of temper to be distasteful. Well then, if that was what it took to get the woman to show her true face, then temper it would be. He picked up a second goblet and threw that, too. Then, holding his arm stiffly out, he brushed off the jars of ink, stands of paper, bowls of fruit, and the mirror still on the table. They clattered to the floor in a noisy cacophony of banging metals and shattering glass.

Eleanor, hands tucked inside her long sleeves meek as a nun, stepped to one side as a stream of ink made its way towards her slippers.

"You are enjoying this greatly," she concluded.

The clattering noise and stormy mess, and Eleanor's pinched expression, freed something in Henry. When the last brass plate ceased careering over the stone floor and all was silence again, he threw his head back and laughed.

"Eleanor," he said, holding out his opened arms. His eyes softened. She hesitated a moment, but then gladly went to him, and let him put his arms around her. She pressed her head against the velvet of his surcoat and closed her eyes. They swayed together, husband and wife, bound by ties that even they could not break.

"When I heard you were dead, I think something started to die in me," he whispered. "Through all that happened, I never thought you would die."

"Yet you must have wished me dead, often enough."

"I did. But that is a different thing altogether. Did you wish me dead?" He hugged her tightly and then lifted her face up to look at him.

"Almost daily. But as you say, that is a different thing altogether. Had you really died . . ." Her voice trailed off.

"Eleanor, what a mess you've made of this."

She stiffened in his embrace. "I? I have made a mess of it? Tell me, my lord. They say Becket haunts you nightly. Is that true, my lord? And what of Rosamonde, the harlot you would have made Queen, had I the generosity to step aside. What of Rosamonde, my lord? You speak wrongly of the messes I have made!" She raised her voice for the first time and the room reverberated with her anger.

Henry released her so quickly, she stumbled.

"Do not speak of Rosamonde," he commanded.

"Not speak of her? The whole world speaks of your harlot . . ."

"Don't try me, Eleanor, I warn you." He turned away and went to the casement.

"It's true, then. Rosamonde is dying." Eleanor sighed and sat down.

She feared a dead Rosamonde even more than she feared a

living one. Dead, Rosamonde would never grow old. Her hair would never grow thin and dull, her face never crease and coarsen, her breasts and belly never lose their tautness. Henry, never having seen her wither, would remember her always in the perfection of bloom. And compare Eleanor to her.

His shoulders heaved; she heard him gasp for breath. He wept now, for the dying Rosamonde, and those tears increased her anger.

"Tell me, Henry, did you want to make her your wife? It was rumored that you would divorce me so you could wed Rosamonde."

"It was true. Rosamonde was the wife I should have had." He lied, wanting to hurt, wanting to make Eleanor weep as he had wept for all things beautiful, now lost. He could not have wed Rosamonde, her family was too base to have a daughter on the throne. But how he had dreamed of it, and hoped for it, that wedding that could not take place.

She believed his lie, that he would put her aside for a common woman. This time, Eleanor gasped with outrage and he smiled with satisfaction.

"Strange that you should call Rosamonde a harlot. That is the very title they give you, Lady. You are Bernart de Ventadour's harlot." His voice was scathing.

"His name is forbidden you," she hissed back. "You banished him once from my court, protesting that a Queen could have but one lord, and a King but one Queen. Tell me, Henry, who were you bedding that week, the time you sent away the knight who loved me? You never loved me, yet you denied me the company of a man who did. You wanted Rosamonde by your side. Perhaps I would have been happier with Bernart at my side."

"Perhaps," he said, suddenly tired. "But happiness is not the point, Eleanor. Dear God. If only it could be the point." He sat on the bench. Eleanor sat next to him.

"No. Happiness is not the point, is it, Henry? It never was." They sat in silence, starring straight ahead at the bare grey stone wall of the room.

"You need some tapestries," he said after a long while.

418

"More than that, I need news. Maingot has let me receive none. How is Richard? Is he in good health?"

Henry slapped his knee, his mercurial mood changing from anger to pleasure. "By the Virgin's milk. He was in strapping good health and venomous as his mother. He's a good, strong lad."

"He turned down your terms, of course."

"Upon your instruction, no doubt."

"But he and Hal cannot win this war."

"No, they cannot. They can hold out for a while longer, but they cannot win. The fledglings tried their wings too soon and will fall to earth."

"And what will you do, when it is over?" Eleanor did not wait for his answer. "You will not injure Richard," she told him. "You will not."

"Eleanor, do you think me a mad dog that would eat my own children? Don't answer that. I will subdue Richard as any beaten knight must be subdued. For his own good. Any knight who loses a battle must learn the humility that comes with defeat. It will make him that much more eager to win in the future. And Hal and Geoffrey and anyone else who crosses my plans will be subdued. But Richard has my blood in his veins as well as yours . . . To hurt him would be to do myself an injury. I wish, though, he would get on his knee to me, and quickly. He is stubborn. Like his mother."

Eleanor ignored the jibe, eager for more news of her son. "Where is he now?"

"He has left La Rochelle, where the town bolted its gates and jeered at him when he tried to enter."

"They jeered? Oh, my poor son, how that must have wounded him."

Henry eyed her sideways and frowned. "His pride is intact. He made directly for Saintes and has made headquarters there. They say he has turned the cathedral into an arms depot."

"The cathedral? That was brazen. And clever. Your men dare not enter." Eleanor smiled in satisfaction.

419

"No, they won't enter. But Richard must leave it sometime, and when he does, I'll be there, waiting for him."

"You won't harm him," she repeated.

"Eleanor, why Richard? Of the sons you bore me, why Richard?" He was not angry, only puzzled. It had always been Richard with her, since the day of his birth, as if the rest of the brood counted for nothing, or at least not as much as Richard counted for in her eyes. Why?

"Because he is the best of them. The Young King is no more than a puppet. You've ruined him, Henry, by pulling at his strings for too long. He'll never dare move on his own, after this. And Geoffrey is cunning . . . too cunning. He will go whichever way the wind blows, and so never walk a steady course. And John. I have nightmares about John. He is your child. He has nothing to do with me. He hates me. I feel it when he looks at me."

"Because you have not loved him. But, Eleanor, you have loved Richard the best, and love is not always given where it is most earned, even if I were to concede that Richard is the best of the lot. Tell me the true reason for making him the choice of your heart."

She hesitated. She must tell the truth, or lie. A lie would separate them finally, and forever. But the truth would earn his pity, and she was in a dangerous position for pity. Yet she chose the truth.

"Because he most reminds me of you . . ."

Henry slapped his knee again and then jumped to his feet. "You admit it, Lady. You loved me." His voice was triumphant.

"And is that the point, Henry? To be loved? But let me finish. You as you once were. Proud. Filled with ideals. Generous. Brave."

"And how am I now?"

"Greedy. Grasping. Fearful."

"There is much to gain in this life. And much to fear in the next," he said, sitting down again. "You are merely pointing out that I am no longer young. Nor are you, Eleanor."

"Nor am I. Perhaps, Henry, that is the point."

420

From below, they could hear the sound of men's voices and heavy steps gathering in the great hall for the afternoon meal. This interview must soon end. Henry must join his men, not dally with his Queen.

"Now what?" she asked. He put his arm around her shoulder. "Do you mean to kill me?"

"Eleanor, you know I cannot. The rebellion continues apace in Aquitaine. Should I murder the Queen of such a disputatious people, I would never have peace there."

"Surely you have dreamed of poison," she insisted, stung that he so openly admitted that her life was preserved only for reasons of diplomacy. "Surely you have dreamed of knives flashing in the dark. Ah. Now I see. That was before Rosamonde took ill. You are afraid now, Henry. Afraid of being entirely alone." She sighed and leaned her weight against him.

"And what do you fear, Eleanor? The same?" He would not look at her.

"No. You have already left me alone too much. I have lost my fear of that. I fear being made less than I am. Your wife. Queen. Mother of a race of Kings."

"You are overambitious, Eleanor. A woman is better off by her hearth."

"You tried to keep me by the hearth, and it led to war, Henry. My ambition matches your own. You would not have taken me to wife, had I been less ambitious. The world has changed. Women are not cattle or mere baby-makers, they are not soulless creatures made for bed sport, nor drudges that can be put aside when it suits the husband. I am your equal, Henry. Cut me off, and you cut off half of yourself."

"Then God help me." His merriment fled, he sighed and scratched at the red and grey beard on his chin.

"You will not let me return to Poitiers, I suppose," Eleanor asked after a moment.

"I cannot. I cannot be rid of you, either through death or separation. You are dangerous, Eleanor. If you return to Poitiers, the war will never end. You will set my kingdom against me, and I will lose my sons. The only way to protect myself from you is to keep you beside me, always." His voice was gentle, but she was not deceived.

"Where?" she asked. "Where will I be imprisoned?"

"England. Away from Poitiers and Aquitaine and France." Away from all she loved, the sun and the South and the vivacious, troublesome peoples of her home. This would be the other part of her punishment.

"England. My God. Perhaps, Henry, you should murder me after all." She smiled grimly and rose with him, as he rose to leave.

"My eagle flies to England," he repeated, taking her hands in his and kissing them.

"To be belled and blindfolded and chained to her perch. You hate me, Henry." There were questions in her voice.

"You are part of me, Eleanor. I love you as I love myself. And hate you in the same measure. I will not forgive you for turning my sons against me." He released her hands and they dropped limply to her side.

"Nor will I forgive you, Henry. But we have each other. For now and always."

"For better and for worse. May God help us."

"And that is my punishment on you, Henry. You are my prisoner as surely as I am yours." Standing, they were eye to eye. They glared at each other, a stormy sea of emotion flowing between them. Henry slammed the door mightily when he left and Eleanor laughed at his anger, but there was no joy in her.

BOOK FOUR

A Man and a Maid

September 3, 1189

It was the custom of the country that since one captive was leaving, all the others got out too. They all blessed Lancelot, and you may be certain that great joy was called for and felt. Those of Logres assembled to celebrate Lancelot and cried so he could hear, "Sir, indeed, you made us happy as soon as we heard your name. Right away we knew we'd be free." The celebration became crowded, with everyone striving and straining to touch him. The nearer they could get, the more inexpressibly happy they were. Joy and wrath were both present . . .

—Lancelot: The Knight of the Cart

1

The meadows beyond the castle keep were filled with the delicate last blooms of the season, and the distant forest was adorned with fiery red and gold. As she leaned out of the casement of the grey tower, a cool wind brushed against her face like the caress of an angel's wing. It was autumn again, as it had been when she lost her freedom. But never had fall colors seemed so vibrant to her.

She was free. Henry was dead. Richard was to be crowned King. The refrain sang over and over in her thoughts, like a rough poem waiting to be polished, as Eleanor waited for her escort to arrive. She had become very good at waiting. She'd had sixteen years of practice.

"Do you see them yet?" she asked her maid, Amaria, who stood next to her and eagerly studied the distant road rather than the colorful meadow. She asked the question more because it was expected, because Amaria could not stand overly long silences between them, than because of impatience. They would come in time. All things came in time.

Amaria sighed and shook her head; Eleanor left the casement, picked up her tapestry frame and contentedly continued stitching a golden edge onto a red rose.

"I see Ranulf de Glanville in the garden, but no sign of the escort," Amaria sighed again, straining to see far into the garden below their apartment.

"And how does my friend look today?"

My friend. How many years since she had learned to call her jailers friend? She had hated them at first, till she realized she merely hated what they stood for: Henry's power over her. In truth, Ranulf de Glanville had treated her with kindness, respect, and even admiration.

She had been allowed the freedom of Winchester Castle, including the gardens. She had not been clothed in sackcloth or fed bread and water, nor even forced into excessive solitude. Eleanor and her jailer had spent many evenings together discussing the strategies of chess, and never between them had they mentioned Henry, or the fact that she was a prisoner. When she had chafed and railed at the confinement, in the early years, he had gently pretended she was in need of guarding for her own safety.

With Ranulf de Glanville as jailer, there had been no knives flashing in the dark, no poison lingering in the sediment of the wine. With his help, she had persevered.

"He hobbles. His gout must be bothering him," answered Amaria, sympathy in her tender voice.

"Then send him some of my own liniment. I would not have him be in pain today. There is a long journey ahead of us." Eleanor painstakingly worked her needle in and out of the tapestry with hands steady and strong. This surprised her. For sixteen years she had thought her hands would tremble when this day came, when the escort would arrive, and they would all of them ride to Westminster Abbey and see her son, Richard, crowned King of England.

Amaria, more obedient than ever . . . she'd had practice too, sharing this confinement with a Queen used to ordering large retinues and even armies . . . took a glass vial from Eleanor's medicine chest and went down to the gardens, to Ranulf de Glanville, glad for a moment in the fresh air.

426

Eleanor, alone, put down her needle and leaned her cheek against the smooth wood of the tapestry frame, allowing herself a rare moment of reverie. Daydreams, she had learned, were dangerous for prisoners. They caused too much pain. So she had hardened herself against them. But now there was no need to be hard, now the dreams could come; indeed, the dreams would soon be fulfilled. She would see Richard crowned. Geoffrey of Monmouth's prophecy would come true: The eagle of the broken pledge shall rejoice in her third nestling.

Her nestling was no longer a soft and uncertain young knight new to warfare and rebellion, as he had been in that summer of '73. He was a middle-aged man now, grown stout in the waist as Henry had, even with the first flecks of grey in his flaming hair. The boy grown to the man looked much as his father had, but of that she would not let herself think. There was too much bitterness there; it was dangerous to let her thoughts stray too much to Henry.

Richard's innocence was also long since over. That had ended in the summer of '73, when he warred against his father and learned of mortality by seeing some of his own and closest knights die by the sword. There had been that one knight, Alberic, who had been killed. It was said that Richard, all these years later, still showed special favor on all knights with that name, in honor of his friend who had died. And still frowned when the Old King was mentioned.

Henry and Richard never reconciled. They were still enemies when the Old King died in July, and Richard showed open disgust when his father was mentioned.

Richard was also rumored to show obvious disgust with women named Alais, and especially with Alais of France, his betrothed.

"He will not wed her. He will refuse," Eleanor spoke aloud. Amaria, already returned from her errand in the garden, nodded her head in agreement.

"Sir Ranulf asks if you will not wait in the great hall, rather than in our tower. There is a fire, and a meal laid out, and minstrels ready to sing for you." In fact, every day since that thrilling day in July, when William Marshall had ridden to the gates of

Winchester to tell them that Henry was dead, Sir Ranulf had put the same question to Eleanor, through her maid, Amaria. Why not leave your small rooms and take possession of the castle, as befits your rank? Henry was dead, and she was prisoner no more. But Eleanor, like an eagle too long kept in its mew, would not move out of her accustomed rooms.

"He will refuse," Eleanor said again of Richard's impending marriage, willing it to be so.

How could Richard marry his father's own mistress? The shame of it would destroy him and her, Henry's wife. It was like the question many had asked years before: How could Henry do it, sleep with his own son's fiancée?

There was no doubt he had done just that. Indeed, Alais had made no effort to hide the fact that soon as fair Rosamonde died, Henry sought comfort in her arms. Alais had not turned him away. Stronger women than herself had been unable to deny a wine-softened, supplicating Henry, the lover. Alais was neither strong nor sophisticated, and she was hot-blooded as Henry himself.

Strangely, Eleanor did not hate the Lady Alais, who was now a middle-aged leftover with neither lover nor husband to protect and comfort her. She remembered that fiery longing of a woman used to love who was required to sleep alone, and she thought that the days must seem very long to Alais and the nights longer yet, with Henry in the grave.

Eleanor disdained and pitied her. But she would not give up her son to her.

"He will not wed Alais," Amaria reassured her. "He would not bring such shame to you, his Lady Mother. Nor does he care for the woman. He never has."

He cares for no woman, her unspoken thoughts continued. And that is well by me, who would die to see him smiling into any woman's eyes but mine, and that never shall be, either. In the sixteen years of captivity Amaria had shared with Eleanor, she had received not one message from Richard. On his rare visits he had not looked at her, nor spoken to her.

Amaria's hair had dimmed from dark to a lighter brown and her forehead was creased, yet there was something maidenish about her, as if part of her had been touched by sorcery, and doomed never to age, never to change. That part was her love for Richard. But the passing years had given her wisdom, and she knew that loving the mother was the closest she would come to loving the son, and being loved by him. She was as content as a pilgrim who comes to salvation by loving the Holy Virgin, who intercedes with her Son.

"There is dust rising over the hill. I think the escort is coming." Amaria peered again out the casement, putting her hand to her forehead to shield her eyes from the eastern sun. "Yes. At least two dozen knights, I think, just as Richard promised."

"Where, Amaria?" Eleanor rose and stood next to her and scrutinized the horizon. She could make out the reds and golds of the field and forest, but she could see neither dust nor men yet, nor would she till they were all but under her window. Eleanor's eyes had grown increasingly bad with the years; she was like an eagle who has had its eyes burned out by the sun.

"Yes, I see them," she lied, sitting down again, waiting again. Again, there was a sense of strangeness. Almost of disappointment. She had always believed that when this moment came, when Richard's knights arrived to bring her to his coronation, she would all but die for joy.

She felt a thrill. That was all. Just a thrill. Not ecstasy, or joy . . . or even, necessarily, pleasure. It would be a long journey for her, and her back would ache, the sun would give her a headache, she would arrive at Westminster dusty and tired and more than a little out of humor.

Suddenly she laughed. "Amaria, do you remember Lady Sophia?"

"The little one who always complained. Yes, I remember her."

"Don't you think I am becoming a little as she was? What foul humor she had, what a long list of complaints! And that other one, Lucie, who never complained. I wonder if she had much joy of her Godfrey. I think that was his name." Nostalgia washed over her. And sadness. There had been deaths. Too many.

Her son, Henry, had died. Slowly, and painfully, and without father, mother or brother at his side to ease his parting from life.

The Young King had spent the years following the end of the war without love in tournaments. Still deprived of power and independence, he reverted to his old pastimes: mock life, mock battle, overspending and loose living. Poor Henry. The boy had had charm, but not clear thinking; popularity, but no power.

If only he had stayed like that. A wastrel son can still be loved. But Louis' son, Philip Augustus, who sensed the means to wound the father through the son, goaded the Young King into a frenzy of restlessness and discontent. Mock battle was no longer enough. The Young King went to real war again, this time against his brother Richard, over land in Clairvaux. The Old King, anxious for a quick peace, sided with Richard. And then Bertran de Born, a trouvère as unlike Bernart de Ventadour as the devil is unlike the archangel, stirred up the Young King's passions further with songs that made much of his craven powerlessness.

> A new sirventes, singer! Music ho!
> I'll cry abroad the Young King's latest deed:
> His father ordered him to quit at once
> His claim against his brother Richard's lands;
> And he obeyed him! Henry, landless King,
> For it I crown you King of cowards!

Young Henry, who thought more of fame and reputation that anything in this life, could not turn back from the path he had started, and there was civil war again in Aquitaine.

Surprisingly, he even took a few castles, including Aix. But he fell sick before he could plunder Uzerche. A summer fever, he told his boon companions and knights. A chill that passes in a day's time. He recovered and, short of money, plundered the shrine of St. Amadour at Rocamadour. But he sickened again at Martel, and sent to his father, saying that he was going to die. Henry, embittered by his son's unrelenting troublemaking, thought it was a trick. He did not go to him.

In the sweet month of June, the Young King made his con-

430

fession before his assembled followers, and sent again to his father, asking mercy for his followers and for his mother, Eleanor, and his wife, Margaret. Then his companions laid him on a bed of ashes with stones at his head and feet, put the Crusader's cloak over him, and the Young King died with neither father nor mother nor brother nor wife at his side.

> Now every grief and woe and bitterness,
> The sum of tears that this sad century's shed,
> Seem light against the death of the Young King,
> And prowess mourns, youth stands sorrowful;
> No man rejoices in these bitter days.

A nice verse, that. One of de Born's better efforts. Eleanor pushed away the remnant pain of her son's death and concentrated instead on the merits of the mourning poems made for him. Truth was, few actually mourned. The Young King had proven himself an eaglet who could not fly a steady course. The public weal came before private affection, and the Young King served his lands better by dying than living. "I trust in God for his salvation" was all Henry said when told of his son's death. Eleanor grieved . . . but not in the way she would have, had the dead son been Richard, not Henry. Poor Henry. He had been a promising knight. To come to naught. Ashes to ashes, dust to dust.

And Geoffrey had died, after making a false peace with his father. He held Brittany, through the forbearance of his father, and feigned contentment. But after the Young King had died Geoffrey, ambitious anew for himself, went again to Paris, to war against his father. He died there, and was buried there, after falling from his horse and being trampled in a tournament.

His death caused no great grief but she had wept for him just the same. He was her son, and now he was dead.

Of her daughters from Henry, Joanna survived and Eleanor of Castille. Matilda was alive but barely, should rumor be accurate.

Deaths. So many. Of her sons only glorious Richard and John remained. Her love for Richard was greater than ever; she still felt nothing for John, except a faint hope that he might yet be useful.

"They ride closer. Surely it is the escort." Amaria, growing eager, leaned out of the casement, so that her words were muffled by the autumn wind that swept the garden leaves into whirling eddies. "Surely we should prepare ourselves."

But Eleanor remained seated. "There is plenty of time, my friend. Plenty of time."

"Even so, what jewels will you wear?" Amaria crossed the room and stood impatiently next to the great casket that contained the Queen's jewels.

Eleanor, closing her eyes, considered. "The ruby cross," she said. "Bring that out."

"The rubies remind me of the red of your mouth," Louis had said when he first tied the cross around her neck. It was the prettiest thing he had ever said to her. Perhaps the only pretty thing, not having a poet's tongue. But she hadn't known that at the time. He gave her the ruby cross at their first meeting, when she was still a *jeune pucelle* of fifteen years. The things she had dreamed at fifteen . . .

She tried to feel sentiment for Louis. He, too, was dead, and being dead, could no longer be a problem. But even dead, he still irritated her as much as he had the first day she had screamed she would divorce him. The monkish Louis had died in a manner so monkish, it would have made her laugh, if it hadn't irritated her instead.

His son, the precious Philip Dieu-Donne given him by Adele of Champagne, had fallen ill of a fever, as children so often do. Louis, panicked, braved crossing the rough autumn channel for a pilgrimage to Canterbury, to implore St. Becket to save his only son. During that pilgrimage, Louis of France had traveled several days with Henry of England. The two Kings had shared the humble bed and board of the pilgrim like old cronies wanting to catch up on the family gossip.

Had they talked of her, those first and second husbands? The days she spent trying to imagine their conversation . . . At any rate, Philip recovered from his illness, and it was his father, Louis, who died instead. He caught a chest cold and suffered a weakness in the heart and brain, and then spent nine months dying. Nine months. A woman can make a new life in nine months. It took Louis nine months to leave behind the old one. Henry Fitz-Empress had not taken so long to die . . .

"No. Not the ruby cross." Eleanor reached up impatiently to undo the clasp herself. She didn't like the feel of it around her neck. It felt of sadness and repentance and guilt. "The chain of pearls that Richard sent." Yes, that was it. For Richard's coronation she must wear Richard's gift to her. It would please him. And the chain was new, it had no memories attached to it, it was like a blank parchment on which new memories would be written, memories made as she and Richard ruled England together.

There was already much talk of Richard's forthcoming Crusade, of his vow to take his army to Jerusalem as soon as the money could be raised. Eleanor approved this plan. The land and the people were starting to stagnate from too much civil strife and local warring; too much was made of even the most run-down castle, and not enough of glory and fame. Chivalry, during her captivity, had all but died. There were no more courts of love, and even the poets worshipped greed, not beauty.

Richard would change that. With her help. She would keep his kingdom safe, while he set fire to the people's imaginations with his Crusade. She would rule again, and this time without Henry at her side, constantly interfering, commanding, bustling, harassing, hurrying, gainsaying. Without Henry.

"My mantle, quickly, Amaria. I hear them entering the hall." For the first time that morning, Eleanor felt a sense of urgency. Timing was important. It would not be wise to be in the great hall when the escort arrived; that would indicate she, Eleanor, had waited, and a Queen should not wait for others. They should wait for her. Yet it also would not do to make them wait for too long. Then she would be tardy and slothful, which were unfitting qualities in a ruler. A moment was long enough, time for the bustle of arrival to die down, for welcoming goblets to be filled, for a sense of anticipation to build.

Amaria quickly went for the ermine-lined red silk mantle and put it around Eleanor's shoulders. "Amaria, friend, it's a rare woman who lives the number of years I have lived, and yet I will live many more, I feel it will be so." Eleanor nodded her head emphatically as Amaria fastened the mantle with a gold brooch. Age was no longer her enemy; it had become her main ally.

"Now we will go to the great hall, and meet this escort. Go before me, Amaria, and carry a torch, for the stairs are dark, but be sure to leave the torch in a bracket before they see us. And don't fuss over me . . ."

There was a lit torch awaiting them just outside the door. Ranulf de Glanville saw to such details. Eleanor, walking behind her servant, followed its golden, smoking trail, and wondered how long it would be before she could journey to Poitiers, to the warm, sun-filled land of her youth, away from this damp and dreary place where the sun was too shy to peek out of cloud or fog.

Henry had never loved Poitiers as she had. He had preferred the North, where the sun was less predictable in its shining and the people more predictable in their politics. Henry. Yes, it was time to think of Henry.

Amaria paused and turned. "Is something wrong?" She heard the noise of consternation deep in her Queen's throat.

"Nothing, my friend. Only there is so much to remember . . ." Eleanor put her hand to the wall for support, suddenly unsteady.

"The bishops will guide us during the ceremonies, you needn't worry," said Amaria, misunderstanding. Eleanor smiled and said nothing and they continued down the passageway to the great hall.

Henry had broken his word to her.

Two years after carrying her off to Winchester, word came that the Old King sought to divorce his wife, Eleanor. He had her lands, and her person in captivity, and he had managed a peace of sorts with her sons, and now he wanted his freedom. He would wed an heiress who could bring him more land, more money, more power. He would put aside the old wife to acquire a new one who could deliver unto him a new dream of empire. It was rumored that he wished to wed Alais, daughter of Louis of France, Henry's concubine, who was Richard's betrothed.

Cardinal Huguezon brought her the news officially, asking her to sign the document stating their marriage was void, that she and Henry had never been married in fact, because she and Henry were too closely related. It was the convenient excuse used in all matters of this sort.

"It's true, then, that Alais has his bastard, whom he wishes to make legitimate . . . thereby making my sons bastards?" Eleanor had responded coolly.

Yes, she had been cool. But inside she had raged with such fever that the flesh melted off her bones like candle wax, and Amaria, desperate, had to plead with her to eat and rest.

She cursed Henry to hell and back and for the first time truly regretted that she had thrown away her life and body on this son of the devil. She remembered how she had lain in his arms, breathless with pleasure, and then the pain of bearing his children that followed the pleasure, and she cursed herself for having been a fool, for having been used.

"Your wealth will endow the abbey of Fontevrault, and you will be abbess," Cardinal Huguezon promised, false hope and obvious fear in his voice.

"A convent? Henry wishes me to go to a convent?" Her voice was deadly quiet. When she laughed, gooseflesh rose on the cardinal's arm. "I will see him in hell first. That is my message. Deliver it to him, little priest, and don't bother me again with this." Huguezon, quaking, backed out of the chamber and was not seen again at Winchester Castle.

He delivered that message to Henry, and others, too, for one day Eleanor's chaplain sheepishly slipped into her hand a sealed parchment. It was from Bernart, who had kept his silence since the autumn he slipped out of Poitiers, sent away that time by Eleanor, not Henry. He had returned to his monastery, and to poems that praised the spirit, not the flesh.

"Reconsider, my friend and my sister," he implored her. "If you agree to this plan, then you can be my wife in spirit, and heart, not Henry's. We would be separated in the flesh, but united in those things that matter. Remember the glory of Abelard and Heloise, whose great love was preserved by the chaste distance between them, and the sanctity of their vows."

435

Eleanor, stung by this betrayal, tore up the letter and wondered if all men were fools, or only those whom she had loved. She was Queen of England. She would die Queen of England, and Henry's wife. No less.

Her sons rallied to her support and made it clear to Henry that, should their mother be put aside, the old wars would continue. The kingdom, only recently returned to a fragile peace, would be torn apart.

At Easter, Henry himself came to Winchester to confront Eleanor with his plan of divorce. He came smiling and bearing gifts; he was all tender concern for her health and promised a new set of brocaded bed hangings when he saw the old ones were moth-eaten.

"Never," she told him. "Never will I give you your freedom. I told you, Henry. You are my prisoner as much as I am yours. Nothing will change that."

He left, taking back the gifts and instructing Ranulf de Glanville to put the Queen on brackish water and black bread, an order de Glanville ignored. But when he left, he was still Eleanor's husband and realized, finally, that he would be till death.

Eleanor waited, and her moment for revenge came one year later, when Rosamonde died. Henry, reeling with grief and sobbing like a child, had actually gone to her, his wife, for comfort. He hadn't looked well. There was too much flesh around his middle, and the shadows under his eyes were too deep.

She had never seen him so deeply wounded as he had been by this loss of his common lover. She was awed by his grief; it awoke the old jealousies that he had never keened so for her. But when he came to her for sympathy, she laughed in his face. He flinched away from her as if she had struck him. He raised his hand to strike her, but did not. He left, and, alone again, Eleanor wept quietly for Rosamonde and all lost love.

She and Henry rarely met after that incident. Henry kept occasional holiday courts at Winchester, with his family, but never was he seen talking to his wife, or looking at her. They sat side by side and worlds apart. They never touched, yet they were locked in mortal embrace like two elks who, engaged in combat, lock horns and starve to death rather than give way to the other. Eleanor felt her heart shriveling in her chest, but never again was divorce mentioned. Only when she thought of Richard was there a tentative stirring of emotion in her chest, faint as the delicate wings of a hummingbird.

And then, Henry died. Henry, younger than her by a decade, hardened by years of war and travel, had died before her. After sixteen years of being his prisoner, he had set her free by dying.

There had been war with France, again, and with Richard, still. During the battles his birthplace, Le Mans, had been put to the torch and destroyed. Henry, more superstitious than ever, saw this as an omen of his own death, and took it hard. He was injured in the foot, and the injury would not heal but instead festered and poisoned him. Too ill to continue fighting, he agreed to the combined demands of Philip of France and his own son, Richard.

Dying, Henry returned to Chinon, to his castle high over the Vienne and the jade green forests where he had liked to hunt in younger days. And there he learned of the ultimate betrayal. William Marshall read the list of traitors who had joined France against Henry. His favorite son, John, whom he had loved beyond all others, was the first name on the list.

"Now let everything go as it will; I care no longer for myself or anything else in the world," he pronounced. His last words were, "Shame, shame on a conquered king."

It was only a month since he had died. Sometimes Eleanor forgot that he was dead and caught herself working on phrases and arguments she would put to him when next they met. And then she would remember that there would be no more meetings and the day would grow darker. He had been her adversary and her love, and there was a great hole where the desire to see him, to revile him, to hold him, to taunt him, had once been.

"Put the torch in the wall bracket. We don't need it anymore," Eleanor told Amaria. They were just outside the great hall. She could hear the escort laughing and boasting of the honor of their chore. They were in high spirits, as was the entire land. Richard was to be crowned King, with Queen Eleanor had his side.

She was free. Henry was dead. Richard was to be crowned

King. The refrain sang again like a love lament whose words are so painful, they steal the breath. She took a deep breath and, gently pushing Amaria aside, entered the great hall.

The escort, which had been busy gulping spiced wine and warming their hands by the huge fire, rose as one and went on bended knee to her. There was one knight, taller and broader than the others, whose flaming red beard made her heart skip a beat, it looked so much like Henry's. Eleanor smiled at him, and then saw that he was nothing at all like Henry, it had been an illusion.

The great hall was silent, and then rose a cry that finally, after sixteen years of waiting, made her tremble: "Long live Queen Eleanor!"

I won, Henry, she said to the man who was not there.

Westminster Abbey was filled to overflowing. All of England must be contained within its stone walls, Dalia thought, pushing against the woman in front of her as she struggled for room.

Yet this was Egypt Day, the third of September, when all affairs, particularly momentous ones such as a coronation, were assured of disastrous endings. This day was, literally, guided by a bad star. What was King Richard thinking of, to be anointed and crowned on such a foreboding day? Did he intend to defy the stars themselves?

"Stop squirming!" hissed Gilbert. He had been standing on tiptoe, trying to see the procession of priests and knights who swayed and chanted their way down the red-carpeted aisle of the cathedral, and Dalia's sudden push made him lose balance. The air was so thick with incense and a curtain of malodorous smells from the crowd that she felt Gilbert's hand reach her shoulder for support before she saw it.

"But she was standing on my toe!" Dalia hissed back. She made a face at her brother that quieted him. Gilbert was the larger of the two, but Dalia always had the last word. If Gilbert wanted to go north and Dalia wanted to go south, they went south. If Gilbert wanted roast chicken and Dalia wanted a pork-meat pasty, they

438

had pork. It had been that way between them since they were born, Dalia a hasty first and Gilbert, her twin, a tardy second.

"You've your mother's nasty disposition," her uncle often remarked. "Stubborn and filled with complaints and determined to go your own way, just like Sophia was."

"If I don't go my way, Uncle, then which way should I go?" Dalia would pertly ask him, unwilling to accept criticism.

"The way you're told to go, woman. Not that you'd ever have the sense to be meek and obedient."

"No, Uncle, I wouldn't have sense to be that," she would agree, laughing at him. Dalia-Does-Not was the name the folk of the manor gave her: Dalia does not want to do that, Dalia does not want to go there, Dalia-does-not, they teased, but in a friendly manner. Dalia had inherited much from her mother, Sophia: intelligence, stubbornness, inability to accept things as they were, and a tendency to complain overly much. But she had also inherited from her father, Sir Foulkes: though she was smaller than most women, she was straight and strong and fair of limb.

"Can you see them yet, are they coming?" she called up to Gilbert, who had managed to climb over benches and onto rafters, so that he now towered above the crowd and had a clear view.

"Now, there's a pretty lad," a serving girl in front of Dalia commented, looking admiringly up at Gilbert. Like Dalia, he had black hair and black eyes, and his smooth complexion was not yet roughened by a beard. "Come down, sweetie, there's plenty to see here." She made as if she would lift her skirts, and the pressing crowd around her guffawed.

"They are not yet in sight," Gilbert said, jumping back down. His eyes were on the flaxen-haired, bold-eyed serving girl, not Dalia. There were so many fair-haired women in this city, with pale blue eyes and pink skin, it was quite unlike the South, where women were darker and warmer-looking. Not that he'd found the women of the North particularly cold . . .

Dalia punched his arm to win back his attention, and wondered not for the first time if they had been right to come here.

It was their first trip away from the family manor in La

Rochelle, and Gilbert had made much of this new freedom. Too much, Dalia thought. He had visited his first prostitute in Tours, learned to gamble with dice in Amiens, and memorized bawdy sailor songs in Portsmouth. He had sinfully careered across the continent and into England, and she wondered what mischief he would get up to in London, all in the guise of wanting to see Richard crowned.

Dalia didn't give a fig for Richard. From all she'd heard, he'd made his old father miserable, and Dalia, orphaned since birth, saved a special place in her geography of hell for ungrateful children. She, never having known the love of mother or father, could not understand how more fortunate children could scorn such love. There was her uncle, of course, who adored her, but he didn't count, whimpering, addle-brain man that he was . . .

No, she hadn't come to see Richard. She came to see Queen Eleanor.

Eleanor. She had grown up in Eleanor's shadow, made famous by the fact that her dead mother had been the Queen's friend and astrologer. Around her neck Dalia wore a gold chain with a pendant cabochon ruby, which had been her birth-gift from Queen Eleanor, imprisoned far away in Winchester Castle. In the fifteen years of her life, she had collected every story, every poem, every legend, told about the Queen, and become a self-taught authority on the Queen of England. Dalia studied the Queen the way her mother, Sophia, had studied the stars and planets.

It was Eleanor who sent the money for the trip to England, to see Richard crowned. "In memory of your mother, my friend," she had written to them. And of course, what could Uncle say, when confronted with a personal request from Queen Eleanor and a gift of gold to pay their way? He had to let them go. Not that he'd ever had any say about it. Dalia wanted to see Eleanor, so she and Gilbert would go to England.

And now, Dalia regretted it. Gilbert, who had always been a part of her, no longer seemed to be. At night, in the inns where they stayed, he sat up late by the hearth, drinking ale and exchanging tales with other young men come to London for the good times. He boasted and bragged and winked so often that Dalia, disgusted with the young man's bravado, would turn away, groaning.

Like other travelers, they shared a bed, but some nights Dalia fell asleep alone, knowing that Gilbert was with a hired woman or a friendly daughter of a merchant.

"You'll get the pox," she warned him. He would laugh and dance away from her, already looking for the next adventure, and her side would ache as if something had been cut away from her.

Now she stepped between Gilbert and the flaxen-haired woman, turning her back to the latter, and stared reproachfully at her twin.

"And in God's own house . . ." she reprimanded in mournful voice, shaking her head from side to side.

"I'm not doing anything," Gilbert denied hotly. "Besides, a church is a church no matter how many side altars it has, and as I recall, you profaned our little Church of the Holy Family often enough. Though now you're fifteen, you pretend to a ladylikeness of manner . . ."

"I did not throw the frog into the choir. It was Albert, I told you . . ."

Just as Dalia was ready to renew this old quarrel, a collective gasp and nervous movement went up from the gathered crowd, and a loud blare of horns announced the arrival of the royal procession. Gilbert and Dalia, using elbows, sharp-toed shoes and pinching when necessary, pushed their way to where Richard would pass, all hot anger and fearful prognosis of shame and illness forgotten for the moment.

Richard, red-bearded and with broad, almost stout chest, dressed magnificently in a red mantle trimmed with grey fur that swirled at his ankles, made his way down the central aisle. He walked slowly and with great deliberation, oblivious to the hands that reached out to touch him as he passed. Touch a King and be healed of leprosy. Touch a King and be healed of the joint aches. Touch a King, and you touch a god on earth, who can heal all illnesses. Hands stretched out and grabbed at his mantle, and his shoes, and all the while Richard continued his slow, stately, mea-

441

sured pace. He did not smile. Nor did he frown. His thoughts were turned inward, to dangerous places.

To the Lady Alais. She must be dispatched back to Paris. He would not have his father's harlot littering his property, and he most certainly would not marry her. Eleanor would see to that matter. She would time it so that the lady could be returned to her brother's keeping in the least shameful manner possible. No need to go to war with France over a woman . . . though if he could have his way, she'd be whipped through the streets.

His chest tightened with anger. Anything to do with Henry still turned his vision red. Would that ever go away? Now that Henry was dead, could there finally be peace between them? No. He didn't think so. He hated the Old King with all his heart. And in that measure did the son also love him, and mourn for him, and his cruel last moments.

Henry had died in shame, defeated by his enemy, France, and his own sons. His body had been stripped and robbed. He had been left naked and alone and plundered, without even coins weighting his eyelids, so that William Marshall found the corpse staring up at the ceiling, as if great secrets were written there.

William somewhere found a makeshift scepter, ring and crown to replace those stolen from the corpse, and Henry's body had been carried in state from the castle, through the silent, fearful town, through the green, birdsong-filled forest south of the Vienne, to the abbey of Fontevrault.

It was in the cold granite church that Richard said farewell to his father. He arrived alone and at night, when the church was filled with the unsubstantial, flickering light of candles. Henry's bier was in the center of the church, encircled by nuns, somber and kneeling, who chanted day and night for the dead King's soul.

The white-faced nuns looked up at Richard, and their eyes seemed filled with accusations, but they did not stop their chanting and praying. The air was fetid and Richard imagined, briefly, that the walls were moving closer together, surrounding him in an ambuscade from which he would not be rescued. He tugged at his mantle, loosening its grip on his throat.

The women parted before him as he approached, making way

442

for him at the bier. Richard felt no fear. He had seen many dead
bodies and knew he would see many more before others approached his own bier. But his steps were hesitant. Henry had
died cursing him. During their last interview his father had given
him a reluctant kiss of peace, and then cursed him.

"May I not die till I have revenged myself on you," the Old
King said, and his eyes, yellowed with illness and suffering, had
glared malevolently at him.

But you are dead, Father. And you have not had your revenge
of me, Richard thought, looking into the bier. It was too dark and
shadowy, he couldn't see. He took a candle from one of the nuns
and held it close to his father's face.

The yellowed skin looked hard as wood; the grey-streaked red
beard was thin and lank. The eyes were finally closed. Thank
God the eyes were finally closed. Henry did not look peaceful.
But he looked resigned and even somewhat satisfied, as if glad to
be done with a long day's labor.

There is nothing to fear here, Richard thought. He has died
without his revenge.

He bent to give his father the customary farewell kiss on the
cheek. And it was then that the nightmare happened.

Just as Richard's lips touched the cold flesh, a gush of blood
issued from Henry's ears. As if to say, I am not completely dead,
my son. Beware of me.

Richard jumped back. A nun, a very old one, took him by the
elbow and gently led him away. "It happens, sometimes," she
tried to reassure him. Richard crossed himself, and was not reassured. In nightly dreams, he saw the blood, mocking death and
life both, flow from his father's face. In broad daylight he saw
shapes flitting at the corners of his eyes, but when he looked,
nothing was there. He felt his father's eyes on him.

Richard was before the altar now, eye to eye with Archbishop
Baldwin, who was to anoint him. The archbishop was nervous. As
well he might be. He opposed the marriage Richard had arranged
for John, to Hedwisa of Gloucester. Damn the third degree, Hedwisa had land and wealth and Richard needed both. They would
be his, through John's marriage.

Richard looked over Baldwin's shoulder to the altar, which was filled with gold reliquaries. The cathedral was surprisingly quiet, considering the many souls gathered there. He nodded and four knights moved towards him. This would be no token coronation, as his brother's, Henry's, had been. The people would know he was crowned king, completely, with no holding back, no clauses, no Old King to stand in his way.

The knights slowly disrobed him of kingly attire till he stood almost naked before the assembly. His whole body was to be anointed with the holy waters and sacred oils, not just his head.

The crowd gasped again, as it had when Richard first appeared, with delight. It was hundreds of years since a King had been anointed in this fashion, perhaps not since great King Arthur himself.

His mother, Eleanor, standing at his right, nodded encouragement. Her dark eyes glistened, her smile was blinding. Richard looked at her, then quickly looked away, afraid too much emotion would show on his face. His pride in her was great. As a child, he had adored her beauty and sweet voice; as a man, he loved the regalness of her. She was majesty personified.

The first thing she had done, when Ranulf de Granville made her the token offering of the keys of the castle to announce her freedom, was set free all other captives in the kingdom. It was an old custom, straight out of the tales of the land, and one designed to win the hearts of the people. It had. There were many prisoners when Henry died. What with the wars, and with Henry's stringent system of laws protecting the property and rights of the land, the dungeons of England had been crammed with people awaiting justice for their misdeeds.

Eleanor did not give them justice. Justice was a kingly quality. She gave them instead the heavenly quality of mercy, and the land rang with the joyous shouting of her name.

This complete anointing had also been her idea. He, Richard, duke of a southern kingdom, was neither well-known nor loved in England. "Such as I see you, this I deem you" was the proverb in Poitiers. "Let them see you naked before them, let them see the

444

body of their King so they will know nothing is concealed, that all is anointed for their protection, for their love," she advised him.

And so it was. Naked, he could feel the newborn adoration of his people surrounding him, caressing him. He was their King, their sacrifice, their beloved, and as the cool oil was poured over him, he felt love grow in his own breast, not the love of maid or knight or music or fighting, but love as a whole, for all people and all things that he would now rule. And they would love him as well as had his own mother.

Love made his heart larger than his own body, he felt himself being stretched, elongated, till his fingertips touched the highest vault of the cathedral and his toes touched the ancient catacombs beneath. His breast grew till it covered the whole land, and his eyes saw the width and depth of the world and showed him what he must do with this love.

He would not marry the unworthy Alais. Nor would he marry any woman soon. First he would heal the land, and the people. He would heal himself and close his father's eyes, once and for all, forever. He would take the sacrifice of his love, his body, to the Holy Land. There would be a new Crusade, and he, King Richard, would lead the army himself.

Henry, you will not have your revenge of me. Father, you will not have your revenge of me, he thought. Let your blood flow in mock life till the second coming, but your curse will not be fulfilled.

He shrank to mortal size as he was clothed again, this time in the new robes of a king to match his kingly heart. The royal mantle was put on his shoulders; the sword of justice was placed in his hands.

Dalia watched the anointing and the rest of the ceremony with a critical eye. She had no doubt that Eleanor had written this ceremony. Her extravagant and poetic sense of drama marked it throughout. It had done what it was supposed to do. The crowd in the cathedral were all but swooning with love for the southern King. Henry had ruled by law and justice; Richard would rule by love and strength of soul.

But would he rule well? Dalia, like her mother, Sophia, had an innate distrust of strong emotion. She preferred the predictable equations of the philosophers. Gilbert, though, watched the long ceremoney with shining eyes and a strange expression, one unfamiliar to Dalia. It made her uncomfortable, and she wished again they had not come.

Later, when the cathedral was emptied, Gilbert remained kneeling, deep in prayer and contemplation. Dalia, restless and shifting from one foot to another—her back was aching from the long hours of standing—never considered leaving her brother's side, but instead poked him or rolled her eyes at him, wanting him to get up and leave with her.

Finally he did rise and look at her. There was mischief in his eyes again, and that relieved the growing anxiety she felt.

"Go back to Dagbert without me," he said, grinning and giving her a quick kiss on the cheek. Dagbert was her uncle's man, sent to guide the twins and see they came to no harm during their journey. He, old and desiring only to sit before a flaming hearth, disliked the journey and the twins as well as they disliked him. Having no interest in seeing a mortal man made divine King, he had stayed behind at the inn, in front of the hearth, rather than come to the cathedral.

"Where are you going?" she asked her twin, frowning.

"Nowhere. Everywhere. To places a maid should not go." He ran from her, his longer legs quickly putting distance between them so that even her shrill yells could not detain him.

Alone, she left the empty cathedral, drawing her skirts close about her body to protect her hidden purse from the thieves who lurked in every English crowd, according to her uncle. Much of the crowd had dispersed, but a group of men still lingered in front of Westminster, wearing long, worried faces and clasping gifts that they had not been able to deliver to their King. They were the Jews of London, and they had been denied admittance to the ceremony, just as the women of the kingdom, including Eleanor herself, had been denied admittance to the feast that followed. Richard wished only the company of his knights.

Dalia, walking quickly away, questioned this policy. Richard, like most other nobles of the land, was heavily in debt to the Jews. Indeed, without them, he could not finance his great Crusade. But to turn them away, and refuse their gifts . . . this made no sense. Until she remembered that gratitude was a rare quality and most men would prefer to turn their backs on those who grant gifts, rather than acknowledge their generosity. The nobles of the land did not like to look upon the Jews; to do so was to be reminded of their debts.

As she walked, it seemed the streets were filled with noises too loud with emotion, both love and hate, and expectation, and she pondered the worried looks on the faces of the moneylenders, and the overexcited faces of the English knights.

She returned to the inn and her solitary room and forced herself to forget Richard, and that this was the cursed Egypt Day, and concentrate on studying her mother's translation of Boethius, which she had carried with her to London. In the back of her thoughts, where study does not overpower primal emotions but merely insinuates around them, she called to Gilbert, willing him to return to her. He did not.

Soon after sundown Dalia, reading by the light of a candle, heard a great turmoil in the street below. Voices yelled "Murder!" or "Mercy," and there was a thunder of horses racing by, and the clanking of swords, and screaming. The tumult was like nothing she had heard before. She seemed to be in a nightmare, though she was not asleep, and when she tried to descend the stairs, to see what was amiss, the porter's strong arm drew her back into the hostel.

"I wouldn't be going out," he told her gruffly. "They're murdering the Jews."

"What? For what purpose?" she screamed over the noise. Outside the very door she tried to go through, she heard the sound of a man being bludgeoned to death, the sound of hurried footsteps following the act of murder.

"They say the Jews tried to enter the cathedral," he said, indifferent. He bolted the door shut and shoved her away from it. "I don't think, though, King Richard will be pleased by this night's work. The Jews were under his protection." He slunk away.

447

"Much good Richard's protection did them, then," Dalia whispered, shaken.

She wished again she had never come to this foreign city, and returned to her room, trembling for Gilbert, who was somewhere in the dangerous night. She huddled in a corner and watched, pale and wide-eyed, as the night grew light with false dawn: the Jewish quarter had been set ablaze. It was Egypt night, and demons and devils roamed the streets of London.

It was almost dawn when Gilbert clambered next to her on the straw pallet, exhausted and reeking of wine, though she could tell by his steps he was sober now, whatever he had been earlier in the evening. His steps were heavy and hesitant.

She pretended to be asleep, and he was careful not to touch her when he lay on the narrow bed. But something in his heart made him sit up again after a moment and look at her long and hard. Her face, in the grey gloom of a London dawn, was small and pale, delicate as a child's. He reached out and tentatively, gently, touched the face that was more familiar to him than his own.

"Gilbert," she said, not opening his eyes but feeling his touch and his eyes upon her. Her side ached again, and there was a clamp of fear around her chest, making it hard to breathe. "Gilbert, they murdered the Jews."

"I know. I saw." His voice was low and grave. She did not recognize it. All youth, all merriment, had fled it. He sounded old and tired beyond physical endurance. "It started as a mere fracas outside Westminster, but some nobles took that as an opportunity to wipe clean their debts. You don't have to pay a dead Jew. They burned the quarter to get rid of the ledgers."

"Were you injured? Oh, you should have been here with me!" She sat up and turned to him, terrified that he be wounded.

"No, I am not injured. At least by no more than a scratch. Received when I tried to turn one knight away from his goal. He slashed the man's throat, Dalia. They were blood-crazed."

They held each other, trying to make sense of this new world, so far from the manor and their uncle, and the soft, long days that knew nothing of such hatred and ignominy.

"What does King Richard say of this?" she asked finally.

"His actions are his judgement. Even now knights known to have committed the deed are being killed in retribution. They have sullied the first day of his reign, and they say anger has turned Richard into a madman."

"And Eleanor?"

"The Queen weeps. They say that Henry cursed Richard before he died, and this is the Old King's revenge. Richard will never outlive this infamy."

"I hate this place," Dalia whispered. "We will go back home, tomorrow."

Gilbert held her tightly, but said nothing. How could he say what he felt? That he was no longer her Gilbert, no longer a boy, but a man who has seen evil. Evil is a door that slams behind you; once it is shut you can't return to the other side, to innocence.

Dalia began to weep, knowing already what was in his mind.

"Don't do it," she pleaded.

"Don't do what?"

"What you were thinking of when you were looking at me a moment ago . . . thinking of how to say farewell." Of the two, it was Dalia who had the sight sometimes gifted to twins: often, she knew what he was thinking, what he would do, before he himself knew.

"You are going with Richard. On Crusade," she accused in a small voice. "You are leaving me. You will take the cross."

"Not you, Dalia. I am not leaving you. I am leaving Uncle, and the manor, and the life there. I have seen things tonight . . . I can't be the same, Dalia. Not now. There must be a Crusade, to cleanse the land, and I must be part of it."

"You are leaving me."

"Would you have me be a farmer?" he asked then, angry. "When the world is large and waiting, and there are deeds to be done?"

"I would have you stay with me, brother." She sat up and stared at him in a way that in earlier years had made her brother meek. Now he was stern, almost fatherly, with her. As if he were the older of the two, not she.

"Dalia, we are grown now. Even if I stayed to plow the fields like a villein, we must be parted. Uncle will be arranging your marriage soon, and no bridegroom will want his brother-in-law as part of the dowry. I must seek my own fortune."

She flinched as though he had hit her. "Arranging my marriage? Is he mad?" She was yelling now, more fearful for herself than Gilbert.

"Not mad. Only concerned. You are of an age, and must be wed." His tone was superior, and that made her even angrier.

"Never."

When he reached to hug her this time, she did not let him. They spoke no more, but kept many thoughts to themselves, unvoiced, and Dalia knew he was right, this time. Slow Gilbert had, for the first time, seen the truth before she had. They were children no longer. From now on they would have to walk different paths. Richard had become a King that day, but Gilbert had grown into a man, separate from her, with a separate destiny that would take him places she could not go.

The anxiety she had felt for many days changed now into a different feeling, a more specific one that was concern and worry, not childish fear. And helplessness. Children are helpless, too, but in a different way, she thought. They think that when they are older, or taller, or more learned, they will no longer be helpless. But a grown maid knows that the helplessness doesn't leave. It just changes.

"You must take care of yourself. Every pain you suffer, every moment of hunger, I will suffer, too," she whispered to Gilbert.

"Then you will also feel my glory, when I see Jerusalem," he promised her quietly.

The pear tree stood on the horizon like a sentinel, its branches adorned with gaily colored ribbons that waved in the wind, reminders of all the secret wishes in a maiden's breast.

Lucie, seeing it again, felt an answering wish rise in her.

"Stop," she said. "Stop. I never thought to see this tree again." But before he could rein in the horse that pulled the cart, she had already jumped to the ground and ran to the tree as if to embrace an old friend.

Bemused, Godfrey halted the horse and then leaped down to the ground, but not as lightly as his wife. It was a long time since the renowned troubadour had had to make do with a simple bowl of porridge for his noonday meal, and he had grown heavier with the years, and slower.

"Again? Have you seen it before?" he asked, wiping perspiration from his brow and joining her in its cool shade.

"Foolish knave." She beamed up at him. "Don't you remember? We passed this same tree years before, that first time we entered Poitiers. It was adorned with ribbons then, as it is now. It must be very good at granting wishes. I tied my own ribbon, here." She reached up and touched a bough that was black and cracked with age.

"You must be right. Yes, of course, we would have come this way. And did you get your wish, Lady?"

"I did," she said, putting her arms around his waist. "I have gotten many of them, since, Godfrey. I have been blessed among women."

"And fruitful," he said a little ruefully. They still had five little ones at home, and their eldest had just presented them with their first grandchild. Hence, this late trip into Poitiers. The celebrations for Richard had begun a week before, but Lucie had refused to make the journey till her daughter had been safely recovered from her childbirthing.

Godfrey, as proud as he was of his family, did not enjoy feeling like a grandfather. And today he did. The sun was warm and tired him; he ached from the long drive to Poitiers. It was years since they had visited the town. Those years had been busy ones, filled with the demands of Countess Marie, who held him to his pledge to make her famous through his songs. He had done so, and in so doing, achieved fame himself. He was knighted, and landed, with two manors of his own, which Lucie ruled with a stern and wise hand.

Lucie pulled at one of the ribbons and looked at him sideways. "We are changed greatly since we last came this way," she said. She had grown proud with the years, and they never discussed the early time, when she had been a bonded serf. But he knew she thought of it often, and wondered at the destiny that had made Lucie of Black Oaks wedded to a rich knight.

"Greatly," he agreed, grinning. "As I recall, you were compliant then, and did as I bid. You have learned to rule, Lady. I fear your tongue above all other things."

"Then you are wise. A lady's law is not to be taken lightly."

"So I have learned."

"As Henry learned." Lucie grew wistful. "I wonder if Eleanor was ever happy as I."

"She must be happy now, if she wasn't then. Richard is King, as she always wanted. The war was not in vain."

"But what a long road it was. Do you think she remembers us, and all that happened at her court?"

Godfrey pulled a blue ribbon from the tree and tied it at his wife's throat, not answering. He knew how fickle fame was, and fame's handservant, memory, was not less fickle.

"I'm hungry. I'd rather have a pear than a ribbon," Lucie complained.

The harvest was long over, but one pear, gold and overripe and starting to wrinkle, lingered at the top of the tree. Godfrey, puffing and panting a little, climbed the stout branches and fetched it.

"Your pear, my lady," he said, bowing and handing it to her.

"Then all my wishes, even those from long ago, are granted." Lucie smiled.

The clerk Godfrey de Leigny has finished The Cart, but let nobody blame him for working on Chrétien's story, for he did it with the permission of Chrétien, who began it. So far he has written, and he will put neither more nor less, for either would spoil the tale.